READER'S COMMENTS...

for *The Breaking Of The Seventh Seal* - published in Czech as *The Return of the Avasthas*.

"For me, the *Return of the Avasthas* is the return to the trust and confidence in my Self. Many times I felt as if behind the situations I used to come through, there was some parallel running game about which I knew within, and as if I knew it beforehand. Experiencing now and then the flashes of recognition that I must have known what I was heading for since my birth, having everything arranged....the situations, actors, powers and possibilities. With somebody directing it, me acting in it and enjoying myself.

But I live my daily life blinded by what I see around, the turmoil which doesn't allow me to put my attention on the subtle and to return inside, to the roots, not just for a while but for some longer period. To be 'there' more and use the energies I perceive stored in my supplies. To be free from my ego and various pains sticking in the mind, without which they cannot exist—how light, safe and free I would be! I'd play with my life so nicely like the children in the sandpit...then suddenly, out of the blue, somebody I never spoke to describes the powers I feel I could have; telling a story about young people experiencing the same as me. People who start 'awakening' and finding out that their short moments of intuition, begin to transform into a real meeting with their own power. A mighty and gentle energy that helps to overcome the hell of this modern world where everything is wrecked so much. To me this book is so precious because I can see that what is happening to me and is so subtle and unobtrusive that one could easily doubt its existence, simply is true. We all have it inside..."
                                                          Jana Michalakova, Moravia

"While the first volume made me feel how beautifully this universe was created, how everything in it is in 'mutual connections' and forced me to go deeper within myself, the second kept taking me into meditation, so that I swept through the whole book as if surfing on the waves of love. Pure, noble, joy giving love. I literally became the part of the story."

Kvetoslava Zgazarova, Czech Republic

"This book is so deep and its message of the truth about ourselves so precious, that it can be hardly expressed by words...because the reading and the reader become one. This second volume helped me to be more forgiving to myself and also to others and consequently to be able to enjoy more the inner beauty of my being. Both volumes of this *Legend* belong to the most precious books in our library."

Maria Skrulova, Slovakia

"One could say, this book cannot be read, because as soon as you open it, you are in meditation! I can imagine this *Legend* being sold in a beautifully carved wooden casket not necessarily just in bookshops but in toyshops or housewares shops...because it's not just a book but a portal...I hope the author will write another sequel and won't spend the rest of his life fishing!"

Lenka P., Finland

"I haven't finished the whole book yet but it is divine! Reading it I feel that what the author describes works within me. Hats off to him! For me, *the Legend* is the most wonderful book I've ever read. I'm looking forward to a third volume."

Lenka Krupilova, Zlin. Moravia

"I was born in the country of 'the teacher of nations,' John Amos Comenius. Owning both volumes of *The Legend*, I was able to go deeper into the knowledge about the Inner World and to use it in the practice of my daily life, not only the wisdom of Comenius but also other enlightened teachers. I'm grateful I could more intensively experience how beautifully we are connected with others, Mother Earth and the whole universe."

Ludek Smolka, Brno. Czech Republic

"The Legend touched the beauty, love and joy inside me that I wasn't completely aware of. It was something like an adventurous journey into my own interior. This is what I felt while reading this second volume. Words fail me to describe it more exactly..."

Jana Cermakova, Slovakia

"The book is so great and energetically powerful, that after having read just a few pages I always had to stop and let it work within me... Thank you!"
Oldrich Kylsan, Bohemia

"*The Legend of Dagad Trikon* speaks to me both in its complexity and simplicity at the same time, and by its beauty. It makes you aware how much those who aren't interested in the seeking of their spirit miss; what adventures they miss. It is simply beautiful reading, when you feel nice warmth in your heart and satisfaction and the desire to be able to keep this feeling forever and spread the joy to others."
Kristyna Kucerova, Bohemia

"*The Legend* makes an immense impression on me – it feels like a sort of entrance gate into the endless inner universe of man, the description, map and the 'fly sheet' of what we really are..."
Leos Malena, Znojmo, Moravia

"To me, meeting the *Legend* was the beginning of a series of small miracles. The story itself started drawing me inside at the very first reading, in the same way as the main heroes felt inevitably drawn into the mystery of Avasthas saga against their will, and gradually I found myself a part of it, experiencing its impact on my own life, made by some higher force to translate it for my countrymen. This is such a powerful and vivid book— it pulsates with inner life and echoes from our ancient memories hidden between the lines, that help us recall what we had once known, it offers many levels on which one can walk through it. A well-known astrologer from Prague didn't hesitate to compare it to the Bible, saying it contains everything important about the history of the Creation and the evolution of man. And for me, the most important message of the second volume is that we can learn more about those who move evolution to a higher level; as one of the conditions of the Game is to recognize them at the end of the day."
Marta Heinlova, Czech Republic

Other titles by Grégoire de Kalbermatten

The Advent

The Third Advent

The Legend of Dagod Trikon

Published by daisyamerica LLC – www.daisyamerica.com

THE BREAKING
OF THE SEVENTH SEAL

Published by daisyamerica LLC
Bronx, New York, 10471, NY, USA
Book design by Sylvia Udar
Cover design by Richard Payment
Printed in the USA by King Printing – 181 Industrial Avenue, Lowell, MA 01852

The Library of Congress has catalogued this trade paperback edition as follows:

de Kalbermatten, Grégoire.
The Breaking of the Seventh Seal / Grégoire de Kalbermatten.
p,   cm,
ISBN: 978-1-932406-02-3

1. Mythology—Fiction. 2. Spirituality—Fiction. 3. Lost civilizations—Fiction
4. Kundalini—Fiction 5. The Goddess—Fiction 6. Hidden treasure—Fiction

First US Paperback Edition 2013
10 9 8 7 6 5 4 3 2

THE BREAKING
OF THE SEVENTH SEAL

Grégoire de Kalbermatten

daisyamerica LLC

This book is dedicated to Shri Mataji Nirmala Devi

G de K

FOREWORD

"Who looks outside, dreams…who looks inside, awakes." Carl G. Jung

Socrates said it is helpful to know what we don't know; but every now and then we don't even know that we know. Books offering tips on how to live a better life are perennially popular. In these times, many are getting the message: our civilization is mortal. It's failing because we believe in having: possessions, relationships, and identities, multiplied by the many portals of the cyber world. To have is good of course, but to be, is much better. Ownership, possessions etc. are not giving us the best out of life. But who are we?

Proposals for greater wellness and self-help methods are many, but the sheer amount of suggestions can seem baffling. Sometimes it looks as if the secrets have been carefully buried within us, hidden perhaps, but still available. Those who seek suspect that they are somehow the key, and that there must be a lock somewhere.

The second book of *the Legend of Dagad Trikon* looks for insights that we store inside us without always knowing or expressing them.

Together with Carl Gustav Jung, let us remember our philosophers and our mythologies. Our predecessors left clues and signs to guide us, tricks that we must learn. *The Breaking of the Seventh Seal* searches for these tips with the reader, explores the path to a destination so close to us, and yet is so completely hidden that it is the mother of all mysteries.

In this quest, we stumble between madness and wisdom. "Better to be mad with the madcap than to be wise alone." It's hard to deny the savvy contained in the maxim of the seventeenth century French duke, François de la Rochefoucauld. How to be wise? Is it to know what is best for us and to live accordingly? Wisdom was the quality extolled by our elders to support positive transformation and self-empowerment, a matter that has interested inquisitive brains for millennia. It concerns us too that the times ahead challenge us to find our meaning and to show resilience. There is no going back and no stopping the clock. In the midst of increasing droughts and rising sea levels, we must make sense of the world that we have created.

I thank Marta Heinlova, who provided me advice while translating the original draft of this book that became in Czech, *the Return of the Avasthas*. Alan Wherry accompanied me during the further development of my writing. I relied on his steadfast support and immensely enjoyed our interactions. Finally, it is somewhat unusual for an author to thank his printers, but Sid and Amita Chinai, of King Printing, have gone beyond the call of duty and professionalism in their support of my work over eleven years, they have printed all four of my books and I am eternally grateful to them.

Dear readers, I wrote this essay in philo-fiction because all those who dare, are the stuff of legends. There is a higher prize to be won in the Inner World to which the companions of the quest of Dagad Trikon now have access.

Grégoire de Kalbermatten, Champex-lac, December 24th 2012.

PRELUDE: A SUMMARY OF THE AVASTHIC LORE

Two cousins, Lakshman Kharadvansin and Lakshmi Vani deciphered Sanskrit manuscripts and Egyptian hieroglyphs containing sketchy references to an advanced civilization that vanished over ten thousand years ago. They located a rocky mountain complex deep in the Sahara Desert that did not appear on any map. It sheltered the hidden dwellings and fortresses known as Dagad Trikon, the Triangle Rock that was the home and last refuge of the lost race of the Avasthas. The Dagad Trikon hideaway was ruled by the secret power of a goddess, the Lady of the Rock.

Avasthas lived by the values of innocence, truth and love. They sought above all to receive the Gift, the elixir of bliss. They were insightful seers and powerful warriors. However, over the millennia and despite their profound knowledge, they could not cope with the sheer wickedness of the evil forces led by the arch devil Thanatophor, assisted by his chief lieutenants Hangker and Belzebseth. Aware of their impending doom, the Avasthas consigned the codes of their magic powers to ten caskets that were entrusted to flying riders and dispatched to secret destinations all over the planet.

The Wheel of Ages turned, and much of the goodness in the world was slowly crushed. Gentleness, honor, generosity, and many of the qualities that keep the heart alive gradually faded away. At the opening of this, the third millennium, the evil effects of the Riders of Thanataphor have penetrated the collective attention of mankind, the darkest corners of the human psyche. Nevertheless, if modern man can absorb the secret knowledge of the Avasthas, the plot of Thanatophor to destroy human civilization and enslave the earth will fail.

The Breaking of the Seventh Seal narrates how the returned Avasthas must solve the riddles of the blue and yellow feathers in order to progress from the Outer World of human interactions to the Inner World of spiritual endowment and powers. It is only when this knowledge is readily available to all that Thanatophor's plot will be defeated on earth and the Great Schism of man's split identity will be overcome.

THE DAGAD TRIKON
LEXICON

This Lexicon has been extracted from the diary of Alexia Ishani, daughter of Ananya, and granddaughter of Jonathan and Lakshmi O'Lochan.

A long time back, during my youth, I went to summer school at the Stealthstar Academy at Mount Uluru in Australia. By then my grandfather was quite old, but he spent time at the Academy as a visiting lecturer and narrated bits and pieces of his adventures. At the time, I found it a bit embarrassing because he shared many stories of our family, and he was open and candid about everything. It was clear from his account that we belonged to the lost race of the Avasthas but that we incarnated again in the human race to bring to others the benefits of the Avasthic knowledge, the Deep Way.

I remember he told me that indeed we had been blessed and normally, in a human context, we should keep it a secret so as not to attract jealousy. However, as the Stealthstars, the returned Avasthas, finally defeated Mokolo at the battle of the Green Horn, he said Avasthas could share their joy without attracting the rampant enmity that was the poison of the witch. He was right because my friends who learned about the saga are not themselves Stealthstars but they do not mind in the least that we are different, a family of Avasthas.

In the Golden Age that has finally started, love can simply flow more freely. Of course, we went through lots of trials and destruction but anyone who understands the Deep Way, knows that how we deal with the difficulties that life presents us with is precisely how we spiritually grow.

In that sense, all the problems we get are heaven sent. So much nonsense had to be removed to leave space for the new world.

Anyway, grandfather also carefully described the diverse beings and characters of Dagad Trikon as he understood them. This is what I noted in my diary during these days:

THE WORLD OF THE AVASTHAS

THE LOCATION   Dagad Trikon, a gigantic triangular-shaped rocky mountain complex in the desert of Africa, which is protected by magic and normally inaccessible to humans.

THE RULER   The Lady of the Rock controls the feminine reserve force called Kundalini, a power of residual consciousness that would come to the fore in the modern age.

THE OFFICERS:

ASLERACH OF ANOR   The Nizam is the ruler of Dagad Trikon under the authority of the Lady of the Rock.

ELKAIM EKAMONON   The Sand Keeper, Lord of the Highlands and the Chief Wizard of the Rock; he is the Master leading the companions through the saga. He is the main character of the saga, known in modern age as Sanath.

PHILTHALAS OF ELNUR   Admiral of the Thalassean Fleet. Took over as Nizam of Elnelok after the departure of Aslerach and his people for the stars.

SERAPIS, GOVERNOR OF SHAMBALPUR   Grandpa said that towards the end, the Wizard, of Dagad Trikon lost faith in Serapis because he suspected that his organizing genius was for control and not for service.

SERNATIL (THE) TITLE OF SERAPIS   the Seneschal Administrator of Dagad Trikon, the highest function after the Office of the Nizam.

CIRCLE OF THE AULYAS   Gathers the foremost knowers of the Deep Way, equipped with foresight; members identified include Alhakim of Golkur, Atha Glaukopis, Habymanyon, and Rasmus.

THE SIX GREAT TRIBES OF THE AVASTHAS ARE CUSTODIANS OF SIX GREAT PRINCIPLES (*TATTWAS*):

KALABHAM (HOUSE OF)   The *tattwa* by which the power of innocence is looked after. And which establishes protective magnetic fields.

FALKILIAD (HOUSE OF)   The *tattwa* of the rules of action through the powers of dynamism and creativity.

ELNUR (HOUSE OF)   The *tattwa* of the art of balance and harmony through the powers of Self-discovery and introspection.

ELEKSIM (HOUSE OF)   The *tattwa* of the protocol of love by absorbing the energy of love directly into our subtle body.

ANOR   (HOUSE OF)   The *tattwa* of synthesis, integration and unity through the power of evolution that leads us towards collective consciousness.

ANORHAD (HOUSE OF)   The *tattwa* of the potential for transformation, by bringing an end to the lower identifications.

THE HOUSE OF NI   This was not a tribe but the destination of all the tribes, the making of a new species on Earth. No information available. "Silence that talks," said Grandpa.

SHERAVALIANS   Amazons of the Lady of Dagad Trikon. Those we hear about are the three sisters Erilie, Esitel, Evenyl born in the House of Eleksim.

YUVA PLATOON (MEMBERS OF THE)   Young warriors who were fated to go through the fall of Dagad Trikon: Etakir, Aliskhan, Lidholon, Hanomkar, Olophon.

All of the above returned to this world as Stealthstars.

THE WORLD OF THE HUMANS (AND THOSE WHO GUIDED THEM)

AVATAR   This is the way we call a divine being when She or He incarnates in human form.

DASKALIAN ASSEMBLY   The college of foremost teachers who provided guidance in the present age of the Earth. The Great Mother says they appeared as the manifestations of a primordial archetype of mastery: Abraham, Moses,

Rajah Janaka, Confucius, Lao-tzu, Socrates, Zarathustra, Mohamed, Guru Nanak, and Shirdhi Sai Baba; they taught mankind about the right path and they command the Aulyas, the Nathas and the Hllidarendis.

HLLIDARENDI (ORDER OF THE)   The Order of Wizards whose initial mission was to prepare the return of the Avasthas and protect the humans but they could not do it because evil in the Age of Iron was too strong. So the Gods on Kailash asked the Great Mother to take her Avatar because no one else could save mankind. The Order dissolved when its members realized She had fulfilled Her mission.

IAN ILDEMAR   Hllidarendi of the Western islands. A Scottish disciple of William Blake who wanted to restore Blake's vision for the spiritual emancipation of Albion.

KHETO   Hllidarendi of Africa who fought to liberate the spiritual potential of his continent. Mostly he fought the black magicians.

MARILUH ATAUI   Hllidarendi of Southern America. She was like a younger sister to Sanath who could fully tune into the powers of nature.

NATHAS   The seers of the human race who took their birth in India, mostly in the Maharashtra region, where the force of the Lady of the Rock is strongest.

THE O'LOCHAN AND JETZLAR FAMILIES   It was the destiny of these two families to be drawn into the quest.

OUTER WORLD   This is the space of the humans when they ignore who they truly are. Because the Outer World is the visible universe, made of matter, perceived by the senses and the generator of desires, the Externalists project their attention and desire outside and, in consequence, end up in materialism. The relationship of man with the Outer World creates the space where the Dark Riders can take their course. It is not evil in itself but it is the natural area for evil to assert control.

THE CONNECTIONS BETWEEN THE WORLDS

DEEP WAY   The knowledge at the core of the Legend is about bridging the gap (the Foul Rift) between the Outer and the Inner World. The art of deciphering the clues from the gods, shaping one's own destiny and accessing the Inner World is learned by the pupils of the Deep Way.

GIFT (THE)   The elixir of blessedness, the Holy Grail, released from the cup at the top of the head when mastery of the Deep Way is achieved.

GRAND SCHEME   An elliptical movement from divinity to matter and back to divinity. The turning point of the ellipse is the bestowing of the Gift on man. Avasthas also call it the Game or evolution.

As if this is not complicated enough, Grandpa explained that the universe is like a rotating wheel and that divine beings come to visit (Avatars). Some Avasthic beings returned to play the Game (Stealthstars).

THE GREAT MOTHER   the Lady of the Rock returned to Earth and manifested the power to grant the Gift to ordinary human beings.

SANATH   Baldur van Jetzlar was the cover for Elkaim Ekamonon, the Sand Keeper, a wizard endowed with a very long life, who revealed himself to the Stealthstars under the name of Sanath. Grandpa said he was an Aulya and that he carried part of the essence of the Daskalians.

OTHERS WHO RETURNED TO EARTH:

THE STEALTHSTARS   Avasthas warriors who traveled in time through the cycle of reincarnation:
- Michael O'Lochan, previously Aliskhan of Anor.
- Lothar Graff von Jetzlar, previously was Hanomkar of Kalabham.
- Sean Chasean Aryaputra was Lidholon of Anor.
- Lakshmi Vani, who married Grandpa in New Delhi was Erilie of Eleksim.
- Lorelei von Jetzlar, who married Uncle Michael in Jetzenstein Castle was Esitel of Eleksim.
- Tracy O'Lochan was Evenyl of Eleksim, she married Uncle Lakshman after the opening of the Casket of the Blue Feather in England. They married in Riffelberg, before the Matterhorn because the Great Mother had blessed this place.

JONATHAN O'LOCHAN   Grandpa was the eldest brother. Auntie Tracy called him Seagull because he always had a deep link with the sea. He was previously an Avastha navigator, Olophon of Elnur, the son of Admiral Philtalas.

LAKSHMAN KHARADVANSIN   who discovered the Dagad Trikon fortress was previously Etakir, leader of the Yuva (youth) Platoon; he was the leader of the quest.

THE WORLD OF THE HEAVENS

ADIVATAR   God, integrating all His aspects and the spectator of the Grand Scheme.

ANANTA QUETZALCOATL   Mythical sacred cobra, he represents energy, for cataclysmic change and regeneration, like the serpent Ouroboros.

ARCHANGEL GABRIEL   Known throughout Asia as Hanuman, the magic White Monkey; he is Hermes and Mercury, the messenger from above who patrols the domain of the Yellow Feather.

ARCHANGEL MICHAEL   Known in India and Nepal as Bhairava, killer of demons: he patrols the domain of the Blue Feather and William Blake was his Avatar to warn of the pitfalls to spiritual ascent in modern times.

BHAKTI   Love in devotion.

DEITIES   When deities from the heavens take a human form they are called Avatars. For them it is a big change, often they switch off their divine memory so they can really become humans. Deities become Avatars out of compassion, to help us in our spiritual ascent.

GODS   Different aspects of Adivatar; they take a separate existence because the need to manifest arises. Beings from above do not force their ways on to humans. It is up to us to pick up the clues (see Deep Way).

GREAT GODDESS   Consort of Adivatar, the Great Mother, housewife of the Universe, She is the one who directs the Grand Scheme to please Him but she is also known to have manifested in Avatar forms, for example, as the Lady of the Rock.

EMERALD KING   He is often represented as the sleeping god although he really is the manager and operator of the Grand Scheme.

INNER WORLD   The map of the heavens contained in our subtle being, hidden within us; getting there is the main purpose of life. The entire domain of blissful consciousness and its properties is stored within human-kind in a potential form that we must actualize.

KARUDAS   The prince of eagles is the vehicle of the Emerald King when he intervenes in history.

KUNDALINI   The magic feminine reserve energy of transformation, the Lady of the Rock (in the triangular bone) within us.

MASTER OF THE TRIDENT   Shiva the Spirit who blesses us with joy. He is the destination of evolution and he resides on Mount Kailash but he cannot be approached if the Blue Zone is not purified. Grandfather would not talk about Him but when the subject came up he would invite us to go into silence and at this point, his lectures would turn into meditation.

NAZARENE MASTER   Jesus, the Christ, was in the light they saw when they reached the Lily of Anorhad, granting access to the House of Ni.

THE SOWER   The Blue Lord - Krishna, he is a later form of the Emerald King and revealed the working of the three feathers in his teachings collected in the *Bhagavad Gita*.

THE WORLD OF HELL

ARAKNA   The spider witch that binds and paralyzes in the blue zone; she weaves webs of attachment and habits that subtly destroy freedom and breeds addictions and dependencies on behalf of Belzebseth.

AZURAS   A variety of demons who gave their name to the region of Assur (Babylon). They respond to the Demon Kings.

BELZEBSETH   Demon King and operator of Thanatophor in the territory of the Blue Feather; he is the sorcerer who loads humans with despair. Together with Hangker, he presides over the Dark Council.

CHUPAQUARNI A SKILLED SEDUCTRESS   who brought the young wizard Elkaim close to destruction.

DARK COUNCIL   The disparate forces of evil always tend to join together and their supreme organ of coordination is the Dark Council. Dark Riders Lust, Anger, Greed, Attachment, Jealousy, Vanity, and Pride: the Deadly Sins on the move create conduits in the psyche to divert attention away from the central channel of the White Feather that carries evolution; they can be eradicated with the help of the Glorfakir, the sword of concentrated attention.

EXTERNALISTS   People who take the substance of human life and project it into the Outer World so that the connection with the Inner World is lost; They played the game of Hangker in creating Urizen, the civilization of materialism.

HANGKER   Demon King and operator of Thanatophor in the territory of the Yellow Feather; he seduces humans to serve his own will, while making them feel they do their own thing.

MLECHAS   Creatures who gained great influence during the Dark Age, both stupid and arrogant, mostly lustful, so degraded that they are in hell without knowing it.

MOKOLO   Chief Kheto said the Green Witch is most dangerous amongst all the Dark Riders because she is the one to prevent tribes, nations and the children of the Great Mother from uniting. Her business is to destroy human relationships through jealousy.

NECROMANCERS   Sorcerers who deal with the powers of the dead. There are many of them but Grandpa did not like talking about them. The include Narak, the chief enemy of the House of Anor, whose job is to bring division and conflict. He passed the task to his consort Mokolo, the Fifth Rider.

TANTRIKA   Term used in India to qualify those who try to control the inner instrument (tantra), mostly not knowing how and causing damage.

THANATOPHOR   Satan, the collective principle of evil. It is not known whether he also can materialize in a single form. Some say he has only a psychic body and thus cannot be seen by man. William Blake saw him but he was no ordinary man. Thanatophor is the chief of all the evil forces. Aunt Tracy saw him in a dream.

TITANOSAURS   Leaders of the Azuras. The forms of the Titanosaurs are not known nor do we know how many of them exist but the Avasthic scholars thought there couldn't be more than five of them. Two were revealed through the story: Abuzinal, the southern Titanosaur: his strength grows with anger, fanaticism, and intolerance. Gorschkak, the northern Titanosaur: his strength grows with greed, and exploitation. Both these titanic Azuras are hyperactive in the modern age and constantly strive for domination, pushing the northern and southern hemispheres towards conflict.

URIZEN   A name given by William Blake for the cold, mechanical, heartless modern world of accountants, machines and materialism.

COMPENDIUM. (OTHER TENETS OF THE DEEP WAY)

AMBROSIA (AMRIT, AMRUT)   See under Holy Grail.

AVIDYA   False knowledge that prevents Self-empowerment. The core of it is the illusion that reality is what we think.

ANGKURA   Sprouting seed of spiritual consciousness.

ANANYA   Love within full union.

AVAHAN   The power and the art of inviting the intervention or protection of the higher forces of goodness.

BANDHAN   Protection.

BARDO   The domain where many dead souls dwell between heaven and hell.

BIJE   Seed of power.

CHITTANIRODH   See under podium.

DEEP WAY   The knowledge that binds man with divinity.

ENEMY   The power that challenges the perfectibility of man.

GUNATITH   One of the most prized craft of the House of Anor; the capacity to go beyond reactivity.

HOLY GRAIL   The aim of the greatest quest of the human race that is revealed in the Gift of Ambrosia (Amrut); it is the highest bliss creatures can experience.

INTROSPECTION   The benevolent use of the Glorfakir sword when turned towards oneself.

KAVACH   Armor of protection woven by mantras (magic invocation of the higher powers.)

KILEDAR   One of the titles of the head of the first House meaning "the guardian of the fort," the Kiledar command over the protective magnetic shield of Kalabham.

NIDRA YOGA   The capacity to be connected through meditation in a regenerating sleep.

NISHKRIYA   The state in which one is acting without action.

PODIUM OF CHITTANIRODH   The platform of consciousness where the attention is fully concentrated, under self-control; it can be beamed like a laser. Hence, essentially, the capacity to retain the attention; full mastery over the thinking process.

PSICHASA Murmuring ghosts used by Mokolo to create envy and jealousy in order to close the flow of the heart between people.

MARYADAS Subtle boundaries establishing the code of right conduct; one of the disciplines of the Deep Way.

RASA Charm of intoxication and shot of energy when accessing higher bliss.

RATAVOLAR Bat-like creatures that suck self-esteem and confidence in the tunnels of the subconscious, as if they were sucking our very blood.

SAO IAMBU Living stones, emitting energy of protective magnetism.

SHRADDHA Faith, based on experience not on belief. *Shraddha* corresponds to our right hemisphere, which is the termination of the blue zone in the brain - the left channel, as the two channels (zones) cross at the Lily of Anorhad. Consequently the yellow zone (right channel) ends in our left hemisphere where we use surrender to enlighten it.

SNEAKY WAY The way in which evil enters into the psyche because it can camouflage into appearances of beauty, truth and goodness.

SURRENDER Quality of merging into the greater whole that deflates the ego. The combined impact of *shraddha* and surrender fuel the Avahan.

SUSAMSKARA Positive conditionings that build self-defense and security: the DNA for the preservation and enhancement of our spiritual potential.

SWATANTRA Mastery of the Self over the inner instrument. The Swatantra Avasthas are the new race created by the Great Mother,

TUNNELS PATHS Opened in our mind; when some of these conduits take us to hell it is the job of the Dark Riders to carry us there.

VANI Power of speech in which that which is uttered materializes.

VIDYA Real knowledge that enables Self-empowerment. The Avasthas and the Greek philosophers also call it *episteme*. Most people think that their opinion (*doxa*) is knowledge, a sure sign of illusion.

VILAMBA The space of silence between two thoughts which marks the entrance to the Inner World; it is under the control of Christ, the Ruler of the narrow gate.

WEAPONS (AVASTHIC) The Glorfakir (attention) and the Sadhan (contemplation).

CHAPTER ONE

RECONNECTING

Where Lakshmi O'Lochan goes shopping with Sean Aryaputra in the Chatuchak market in Bangkok to find a special statue, and how he mentions the return of the Great Mother.

Sometimes Lakshmi O'Lochan would close her eyes to see better. She would do so when, for no particular reason, a pressing urge would suck her attention inside. She felt a pleasant relaxation in her chest, a slow rise of expectation and the protection of an invisible presence softly embracing her.

She took a deep breath and exited the subway train. The rush-hour traffic of Bangkok was deafening. She braved the motorcycles zigzagging through the congested traffic and took a cab to her destination on Soi Settabhut where, in a meeting arranged by her cousin, a Thai businessman not previously known to her, would take her out to see the famous Chatuchak market.

A gardener opened the door, and she was greeted by the barking of an agile, miniature pincher that sniffed at her, and satisfied that she'd passed muster, became immediately and exuberantly friendly. Lakshmi followed the dog, which stopped now and then and looked back to ensure she was still following. The bamboo screen along the alley provided a refreshing canopy to a garden of respectable size by Bangkok standards. The lawn was shaded by a variety of palm trees of differing shapes and sizes. Begonias and orchids added a colorful charm to this secluded place.

The ancient house, miraculously spared from the recent real estate boom, was built on two floors with large wooden terraces. It was of a traditional, light Thai structure with the basement in stone and the upper floors in teak. A large mango tree, whose generous shade was much appreciated during the summer months, flanked the entrance.

Her host appeared, and in a quiet voice said, "Putzi, calm down." The dog responded immediately and stopped his playful pranks. Her host, a handsome man with finely chiseled traits, fair skin, soft eyes and a pleasant smoothness that exuded discrete distinction greeted Lakshmi. There was a familiar air about him, a sense of déjà vu. He welcomed her with an engaging grin.

"Welcome Mrs. O'Lochan, I just had your cousin Lakshman on the phone. He wanted to make sure we take good care of you. My name is Chasean, but you can call me Sean; it's more appropriate."

"Delighted to meet you. Please call me Lakshmi. If you don't mind my asking, why do you consider Sean more appropriate?"

"In Thai, Chasean means 'the chief of hundred thousand soldiers' while Sean simply means one hundred thousand. My Western friends call me by the Irish name Sean.

Lakshmi responded with a warm smile to the gentle welcoming.

Sean proposed, "Your cousin Lakshman told me that you probably need to do a bit of shopping before you fly back to Washington. You can find everything in Bangkok, and good quality too. Would you like to come with me to the Chatuchak market?"

She was grateful for the offer, and they left immediately. They found a dusty parking spot and walked through a labyrinth of narrow alleys and stalls displaying goods of every possible kind. The crowd was so dense that Lakshmi feared getting lost, and so she walked closely behind her guide. As her cousin Lakshman was arriving that night, Lakshmi wanted to welcome him with a typical Thai gift. She also wanted to shop for her husband and was thrilled about being shown around by someone who knew every nook and cranny of the market.

As they arrived at the covered section of the market selling ornamental objects and handicrafts, Sean pointed to a stall. "Look at this display: the owner is the only one left here who has genuine antiques, and she has some really fine specimens I want to show you."

They examined an array of Buddha statues of Thai and Burmese origin scattered on the floor, some in bronze, and others in gold, or ochre colored wood. Most were modern replicas; a few were originals, probably coming from the hills above Chiang Mai in the north or smuggled across the Burmese border. Many statues showed a long undulating flame shooting from the apex of the crown.

"This flame surging from the top of the head of the Buddha, dear Lakshmi, is the rocket I was talking about; it can transport us through the etheric plane and beyond, so that we may enter collective consciousness. Look at the details," said Sean, holding one particularly fine statue up for Lakshmi to get a closer look. At the base of the central flame, she noted an engraving that appeared to be a comma.

"How much did they know of the secret energy?" she asked as she pointed to a wooden sculpture that had come from the roof of an ancient temple. It also depicted an undulating flame springing upwards from a half coil.

"Who knows?" Sean shrugged, "This is also shown on the royal state crest of the King, but today they have no clue what it means; this comma suggests the half part of the three and a half coils, the sign of the sacred serpent, unfolding at the base of the ascending flame. Regretfully, in these times no one pays attention to the meaning of symbols; most are just interested in selling their goods," he added with a glance in the direction of the saleswoman.

She looked like a village woman in simple attire, sitting on a small piece of worn-out carpet on the floor, her hair covered by a scarf and her head resting on her crossed arms above her raised knees, without paying particular attention to her potential clients, or so it seemed.

"I'll buy something for Jonathan. Come, let's have a look around and we'll come back later."

As they turned away, they heard a voice asking in English, "Why did they kill Pythagoras?"

They froze in their steps and turned in the direction of the voice. The saleswoman was not looking at them; she still had her head buried in her arms. It was surprising enough that she spoke fluent English, but this was Bangkok, not Athens, and not the place where you would expect to hear remarks about the fate of a pre-Socratic philosopher.

"I beg your pardon?"

The woman slowly raised her head; her piercing glance surprised them by its sheer intensity; her voice was vibrant and a baffled Lakshmi sensed a power in her, a power that was now calling, "Why did they persecute Heraclites, the Ephesian? Why did they kill Zarathustra and why did they butcher Hussein in Kerbala, sending horsemen to trample over his body? And do you remember what they did on Golgotha? Why did they burn Joan of Arc? Pardon always comes, Daughter of the Lion, but to what avail? They go on killing all those who were sent to show the way. They never learn. And they are still after us. They are after you." The woman said with a shake of her head.

Sean and Lakshmi stood still, mystified by this diatribe. Their strange interlocutor was old, with slanted eyes; high cheekbones and skin too brown for the average Thai, maybe indicating the woman came from a remote mountain tribe. They didn't know what to say, and fortunately, a group of American tourists gave them some respite by elbowing them to one side and enquiring rudely about the price of some items.

Sean and Lakshmi shared a glance and a premonition that some-thing was on its way. For Lakshmi, the legend was again knocking at the door. Now the door was opening but having heard the warning of the saleswoman, Lakshmi registered the diffuse perception of a threat-ening presence approaching. It reminded her of the vigil in the hall of Jetzenstein Castle, before the demons and their Japanese bodyguards interrupted: the sensation was weaker, no doubt, but of the same nature, gripping the stomach, and accelerating the heartbeat slightly. She had not felt the presence of any precise threat for the past year, and she intensely disliked being reminded of the sensation. She took a deep breath and, deciding consciously not to show fear, she turned around.

Lakshmi methodically scanned the crowd of people around her and focused on one silhouette in the shade of the shop next door. It was of a shaven-headed monk wearing sunglasses, peering from behind a group of tourists. He seemed to be scrutinizing the old woman's display, looking for something. Despite his attempts to be discreet, she could now distinguish his face and noted a thin mouth that expressed harsh-ness. Lakshmi felt uncomfortable; she had the impression that she had seen him before and recalled that she'd registered his hostile attention as she'd entered the Chatuchak market. He'd been pretending to examine trinkets at one of the small stalls near the entrance, and she had sensed that he was furtively looking at her. It is not that rare for men in the street to look at young women, but this was something different and Lakshmi shivered slightly. She turned as if she had not noticed the monk and whispered discreetly, "Is that fellow in saffron clothes follow-ing us? He gives me the creeps."

As though sensing menace, the woman quickly placed a cloth over one particularly old statue that had drawn their attention. Sean raised his head inquisitively in the direction of the monk and to Lakshmi's surprise stepped purposefully in his direction. Unwilling to take the challenge, the monk swiftly retreated and disappeared into the dense crowd.

4

The Americans left soon afterwards, and the saleswoman turned to Lakshmi and Sean, gestured for them not to speak, removed the cloth and revealed the greenish brass statue of a sitting Buddha in meditation with a gently serene expression. The posture was gracious, the work delicate. Lakshmi noticed at once the crown of flames around his head.

The saleswoman, who'd been keenly observing her, spoke in a quick tone, "Here you are, take this one, it's a genuine piece from Mandalay, eighteenth century. For you, I will make a very special price, only five hundred dollars. Please hurry otherwise, there'll be trouble."

The statue was not as old as Lakshmi had first imagined, but it was an interesting piece with intricately carved, lateral volutes coming out of the Buddha's temples in the Burmese style and a single higher flame coming out of the center of a crown of smaller flames. Bemused by the unexpected turn of events, Sean did not hesitate. His expert eye could recognize a good bargain.

"I do not have the full amount with me. Could you bring it to my house tomorrow evening? Here is the address."

The saleswoman nodded, and Sean scribbled feverishly on a piece of paper. She took the paper and the statue and vanished behind the curtain of a neighboring dwelling. A girl appeared to watch over the display, and with an air of perfect indifference, indicated clearly that she would have nothing to say to them. As they walked away, Lakshmi, ignored the other stalls and merchandise, trying to make sense of the strange encounter.

"Lakshmi, I don't understand any of this. Why did she call you 'Daughter of the Lion'? Let's ask her."

"The lion is on the coat of arms of several countries; for example, the United Kingdom or Bohemia. In Jetzenstein, I saw a lion on the emblem of Eleksim, the Fourth House of the Avasthas, to which I am supposed to have once belonged. I found out about my past from the demons that had come to kill us. This is the only reference that makes sense to me because I have no connection to a lion except for this one! This is eerie and besides, did you notice? She gave us the only Buddha with a crown of flames around the head, springing from the limbic area of the brain. That'd be my guess, but I don't begin to understand it. Lakshman will probably be tired when he flies in tomorrow night but what luck that he can be with us to see the statue."

"I'm sure he won't mind, from what you told me he wouldn't want to miss this woman. I really want him to see the statue too. It's hard to find such excellent workmanship these days."

"It's always exciting when Lakshman is with me. Things happen when we are together, adventure seems just around the corner," Lakshmi said with a vibrancy Sean didn't expect. As they were about to get into their car, Lakshmi looked in a pocket mirror as if to check her make up. "I don't like the look of him. There he is again. Don't turn, Sean, he is still watching us."

"Whom are you talking about?"

"That young monk. What's up with him?"

"OK, get into the car. I have a camera on my cell phone. I'll pretend to be on the phone." Walking back and forth, gesticulating as if engrossed in a captivating conversation, Sean took a picture of the spying monk who did not suspect the maneuver.

As they returned from the market, Sean invited her to stay for dinner. They entered the house, and he introduced Lakshmi to his mother, sister, wife, and their children, two lovely daughters who evoked the celestial dancers of Thai legends.

A large combined living and dining room sustained by white pillars in the middle occupied the ground floor. Lakshmi, comfortably settled in a bamboo armchair and sipping a tumbler of fruit punch, surveyed her surroundings. She noted the large beige, and light green silk cushions scattered on the floor. The dark reddish texture of the teak floor and staircase allied to the delicate woodwork of the mahogany lattice separating the living room from the dining room gave a sense of intimacy to the space. Large French windows, through which a light breeze flowed, provided a natural coolant.

They spent the evening over a light meal. Sean was a business-man, Sales Manager for a Japanese luxury car brand. During small talk, they got to know each other faster than they had expected, and Lakshmi found that interactions between members of the family were affection-ate and relaxed.

More interestingly, she found out her host was a committed student of the Deep Way. Lakshmi understood why Lakshman had wanted her to meet him. Sean told her that a woman was now teaching it in these modern times, and that many invisible enemies opposed her work of emancipation. As he related his experiences, it became clear that he was talking about the lady she'd met in the sari shop in New Delhi.

Lakshmi registered a diffuse oppression in her chest. She breathed deeply and focused her attention to dispel the unpleasant sensation. She knew that she'd often pick up these signals when forces of good and evil battling in the invisible world would come close to her. Lakshmi felt goose bumps on her arms, sensing she was again connecting with the one whom, as the Lady of the Rock, had been the protector of the Avasthas.

Sean called this lady, "the Great Mother" and explained that She had been the ruler of Dagad Trikon in command of the transforming power of the magic serpent. Lakshmi now knew in her heart that She was the same as the Great Mother who was taking Sean and his friends through the greatest spiritual transformation of all time.

When mentioning her name, Sean imperceptibly switched moods: his usual lightness of touch faded to something approaching reverence. Lakshmi was excited and hopeful that meeting up with the lady again was now entering the realm of possibility. This was the moment she had been waiting for since her first encounter with the mysterious lady in New Delhi. She was finally reconnecting with the quest, but this time in a contemporary context that would, with any luck, be more accessible than the itinerary of her past adventures.

"What are you looking for Sean? What is it that you want, and why do you follow Her teachings?"

"I want true freedom. Freedom between this and that is not real freedom at all; it is often confusing and true freedom of choice is limited. I know for most people freedom is about making choices and this understanding inspired political democracy and market economy. All this is well and good, but it did not prevent the present mess that we see in this world when we look around. I want full freedom, freedom from ignorance, from darkness, from stupid desires. I am fed up with all the chains we carry in our head. My thoughts forge my chains; my emotions are my bondage. I want the freedom that is spiritual, the freedom of my spirit, and I want it to soar in light."

"Soaring in the light? You remind me of my husband Jonathan. His sister Tracy calls him 'Seagull' because he carries the same nostalgia."

In the ensuing conversation, she narrated her trip to Delphi with Lakshman and Ivan Sadaka when they visited the Rock of the Pithy. Sean asked when these events had occurred and laughed.

Sean explained that he had participated in an international event in Delphi on the very same day. It had been one of the mystical festivals that the students of the Deep Way regularly attended in order to raise their level of spiritual energy.

Lakshmi remembered seeing a gathering of people who seemed to be camping in a large tent just below the town. It turned out that Sean had been one of those who had gathered there with the Great Mother. Lakshmi wanted to know more about this event but postponed her questions, as she wanted to tell her own story.

It was easy for Lakshmi to open up to her host. There was something cozy about his family; the fondness among them was contagious. Late into the night, she shared the extraordinary adventure Lakshman and she had experienced in the unfolding Dagad Trikon legend. Sean soon became engrossed in the lore of the Dagad Trikon and the Lady of the Rock. Lakshmi was surprised not to find him more skeptical in his response to her story, but he seemed to care deeply about how the dimension of self-empowerment revealed by the Deep Way could be applied to daily life. This was indeed the reason for the interest he had in the spiritual path he was following.

Sean said, "There is much I have yet to figure out. Our small community in Bangkok is trying to help people to understand the basics. The common folk must reconnect to their ancestral heritage, as our King urges us to do, because there is much knowledge of the Deep Way that was already here in ancient Thailand. For example, our folk art is filled with stories of the White Monkey that Lakshman told me about. Moreover, we used to know a lot about the serpent power but today all that is left of this heritage is the belief that one should burn incense in front of the Buddha's statue in order to get a better job or to marry the right girl. Important, agreed, but don't you think we should realize by now that there is more to it than that?"

"You seem to be a very knowledgeable group," Lakshmi observed with a trace of surprise.

"Yes and no, it is quite bizarre. The students of the Great Mother come from all walks of life. She gives them the cards but lets them play the game; there is quite a bit of randomness. Many people who receive the experience do not prepare for it. Some are fine, quietly minding their own business, nurturing their families and trying to share access to the Deep Way whenever they can. Others are more flamboyant, eager to speak, tweet, or blog about it but sometimes slower to imbibe its deeper meaning."

Sean noted the surprised expression on the face of the young woman and continued with a grin, "Our numbers are still rather small. It looks at times as if many who were meant to join missed the boat, while others unexpectedly found themselves sailing with it. Sometimes I feel that some had their appetite for spiritual growth spoiled by the good things of the material world: success, fame, wealth, or popularity. I have entertained managers, lawyers, even one or two pop stars but most seem too self-important or too distracted to accept the priceless gifts of the Great Mother."

"Well, if they aren't asking, how could they receive?"

"Others who were hungry got lost in their own search and ate at the wrong table. So finally the Great Mother sent Her people into the streets inviting all those who are willing to come to the meal. They are distributing leaflets in shopping malls, in car parks, train stations and other public places. This has been happening worldwide for many years."

"It sounds rather like the invitation to dinner in *The New Testament* parable. The *Bible* says the guests who were expected got lost on the way, but then the master of the house sends his servants to the crossroads to invite whosoever wanted to come. And so, at least other people had a chance to have a seat at the table."

"Perhaps but not everybody seizes the chance that is offered and, by the way, merely sitting at the table is not enough."

Lakshmi registered a paradox in Sean. On one hand, he clearly knew what he was talking about, expressing himself with an easy elegance, with clarity, and without pretense. He was insightful in his grasp of the mechanisms of the mind and balanced in his judgment. However, she could spot something like a touch of melancholy in him. The exchange was uncomplicated; she felt that both recognized that they shared a sense of complicity. Lakshmi was appreciating the ease that is enjoyed in the company of those who had accessed the Deep Way. If all the students of the Great Mother were like Sean and his family, she thought with a trace of envy, they would be enchanting people to be associated with.

Sean's voice now carried a new vibrancy, "We have much catching up to do. I have something really important to tell you."

"Important? Like what?"

"Like finding the right thread. Many pearls make the necklace, but it is the thread that maintains them together. Find the thread and reach all the pearls. Find the core of all men and you shall reach the great oneness. This is the Ariane thread, the thread that takes us out of the labyrinth of our own thoughts."

Sean's words caught Lakshmi's full attention. For a split second that was beyond human time, she sensed within herself the presence of a strange force.

Sean continued, "The old forms must fade to give way to the higher beauty of the new ones. What will happen now is the transformation that comes with the changing of ages, as it does every time evil comes close to victory but is even closer to defeat. This moment was to come, and it is coming."

"You mean, like the big one, the moment they expect in California, sitting on the San Andreas fault?"

"This is not about destruction. In the heavens, there is a bottomless lake of joy waiting to be released for the benefit of the human race.

It will pour down with a tremendous force and the channels within the human brain must be cleaned out so that human beings are able to receive it. This is living alchemical work, and the entire creation is involved in a great churning, a formidable transformation to bring about this break-through. Everything contributes to it, good and bad, from the melting of the glaciers to the sound of clapping hands in musical festivals."

A spiral of coolness ascended within her spine, and she shivered. Somehow, she felt that this man was pointing to the destination of the Stealthstars who, coming from the stars of a higher world, were Avasthas who had returned in the human race, but needing to move stealthily and hide from the devil. How was it possible that he could have such an effect on her?

CHAPTER TWO

THE TALE OF MARILUH

Where Sean explains a dream and Mariluh Ataui, the seer from South America, tells of reviving all that was good, powerful and holy in the past and brings Sean to meet the wizard Sanath at the Oriental Hotel.

The next morning Lakshmi was back at an intergovernmental meeting in the sleek, white building of the UN Economic Commission for Asia and the Pacific in Bangkok. The meeting was dragging on and on, and its monotony was making her restless. She'd much prefer to return to her rented flat and play with her baby Ananya. Her daughter was now one-year-old and quite a handful but friends had recommended a good nanny, which was lucky.

Her attention drifted longingly to her Jonathan. Lakshmi needed to admire the man she loved and her husband made it easy for her. He was intensely sincere, a man of principle, sensitive with an alert intelligence. She appreciated his honesty, how he managed to remain true to his convictions. Lakshman had been such a darling for having introduced her to the man who'd brought her such contentment. And her marriage had strengthened the already strong friendship between the two men. She was thrilled that Lakshman was now on his way to join her in Bangkok.

The Fijian delegate's speech proved to be a good time to make a discrete departure. Outside, she called her husband, eager to share with him what had kept her mind busy the entire day and her expectations of the evening to come.

"This meeting is boring me to tears but it'll soon be over. How is D.C.? One more week and I'll be back in the States, my love! Yes, the baby is fine. Great news: Lakshman has arranged a dinner with a nice guy whom I met yesterday. His name is Chasean Aryaputra and I'll see him again tonight. Lakshman arrives from Mumbai and will join us. I have such a good feeling. I think we shall finally meet the Lady of Dagad Trikon."

Lakshmi rushed home where Ananya, a sparkling little beauty, with Jonathan's forehead and Lakshmi's eyes, welcomed her with sweet gurgles and accepted the last milk of the day without fuss. Lakshmi, hardly able to control her enthusiasm at the prospect of the evening ahead, sang somewhat heartily what would otherwise have been a gentle lullaby. Leaving the sleeping baby with the babysitter, she took the overpass Sukhumvit metro line and descended at Ekamai station from where she reached the Aryaputra home by taxi.

Dinner was served, and Lakshmi enjoyed chicken soup with lemon grass and coconut prepared by Sean's mother, followed by delicious seafood. After dinner, while Sean's children watched TV, Sean and Lakshmi sat on the cushions spread around a low Chinese table. Soon the conversation turned to the core of the matter.

"The meditation the Great Mother teaches brings us to our essence," Sean began, "We reach the depth of our being where we connect with something greater than our individual selves, like the part finding the whole. Sometimes I have strange haunting dreams, flying in the air or even through the earth itself. Last night, as I knew I was meeting you again; I dreamt of oneness. It was quite a surprising situation.

"I don't particularly like soccer but in this dream I found myself in a football stadium. It was a grand occasion, either the final of the World Cup or the European Cup. The excitement around the taut, tense field of play was palpable. This was the turning point in the tournament; impending defeat turning into triumph. One side gained the advantage, mounted a coordinated attack on a crowded defense. A deafening ovation came from the fans as an attacker sprinted between the rallying defenders, guided the ball delicately with the outside of his boot between the legs of a defender, and scored a goal with a crisp, low shot.

"At this moment the red and gold wall of fans released a fantastic roar. Spectators jumped to their feet, their arms in the air. The players hugged each other, and raised their arms in salute to the fans who responded in kind. Waves of energy were released from this celebration.

"And then something clicked in my head. It was the synchronicity of the movements, minds and feelings that was emitting a formidable psychic force. It was profane jubilation, no doubt, but with a kind of ecstasy nevertheless. In this pitched moment and for a little while after, the fans had become a collective being, setting aside their individual personalities as the juice of euphoria flowed through them.

"A witness to this colossal scene, I realized it had nothing to do with soccer. Yes, this was a sports stadium but soccer was only the chosen pretext, the powerful trigger. In this brief form of exultation, players and onlookers broke into a new dimension. They had become one, and they felt that joy. They were in it, yet unaware of it. My sleep was bathed in the feeling." Sean paused. "I realized it had started; it is happening."

Lakshmi's face betrayed her puzzlement.

"I mean the new dimension," Sean explained. "I could feel it—how the jubilation of the players and the fans was melting, merging into one. And so I found myself murmuring *Akasha*, ether. I checked when I woke up and indeed, *akasha* means ether in Sanskrit!"

"This is cool but what has the element of ether to do with the crowd in the stadium?"

"We are separate individuals, each one living in our own body, our own mind, our own world. To go beyond the elements of matter that divide into unconnected forms there is a solution: we must reach with our consciousness, the plane of the element that permeates all in order to access union. Ether is the carrier, flowing into everything, omnipresent and invisible. The subtle dimension of ether carries the potential of a gigantic union in the material world."

"It certainly carries the advent of the brave new cyber world with its electronic town hall, everybody chatting on the Internet as though they were neighbors."

"Yes, but let's go a step further. Converging, commonality of hearts and minds, all this works for the Inner World. It opens the space to release the spiritual energy of the new age. This is the Aquarian step of evolution, the omega towards which we converge: merging into oneness. Collective consciousness is going to be possible in the material world through the etheric plane."

"Are you saying it is really going to happen – without a soccer match?"

"When I woke up, I remembered the Great Mother's words. She once said that we were becoming aware of the whole that we are going to become. With this heightened ethereal sense, the children of the Great Mother will become perfectly connected between themselves. They shall then become a wide enough channel through which the forces and the visions of the heavens can be released. The future has begun. It is baffling;

I had this insight on the evening of meeting you; this encounter of ours has a meaning."

The insight affected Lakshmi too. She felt the energy rushing through her throat and spreading on the lower plate of her brain like a misty cloud. She thought, "He speaks like an Avastha; we are indeed regrouping."

Lakshmi asked, "For millennia the mystery has been: how to achieve oneness? Yes, I agree with you. It should be the next step. Are the soccer fans pointing the way?" She laughed merrily, "How did your dream end?"

"Not too well. We are women and men of the telecommunications age and we have discovered the powers of the Outer World hidden within ether. I saw it filled with sparks of electricity. Digital data cascaded across computer screens. Images of network news and TV channels flashed back and fro, reporting on conflicts and wars. A web was undulating. It was the World Wide Web flushed with billions of messages. Then ugly, hairy, brownish worms crawled in to devour it. Computers crashed all over the world in a ruthless cyber war and finally, during a gigantic solar storm, the magnetic field of the earth was smashed. Electricity supplies failed, and all the lights went out."

"Wow! We either go forwards or backwards don't we? Nothing in between!"

"Yes and I think we do not have much time." Sean said, his face somber, "Negative forces, rushing to block this path, are also active."

His entire discourse had been pointing to a bright outcome but now Lakshmi realized that the achievements of a grand spiritual pursuit could not be taken for granted. She felt again the unease in her chest, as if finding herself at the eve of a great battle. She chased away her fear.

They did not notice the time going by while sharing the intensity of Sean's insights. "Your cousin should be arriving anytime now and the lady from the market is late. I do hope she will come."

Later that evening when Lakshman arrived at the airport, he marveled at the ornate wooden statues and orchid arrangements in the middle of the conveyor belts in Baggage Claim, happy to rediscover the artistic resourcefulness of the Thai people. He called his cousin and agreed to meet her at the Aryaputra residence.

He reached the house around midnight where Sean and his family warmly welcomed him. Lakshmi hugged him and took him to the veranda to enjoy a light monsoon shower that freshened the air. With the excitement of a schoolgirl, she took him aside and told him that, since meeting Sean, the old magic of the Rock had begun again, with a strange new urgency. As they rejoined Sean in the living room the discussion continued, they spoke about Delphi and Sean spoke of the spiritual festivals known as pujas that were held by the followers of the Great Mother.

"Can you explain?" asked Lakshmi, "If people travel from all over the world to celebrate what you call a puja, it can't just be for the music or for feel-good entertainment. There must be a subtle effect of a puja that makes it worthwhile. What would that be?"

"Synchronized give and take!" said Sean with a warm smile. "We give, we receive. I am glad you ask because this subject is dear to me. Where to start?" He paused to chose his words and then continued, "You see, life is not absurd; complete self-fulfillment is the destination. But to reach that state we need to go deep within ourselves, into a plane we cannot normally access. So what to do? The beauty that is buried within us also exists outside, at the highest level. It is the world of the heavens. The word puja that we use for these celebrations means worship. We project our devotion outside because this invites the depth inside to emerge. The very movement of approaching the heavens above brings us nearer to our own heavens hidden within. With the rites, the decorations, the prayers and the music, we direct our devotion and love to a world of purity, which responds in kind and we receive. This purity then manifests within. We feel light, joyful, loving, we touch this beautiful state inside where we are completely fulfilled."

Lakshmi leaned forward, obviously enthralled by Sean's words. "We understood that in the days of the Avasthas these festivities released a flow of energy that invigorated those who attended them. Going back to your dream in the stadium, it all points to oneness, but this time at a level ordinary people can consciously feel. This depth of unity can bind a crowd in the wonder of a collective state."

A dog barked outside, breaking the silence that had ensued. A maid entered and announced the arrival of a visitor who had come to deliver an antique statue. Sean, realizing it was the woman from the Chatuchak market, urged the maid to invite her in.

The visitor left her dripping umbrella on the sheltered terrace outside. As she entered the room, she seemed to be taller, more impressive than in the market. They exchanged greetings and presentations. Lakshmi paid for the statue and asked, "We are most grateful madam that you came in person to deliver the statue, but can you please tell us why you mentioned Pythagoras to us?"

"We are guided in ways we don't know, Mrs. O'Lochan, or as I said," she added with a disarming smile, "Daughter of the Lion! Sometimes hints and coincidences are provided, so we recognize the moment. The time for the persecution of the holy ones is ending. Instead, they must now be acknowledged."

Sean was as keen as the cousins in his determination to figure out the implications of this encounter, and he asked, "You seem to know us but we don't know you. If Lakshmi is the Daughter of the Lion, can we please know who you are?"

"I am a member of the Most Venerable Order of the Hllidarendi. I came from Colombia to Thailand at the bidding of the Grand Master of the Order. I am the priestess of the Kogis known as Mariluh Ataui."

They were dumbfounded. The cousins had been worried about not having heard from Sanath for a very long time and there was no hope or means of contacting him so they simply had to wait for him to pick the right time to visit them. Lakshmi cleared her throat and asked, "You know Master Sanath? Do you know where he is at present?"

"Yes, this is why I contacted you. The Hllidarendi Master is at the Oriental Hotel, here in Bangkok. I told him I'd met you earlier than expected, and he was pleased. He would be most grateful if I could bring Mr. Sean to him tonight, and he will be overjoyed to meet with you all the day after tomorrow. But he asks you please to be discrete."

The room was hushed as they absorbed the woman's words. Lakshmi and Lakshman had never met another member of the Order besides Sanath.

Lakshmi was the first to speak, "You are telling us, respected lady, that you have been sent by the Hllidarendi, known to us as Master Sanath? We have not heard from him since he held a memorable council of your Order at Jetzenstein Castle on the Rhine valley some years ago. Now you are telling us he is a few kilometers from here? It's all a bit baffling. Could you tell us more about the Master's recent whereabouts please?"

Mariluh had an open face with large cheeks framed by black hair that reached her shoulders, and her attention sparkled in her slightly slanted eyes. Her glance was lively, scintillating, yet calmly resolved. Rivulets of small wrinkles, suggesting an advanced age, covered her sun-tanned skin.

"As I said, he just returned here from China and is now resting at the Oriental Hotel, more precisely in room 102. He asked me to convey to you his warmest greetings and an invitation to join him there for lunch the day after tomorrow. Now he needs to sleep, but he would appreciate a meeting with Mr. Sean in order to clarify the record, so to speak, and to prepare him for the next steps of your adventure."

She turned to Sean with unexpected kindness, "It was the Master who told me about you but while he knows your guests, he did not yet have the pleasure of meeting you. Please do not ask me more about this; a car is waiting outside, and it will bring you home later. All is well really, but he asks you to be careful. Our enemies heard about a possible gathering of the Stealthstars in this country, the land of the White Elephant."

Lakshman narrated how the wizard's house had been blown up in Holland and how he'd managed to escape and, in consequence, Sanath had talked about humans in the service of the satanic Thanatophor and was now very careful. The cousins were overjoyed to hear about Sanath and happy that he had invited their new friend.

Lakshmi asked the Columbian priestess, "My lady, are you like our Master Sanath; one of the ancient beings?"

"How old does one need to be to be called ancient? At the time of the Incas, I used to walk the high country between the Machu Pichu fortress and Lake Titicaca, and I was a peacemaker among the tribes. In those days, we were using two thousand varieties of potatoes, fifty-two species of maize and countless varieties of quinoa. However, when the Spaniards arrived, they forced the Andean people to eat only wheat. We all became impoverished in many different ways. I started to understand the plan of the Evil One, but it was already too late. When the Great Inca Atahualpa was captured, I took refuge in the north and later wandered the sierras of the Kogi people."

Mariluh eased herself into one of the large green armchairs. Lakshman asked her for more details, urged on by his native curiosity. The archeologist knew about the Kogis, their pre-Colombian knowledge system and their intimate connection to nature.

"The enemy of our race, Thanatophor, wants to abolish diversity. The 'younger brothers' as the Kogis refer to the white man, followed his lead when they indulged in slavery, racism and conquest, cementing their empires with our blood, making everyone fit into their norm. To this day, the followers of the tyrant Hangker are at work to produce a world that is subdued and sanitized, where men eat the same food, churn the same thoughts and, if possible, dream the same dreams – and of course, consume more. They become plugged into a robotic system that he controls. That system mercilessly plunders Mother Earth. I helped the Kogi tribe to resist the money regime, which promotes monocultures to wipe out the life-style of indigenous people."

"Do you mean that we should now re-learn the ancient ways?"

"Of course. The Kogi systems of cropping, grazing and agro-forestry represented diverse languages in the dialogue of our race with Mother Earth. We addressed her with tender respect, and she responded as a live entity with intelligence, bounty and love. What your experts today call the services of ecosystems was quite simply to us the multiplication of her response, of her gifts. These languages are dying now, known only to a few elders, but they were mastered by the earlier Hllidarendis."

"Still, I do not quite understand why it is so important for the devil to eradicate diversity, do you?" Lakshmi asked turning to Sean.

"Look at the madness of the twentieth century," he responded. Thanatophor drove the masses into the deceptive security of conformism. He generated leaders who wanted to mold people and entire nations into a phony external uniformity. This is the opposite of living in unity. Enforced uniformity is a tyrant's fantasy, a parody inspired by the devil to poke fun at divine unity."

"I agree with Sean," said Lakshman. "The Evil One's political plot brings power hungry rulers to ridicule the totality of God by creating their own little totalities. Goethe was making fun of this. Gorshkak, the northern Titanosaur, and his agents perfected this job. Remember Mussolini, Hitler, Stalin and Mao? Totalitarian ideologies trampled men and women, millions of them. Charlie Chaplin showed the dictator as a clown but not all clowns make you laugh. It seems the younger brothers too have been punished as well, this time by those regimes that turned against their citizens. This is an unexpected twist don't you agree?"

Sean turned again to Mariluh with a hint of perplexity animating his intelligent face, "Diversity, unity, how does it all fit together?"

"In essence, the invention of tyrants is the devil's mockery. The rulers play god but practice evil." Mariluh had carefully followed the exchange and was pleased by the insights. "Diversity was meant to nurture inter-actions and play. Adivatar created differences; he deposited his beauty in a variety of creatures and diverse forms of human life. Interactions between races, tribes, places and ideas were to sustain a beautiful variety. Diversity provided the elements to propel his creation towards higher col-lective organisms. We were to reach the synthesis of integrated societies and finally, we, his children through our discoveries, would merge in a new state. A majestic spiritual consciousness would eventually result from this play. This was the secret of living unity that the Avastha elders had entrusted to the House of Anor. And this is what the demons are now determined to prevent."

Clearly, Mariluh was not merely a village saleswoman from Chatuchak. There was an authority in her words, a power that carried conviction, a sign that she was indeed a member of the highest order of wizards. Penetrating and articulate, she knew about the lore of Dagad Trikon as well as what was going on now.

"What is your story? What is your mission as a member of the High Order?" Lakshman asked?

Mariluh continued her tale, "When the Avasthas retreated to the subterranean fortress of Elnelok, they stayed there for some generations, but they aspired to return to the light of the sun. Eventually, they decided to leave, and a great migration took the last of them through white and grey sands to the mountain the Touareg tribes of southern Algeria later called the Atakor, in the heart of the Hoggar from where the water flows. In this immensity heaven and earth appear to be one.

"This is where I connect with my first memories. I was the attendant of Evenyl, an Avastha princess, the only one remaining from the elders of Eleksim. While others were fast losing their Avasthic memory, the princess remembered the glory of her race and could see the future. She told me I would take birth in the far away islands of the setting sun. Indeed, I carry both Inca and Aztec blood and had to witness also the fall of both these kingdoms. I saw the emerald god of the Avasthas visiting the Andes on a condor and he came to me in my dreams. He told me to sustain my people. As a young woman, I lived in osmosis with Cochabamba, Mother Earth, and gave sustenance to the land and people of the high sierras. However, I got into trouble for I cared too much about others and not enough about myself. This was my mistake and thus I discovered and experienced decay.

"I felt the pain of others within my body. Then, every patch of forest that was cut, every brook that was polluted, and every field that was ruined became a wrinkle on my face, and this is how my age started showing. The burden was too heavy, and I was about to die. The great wizard snatched me up from the jaws of death; he stayed in my village and trained me. I would have preferred to stay in the sierras with my people but I was getting drained of my strength. He taught me how to look after myself better.

"I was called to join the Hllidarendis because I could feel the electro-magnetic fields of plants, animals, people and invisible beings. In that intuitive knowledge, my task is just to take care, to give and to love. This knowledge is much wider than all the thinking and science that so captured the little brothers, those modern minds. Alas, it is harder to love when the little brothers take only to the culture of selfish grabbing."

The sincerity of the Columbian was touching. She looked much more present and majestic than the person Sean and Lakshmi had seen in the market. She was revealing herself to them slowly as she continued, her voice calm but firm. She had spent her life hiding her status as a member of the Secret Order to foil the plots of Belzebseth, the head of the league of the necromancers and an archenemy of the Order. Sanath had told the members that the devil knew of the existence of the Order and that he would stop at nothing to capture one of them. But, now that Mariluh was in the company of the cousins and Sean's family she felt comforted, sensing they were all on the same side of the cosmic fence dividing the camps of good and evil.

"Since I could no longer protect myself Master Sanath took me away from the land of the Kogis, assigning me the task of rediscovering the lost paths. He told me I carried within me the intuitive wisdom of the older brothers, the Avasthas, and must reactivate the inner lives of local and traditional knowledge systems, so that people can be reconnected to the ancient genius of their race!"

"Now I understand better why the Order wishes to preserve diversity, my lady, but what is your errand in my country?" Sean asked. "I love Thailand but what can be done here? I can see there is potential, but the country faces immense challenges. Here like elsewhere in Asia, people are struggling hard to make a living in uncertain circumstances. This effort absorbs most of their attention and energy. It is hard to let them know they have a right to expect more and better from their lives."

"Keep hope, this land has been blessed," Mariluh assured him. "The primeval flame of the Buddha is worshiped here because the Emerald King himself walked barefoot for five years on this land. The sovereign of the worlds switched off the memory of his divine origin to share in our human life. Thai people know him in their national legend as Rama of Ayodhya. He came here as he was looking for his wife Sita, who had been abducted by the demon, Ravanna of Lanka, who rode in a carriage drawn by pride and lust. After Rama came to these shores, the seers sighted the White Elephant in the forests of Thailand, an augur that a great transformation was in the offing."

Lakshman waited patiently for Mariluh to finish; he was not going to interrupt a member of the High Order. "This was over ten thousand years ago or so. We are still waiting—but what has all this to do with time anyway? I trust the Master will reveal more."

Mariluh moved as if to get up from her seat. Sean sensed that the visit of the Kogi priestess was coming to an end, so he hastened to ask a last question, "I would be grateful if we could quickly go back to what happened today at the market. Please tell me, do you know this fellow?" Sean showed the photo of the young monk to Mariluh. Her expression became severe.

"I don't," she responded after carefully studying the photograph, "there are evil monks although I do work with good ones who did not betray the Buddha. This one seems to work for the Externalists."

"Externalists? Who are they?

"The Externalists is the name the wizard uses to refer to those who, across centuries and continents, have appropriated knowledge and religion to strengthen their own power. Religion is about going inside and sharing this inner wealth, whereas they are about ruling outside and robbing material wealth. Religion is the passage between the Inner and Outer Worlds, but that passage was blocked with an iron fence of institution, prestige, money and control, because this is the way they dominate the faithful. They want to be feared; they do not want to be loved. Externalists follow the scheme of Hangker, the elder son of Lucifer.

"Should we go now?" she asked Sean and then turned to Lakshmi, touching her hand gently, "Please, when you meet the Master, bring the statue that you have just bought."

"Is this statue a special object?" Lakshmi asked.

"Of course, but you shall know more in due time."

On this hopeful note, Mariluh graciously took her leave, and Sean left with her. Lakshmi, on the way home with Lakshman, showed him the statue.

"Look at the decoration on the top of his head. Doesn't it point to the Seventh House, the one that was a mystery even for the Avasthas?" asked Lakshman.

"But this knowledge was within the reach of Siddharta Gautama. This indeed is the origin of his title: 'Buddha' which means the Enlightened One…" Lakshmi paused, "because he was eventually able to break into the Seventh House and became enlightened there. He reactivated the knowledge."

The cousins exchanged a glance. Now they could see Mariluh's point: the past informs the present.

They were greatly looking forward to seeing Sanath again, so much so that Lakshmi could hardly sleep that night. However, Lakshman, exhausted after the journey and all the excitement, crashed into a deep sleep on the sofa in the living room of the small rented studio.

When he awoke, at first he did not register the gurgles of baby Ananya, but when he picked her up he marveled at her deep, shiny, black eyes, which Sanath had once told him, were typical of children born to former Avasthas. After breakfast, the cousins played with the baby and later went to the nearby Tesco Lotus supermarket on Rama IV Street for a relaxing Thai foot massage. "Why were so many staff members and shoppers wearing the same style of yellow T-shirt? Lakshmi wondered. With the unanswered question still in his mind, he went off to buy yellow sapphires stones for his jewelry business in the Shilom district while Lakshmi returned to the UN Conference center.

Sean's night proved to be much more eventful. It was two o'clock in the morning when he arrived at the Oriental Hotel with Mariluh. They asked to be announced to the client in room 102. The receptionist phoned the room and nodded, "You are expected; this is the room for VIPs, the one which was once occupied by the writer W. Somerset Maugham."

The meeting between Sean and Sanath was not unlike the first encounter of Lakshman with Sanath in Iceland. Sean felt intimidated by the presence of this great man but Sanath's amenable manner immediately put him at ease. Sanath gave him a forewarning of the significance of the moment combined with a sense of security. Sean was curious to learn the reasons for this late evening encounter. As if sensing Sean's state of mind, Sanath turned to Mariluh and asked her if she had shared the fruits of her enquiries with him.

"Not yet," she answered and then proceeded to explain to Sean the investigations that brought her to Thailand in the search for the markings of the Deep Way, "In short, some black magic practices in monasteries are emitting a scorching, vibrational heat that spoils the magnetism of the country," she told him. "This heat has nothing to do with the flame of the Buddha that radiates, in fact, a cool energy." She took a deep breath, "And now comes my most important observation. Sean, whenever you and your sister organize a meeting to share initiation in the Deep Way in your gathering place in Bangkok, I registered that the energy of the statues in the nearby temple cools down somewhat."

"Normally nobody can influence the flow. There is a reason for this." said Sanath confidently.

As he listened transfixed to what Sanath was telling him, Sean's curiosity blossomed into premonition. "Sean," Sanath continued, "you are blessed to be one of the very few human beings who are able to recognize the Great Mother. Your connection is fully operational. This is why you must share it with other people."

"But there is such a distance between their minds and themselves; will they accept the Gift? That is the question, isn't it?"

Sanath's face registered that indefinable sadness that Lakshmi had come to recognize. His tone now felt protective. "It is, dear Sean. Once upon a time, the Avasthas, the greatest warriors and sages who ever walked on this earth fell, and their fortress of Dagad Trikon was invaded by demons. Even for some of those who have found the Great Mother, the paths of this world are fraught with uncertainties. You need to understand what happened in the past so that the people She raises do not fall again. We do not want us to let Her down, do we?"

"No! Most certainly not!" A shout escaped from Sean's breast, a reaction to a pain experienced from very far away, from the remote past, and it was now his turn to sense the same sadness Lakshmi had felt in the wizard. It brought them together; "But what can we do, what can I do?" Sean asked in desperation?

"Do you wish to know? First, I have to test you. Are you ready?"

"Of course, you can test me." Something beautiful was coming alive in this moment, and Sean trusted his own innocence. He laughed like a child. He was fascinated by this encounter and inexplicably attracted to Sanath, who had managed to win his trust in such a short time.

CHAPTER THREE

RETURN TO THE BEGINNING

Where Sean, equipped with the magic sword provided by Sanath, goes back through time to learn that he is the heir of the Fifth House and to witness the fall of Dagad Trikon and how, after taking refuge in the den of the wizard, Evenyl is healed by the properties of the Book of the Kavach.

T he wizard gestured to Mariluh, who took a long black rectangular box from a cupboard. She brought it to Sanath who invited Sean to open it. Inside was a sword, most unusual in shape, and of an alloy he could not recognize. But, he felt a shiver along his spine.

Sanath said, "This is Glorfakir, the sword carrying an Avasthic force that opens all frontiers to our attention. I equipped it with a potent spell." The mood of the moment in the Oriental Hotel was solemn and yet Sean felt secure, full of expectation.

With carefully chosen words, Sanath evoked the end of the ancient race, the Avasthas. Some of the earlier born had not been fated to access the higher worlds. Through millennia, a few of them had remained within a human existence because the seeds of a new world to come had to be left behind on planet Earth. He explained that there are various portals between the world of our daily perception and the world of magic. This weapon, Glorfakir, was one of them, and it operated beyond time and space. He offered to demonstrate the procedure to Sean, who readily agreed.

Sanath asked him to lie on the bed, holding the hilt of the magic artifact on his chest in the manner of a knight who had died in battle. Sean did not hesitate. The blade glittered briefly. His keen eyes registered that Sanath and Mariluh sat in armchairs watching him with concern and affection. Shivers that began in his clasped hands pervaded his entire body. He closed his eyes, and within seconds fell into a torpor that gradually dissipated to become a pleasant sense of immense vacuity. The sensation in his body was now extremely light, almost floating as if he were traveling through a new dimension of changing colors and shapes.

The sword provided a window through which his attention traversed the mystery of time, connecting his consciousness to a faraway past. In this living dream, Sean Aryaputra realized that he was an Avastha. His last perception of his body in the Oriental Hotel was the fading voice of Sanath, "We shall meet soon, son of Aslerach." Aslerach of Anor, was the last Nizam of Dagad Trikon, and with this greeting Sanath signaled that Sean was going to a place that had been his own, long, long ago. He found himself on the fateful day of the fall of Dagad Trikon. The final drama of the Avastha race rushed upon him.

A young woman sitting on the stone floor addresses him, sobbing, "Lidholon, I am finished, I cannot go on anymore." He feels pervaded by a sense of utter helplessness.

The sun is setting in bleeding splendor. The warrior is surrounded by the rocky landscape of Dagad Trikon, the last refuge of the fair race of the Avasthas on Earth, but he senses that something sinister has penetrated the splendor of its magic. The crimson walls of the canyon cliff lie bare before his inner eye, dwarfing his silhouette. Despite the heat, he shivers. Memories come to him with chilling precision. He knows the place, the names, the feeling. Two days ago, the hosts of Thanatophor emerged from underground tunnels, like slime vomited from hell. He can smell the stench. The dark hordes have been guided to the precise location of the central canyon of the Avasthic rock through the craft of some untold treachery. The élite archers of the Yuva Platoon, young fighters with exceptional military skills, have pierced thousands of assailants with their crystal arrows, but the unequal battle is drawing to an end. Their foes are too many, carrying hate that is too ardent. The scouts of the first legion of Hangker, commander-in-chief of the demons, are heading for the mountain where he, Lidholon and his companions have sought refuge. He watches them, speedily climbing the flanks of the gorge like enraged ants. Hounds are sniffing the traces of blood left behind by the wounded fugitives.

Lidholon of Anor is pale, exhausted. Dark patches of coagulated blood in his blond hair give him a fearsome appearance. He sways with fatigue and wipes away the sweat and blood that runs from a wound in his scalp. Sean keenly feels the torment of this moment; searing pain courses through his head but there is no exit for him now. The vision continues.

The narrow cornice Lidholon has reached in his flight is a dead end. He has nowhere to go. Two young women, wearing the battle armor of the Sheravalian Guard of the Lady of the Rock, are sitting next to him.

Their Mistress was the ruler of the Avasthic kingdom, Master of the serpent that carried the sacred mystery of the inner transformation. However, She has left and in the absence of Her light, the shadows of darkness had crept in. He leans over the crag. The glow of the fire that engulfs the once splendid capital city of the Avasthas is now half-hidden by billowing, black smoke. More troops are progressing like a surging tide through the gap of the Gundaldhar Canyon, setting fire to the giant banyan trees that have been for so long homes to the gentle inhabitants of the lowlands. The blazes delay the shadows of the approaching night in the abyss below, and he can see lines of combatants in the valley, the vanguard of Hangker's army.

Shambalpur's beautiful dwellings are now empty as most of the Avastha folk had congregated a few days ago at the launching pad of the cylinders of fire hidden in the crater of the Givupatlast volcano, on the southern edge of the mountain complex. Following their leader, the Nizam Aslerach, they left for the stars according to the plan that Adivatar, the Omnisicient, had reserved for the Avasthas on the completion of their earthly age cycle.

Esitel, beside him is moaning from her wounds. Despair grips Lidholon as he sits back, worn out, burying his head in his arms. Behind his closed eyes, his mind reprises the scenes of the past hours.

The limited garrison in the deserted citadels of the Dagad Trikon had retreated to the highlands. The slaughter of his people before the holy cave of the Lady of the Rock, the hammering they took on a doomed bat-tlefield has broken his spirit. His endurance is spent, his sense of personal failure, total. He cannot free himself from the image of Hangker, flanked by his lieutenant Abuzinal, the Southern Titanosaur, emerging like a living terror from the mistiness of the blessed woods in the Gundaldhar Canyon of the High Lady. He cannot take his mind off the dreadful images of the last hours.

The regiment of the Blue Watch, the former lifeguards of the Nizam, had taken defensive positions to protect the Cave of Wonders, which had been the residence of the Lady of the Rock. Units from the Yuva Platoon and a company of young women warriors from the now disbanded Sheravalian Guard had been attached to the Blue Watch. This small élite troop had fought valiantly but had been overwhelmed by the savagery of the enemy onslaught.

Foot soldiers and a pack of giant beasts had surrounded their party before the holy cave; the Yuva Platoon had been heavily outnumbered.

Tears well up in Lidholon's dark eyes. In that fatal struggle, his two best friends, Hanomkar and Aliskhan, pierced by poisoned shafts, had fallen by the throne of stone before the entrance of the cave.

The fierce defense mounted by their brothers had given a few moments of respite to the surviving women of the disbanded Sheravalian Guard. From the depths of the forest, new enemy battalions constantly streamed into battle. Abuzinal, wielding a huge mace, attacked the survivors of the Blue Watch. Lidholon emptied his quiver of crystal arrows and activated the secret mechanism of the cave's entrance. The Sheravalians and a handful of warriors managed a desperate escape into the cave. Before the thick stone gate closed, Lidholon saw Etakir and Olophon, two of the foremost Avasthas warriors, breaking through the circle of enemies and fleeing into the woods, while discharging their terrible light-bolt shafts.

Lidholon's group, sheltered in the holy sanctuary, entrusted the bodies of the fallen warriors to the indigo blue water of the bottomless pond at the center of the abandoned cave where their earthly remains would rest in the holiness of this liquid shrine. At dusk, they climbed through ascending tunnels and steep trekking paths to reach the highlands, destroying the hanging rope bridges behind them as they went. The fugitives scattered in several directions to confuse their foes who had spotted them and set off in pursuit. Lidholon, Evenyl and Esitel were frantically trying to reach the abode of the wizard. But the stone arch over the ravine leading to his base had disappeared. They were trapped.

In the hotel room at the Oriental Hotel, the fatigue and the horror of this ordeal was visible on Sean's face.

"Why have we been left behind, abandoned by our elders? Why do we have to face this horror?" Esitel gasps; her face bathed in tears. Her right hand is clasped to an injury on the left side of her abdomen. The thin camouflage cloth covering the armor on her left thigh is soaked in blood. She leans on Evenyl, who lies on the ground, panting. Esitel had fought furiously, but now her energy is spent. "I wish Erilie were here," she moans, "she always knew what to do. She left with the Casket of the White Feather and never came back; they all left us to face this dreadful misery alone at this, the very end of Dagad Trikon. They left us, us, the youngest of them all!"

Lidholon opens his eyes. Shambalpur is ablaze. The fire in the valley below is gradually lighting up the lower walls of the canyon. The three warriors feel utterly abandoned, and their despair fills the purple skies of dusk. The son of the last ruler of Dagad Trikon knows he has no strength left to protect the young women from the imminent assault. He shakes his head, as if that would somehow loosen the sense of loss, the unbearable grief.

There are places in us that we're not aware of, until pain enters them to make them exist. Lidholon feels he has reached the end of history.

His two Sheravalian sisters are staring at him. He draws his sword, "Let us rise for a last stand before we die." A quiet fury blazes in the dilated retinas of the two Sheravalian fighters. "Why didn't you let me die with Aliskhan?" Esitel asks of Lidholon. "I cannot be captured alive by this scum. I'll finish it off here."

Crying, Esitel draws her dagger and points the weapon at her breast but stops as a voice thunders behind her. "Not so hasty, maiden of Eleksim. This moment is neither of your doing nor of your choice. Listen first and then decide."

Lidholon turns with a tremendous sense of relief, rises as swiftly as his condition permits. The young women turn around. The three face an elderly shape wrapped in an ample, olive-green mantle. Elkaim Ekamonon, Lord of the Highlands and known to the Avastha folk as the Sand Keeper, had stealthily emerged from an invisible door of stone carved in the side of a large boulder and stands before them. He is one of the mightiest lords of the Avasthas, commanding supernatural weapons and knower of buried secrets.

Lidholon addresses him in a shocked tone, "Master? How glad we are to see you! We thought you too had left this planet with my father and the rest of our people. It's all over now. Aliskhan and Hanomkar are dead, and without them, I cannot exist."

In an instant, Elkaim perceives the depth of the wounded warrior's distress. Aliskhan was skilled; Hanomkar was strong, Lidholon was an élite yuva warrior of insightful subtlety. For so many years, they had complemented each other admirably and had functioned as a single fighting machine at the core of a larger team. Without his yuva brothers, Lidhholon feels empty, hollow, vulnerable, a shadow of his former self. The empathy in the voice of the elder brings little solace.

"Heir of Anor, it is not quite what it seems to you right now. Death is just a change of clothes. For an Avastha, death occurs not when the heart ceases to beat but when it ceases to love. By now, your friends are being welcomed into full glory by the angels. When they come back you should be ready to join them. We have some serious work to do and..." turning towards Esitel he adds gravely, "taking your own life now is the sure way never to meet Aliskhan again for you shall win him only if you do not succumb to the creeping folly of this evil that is now sweeping our valleys. Be sure of one thing, dear Esitel; when love is pure, the power of fate yields to the power of love."

Esitel drops her dagger and stares in disbelief. No one knew, or so she thought, about her love for Lidholon's cousin, Aliskhan, the handsome esquire of Anor. Lidholon however, spares her the need to reply as he asks, "Why did you, the High Wizard, stay behind with us in this wretched world when hope itself has departed? What is this work you possibly want us to perform as we witness the unchallenged might of evil, the rise of the age of demons?"

As the sun sets, the deepening darkness of dusk comes alive with awful growling, the sound of running steps and the dancing glow of torches. Evenyl shouts, "The birds; the accursed birds are coming." She has the gifts of far-sight and far-hearing and perceives the sound of flapping wings high in the sky above their heads. Pterodactyls carrying the spies of Belzebseth, the necromancer king, are rushing towards the cornice, equipped with weapons of sorcery. Elkaim prompts the three with a pressing voice, "Hurry, come with me, let's vanish into this corridor. No use fighting. There are simply too many. This is no longer our field and not yet our moment. We'll choose the place and hour of the next contest ourselves."

They disappear behind a boulder into the dark mouth of the secret passage, and the stone gate closes as the first hounds, hyenas and jackals, barking furiously, rush forward to the cornice.

The exhausted warriors walk hesitatingly for fifteen long minutes through the dark tunnel, Lidholon helping his sisters. As they advance deeper into the mountain, the temperature becomes pleasantly cooler. The wizard, holding a small torch, is waiting for them whenever there is a turning in the corridor or a flight of stairs. Following the flickering flame, they finally reach the end of the tunnel where they face another stone gate. The wizard enters a code to command the gate's opening, and they find themselves in a large, brightly lit hall. Lidholon and the two Sheravalians pause, dumbfounded at the astonishing sight.

They have entered the lair of the Sand Keeper, a sanctuary of great magic. Under the tall dome, the hall is bathed in a mellow light; the limestone walls, displaying patterns of apricot and peach hues, seem to reverberate softly. They notice a surprising wooden structure that fills the volume of the cave almost entirely. Beautifully carved monumental pillars support sturdy beams at different levels, a succession of separate floors, with flights of staircases and arched bridges linking the elements of the multi-storied construction.

Silhouettes appear before them, seemingly from nowhere, distracting Lidholon. He has lost much blood; he is about to faint and they rush to help. From their earrings, he recognizes them as scholars of the House of Falkiliad, the guardians of the library and archives of the Sand Keeper. Elkaim addresses his attendants, "Please bring them to the chamber of healing right now; we shall see what can be done immediately."

They pass into a smaller, undecorated, rectangular dormitory, and the young soldiers are laid on thick mattresses of dried grass that emanate a delicate aromatic fragrance. Their armor is carefully removed. Elkaim's attendants speedily select unguents and oils from a cupboard from which they prepare ointments. Elkaim washes Lidholon's and Esitel's wounds with a wet cloth saying, "This is magic water from the fountain of the blessed cave of the High Lady," he explains, and as an afterthought, "its entrance is sealed by the highest locking magic and these fiends and beasts will never find access."

The light glowing from the walls of this sanctuary bathes the space in soothing shades of greenish blue. Its soft palpitation, combined with the lapping waves of a circular fountain, provides a gentle aquatic mood. The bedheads are oriented towards a little black basalt monolith in the middle of the room. Fresh air flows through a small, round window, camouflaged on the outside by creeping bushes growing on the flanks of the vertical cliff. The air mixes with a subtler breeze coming from the stone.

"This is the Sao Iambu," says the Sand Keeper, "the living stone of the Triangle Rock. I established my den here because of the presence of this enchanted stone that stores and emits energy. Avasthic magic deals with vibrations: the walls of the grotto, the water and the stone vibrate softly. They emit a comforting and healing energy, but you are all in a bad state and you will need more than this." The Sand Keeper sounds concerned. "Sorcery has entered through these wounds. I must warn you, Lidholon, since you have enough courage to hear this; that through the lesion in the right side of your head, the curse of despair has entered. It will try to rob you of a precious strength, your faith: faith in yourself and the goodness of life, and faith in the protection of the gods. And you, my dear Esitel, you have been hurt on the left side of your stomach. The curse of the demon that threw this spike at you is to deny you the family happiness that you would have been entitled to. You will find it hard to find men at your level. Do not fear: both of you have the powers within to overcome these evil spells and," he assured the young woman, "if you heal well now you will be united, albeit in a distant future, to the one you really seek."

They hardly hear him: in sheer exhaustion, they float in a state of half slumber. At this point the youngest of Elkaim's four attendants points at Evenyl and says, "Look here Master, this lady seems the most severely hurt."

Evenyl's slender body appears frozen, yet it shivers slightly. The harrowing clash before the stone throne in which Aliskhan, Hanomkar and many other heroes had lost their lives has sapped her power. The dreadfulness of what she has felt and seen has penetrated deep inside her, in the form of a black presence, a murmur of terror that is now lodged in her sinews. Evenyl's eyes are open wide but can no longer see anything outside. However, she sees, and what she sees brings tension and fear on her face. Her hands are sweating, her breathing is fast, her pulse racing.

"Don't look, don't look at this!" The Sand Keeper immediately sees the gravity of the threat, "When children of goodness face the unexpected fierceness of evil, it can enter them through the surprise of that shock."

Evenyl's head tosses from side to side; she feels the slow surge of an unbearable panic, a dizziness in which her very being would splinter like breaking glass. The Sand Keeper turns towards his assistants and shouts, "There is only one cure possible. Run quickly to the library and bring me back the *Book of the Kavach*."

An attendant hurries off, climbs the library staircase and returns holding a small red book. "A book, that's all?" Lidholon looks worried.

"The *Kavach* is a book of mantras, magic names that provide heavenly protection for every single and every part of the human body. It will free her from the terror in which she has been drowning and dissolve the insidious sorcery of Belzebseth, the chief sorcerer of Thanatophor."

The wizard of Dagad Trikon begins reading. He chants the potent psalmody in a rhythmic tone, pausing between each name to let its power operate. He starts by invoking the protection of the guardians of the four quarters of the horizon. As he reads the names of these guardians, specific forces construct a protective shield of magnetism in front, behind, above and below Evenyl. Another appellation weaves the sheath of protection in ten directions. The names target precise locations: the forehead, the eyebrows, the space between the eyebrows, the eyes, the eyelids, the nose, mouth, tongue, ears, roots of the ears, lips, lower lip, sound box, windpipe, outer part of the throat, neck and so on.

The effect of the magic names on the hazy consciousness of the wounded warrior is immediate and Lidholon can register in his own body what she's experiencing. When the wizard takes the name for the area of the shoulders, Evenyl feels as if she is wielding a deadly weapon in her hands. The might of the fighter she used to be again strengthens her muscles. When he invokes the name for the arms, the level of this force rises as if she is holding a thunderbolt. With the name for the fingers, she feels her arms ending with hands like deadly pliers ready to strangle the demons. With the name for the back she is suddenly carrying a quiver full of lethal arrows.

The attendants are visibly taking heart as the *Kavach* reveals its mighty effect. With each utterance, a stream of power flows from an innermost state within Evenyl; her inner strength is now fully released. The living names are both beautiful and melodious.

The utterance of the *Kavach* gradually covers her entire body from the crown of her head down to her toenails. When the Sand Keeper reaches the name for the feet, it seems to Lidholon that they are radiating a faint light. During the reading of the *Kavach*, Evenyl feels a searing pain in her left thigh, her body shivers with sensations of pressure and finally, burning around both the sides of her head. Now conscious sight is back in her eyes. The protective coat of the *Kavach's* holiness infuses energy in every named part of her shattered body.

By the time Elkaim finishes reading the *Book of the Kavach*, the grip of tension and fears is loosened, and Evenyl has fully recovered. The rhythm slows; he has reached the end. His voice now rings in the ears of the wounded Sheravalian.

"Come back Evenyl, come back. These are the names of power, the sounds woven in the texture of the shawl of the High Lady, the magic shawl of Eleksim. Eleksim is your house!"

A voice speaks from behind the Sand Keeper. "The outside is within. As in the heavens, so it is below. The power that made the stars also resides in our cells. That which is immense can make itself minuscule. Why build temples? We are the temples."

Lidholon is sitting cross-legged on his bed, leaning back on the wall behind. A radiant glow has returned to his ashen face. He has fully absorbed the *Kavach* incantation and the healing impact on his own wounds. The recognition of its power has compelled him to speak. He is still pale, but his eyes are flashing. Esitel too, her eyes closed, shares her relief, "I experienced the names, multicolor jewels of sounds, carrying waves of breezy grace. Each name resounded with delicate echoes, granting progressive liberation. May the *Kavach* protect us through the shadows, to the end of night, until stars shine again and a new world emerges."

At this moment, the blessings of the *Kavach* further manifest in an unexpected way. Another voice, a voice they know well, comes from the entrance of the Chamber of Healing. "Well spoken, sister. The Deep Way is alive and well."

A fierce looking archer is standing before them, his hair in disorder, his cheek marred by the dried blood of a wound. He is tall and carries a mighty bow on his back. His bloodstained and dirtied, tattered clothes tell of the fight he has been in. He is Etakir, Commander of the Yuva Platoon, one of the few Avasthas who knows the access code to the sanctuary of the Sand Keeper. A radiant smile appears on the face of Evenyl. Lidholon and the two Sheravalians arise. They stare in delight and disbelief. They had thought that he too had perished in battle. He is tired but happy to have reached momentary safety.

"Etakir, Etakir, my goodness..." The four hug each other, heads against heads, arms on each other's shoulders. They sob for those they have lost, for the many daring fighters and fair Sheravalians, never to be seen again.

The friends talk late into the night and although they thought they'd emptied themselves of tears, Esitel and Evenyl weep again when Ekatir describes how the heroes of the Yuva Platoon perished. Hanomkar had smashed so many foes, but Abuzinal ordered his bowmen to target him simultaneously. A volley of arrows pierced his body; Aliskhan was fatally wounded in a vain attempt to shield his dying friend. Etakir narrates how he, Olophon of Elnur and the great puma of Erilie, rallying all the remaining felines of the Gundaldhar Canyon, had wounded the titano-saur Abuzinal, creating a commotion in the enemy ranks. He saw how Lidholon and the Sheravalians escaped, and he covered their flight. They then fled through the secret trail on the high branches of the banyan forest. At early dawn, fugitives in their own land, they visited the deserted ruins of the capital before leaving for the highlands.

Lidholon sits and looks at his companions. Evenyl, feeling serene since the arrival of Etakir, lies down to rest. Esitel is mournful, gazing beyond the room into an unknown land, as if to locate a trace of Aliskhan; her departed love.

Perhaps because of a newfound proximity or the gravity of the circumstances, Lidholon feels much closer to the mysterious Sand Keeper who now reassures him, "The Lady of the Rock foresaw all this. Fear not. The time has come for us to discover the whiteness, the purity of the paper on which we write this story. You and your friends shall one day break the innermost code of the Deep Way. You will achieve it for yourself and for the sake of the race that shall come after the Avasthas."

They rest the next day too. In the evening, the wizard's attendants bring two wounded guards of the Nizam's lifeguard regiment to the Chamber of Healing. Esitel and Evenyl move to another room to leave them space. The soldiers are overjoyed that Etakir and Lidholon have survived. They bring a grim update on the waning battle.

"The Blue Watch has been wiped out, my lords. The accursed horde is flooding the lowlands. They have taken the ponds, the canals and the underground water reservoirs. Columns of troops control the mountain trails. They want the upper floors of the canyons and the mountains. These rascals are swarming all over this very peak. There is a bunch of sinister looking fellows dressed in long robes, high sorcerers I'd say..."

"I think they are looking for our secret weapons in the hidden base of the great wizard," the other soldier added.

"The entire city of Shambalpur was burning. While enemies were ransacking the downtown houses, I managed to run to the temple of victory in the citadel," says Etakir somberly. "It contains the sacred weapons that the gods bequeathed to our ancestors during an ancient October Pujan festival. I grabbed the Sadhan shield and the Glorfakir sword from their ceremonial cases, buried them deep in the vaults under the backyard garden of the temple and put a strong cloaking spell on them. Let's pray and hope that they'll never locate these prizes."

"Let's pray it's so," the soldier agreed, "a few areas are still safe. The survivors of my regiment followed Lord Olophon on the Western peaks and have joined the rangers of Kalabham. They still hold the gorges around the three music towers. Yet, where is hope?"

"The damage brought to our land is fatal: this is precisely what happens when evil takes over a land that was once holy. The water is turning brown, the vegetation withers in dryness; the very air carries a foul stench, Mother Earth expresses her displeasure. For now, let your minds be at peace. Lie safely in this Chamber and take respite," says Etakir affectionately comforting the soldiers.

He attends to their wounds, with Lidholon and the helpers of Elkaim. The wizard comes back from the library to check on their condition. The guards of the Blue Watch try to stand but he signals for them not to exert themselves. The Sand Keeper examines their wounds and gives a few instructions. The elder soldier is still suffering from the fright of the harrowing pursuit. Hesitatingly, he asks the Lord Wizard of Dagad Trikon,

"Your Lordship, we are so blessed to have found your abode. If your scouts hadn't found us and taken us through the secret passage, we would be dead by now or worse, questioned under torture. Forgive me for saying so, but aren't you afraid your abode will be discovered by the enemy very soon? Hundreds of them are now digging tunnels around this stronghold; they are probably close by now. How do they know we are here?"

"Treachery!" murmurs the wizard somberly. "One who knows the secret maps has already betrayed us. I reckon Belzebseth dearly wishes to find the Avasthic library. I sense he is on his way, he is near," says the wizard with astounding detachment. And without another word, without bothering to reassure them, he turns around and walks out of the room.

In the Oriental Hotel in Bangkok, Sanath followed the progress of Sean's awakened dream, through his own clear sight or sometimes by watching Sean's face, which registered the properties of the vision, the steps of the discovery. He whispered to Mariluh, "He has seen the destruction of his race, he his now safe in my lair but the worst is yet to come." She nodded. Her task was to keep evil spirits at bay so nothing would disturb Sean's grip on the hilt of the Glorfakir sword.

CHAPTER FOUR

THE BURNING OF THE AVASTHIC LIBRARY

Where Sean, as Lidholon of Anor, discovers the properties of the magic library that keeps the secrets of the legend; where the Sand Keeper intends to burn it so that its knowledge does not fall into the wrong hands, and how the Avasthas discover the presence of the arch demon Belzebseth and his accomplice who betrayed the Avastha kingdom.

The following morning Lidholon meets Agnorth, the secretary of the Sand Keeper, a highly learned scholar of the school of Falkiliad. Despite the urgency of the moment, the Sand Keeper instructs his assistant to show the extraordinary library of the Rock Avasthas to the four companions. This offer from the Lord of the Highlands is an uncommon privilege for his visitors and a mark of the esteem in which he holds them. Agnorth is the warden of the library and rare are the occasions when he can present its contents to outside visitors. The affable librarian is eager to oblige knowing that they are warriors of renown whose praises have been sung in happier days by the minstrels in the festive halls of Shambalpur.

Agnorth explains, "The effect of the magic of the Gnostic library on those who have not received advanced training in the Deep Way is unpredictable. It is said that the library has several levels of magic. It can print the content of the books in the memory of the readers, or, even better; some superior works can translate knowledge into direct experience. However, it can also infect their brains with false concepts that can corrupt their lives."

Lidholon is intrigued by the explanation and hopes to hear more. Not knowing what to expect but full of curiosity, Etakir, Lidholon, Esitel and Evenyl follow their guide. Agnorth opens the door of the library hall and they admire the sight of the vertical structure that fills the central cavern of the wizard's retreat and reaches a height of forty meters. The wizard joins them briefly to comment on the supernatural properties of the library. "Can you imagine a book you read not only with your eyes but with your entire being? The alert reader does not register the matter in the form of bookish knowledge; he assimilates the content. In the Gnostic library, we have a few of those. They deal with perception, not erudition. You don't read these books. You absorb some; you drink others. This is where talismans are stored, and riddles are solved. I just love these books. I can simply touch them, look at them, feel their presence, and they keep me company."

"How so?" Evenyl asks. Raised in the clan of Eleksim and thus well trained in the subtler aspects of the Deep Way, she has the capacity to imbibe knowledge quickly but her clan never relies on books. She has heard however that many secrets of her race are hidden in the library of the Sand Keeper. Her father told her that even the high Avasthas have not accessed all the inner powers consigned within some of these manuscripts.

"Let me give you a simple example," the wizard replies, "on the shelves of the library of Elnur there is an essay on pineapple fruit. When an advanced reader is thirsty, sometimes he reads this book and his mouth tastes and enjoys the juicy flavor of pineapple, in which case he is refreshed and satiated for a couple of hours. In short, the content of the Gnostic works registers directly on the central nervous system. More wonderfully," he adds with an untypical tone of longing, "in the library of Eleksim, there is a magisterial work, a voluminous treatise on the one hundred and eight flavors of bliss. You cannot imagine what a feast this will bring to the fortunate reader. It is quite delightful. Of course, access to this specific treatise is restricted to the purest hearts, and I know of nobody today with the training to absorb its contents."

"Master, is this how the *Kavach* worked on me? Is it because I received the names of power on my central nervous system?"

"Quite so, Evenyl. When the nerves are purified, evil has no support to stay in one's thoughts, emotions or limbs. It worked fast for all of you because of your advanced level. The force of the *Kavach* comes from inside. You did well," he adds as an afterthought and with a smile at the young woman, "because you always strived to cover more ground in your self-enquiry. Now please follow our esteemed Agnorth to have the last glimpse at the lore of the Avasthas."

Each floor of the aerial wooden structure contains the records of the knowledge of one of the great houses. On each floor, the library displays bibliotheca of various baroque shapes and sizes aligned in a pre-ordained symbolic order. Each floor accommodates visitors and includes space with richly-colored carpets, embroidered silk cushions and gilded lamps. Higher up and on both sides, arched bridges lead to structures containing the material relating to the Blue and Yellow Feathers, symbols for the energies of desire and action that cover the domains of emotion and thought. Multicolor prayer flags carrying magic formulae hang from two long ropes connecting the pinnacles to the domed roof of the central structure.

As they begin, the librarian comments in detail, "On the ground floor, the records of Kalabham are contained in these richly-engraved orange, salmon pink, and ochre-colored books. Kalabham is the house of the pure and the wise. You will find here the compendium of the essential principles of the Deep Way and a description of the foundations of Avasthic culture. It includes children's drawings and sayings, which are mostly a collection of aphorisms. We can learn about the fountains of wisdom, spontaneity and their relationship to the atomic nature of innocence."

"Atomic? I don't understand," says Lidholon.

"If you break an atom you release a destructive energy. They say it is the same if you break innocence," answers Agnorth, matter-of-factly, as though it were obvious.

Here and there, on the walls, they see ornate maps describing the landscapes of magnetism within stones, plants, the human body, the continents or the planets. Subtle perfumes and exquisite scents float in the air, and the atmosphere reminds Lidholon of the blessed cave of the Lady of Dagad Trikon. The librarian adds, "The House of Kalabham worships the gate keeper of wisdom, the Primordial Elephant. It maintains on earth the protocol of the subtler magnetism, which binds the universe together. Only by riding the waves of the elephant's magnet can Avasthas and men reach the heavens. The wizard told us that children are best at deciphering its cryptogram." They climb the stairs to the second floor, where their guide continues his explanation of the importance of the library.

"On the second level, the yellow and golden books contain lessons learned from the lives of Avasthas who have achieved excellence in their field of activity. Here you can also admire the large collection of the Precepts of Falkiliad, which, as you know, is the House of the Doer." He adds proudly, "You can find everything that matters in achieving brilliance in music, poetry, art, architecture, literature and science, and how to combine efficiency and elegance while mastering the art of effortless action. As you can see, this lovely arched bridge from the second level takes you to the section dealing with the golden provinces ruled by the Yellow Feather; the subjects are clearly related. This section explains the system governing the creation. Access through the bridge is restricted. You know; this knowledge is dangerous if it falls into wrong hands. The drive for action is addictive; many are under its spell."

They admire a delicately sculptured statue of a monkey in white marble on the other side of the bridge. Most volumes are bound in fine leather carrying the colors of the House of Falkiliad, with embossed titles in dark, pink gold.

Agnorth continues, "When people are under the power of this feather; its color is yellow. When higher beings such as the Aulyas control its power, the color is golden as it is on the helmet of the Lord Kartik Senapati, the commander-in-chief of the heavenly armies who was born of the fire. He has many names, of course, such as 'golden-hued,' 'splendid,' 'effulgent,' and 'the slayer of mighty foes.'" Despite the seriousness of the circumstances, the librarian is enjoying the moment. It isn't often that he can display his knowledge.

"What do we gain when we master the Yellow Feather?" Agnorth walks on a couple of steps, choosing his words carefully to provide the best answer to Esitel's question.

Finally, he replies, "In a practical sense; mastery over this feather permits us to use the considerable properties of the frontal cortex of the brain more fully. You may recall that the golden domain deals with cognitive process, reason, thought and will. So, in the end, clarity dispels confusion and illusion; we achieve complete precision; we move in command of our faculties. This is the feather for those who want to act, to lead, to be the winners." And as an afterthought, he adds, "You can also find some material cross-referenced on the fifth floor where we keep the records of Anor because that is where we store our scriptures on effortless action and the wonderful art of playing."

Lidholon stops before a series of six golden volumes bearing the title, *About the Use of the Glorfakir Sword*. "Etakir," he exclaims, "look at this one, I wish you would have taken this sword with you!"

"I did not have permission. With such weapons, you simply cannot improvise," replied Etakir. "I must confess I hesitated, but I was afraid of being caught by the invaders. Maybe our guide can tell us more."

"I can see you have a sharp eye. This is the opus magnum concerning the attention. It tells you how you can beam it anywhere, to be able to catch anything, and to open all the hidden messages carried by the flow of hours and circumstances. The Glorfakir equips you to be a seer. It cuts the knots of illusion. You can use its power to go into the inner silence that Avasthas seek. However, we must go on. Any of these volumes would absorb you for a few days. I must say…they do capture your attention."

"What a pity to leave this behind," says Etakir, longingly caressing the finely engraved bands of the manuals. Agnorth turns to Lidholon with furtive awe, "They say your father, the high lord Aslerach, had absorbed the power of the Glorfakir into his eyes, so that he can turn them into diamonds during battle, and the light they projected killed his enemies. Perhaps some do not need the sword after all." Lidholon keeps silent. He feels the pain of being separated from his father.

The tone on the second floor is creative, mobile, dynamic, and they feel energized. They would like to stay longer, but the librarian is under instructions from the wizard to hurry. "Follow me," he says, while climbing a steep ladder leading to the third floor.

They marvel at the green, silk jackets of the large volumes of the Elnorian collection, with golden engravings displaying many unknown signs and symbols. "Here, in principle, you could find what you need to know in order to manage the universe," whispers the guide with a trace of wonder in his voice. "The annals of Elnur speak of the Emerald King, of his giant serpent and his bird of light, of the maxims of the Daskalian Masters, the conventions of the Aulyas, all the fine rules to keep everything in proper balance and how to progress on the white channel of evolution. Here you can see a miniaturized version of the records of Dikayoson, the herald of the Chamber of Maat. He operates the Wheel of the Law: action, reaction, sowing, and gathering, how to achieve balance in order to move forward."

"Trial and error. The precepts of the cosmic order," observes Lidholon.

Agnorth continues, "The Lord Wizard recently consulted this document," he says pointing to an old parchment from the astrology section that is stored in a niche. "He confirmed his understanding that our cycle of history is over, opening avenues for a few possible futures. The method of selection among options, futures and choices is contained in the accounts of the White Feather whose records are stored here in this vaulted division."

At the rear of this floor, they see a golden pipe bringing water to a small fountain made of malachite. Lights dance on the surface of the water. A gentle dampness floats in the air; the atmosphere is bathed in a misty freshness and carries a majestic serenity.

"Avasthas worship water, carrier of the codes of life."

Reluctantly, they leave the comforting moisture of the floor of the House of Elnur. They progress to the fourth level through a narrow spiral staircase situated in the center of the Elnorian floor. This floor is connected by another arched bridge leading to the library section for the domain of the Blue Feather on the left side. An ebony statue of a tall, winged creature killing a dragon decorates its entrance. The brightness of the floor exudes pleasant warmth; the pervading color is red in its many hues from pink to dark burgundy.

"This portion of the Gnostic library keeps the accumulated wisdom of the House of Eleksim. Everything here is about love, its art and its power," Agnorth says in a sententious manner as if too shy to talk about love. "How to access blessedness is the greatest riddle, but it has something to do with love. Eleksim is the house of those who live to give love. We have entered the area of enjoyable feelings. It is here that I searched for the *Book of the Kavach* yesterday since the *Kavach* contains the magic of the motherly shelter."

He sums up with an admiring smile. "It worked so well for Lady Evenyl because this lore belongs to her house. There is also a collection of poems on the shawl of Eleksim, the shawl of the High Lady. I was told that it is an envelope of gentle magic and grace that comforts the heart."

The thought flashes through Lidholon's brain, "Why was he told? Is this not a matter of experience? Can't he feel it?" But then he remembers that even the librarian may not have free access to all the enchanted works.

They pause to relish a fairylike charm, a dreamy feeling of tenderness, astounded at how their moods are shifting as they climb from floor to floor. Lidholon realizes that the Sand Keeper has also sent them on this tour for the purpose of healing. The terrible ordeal of the last days no longer weighs on his consciousness. They walk past rows of books, admiring the magnificent display of bindings in crimson, scarlet, ruby and cherry shades.

They see a bridge crossing to the section of the Blue Feather. Agnorth gestures towards the statue in black ebonite at the entrance, the winged warrior slaying the dragon, "This represents Bhairava, the Archangel who patrols this area; he defends the access code to pure love, the one that releases blessedness.

"What is pure love?" asks Esitel sadly. The pain of her loss suddenly returns and Lidholon senses how acutely she misses Aliskhan, a loss expressed in her next question, "Is it passion? Is it fusion?"

The question is obviously embarrassing for Agnorth. How can he talk about such things with a beautiful Sheravalian? He hesitates, "I wouldn't...I don't know, my lady; for most of us it is an aspiration, I suppose."

"The dragon slayer helps if we want him to," says Etakir, as they observe the ebony statue to distract the attention from the embarrassment of their guide. "He destroys useless desires, those which bind in dependency, the cravings that keep us small and wasted."

Agnorth continues, "Precisely my lord. This is why, beyond this bridge you'll find the conventions to handle, contain or liberate the fiercest of all powers: desire. Many files relate to matters of the past – feelings and emotions, bonds and trappings. The Blue Feather library is a restricted area; we cannot cross this bridge. Releasing the Blue Feather can create deadly floods and storms. Besides, no one else can afford to approach the perils of the forbidden books in the *Bibliotheca Diabolica*.

"The *Bibliotheca Diabolica*? What sort of devilry is that?" asks Etakir.

"The devil keeps his own files. It is the works of doom, stored under the vault at the end of this passage. Its purpose is to teach how to throw people out of their personal axis, to disconnect them from the place of their being where they are in touch with their own depths."

"I can't believe Avasthas would make this sorcery available."

"The black and violet tomes of the forbidden bibliotheca are locked behind an indestructible glass encased in black iron. These treatises belonged in ancient times to the Council of the Necromancers and were stolen from the donjon of Thanatophor in the great siege of the previous age, when the Avasthas of yore under Nizam Irene the second of Anorhad defeated the army of the demons. They obtained the library of Belzebseth, the Witch Master. The Lord Irene wanted to know how the enemy operated and now this chief of the sorcerers sorely wants his books back."

The very mention of these works is enough to make Lidholon uneasy. Agnorth notices the puzzled look of the companions and feels he needs to provide some added explanation. "The *Bibliotheca Diabolica* contains the treatises of the dark arts divided into two sections: witchcraft supremacy and battlefield sorcery. It contains, for instance, a compilation of the ways to sow abominations in unsuspecting minds or seeds of hate between clans. The handbook deals with the knack of turning goodness into serving evil—very useful for all the wrong kinds of rulers. The manual explains how to influence minds and enslave them without it being noticed. There is an illustrated writing on witch supremacy through the craft of seduction and the fascination of lust. The section on battlefield sorcery includes the science of all poisons, from cyanide to jealousy, the ability to possess someone or kill at a distance and, of course, how to trigger all sort of sicknesses."

"Why keep books containing such awful things?" asks Esitel.

"Even my Master the Sand Keeper, to my knowledge, never ventured to open the books of the forbidden bibliotheca because they are so toxic. But it is reported that some Aulyas sometimes consult them to gain inside knowledge of the enemy. Few can face such evil without absorbing it."

"Reading this material must be dangerous, although I can see how some may be tempted. Understanding the craft of the enemy is always an attractive proposition for a warrior." Lidholon nods in agreement to Etakir's remark, but he keeps his thoughts to himself.

Casting a furtive glance at the structure beyond the bridge, they feel an insidious pull, the call of those who came before, the desire to cross the bridge, but instead they hurriedly return to the main corridor. A longer spiral staircase of wrought iron takes them to the fifth floor, and they approach the high vaulted ceiling of the grotto. The delicate silver colonnades flanking the access door to the floor are enshrined with large sapphires. As they cross the jewel-bedecked entrance to the fifth level, an ethereal ambiance of greatness surrounds them. The colors of the books represent a gradation of shades of blue from lavender to cerulean, azure, turquoise and cobalt.

"Son of the Nizam, this is the floor of your house," the guide turns towards Lidholon. "Anor is the House of Unity. A lot about it has a royal feeling and is shrouded in mystery. The wizard speaks of something immense yet to be revealed. These chronicles are about the wonders of bringing people together, the art of achieving it, about the deeds of the god with the peacock feather, the sower who weaves legends, myths and history."

"What is this?" asks Lidholon, staring at a thin volume titled *The Gunatith Manuscript* or *The Lore of Being Motionless*. "It's most sensitive of you to note this," responds Agnorth, surprised at the knack with which the yuva warriors are regularly picking out the strategic writings. "This work teaches a difficult art, how to stand on your own, without actions or reactions, undisturbed yet connected, seeing all without being seen, not affected by anything, yet having an impact by the mere fact of standing on one's own ground."

"It sounds like shooting on a good day on the battlefield. In such times, when I shoot volleys of arrows, it is as though I don't do anything, I am completely silent, almost absent, but somehow, all targets are reached and the enemies are killed. That's all."

"I would not know, my lord," responds Agnorth, awed by the fame of Etakir, a formidable archer whose prowess few can emulate. "It is said that in the motionlessness of the Gunatith state, the trained Avastha can call into motion greater powers than his own. This is the state reached by the Aulyas, our mentors, firmly anchored on their axis, the central path of the White Feather.

Your father, Aslerach, sometimes came here to meditate." adds Agnorth, pointing at an alcove with large lavender cushions scattered on the ground. Lidholon remembers the last words of the Nizam as he boarded the spacecraft, "You cannot come with me, Lidholon, for the task before you is one that I could not achieve. It is our yuvas who must bring to mankind the seeds of the new world."

He sees the diamond eyes with a touch of blue, glistening tears. What is it that his father, first among the Avasthas, cannot do? Lidholon is distracted from these wrenching emotions by a question from Etakir, who is looking at the intricate stone rose at the center of the empty ceiling above their heads, "What about the records of the House of Anorhad and where is the Seventh House, the House of Ni?"

"We have nothing on the Seventh House. I think the knowledge is transmitted telepathically, or through some deeper vibrations, I am not quite sure. The Lord Wizard does not speak about it. As for the Sixth House, the Anorhadans took their records with them when they left Earth. Can you see the two ropes coming from these flanking turrets, with all the hanging flags carrying the magic formulas of the two feathers? They are attached to this floor where all magic of the feathers ends, and the new magic of Anorhad begins. So much about Anorhad is different. Their books contain affirmations and negations that cannot be apprehended or understood by human thought. Anorhad is the house of those who pacify contradictions because they reach beyond thoughts. It is said their books are living in their third eye and would self-destruct in their absence. Anyway, there were only a few books, as they did not believe much in words. See, we can still see their sign: the tricolor Lily of Anorhad carved on the shield crowning these empty shelves."

Etakir whispers to Lidholon, "Look at the shape of this crest on which the lily is engraved; it is made in the likeness of the Sadhan, the magic shield that forms the walls of silence around the Inner World."

As they descend from the top floor, they hear a commotion; the wizard's attendants are hastily spreading the contents of barrels of inflammable naphtha. The mournful attendants tell the companions that the entire library will be set on fire the next day on the direct order of the High Wizard of Dagad Trikon. Agnorth looks livid. Horrified, the young women run to the Sand Keeper, who is issuing instructions.

"We beg you, Master, burn the devilish books, yes, but not the rest." They offer a flood of arguments, imploring him to save the Gnostic library.

"I must be firm on this. The contents of the Avasthic gnosis are not that simple; transfer of knowledge comes from the giver, but we always forget how much of the transfer depends on the one who receives. A writing of the gnosis delivers its substance only if the receptivity of the reader stems from his or her proximity to the Deep Way. It is when such is the case that the content of the pages blossoms in the mind of the reader as an experience of recognition." The sadness and gravity of the Sand Keeper does not convince Evenyl who remembers her recent recovery. "It is amazing; the healing hand of a mother from above was working through the *Book of the Kavach* and snatched me from the very jaws of hell. I beg you, do not destroy such treasures."

"Alas, trained Avasthas and accomplished readers have now disappeared from the Earth. In the wrong hands these books are like a cypher that cannot be decrypted; they are useless, worse; they are dangerous. At best, people getting hold of them will forge mental constructions about matters they neither grasp nor experience. They shall impose their interpretation on others with all the authority of borrowed magic.

"Is it so that in the next cycle the race that follow will have to experiment, fail and have to learn all over again that which will be lost? If so, that seems absurd to me," says Lidholon.

"It would be more absurd to feed them food they cannot digest. What is the use of putting the knowledge of reality in little packages of thoughts where it will merely be broken down and dissolve? Do you want, down the alleys of time, to meet only the proud guardians of empty boxes? Readers who are not prepared are likely to twist and distort the meaning of the discourses, including the teachings of the Daskalians, who are the Primordial Masters. What would they make of the words of the greatest seers, our Aulyas? At worse, the magic powers of the Gnostic books would be misused and manipulated. And what if the demons can finally force the gate of my lair? No, I cannot risk this."

"Master, why didn't you share this knowledge when you taught at the Shambalpur Academy? Will there be a way to regain this treasure?" Evenyl interjects. "I cannot bear the thought that the Gnostic library of the Rock Avasthas will go up in smoke. We have achieved all this incomparable knowledge and to what avail?"

"The dominion of the demons will be short-lived in the greater scheme of things. The next cycle belongs to mankind, but the demons will try to retake control. Believe me, we must destroy the work of the Avasthas even though we do so with a heavy heart. The human mind is restless, a twister of truth. I fear what human beings might do if they get hold of sacred books. What was a message of love could end up as hate. There might be a path opening in a far-off future to impart this lore in a new way – but definitely not through books."

Their hearts feel like stone. The wizard is visibly sorrowful too but he does not wish to transfer the Avasthic legacy in a manner that can be tampered with.

"Honor and home, my friends, and now the knowledge of my race, all gone," Lidholon sighs, "then everything is lost."

"On the contrary, Lidholon, everything is saved; everything will return but it will be different: everyone will have the answers. Knowledge will blow in the wind, in the breath of the new life."

Lidholon approaches the Sand Keeper as they leave the cave and asks, "Master, I trust no one has the clearance to access the *Bibliotheca Diabolica*; is that right?

"Quite so," replies the wizard in a surprised tone; "No one has permission to even look at it. Why do you ask?"

"Oh nothing, I just wanted to make sure."

They retreat in a state of frustration at having been shown such a treasure that is about to vanish. Harsh reality is back again, like a sticky nightmare; their enemies are surrounding them and everything they have ever cherished has been or is about to be destroyed. How long can they feel safe in the cave of the Sao Iambu, under the protection of the Sand Keeper? They go to bed that night, nostalgic about the past glory of the Avastas and anxious about the fate in store for them.

The next morning, Hangker's troops have completely sealed the mountain that shelters the wizard's den. They can be seen, in porcupine-like brown and grey leather armor, swarming like cockroaches, with bizarre horns on their helmets serving as searching antennae. The mood in the underground refuge is somber. Lidholon spends most of the next day in the Chamber of Healing, resting or chatting with Agnorth. He wants to engage the young librarian who has strong academic qualifications from the Falkiliad College of Creative Projection.

"I am intrigued by the forbidden books. Why all the secrecy? After all, knowledge is only useful if it can be shared!"

"The lore of the Deep Way is somewhat treacherous you know." The young scholar sips cinnamon tea while scrutinizing the face of the warrior. "Treacherous? What do you mean?"

"It's full of tricks for the tricksters and locking mechanisms for the rest of us. We cannot ascend if we don't find the right entry point and there are several narrow passages leading to nasty places we need to cross before getting there. The wizard could only give one-on-one lessons because the Deep Way is so subtle. The teacher of the Deep Way is very selective; he has to keep an extremely close eye on the disciple to make sure that he or she properly understands its subtleties."

Etakir, followed by the Sand Keeper, bursts into the room and walks quickly to the only small circular window in the cave. Besides providing light and fresh air, the window of the Chamber of Healing serves also as an observation post. Carved high in the cliff, it overhangs a nearby spur from which one can see the neighboring foothills.

Taking an arrow from his quiver, Etakir slowly moves some overhanging branches that camouflage the window from outside. In clear weather, the wizard's sentinels can see the high walls, golden domes and minarets of Shambalpur far below in the valley formed by the Gundaldhar Canyon. Now a mournful haze hides the view of the bottom. He addresses the elder in a low, tense voice as they peer outside. "Look at that pterodactyl down there. It was circling in front of this window about half an hour ago. Its rider even tried to peer through the creepers. If I had fired an arrow, they would have found our exact position. The eagles have gone; we are defenseless against these horrid birds. It has landed now and its rider is reporting to a group on the bluff to the left, about two hundred meters below."

Lidholon joins them and carefully moves more foliage. Three heads are now straining to see the movements of the enemy below. They can make out a party of some thirty troopers of the demonic horde. The flying spy is kneeling before two silhouettes in the center who look like the leaders of the group. Etakir's glance is piercing. He strains his eyes to get a better look and jumps back with a shriek of horror. Turning to the Sand Keeper he asks in a strangled voice, "My Lord, do you see what I just saw?"

The wizard does not respond. Lidholon is a Yuva Platoon fighter with excellent eyesight. He notes that the enemy is wearing the brownish armor of the troopers of Hangker, except for the two men in the middle. The tall one on the left is draped in a large violet robe. The other silhouette next to him however, is wearing the long tunic worn by the dignitaries of Dagad Trikon. "What can you see, children?"

"Oh no! It's impossible." The son of the Nizam has just recognized the person in the ceremonial tunic bearing the embroidered crest of Shambalpur. Etakir is too shocked for words. The wizard swiftly replaces his binoculars in the ample pocket of his mantle. Grabbing the two yuvas by the shoulders, he pulls them back from the window.

"Step back. Don't talk. He senses my presence now. The witch lord is here, hardly two hundred meters away. We have finally reached this moment. As I trained my sight on him, he began to stare in our direction. Agnorth, please engage the locking mechanism to seal the window. Ah, I feel his attention is here but he won't be able to follow us. The vibrations of the Sao Iambu will stop him and cleanse the air for a while. Come with me to my private chamber, deeper within the mountain." And without paying further attention to his shaken companions, the wizard leaves the Chamber of Healing and takes the faintly lit small corridor that goes up a flight of stairs to his apartment.

They hurriedly cross his study lit by a glow from the ceiling. Large stones that fit the opening of the windows now block the view of the valley below so perfectly that it is impossible to distinguish the shape of the window from the wall. They follow yet another narrow tunnel that turns into the mountain and enter the bedchamber. The room is Spartan, furnished with a bed, a desk, an armchair and a few chairs. Only two wall hangings decorate the walls.

One is a lovely painting depicting a beautiful lady dressed in red sitting on a tiger. Etakir and Lidholon know it is a representation of the Lady of the Rock, Sovereign of Dagad Trikon and Commander of the Sheravalian Guard. The other hanging, above the head of the bed, is a white towel that carries the red imprints of two delicate feet. Standing before the bed, the wizard tells the yuva bowmen, "Stretch your hands towards the footprints of the Goddess. She stood on this towel after a pujan festival, and I kept it. Feel the power if you can. It will bring peace back to you. For now, try to forget what you saw."

Still in shock, the two friends stretch their hands towards the towel hanging on the wall of the bedchamber. They stand with closed eyes to aid better concentration. Lidholon chases away images, fighting tears in his eyes and starts relaxing only when he feels a soft cool breeze flowing from the towel into his hands. This gift of energy, this sign of living protection from the sovereign Lady of the Rock, brings back serenity. He opens his eyes and notes that the expression of disgust, which had distorted Etakir's face a few minutes ago, is almost washed away. Opening his eyes bring his attention back to his surroundings, and he remembers his distress.

The wizard positions himself on the bed and the friends sit cross-legged on a carpet at his feet. Adversity drapes the elder in an expression of a grim resolve. His tone is somber but resolute. "The silhouette we saw in the violet mantle is my ancestral foe, the chief sorcerer of the Dark Council, Belzebseth himself. My spies had told me he recently arrived on a giant purple lizard. He is close to realizing his dream, hunting down the Highlander of Dagad Trikon in his lair. He senses that the prize – the magic library of the Avasthas he always wanted – is finally within his grasp."

Looking at Lidholon, again restless, he says, "You may speak, son of Aslerach." This moment of reckoning twists Sean's face as he lies in Sanath's room in Bangkok. "We come to it," The wizard said, observing the disgust and pain. "It will not take long until he returns to us."

CHAPTER FIVE

THE PERILS OF BEING TOO CLEVER

Where evil takes the mighty away from love, for only the higher power of love can subdue the craving for might.

"Avasthas are those who fight evil, not those who compromise with it!" The shock in Lidholon's voice reverberates in Sean's head. "Master, it's Governor Serapis by his side. I recognize the colors of Shambalpur on his tunic and his long white hair. He is chatting with the violet sorcerer, looking on quite friendly terms with him, I'd say."

The yuva warriors are stunned, enraged. Serapis the Sernatil, Seneschal of the lowlands and Governor of Shambalpur is the second highest officer in the government of the Avasthas after the Nizam.

"It is true; I recognized him too," Etakir says in a tone of disgust. "The presence of Belzebseth is dark tidings, no doubt, but seeing one of our own high lords next to him makes me shiver from head to toe."

"I played at his feet when I was a child. Aren't you shocked, Master, or have you foreseen this too?" Sean shakes his head as if to chase away Lidholon's nightmare.

"I have suspected trouble for some time," the Sand Keeper responds slowly, "but I did not sense it would come to this. However, recent events confirmed my worst fears. Remember that the Rock is hermetically sealed from the surrounding dunes of the desert. No foreign being can penetrate the Rock on foot without our permission. You know that the labyrinth of underground passages towards and under the Rock is complex and runs for hundreds of kilometers. Yet Thanatophor's legions found the passage easily without losing their way. They even managed to open the normally impassable portals, something that has never been achieved.

"Normally Thanatophor's army might have penetrated our fortress through the main underground passage but that tunnel leads to the cave of the subterranean lake that belongs to the House of Elnur. The Sernatil did not have the access code to the giant gates of the cave's outer wall because it is under the sole control of Elnur. The troops of pestilence broke through directly from the undisclosed entrance cavern of Shambalpur at the center of the Gundaldhar Canyon. That is the passage under the control of the Seneschal of the Lowlands."

"Is that irrefutable proof that Serapis helped them?" Lindholon asked, hoping to a clearer explanation from the wizard, He still cannot comprehend the presence of a much-revered Avastha lord by the side of the enemy.

"No, it isn't. But the day before I rescued you, I received a secret message written in a coded script known only to members of the Avastha War Command. It read 'The Nizam and his people have run away. Elkaim, join me and together we can defeat Thanatophor. This is the only way. Lord Belzebseth is smart, he greatly values our knowledge, and it is entirely to his advantage to spare us. Do not do anything rash but answer my emissary.' It was signed Serapis Sernatil. A bodyguard of his household carried the tablet on which the text was engraved with the Governor's seal."

Still the young warriors are incredulous, "Why? Was he not meant to leave the Rock with the rest of our race who departed for the stars?"

"The Avasthas have been assigned the task of colonizing another galaxy, but a small party is being left behind with the mission to assist human beings to acquire the Avasthic knowledge. Sernatil however, wants to secure his position of power on Earth in the age to come because it will be an age when everyone, high or low, will be free to grab and abuse power. He is a mighty lord commanding many spells. The demons will be flattered and strengthened by his allegiance. It is a game of who cheats who and who will come out on top, a game Serapis is ready to play."

"When did you realize he had not embarked on the fleet of galactic ships that were waiting at the base of the Givupatlast volcano?"

"When I received the tablet. Serapis gambled on revealing himself to me but in the high-stake games he is playing now, he needs the library. He knows some of the books hold the secret to release terrible spells and weapons. He needs them."

"But why? How is this possible" Loyalty was so much part of the Avastha breeding that they could not fathom the notion of betrayal.

"For some time I suspected that Sernatil sought to build a following for himself. Did he wish to rule Dagad Trikon? With the Lady of the Rock gone, all he had to do was gain my acceptance and there would have been no resistance left. He asked for my response, and I told him that I would send a sign. I am in no haste to oblige. He must have lost patience. I suspect he has decided to lead Belzebseth to my refuge so that together they can defeat me. Perhaps then, through some plan of his own, he wants to defeat Thanatophor. What he doesn't realize is that if he were to succeed, he would become just like Thanatophor himself. However, he will not succeed; he has underestimated both Thanatophor's powers and mine. It is a deadly game, balancing between the Sand Keeper and the Master of Evil.

Lidholon's mind is racing, trying to figure out what is happening, "Is this about the *Biblotheca Diabolica*? There is something I wanted to ask…"

The wizard interrupts him, absorbed in his own train of thought, "The prize of the library is probably how the Sernatil enticed Belzebseth to join forces with him to defeat me. He knows it is under my jurisdiction as the lord of the highlands, and that, in the absence of the Lady and the Nizam, I can decide on its fate. He must have foreseen that I might destroy the library. He also knows that the highlands are remote and not as easy to conquer as the floor of the canyons, so he is under some time pressure to get his hands on these books. And, yes, the *Bibliotheca Diabolica* is probably of immense value to him."

"How can you be so calm, my Lord? I don't understand. This is Serapis, one of the high Avasthas!" Lidholon, having never faced or heard of such treachery before is so outraged he feels like shouting his war cry and rushing out to attack the traitor on the spot. Etakir on the other hand, tries to contain his anger.

"No doubt Serapis Sernatil is of high lineage and revered by the dwellers of the Rock. He was also a friend of your father, Lidholon. Perhaps one of the great differences between him and the other great lords of our race is that he never married. This difference seems trivial perhaps, but in reality, it is not."

"Pardon me? Master, I don't see how that is relevant. Forgive me but isn't the same true of yourself, did you ever marry?"

"No," responded the wizard, "but I loved my students as if they were my own children. Usually it helps to have people around to love, here and now. The exchange of affection keeps the flow of love going. We give; we receive, and the heart increases its capacity to love. This is not an abstract thing, and like all arts, it grows with practice." The bemused look of the yuva warriors clearly indicates they need further explanation.

"The Seneschal didn't have enough respect for women to understand that a good woman is the source of her husband's strength. Men in power need the balance brought by a feminine partner. A good marriage keeps the practice of love alive, in small gestures and daily moments that keep the heart contented. It is common sense. Your mother Annada, was of enormous help to your father, dear Lidholon. In the household, he found peace as she soothed him through the safety of her love. Serapis's love was for himself, his role and his function. His self-importance became more important than himself. This is, I believe, the way in which he became lost. He avoided the company of others and fully immersed himself in the task of ruling."

"That doesn't make him a traitor!"

"The capacity to grow spirituality depends on the capacity to love. Without family or friends or anyone with whom to share love, it is hard to balance the might of the Yellow Feather within us. The Governor of Shambalpur's capacity to love dried up in the heat of his urge to be in command. What I can tell you is that for some months, I was uneasy; I could detect that a poison had entered his mind—was it ambition for his own glory? Was he maneuvering to replace the Nizam? Of course only a few of us became alerted. Isaprem, the head of Anorhad, was the one who first saw his game and secretly brought it to my attention. Don't ask me to explain or to understand Serapis. If I could, perhaps I would have helped him. In fact, I tried to help when I perceived the first deviations. He was deeply suspicious of me. Those who are power-hungry, unconsciously think that everyone else with the capacity to govern is the same. They perceive others as threats."

"This happens with human kingdoms, not with ours. Did my father notice?" The peace Lidholon felt when absorbing the vibrations of the hanging towel is now completely gone. The wizard's comments cannot dispel the bite of his desolation.

"Serapis was too clever. The Nizam cannot be endangered because he is under the direct watch of the Lady of the Rock. On the other hand, Aslerach was simply too straightforward to see the slow motion of such deep craftiness."

"So you must have told him?"

"I simply was not sure, and I kept my observations to myself. Your father was the head of Anor and Anor lives for the unity of our tribe.

I needed to be sure before I would hurt him, so, I resolved to take the counsel of the High Lady. This was a matter of the security of the state."

This latest revelation captivates the yuva warriors and reassures them. They almost forget their grief. Surely, if She knows about it, it means the situation must be under control, bleak though it may seem.

"What did our sovereign say?"

"She interrupted me before I could open my mouth. She said, "I know about your friend the Governor." I realized once more that She is omniscient. She knew so much more than I do on the subject of Serapis's treachery. She explained that the Avasthas crossed the Lily of Anorhad and surrendered their fate to Adivatar. This allowed them to complete a glorious leap in their evolution and to move to higher worlds. She told us that the Governor was going his own way, as a human would do. Serapis was not beyond the perils of his vast intelligence and his extreme cleverness became his curse. He was the first to decrypt the signs of the stars and foresee that our age was coming to its end. If the temptation for power could distract the angel Lucifer, the carrier of light; it could also corrupt an Avastha. She told me that when the time came, Serapis did not want to obey the plan of Adivatar, which the Avasthas were following, by migrating to another galaxy. He wanted to secure his share of dominion and fame on this bounteous planet. To this effect, he made a deal with the devil, thinking he could outsmart him."

"What else did She say?"

"She said that Dagad Trikon was drawing to an end and that She would let each of us follow the path we chose. She said, and I remember it so clearly that I can quote Her. She said, 'I do not understand this craving for power. Power is useless unless you misuse it.'"

Lidholon stares at the wall with blank eyes. The Avastha kingdom is falling into ignominy. The young warrior begins to cry, sobbing like a child, his entire body shaking. The shock caused by the betrayal of one he greatly admired, the grief of the death of his companions; the losses of the last days overwhelm him. The water in his body releases the pain swelling up in him. The squire of Anor cries over lost greatness. He mourns the ending of a fair and gentle folk, the departure of the Lady of the Rock and the loss of the innate nobility that adorned Her people. Finally Lidholon cries for himself, a child left by his mother in a world that does not want him anymore.

In room 102 of the Oriental Hotel, Sanath and Mariluh watched Sean's body tremble and twist with grief; tears flowing profusely down his cheeks. The knuckles of his hands clasped on the hilt of the Glorfakir were white from the force of his grip.

They witnessed his struggle in silence. The wizard had to drink the bitter cup of experience to the very bottom, reliving with Sean the burden of memories that carried the pain they had endured during the disaster of the fall of Dagad Trikon. It wasn't easy for Sanath to relive this episode but any interruption at this point could be harmful for the young man. The only thing Mariluh and he could do was to watch as custodians of the Sean-Lidholon's body and wait patiently for the end of the vision.

In the cave of the highlander, Etakir looks away. The Sand Keeper stands motionless during this outpouring of grief. After some time, Lidholon asks him in a quavering voice, "What did you do then? It must have been so dreadful for you."

"It was. I was devastated; I never thought that such a high Avastha lord would fall. Something died in my heart when I found our oneness was broken. This is when I knew our fate was sealed. The Lady told me not to let Serapis know I suspected him. This is why we did not arrest him, we had to leave this world anyway. On Her orders, though, we took some precautions. We accelerated the schedule for our people to depart for the stars. Then we took care of our most precious belongings. We dispatched the caskets but I fear Serapis may have tampered with the contents of one of them."

CHAPTER SIX

THAT SAME OLD THING

*Where treachery could be introduced in Dagad Trikon through the
Governor's yearning for supremacy, where the Sand Keeper announces the
arrival of an Avastha reserve army and how he prepares for the escape from
his highland den and foresees the return of the Avasthas in an age yet to come.*

In his hotel room, Sanath was decrypting the progress of the vision on
Sean's face. Unexpectedly Sean opened his eyes and for a few seconds
blankly stared at Sanath. His attention was back in the room of the
Oriental Hotel, which suggested to the wizard that Sean was experiencing
something to do with modern day Bangkok. But, with his hands clasped
firmly on the hilt of the sword, the magic of Glorfakir returned him to
the faraway past to see a grim Etakir shake his head and break his silence.

"The more I hear, the less I understand. Why is power so alluring?
Can you answer this question, oh wisest among our race? You must have
pondered this in the solitary hours of your vigils, waiting for the treachery
to deploy its full effect."

"Dear Etakir, mind my words: there are only two ways for a creature
of Adivatar to obtain supremacy. One is to merge into the supreme
power, which is the way of the Avasthas and higher humans. The other
is to assert supremacy over creation, which is the way of demons and
lower humans.

The first approach can succeed, but is rarely tried. It is the path of
the Deep Way. The second approach is attempted, time and time again,

56

but always fails. It is the favorite way of pride, the mightiest of all the Dark Riders.

The way of the Avasthas is to consign their fate to Adivatar, a sensible thing to do because his help is of paramount importance for our ability to control our own lives. Serapis ceased being an Avastha when he tried the lower path. I am truly sorry for him."

For a moment, Elkaim Ekamonon, the Sand Keeper and prince of wizards, looks as ancient as the world, so much older than the episode they discuss, tragic as it may be. He is standing on the axis of a whirling world and through their proximity to him the young warriors feel their strength being pulled together and their energy returning. No one breaks the silence but they hear the sound of light footsteps running into the study. Esitel and Evenyl arrive hurriedly and compose themselves as they see the wizard.

Walking slowly towards the bed, Esitel addresses the Sand Keeper.

"Venerable Master, we were resting in our room when we heard some muffled hammering. We called Agnorth. He told us to report to you that the enemy army sappers are digging a tunnel and are approaching the second gate. He says it is a matter of hours, not days, before they pierce the wall. Agnorth says there is witchery at work otherwise they could not progress that fast. He is setting up the mechanism to block the passage and is busy packing food for a couple of days. Master, is there something we can do to help?"

The presence and craft of Belzebseth seem to give an edge to the enemy. Etakir turns to the wizard.

"You said that you discussed with the Nizam precautions to be taken against the oncoming treachery. Is it anything that can help us now? Surely Master, you must have a plan?"

The Sand Keeper stands up slowly. He seems to grow in size, like a black cloud filled with the threats of lightning and the rumbling of imminent tempests.

"The invasion of the Dagad Trikon fortress is a sinister moment, albeit a passing one. The demons will soon have other things to worry about than my magic library. As I speak to you, a strike force is approaching, ready to hit back. The Admiral of the Avasthic fleet, Philtalas of Elnur, father of Olophon, is coming at full speed to the rescue, his magnetic ships sailing swiftly through the expanses of sand of the Hasara desert. On the last orders of the Lady of the Rock, he brings well-armed Thalassean sailors and ten regiments of Elnorian troopers. No one facing the wrath of Philtalas has ever survived. Waiting for the landing of the rescue legions of Elnur, thousands of undefeated fighters of the House of Kalabham are rallying to surge in the dead of night from secret refuges. Hidden from the sight of Serapis, they are now regrouping in the sanctuary of Elnur below the surface of the earth, the giant underground cave with the large stalactites and stalagmites, converging on the shores of the lake where your friend Olophon took refuge. Kalabham is the guardian of the purity of the Triangle Rock. They master terrible weapons. Their assault will be formidable and their fury deadly."

"These are glad tidings." They are all greatly surprised at the news having thought that all the Avasthas had left Earth."

"Thanatophor's throng is very large and has spread everywhere. Do you think our troops will be able to defeat them?" Esitel asks anxiously? The Sand Keeper looks into the distance, as though trying to visualize something in the direction of the three, high, red stone towers of Dagad Trikon.

Etakir captures his glance, "You mean, the towers, the music towers that can broadcast the harmonies of death?"

"We were suspecting treachery, but we did not expect it to be so terrible or so fast. Your friends would have survived had we not been taken by surprise. Our unfortunate Hanomkar did not have time to activate the emitters of the Rasa music but the spell on the music stations is still intact. The Seneschal thinks we dismantled them before the departure for the stars as per the plan, but the Nizam secretly gave orders to keep them fully operational. The rangers of Kalabham have maintained control of the three music towers and are now setting up the broadcasting machinery. Lord Chanta, Warden of Kalabham, is commanding them. He knows how to release the waves of the killing sound that will throw Thanatophor's soldiers into madness. Remember, music is the ultimate weapon of the Rock Avasthas."

"Yes, let them face the music," adds Lidholon, a spark of fire dancing in his eyes. "The Kalabham organists will play a grand requiem for Aliskhan and Hanomkar."

Etakir is happy that his tribe's land will not stay in the possession of the loathed enemy. His voice is like velvet on steel. "I am happy that Lord Philtalas is on his way. Kalabham and Elnur will give a good hammering to this scum." He adds with a mean smile, "Punishment is overdue. Thanatophor will, for the last time, feel the full might of the Avasthas."

The wizard nods in assent. "The scions of evil shall not rule over our beloved Rock. It belongs to the Lady and to Her alone. None who are unauthorized have ever been able to approach the power that dwells in Her abode, the reptilian energy of the Ureus, her sacred cobra. The Cave of Wonders is sealed forever, and it shall sink into Mother Earth."

"For all practical purposes, the history of the Rock Avasthas came to an end when the cylinders of fire, as we call our trans-galactic spacecraft, left the Givupatlast crater," added Etakir somberly. "You know the god of water, Jaladhar, has withdrawn his blessing and the sources are drying up fast. The holy vibrancy of the Triangle Rock cannot be restored. Even if Thanatophor doesn't rule this beloved rock, the desert mountain is still finished, its magic broken. It will remain a dry and desolate place, shrouded in the spell of its own loneliness..."

"...until the day when its magic is reactivated in a new and unknown way," completed the wizard.

"I wonder if and how this will ever happen," says Etakir doubtfully. "How can he fathom that the Rock will still play its part in the unfolding of the legend?" How indeed can he foresee that, millennia later; he would be the one fated to rediscover the Rock as the archeologist Lakshman Kharadvansin?

In the meantime, Lidholon pulls himself together.

"I did not know the Avasthas kept a reserve army on this Earth. I am glad our friends will be avenged. The trend of the age is against us. You are telling us that whether or not we remain the masters of the battlefield we have already been defeated. We have lost the magic of the Rock. We are now fugitives on this Earth." Lidholon pauses then continues in a strong, determined voice. "Then, I salute the last hooray of the Elnorians; it is important to end in style."

The wizard concludes, "The House of Kalabham is fiercely loyal to Mother Earth and will be only too happy to give her a little respite. The last attack from our people will simply be a parting work of cleansing. For a few millennia perhaps the living creatures will also benefit. Who knows? Some righteous kings of men may for a little while try their hand at the art of just and equitable government. We have reached the end of our cycle in the pre-ordained succession of ages. No one can win against the passing of time, not even me, who received the name of the Sand Keeper from the Aulyas. Why? Because it was said that the sand of so many centuries flew through the hourglass without affecting me."

"Master, the knowledge of the Deep Way is waning. Are you saying we can sustain this fight?"

"No," the Sand Keeper shakes his head sadly. "We cannot. The crooks and the greedy will take over and ultimately, you are right, the demons will win."

A long silence follows. Evenyl whispers, "What will such a world look like?"

"Well, I can tell you. I used to converse with some of the Aulyas, who could see the future: Humans have technical skills but no strategic sense. Man and nature fall apart. None stays in its proper place. Value comes from connection to machines, not people. Food and thoughts are tasteless and polluted. Women and emotions are cheap. Men either soil the name of Adivatar or forget him. Mostly, between license and violence, they turn vulgarity into one of the beaux-arts. The ghosts of the Mlechas, worst among the demons, enter their brain. Many that are filthy are honored; the few who are clean are ridiculed. The wealthy…"

"No," shrieks Evenyl, "please stop! I can see it all before my inner eye as you speak. I feel nauseated; I sense the return of the horrible fear I had before you read the *Kavach*. Please stop, the demons are stirring in my head."

"Forget it!" the wizard forcefully interrupts to call Evenyl back to her senses. "The wheel moves for them too, and truly, I am telling you, it is when they are at the apex of their rule, in some ten thousand years from now, that we shall return and reclaim the Earth. Do not fear destruction: an age must end before the next can be born. You shall live to see the rebirth."

"Master, will you be with us on the day of the Avasthic redemption? I sense it will be so!"

Wind blows over their heads. Evenyl, the damsel of Eleksim, has spoken spontaneously without realizing her words carry the Vani spell of prophecy. When she utters these words, she feels instantly liberated from the insidious evil she had glimpsed. Lidholon looks gratefully at the Sheravalian warrior and feels a new courage surging from his heart. The Vani spell of prophecy is a property developed by the Avasthas when they are initiated in the lore of Anor. Their throats carry the power to utter the truth, in the sense that what they speak becomes the truth.

The Sand Keeper emits a subtle radiance, and a white-orange spark dances above his head. His face is glowing.

"I swear by the discus of Anor that our people shall come back. I shall be appointed to prepare their arrival, and I shall then bear the celebrated name of Sanath, the Hllidarendi. Thus speaks the Sand Keeper. When the tree has grown from the seed and the meaning is extracted from the riddle, when the end gives birth to the beginning and the chick breaks the egg shell, then the secrets contained in the Gnostic library shall be deciphered within the bodies of human beings."

They are listening intently and Evenyl says, "Hail to the Lady of the Rock, the Sand Keeper has prophesied. Normally, he does it only within the Circle of the Aulyas. We are lucky to have witnessed this; great work is at hand."

The wizard turns and looks at her, still carrying an aura of great majesty. "Have a rest now. Tomorrow we must leave these ancestral grounds for good. And then the great library will be set ablaze."

This time no one protests. The Sand Keeper's guests return to the Chamber of Healing and fall into an uneasy sleep, a sleep punctuated by the sound of muted hammering. The Sand Keeper and his attendants labor in the launching pad located in a circular room, above the pinnacle of the library cavern; a sleepless Lidholon joins them. They are preparing three small pentagonal Pushpak aircraft, loading the supersonic vehicles with everything necessary for the imminent evacuation.

During that night, the surroundings of the Highlander's den are overrun by patrols of enemy soldiers and hyenas. Columns of the devil's troopers are at the entrance of the tunnels, awaiting instructions from the engineers who are digging through the mountain walls. Equipped with clear sight, the wizard can observe and sense that Belzebseth himself is directing them, feverishly looking for the secret access to the refuge of the wizard lord. The sorcerer utters curses and casts spells, aware of the proximity of the invaluable Gnostic library, enraged by the scent of the prey, the nearness of the loot, so close, yet so far.

During the last hours of the Gnostic library, some of Belzebseth's malice reaches its destination. During this night, the floors of the magic library are busier than they should be. Sean can see through Lidholon's eyes, and the young Avastha knight stays awake. Descending the launching pad through the hall of the library, he spies a shape, coming out of hiding, cautiously emerging from a dark corner of the great hall of the library. The face is hidden. This intruder is heading for the *Bibliotheca Diabolica*.

The sun has not yet reddened the peaks of the music towers in the early morning when the Sand Keeper briskly awakens his group.

"Hurry, grab your belongings and let's go. Philtalas has arrived. The green standard of Elnur has been unfurled on the Western peak. The grey war banner of Kalabham has been raised on the music towers. The Avastha reserve army will attack in less than an hour. My flying Pushpak chariots are ready; they will take us at great speed, far away beyond the great sea, onwards to the snowy regions of the Himavat Mountain where we'll be safe. I have a strong longing for its white, mountain peaks glittering in azure skies. You will enjoy walking through its wondrous forests of rhododendrons. We shall forget all evils when bathing in Ganga's bubbling mountain streams. Come, you too will be refreshed. Our mission is to leave what we know in order to prepare for the unknown of the next age. Besides, I need to consult the Nathas. I will be able to find some of them there."

The air is cold. From under her blankets, Esitel, still half asleep and yawning, asks, "Who are the Nathas?"

"Human beings. I mean, they are not Avasthas but they are foremost among the knowers of things that were hidden from the multitude. They have achieved towering heights in the understanding of the Deep Way. Like the Aulyas, they take their directions straight from the Daskalian teachers, and some of them can even speak with the gods. Men can ascend very high if they chose to."

Bothered by a sudden intuition, Lidholon asks with a worried look, "Are we now supposed to become human?" He pauses and adds, "That's a really scary thought."

Sean Aryaputra's body started to move. He woke up in room 102 of the Orient Hotel, his hands releasing their hold on the hilt of the Glorfakir. He slowly eased himself to a sitting position. Both Sanath and Mariluh remain immersed in meditation.

His first awareness of consciousness was the unease of being an all-too-human, human being. Despite the sorrows of Lidholon, Sean had experienced the lightness of the body and the clarity of the being of an Avastha. The human condition had a weight and a fog entirely of its own.

The Glofarkir sword had taken his attention into a deep slumber, revealing the secrets of his past, many lifetimes away. Looking somewhat haggard, Sean said, "It is that same old thing: Dagad Trikon fell because one of us lusted for power. It is the Lucifer story."

Sanath opened his eyes, and said, "The Seventh."

"What do you mean?"

"The Seventh Rider – Pride is the strongest of the Dark Riders."

"Finally, it was pride that destroyed the higher race, wasn't it?"

The wizard nodded sympathetically, "So it had to be; let us pity those who have an unpleasant role to play on the stage of life. A long time ago we witnessed together the end of an age, and together again we see the birth of a new one. Finding you is one of the reasons I came to Bangkok. Many Stealthstars are lost by now, covered by the shadow. It was important that you know for you carry the light of Anor and the Lady of the Rock intends it to shine. You must rest now. I've ordered a car for you, and we will meet again very soon. What is yet to come will fill you with awe."

CHAPTER SEVEN

THE ELDER ON
TABLE MOUNTAIN

Where Kheto the Hllidarendi from Africa meets Michael and Lorelei, explains his role, and why the wizard now summons the Stealthstars to prevent the ultimate peril, the War of the Two Feathers.

The noonday sun stood in motionless brilliance in the African azure sky. Michael O'Lochan and his fiancée, Lorelei von Jetzlar, were strolling, hand in hand, in the crowded Victoria Wharf shopping mall in Cape Town harbor. It was the last day of their vacation in the Republic of South Africa. Michael, always careful with the effects of the sun, wore a cap and sunglasses. Dressed casually in faded blue jeans and T-shirt, Lorelei nonchalantly sipped a cola drink as she walked along, her disorderly blond hair in glorious contrast to her tan; looking very much like one of the mythical holiday sirens that sometimes visit the dreams of young men. Michael wasn't the jealous type and didn't mind the furtive looks at Lorelei from male passersby. He was insulated from any suspicion or jealousy by the enveloping comfort of her ardent feelings for him. Loving and being loved, all in one and with the same person, was very much at the core of the happiness he had discovered with Lorelei. After all, hers was an enduring, ancient love, dating from the time of the legendary Dagad Trikon fortress in North Africa, when his name was Aliskhan, a warrior of the House of Anor, unaware of the yearnings of Esitel, the young Sheravalian Amazon who was Lorelei in this lifetime, far in the distant future.

They wanted to purchase an engagement ring, something more imaginative than a diamond, and they found a dark-blue, tanzanite stone, alive with a dancing lavender flame set in a ring of white gold. They admired how it flashed in the midday sun, took a deep breath and bought it for a good price.

To celebrate their purchase, they had a Cajun hamburger lunch at Emily's, a sunny wooden terrace on the waterfront near the old, red clock tower. This was their last day together for some time. Lorelei was about to fly back to Jetzenstein Castle on the river Rhine via Frankfurt, while Michael was bound for Washington, D.C.

His sunglasses hiding a mischievous glance, Michael returned to one of his games, playing Doubting Thomas, "Not much has happened during the last year, no move on the Dagad Trikon front, and I wonder sometimes if we have really achieved anything, I mean, anything lasting. I cannot feel the deep peace any longer, unless I am in a pristine environment, away from human beings."

A smiling Lorelei would have nothing of it, "Come on. We can often feel the gift of the Lady of the Rock, when we are together, with Tracy, your brothers or with Lothar. You know that if we desire it enough the legend will unfold. We will connect to it again. Please don't start your little lost doggy act so you can get more cuddles!"

"What I like about you my darling is the faith you have in your own desire and the way it works out."

Happy with the comment and the moment at hand, Lorelei changed the subject, "Put some sunscreen on your nose, honey. I read in the newspaper that the sun's UV rays are particularly nasty between 11a.m. to 3p.m. because of the hole in the ozone layer down here."

"I do tan my dear, although not as well as you. Don't worry. But I must pay attention to the bill. The waiter owes me another fifty rand."

The waiter apologized, gave the correct change and added furtively, "A young African woman in a red dress asked me to give you this envelope, but she did not want to wait." They turned but saw no one fitting the description. This was unexpected. Lorelei opened the envelope and read aloud:

"Greetings, my name is Kheto, I am the African Hllidarendi. The Grand Master has now summoned the remaining members of the Order. I am contacting you as per his wish. Please kindly meet me tomorrow at 1 p.m. at McClear's Beacon. I have asked my granddaughter to carry my invitation because I cannot show up in town."

"Wow! Instant and telepathic! What do you make of this?" Michael glanced at his fiancée with a puzzled look. She smiled broadly and sounded thrilled, "This is exciting! Sanath is making contact with us again. Where on earth is this beacon?"

"There," said Michael, pointing with an expansive gesture at Table Mountain.

Flanked by Devil's Peak to the east, Lion's Head and Signal Hill to the west, the spectacular Table Mountain overlooks the city of Cape Town. The astronomer of the same name, who wanted to accurately measure the circumference of the earth, erected Maclear's Beacon on its summit in 1843.

Lorelei added firmly, "I don't know why this person is so shy but surely no one here knows about the Order of the Hllidarendi? I think it's an answer to your eternal doubts." They looked at each other, energized, with emerging determination.

"Let's do it then, and hope it's not something phony," responded Michael. "You and I both know there are creepy creatures in this saga. Lately, I've dreamed of a tarantula walking on my body and the next night, of a scorpion coming to get me. I woke up just in time. It wasn't nice at all."

He looked uneasily over his shoulder as if making sure he was not shadowed by foes of the wizard of Dagad Trikon. Walking back to their hotel, they stopped by a group of young Africans on the wharf who were singing and playing drums with the polyrhythms so typical of Africa. They marveled at the spontaneity, the graceful simplicity with which their bodies undulated with the music; musical language that spoke to the former Avasthas. It was such an essential part of the vanished culture of Dagad Trikon.

Michael called their travel agent. Fortunately, Lorelei's booking on South African Airway's morning flight to Frankfurt could be rescheduled without additional charges, but Michael was now wait-listed to D.C. through London. He felt unhappy about it, but it was difficult not to take the bait to get back into the legend. Besides, Table Mountain had been on his destination list, a National Park renowned for its scenery and unique flora.

The next morning, equipped with trekking shoes, backpacks and sleeping bags, they reached the western end of the flat-topped plateau by cable car. Under the uncompromisingly blue African sky, they hiked through unspoiled landscape, admiring interesting geological formations and enjoying the breathtaking view of Cape Town and the ocean far below. They chatted about their past adventures, noting that this was the continent on which the mountain fortress of Dagad Trikon was located.

Maclear's Beacon is a remote but magnificent spot for any meeting, more than a thousand meters above sea level. At the nearby restaurant, on the highest point, an elderly African rose to his feet as they entered. As their eyes met, they sensed that he was the one they were looking for. His eyes were penetrating and insightful. He was a Xhosa of average height, with short curly gray hair and a light-brown complexion. There was an air of great alertness about him. Michael and Lorelei felt a commanding presence. The African elder, wearing a worn beige suit and a light green shirt, greeted them in a warm voice, using the name given to the Avasthas who had returned incognito in the modern world.

"Greetings, young Stealthstars. My name is Kheto. You can call me Uncle Kheto if you wish. I have been looking forward to meeting you since the Master told me about you."

They weren't used to being greeted in such a manner by a stranger and looked around feeling embarrassed but none of the other diners were paying attention to them. Kheto seemed genuinely pleased to meet them.

As they dined, the elder told them about his initiation sometime back by the wizard Sanath. As a teenager in Pietermaritzburg, he had worked in the company of an Indian lawyer bearing the name of Gandhi, who had thrown a challenge to the might of the Afrikaners and subsequently to British rule in India. Like other wizards in Sanath's Order, Kheto didn't age like other humans and was far older than he looked although not as ancient as Sanath, who was after all, the Grand Master. He continued with his story: he had been a trade union activist, a freedom fighter against the Apartheid regime, a journalist and for ten years, a taxi driver in Paris where he took refuge from the South African secret police. His daughters still lived in France. He chatted for a while with Lorelei in the language of Molière and she found his French excellent. Kheto's manners were serene and jovial; they enjoyed his natural simplicity. At the same time, he exuded the quiet dignity of an African chief.

"What exactly is your job as the African Hllidarendi?" Michael was curious about the workings of Sanath's mysterious Order.

"To help the conquest of a truer freedom. You see, Africans have an advantage compared to some other races: they feel more. They are more musical less mental. They can tune in and melt into oneness more easily than others. Overall, they are more adept at flowing with the Deep Way, but they need to achieve the balance to access the gate to the Inner World. To do so, they must reach beyond their present conflicts; and this is the challenge. I am trying to find the key to help my people."

The elder explained the heritage of his continent. Kheto's tribe knew about a kind of electromagnetic energy. It was identified with the strength of the giant python that rises within the spine and emerges at the top of the head. The name sounded like Umbili. Sanath had told Kheto that many ancient people, from the Dogon astronomers of Mali, to the Celtic western druids or the long vanished seers from Ukraine were all familiar with it and knew about it at one time. The legend appeared in form or another in many traditions around the globe but no one, Kheto agreed, knew how to activate the dormant power.

"Tracy told me that the U.S. Congress withdrew funding for the global Oikos research project which was meant to rediscover this knowledge.

It was most unfortunate," Michael observed, "Carl Gustav Jung, the Swiss psychologist, studied this subject. His area of research, the field of the universal unconscious, seems to be the area in which your Order operates. He wrote about the electromagnetic energy, called Kundalini, as the transforming force."

"Jung could not cross some barriers, and was aware of his own limitations. Reality cannot be captured by analysis. Thoughts can describe the map, but they cannot take you there."

The African Hllidarendi was articulate and knowledgeable and the couple responded warmly to Kheto's genuineness and openness. While asking about the purpose of their encounter, Lorelei had a premonition, "Do you mean that we need to find the missing caskets?"

"Precisely. The opening the Casket of the White Feather in Iceland and Holland cannot deploy its effects on global consciousness if it is not balanced by the revelations of the two complementary caskets. The great schism, the split between the Outer World and the Inner World cannot be overcome if the two other caskets remain hidden and closed. The Grand Master asked me to contact you because your little group must help him to prevent what he terms the War of the Two Feathers.

"The opening of these three caskets, of the White, Yellow and Blue Feathers, is a condition for the release of the pure knowledge. In order for this race to overcome its conflicts through the central channel of the White Feather, that is, the middle path of harmony, the caskets of the Blue and the Yellow Feathers must first be secured. This process has started.

"Pure knowledge is the path that takes us to the inner axis of the truth. Only when we are grounded in the truth can we achieve unity. Otherwise, calls for unity, solidarity and love sound false and merely serve the purpose of hypocrites and politicians who want to be popular and gain adherence to their cause."

"We are more or less aware of this," commented Michael politely while waiting for Kheto to disclose the purpose of their meeting.

"Listen to history; Kheto exhorted, "it tells us that the next evolutionary leap into greater brain power requires mastering the qualities of the three feathers."

In the majestic silence of this lofty place surrounded by the ocean, the couple felt that history was gently letting them know that its purpose was alive and well. "Thousands of years ago, the ancient people who knew about the Goddess developed the energy of emotions, mostly under the sway of the Blue Feather. For instance, the sedentary populations were worshipping the Goddess in the Middle East, where the exchanges between Asia and Africa took place. They developed societies by the power of feelings and empathy, forging a bonding that helped them to endure and overcome adversities. With Belzebseth being active, these civilizations slowly degenerated, like Atlantis, into all manner of excesses such as fertility cults and black magic."

"Atlantis existed?" Michael's voice betrayed his surprise.

"Indeed and the Thalassean fleet of the Avasthas was trading with them but their continent collapsed into the sea as Mother Earth would no longer endure their excesses. Atlantis was an empire that carried the might of the Blue Feather."

"What happened?"

"Some seven thousand years ago, the Indo Aryan civilizations evolved from sedentary populations with iron, horses and their male deities. This marked the end of the age of the Blue Feather, and most of its secrets were lost. The shift was brutal; the ascendancy of the new age of thought, the age of the Yellow Feather, would prove irresistible. It continued over millennia, fearsome and ever accelerating: witness in a few recent centuries the explorer navigators, the inventions of industry, technological acceleration, and virtual finance! At the end, the worshipers of thought and action produced the burned-out world in which we live today and threatens to collapse around the town of the betrayed Nazarene Master, Jerusalem."

"My brother Jonathan who was posted in Cairo for a time, agrees with this grim conclusion," said Michael who continued, "Sanath once told us once that bringing the three feathers together will bring minds together. But why please, did you choose this place to meet us?"

"This was formerly called the Sea Mountain because, further to the south, the Cape of Good Hope is where currents of the Atlantic and Indian Oceans meet, causing stormy waters. This region is a place of both separation and meeting. The Goddess emerged from the sea on the west coast, and landed at a place now called Langebaan Lagoon, about sixty miles north of Cape Town. The imprints of Her footsteps in the limestone are about a hundred and seventeen thousand years old. Since then, the area has been covered with fields of daises. This is the true reason why the city of Cape Town came to be known as the Mother City in South Africa, not because it was the first city of the Dutch settlers. It was where mankind was meant to unite, until the Afrikaners invented apartheid. Whatever was holy has since been soiled."

"But we could also have met downtown, couldn't we?"

"I usually work in the townships, but it would have been too conspicuous for you to join me, for example, in Crossroads. Here the mountain protects us. Kheto paused and added, "Let me tell what you need to know. The moment is precarious. You witnessed in Germany how the arch demons Hangker and Belzebseth were thrown into hell, but they have successfully multiplied themselves within their followers. They are still around, trying to stop and prevent the ascent of man. Men go about their ways, unaware of the evil that they are contributing to the dominion of the demons. Even some Stealthstars have been led astray, many seduced by witches. Others wanted to get back to Dagad Trikon and took drugs to get there, in the hope that doing so would help them, but landed instead in the prisons of Thanatophor. This has been such a sad story. We need to overcome this sorcery in order to achieve inner progress. More to the point, one of the main foes of goodness is chasing me.

"The ghost cavalry, you mean, one of the Dark Riders?"

Kheto pondered. His attention could usually sense within a radius of half a mile around his body, and he had registered some unease, a premonition that they would be disturbed. Everything was fine here in the inn yet he sensed an approaching hostile force outside. Although he did not have much time, he refused to be rushed.

The African chief continued, "The Master told us that the six Avasthic Houses in the days of the sacred rock lived side by side, complementing each others' talents and skills in full harmony. Without this strong sense of togetherness, only scattered individuals would have known the Deep Way, not entire communities and well-functioning tribes. This is not enough to change the course of history. The awakening of our common destiny and purpose must now happen in entire villages, cities and nations. I am located in Africa to help as I can."

"Well done! Apartheid is finished, and a new country has been built."

"Yes, but the work is a long way from being finished. In South Africa, we call ourselves the rainbow nation because of our many colors, but it is the moisture of love that makes the rainbow visible. Now we are living in parallel communities, not in unity. We must at least face the true state of affairs: we still have inequalities, violence and corruption.

"Thanatophor has a plan for each continent. The alchemy of plagues he reserves for us is quite subtle. The devil fears that Africa will manifest its potential and its true greatness. In essence, as I told you, we flow with the pulse of life; we celebrate our integration with nature, the rhythm, joy and the maker of it all. We go to the roots of knowledge. This is our sacred destiny. True knowledge, or *vidya*, brings us into oneness. False knowledge or avidya separates and divides. Jealousy opposes oneness. The fifth wraith operates across the entire world, but she wants to bar man's access to genuine knowledge by hampering progress on my continent. She is insidious and crafty; she knows how to invite herself unexpectedly, and her victim does not know how to chase her away.

"She? Who is she?"

CHAPTER EIGHT

THE SEASON OF THE WITCH

Where Chief Kheto exposes the craft of the fifth Dark Rider while explaining that something as petty as jealousy can destroy something as important as a community, and how Michael discovers the effects of Psychic Compulsion Viruses (entities).

They heard a commotion outside and went out to see what had happened. A group of tourists were standing around a young man who had fallen to the ground, shivering and shaking in front of the restaurant. Kheto stayed in the background but Lorelei and Michael joined the group. The young man was dressed in sports attire, wearing a T-shirt with an image of a flying Superman. His eyes were open and foam was coming from the corner of his mouth. Lorelei was frightened and hid behind Michael. He was making the noises of an animal growling. "Is there a doctor here?" someone shouted, while others dialed for help on their cell phones. It looked to Michael like an epileptic seizure.

Then something strange happened. After their encounter with the Goddess in Delhi, the Stealthstars sometimes used their vibratory awareness. Instinctively, Michael extended a hand, palm upward, toward the young man lying on the ground as if to test his condition. The man instantly began convulsing; his prostrate body jerked off the ground. His distorted mouth emitted a horrifying gurgle and a piercing shriek. Nobody had noticed the correlation between Michael's hand gesture and the wild reaction, or so he thought. He himself could not believe it. The man on the ground was now breathing heavily. Intrigued, Michael waited for a few moments then extended his hands towards him again.

This resulted in new screaming as another jolt propelled the entire body a few centimeters above the ground. Growling and foaming, the unfortunate fellow immediately started to crawl, trying to hide behind the legs of people on the opposite side to where Michael stood.

This should have sufficed, but Michael was still in a state of disbelief; the coincidence between his brief movements and the extraordinary convulsions was astonishing. Just to be sure, he took a step forward. Moaning with more animal growls and sounds, the young man hurriedly crawled away from Michael and hid behind a nearby boulder. Michael's mind was processing, "This is extraordinary!" And with another small gesture of his hand, he caused another fearful bestial growl. "My movements really do have an effect."

"Stop it, stop it! What are you doing?" a young woman shouted angrily at Michael. She had noticed the link between his hand movement and the desperate response. The connection seemed so unbelievable that Michael had no difficulties convincing the group as he plaintively protested, "I'm not doing anything at all!" The group looked at him with a certain diffidence. What could they say? The woman's claim was not plausible.

Kheto seemed annoyed by the commotion. He took Michael by the arm and pulled him back into the restaurant. They paid for their meal and left discreetly taking a trail in the opposite direction to where the young man was. They walked briskly to put some distance between them and the scene of the epileptic seizure.

After a while, Lorelei observed, "The woman who spotted your hand movements must have been his girlfriend. Perhaps you might have been more discrete."

"Honey, how could I possibly have known?"

"Those spasms were awful. It was so, so scary." Lorelei shrugged. "I guess this is what Tracy reported from the Oikos project, these PCVs—Psychic Compulsion Viruses. It must have been a possession that could not bear your proximity because of your vibrations. It's the first time I saw a possession with my own eyes. It was ghastly!"

Kheto added, "I know the fellow with the Superman T-Shirt. He is a young lawyer from Cape and works for the witch Mokolo. He must have traced me to the cable station and attempted to find me on the Table plateau. The scary part is that these poor people do not notice anything, for the PCV penetrates them unnoticed. They did not know that the witch Mokolo had put this stuff into him. They are landing in hell without noticing it—vintage Thanatophor."

"So this Mokolo is the one you call the Fifth Rider, correct?

The elder Xhosa signaled them to sit with him under the shade of a large boulder and continued his tale, "We call the fifth one the Mokolo witch, a female wraith riding the greenish horse phantom of jealousy. The demon kings turned over the execution of their plot of divisiveness to Mokolo. She is the widow of the titan Narak, who was killed a long time back by the Emerald King. Mokolo seeks her revenge against the human race. Her method is old, well tested: she provokes separate groups and sects, bringing discord and divisiveness. Now she has been given the task of dividing the human followers of the Goddess."

"I hadn't a clue that jealousy is so powerful." Lorelei said.

"But indeed it is," Kheto continued, "it is truly a plague. Passive jealousy disturbs the inner peace, and active jealousy disturbs the peace of others. Those who cannot do better use jealousy to express their nuisance value."

"Does the name of the witch have a meaning?"

"Master Sanath told me you are quick!" Kheto smiled at Lorelei. "In the language of the ancient pastoralists who arrived here with their domestic animals about two thousand years ago, Mokolo means 'nasal excrement.'"

Michael and Lorelei's puzzled faces indicated to Kheto that his explanation left them none the wiser.

"Demons are excrement and vice versa. Let me explain. In the world of the ancients that is still understood by the last guardians of the Order, the whole universe is one body made of diverse energies. Energy produces waste. The demons are nothing but waste, the by-product of these energies and this is why in many traditions, hell is a place where this waste is collected, the sewage of the universe.

"Similarly, our own bodies are crisscrossed by flowing energies, which generate various forms of waste. The physical waste is evacuated when we excrete. There is a subtler waste of thoughts and emotions that humans do no know how to evacuate: the compulsion of lust, anger, greed, attachment, vanity, jealousy, and pride. You know them as the substance of the Dark Riders. They ferment and can penetrate the mind. When the gates are wide open, the horses of doom ride out to find us."

"And in the case of this witch, how does she manipulate jealousy? And why is that so important?"

"The orthorhinolaryngological complex in our faces is the seat of the power of communication, which can bring the human tribes together. Communication should work for what had been the purpose of the Avasthas, the return to oneness. It is a tremendous tool for good but Mokolo can also make it work for evil." He shook his head. Kheto's otherwise radiant face looked more somber now, as if the topic was bringing the weight and weariness of a long drawn-out fight. Lorelei noted a cloud pass over his noble and gentle features.

"Please, what has this to do with you summoning us today?"

"Quite a bit, unfortunately. Mokolo has not been able to penetrate your group, but she is the ancestral enemy of the Fifth House. She works mostly through selfish and ambitious people whose business is to keep the masses in poverty, and to turn people against each other, so that they won't challenge the exploiters who remain in power. You are a scion of the Fifth House, the House of Anor, dear Michael, and its magic was to keep alive the organic bond between all the houses. The Avasthic civilization could not have existed without this collectivity, let alone matured."

"I understand a bit better how this battle must be won in Africa for all of us; but why are you in hiding Uncle Kheto?" Lorelei asked, for she sensed the importance of the subtle, but formidable battle now taking place on the continent where the Dagad Trikon fortress had been located.

"Mokolo wants to get rid of me. Though she cannot easily pierce my disguises, she has many spies in town, and they look for me day and night. You see; the witch received word from the Dark Council that the Order of the Hllidarendi is now reactivated. The necromancers know we are few in number and that I am living in this country. They don't want the Order to obtain a footing on this continent. They need to find me because Belzebseth wants to work out of Africa through the practice of sorcery. He takes advantage of the cult of the ancestors to capture the souls of the dead, helped with body parts of animals or humans, a sinful art that we must foil. By the grace of the Lady of the Rock, I'll be successful and sap his strength. We need to meet the black arts with more Avastha magic. Master Sanath says that I have a respite because Mokolo is now turning her attacks on the followers of the Mother who are young and inexperienced in the Deep Way. She wants to split their community."

"How can it happen? Lorelei wondered aloud. "Surely, with all the knowledge they have acquired, they must know better than to quarrelling amongst themselves."

"Remember what I told you about the power of the witch? She uses communication for malevolent purpose; she creates waves of gossip, promoting the formation of hostile groups, splitting clans, and causing conflicts. The psichasa are these murmuring ghosts whose powers she uses to insert her messages in our brains.

"She works her devilry though these murmuring souls, whispers in our ears, and on the Internet, she, sows doubts, treachery, and breeds hatred. Lies, defamation, insinuations, and character assassination are all part of it. It is all filth, thus the connotation of nasal excrement. The witch patiently sows dissent, resentment or even diffidence; her mission is to divide and conquer."

"What about the poor fellow having an epileptic seizure?" asked Lorelei.

"Narak taught Mokolo a few tricks in the service of Thanatophor. She gives her students special mantras, names that they repeat a thousand times a day, without knowing that they are the names of evil entities. These entities, being called, respond and enter. The overload creates the conditions for epilepsy. Of course, there is quite a bit of black magic behind it all."

"This gives me the creeps," said Lorelei, her blue eyes wide open and her mouth twisted in an expression of disgust, "but there is another magic to stop them, isn't there?"

"Correct. In this particular case, the mountain ghost frog prevented them from finding you." They arose and made their way along a scenic mountain trek. The Xhosa elder talked about the importance of animals. Some warned Kheto of the movements of enemies: indeed, the frogs on Table Mountain were particularly helpful in this respect. "This mountain ghost frog only exists here, and it took us a long time to work out this net of protection," added Kheto with unconcealed satisfaction. "In this way, I am pleased to say, the park is quite safe for us. I have loaded the local biodiversity with a bit of my magic; when the followers of Mokolo come in the presence of a frog, the PCVs as you call them, emerge. I had asked the frogs to surround the restaurant," he added, as if it was the most natural thing in the world.

They walked faster, Kheto leading with sure footsteps and a surprising agility for a man his age. They were followed, it seemed to Lorelei, by a bunch of hopping frogs, but she could never see them clearly.

The Xhosa elder hummed an ancient song, it was melodious and rhythmical, his voice gradually rising, vibrant and nostalgic. Slowly, the song took away the memory of the disturbing event with the young man. They were back into their own peace, absorbing the view of the ocean and the magnificence of the scenery of Cape Town bay below. The late-afternoon sun painted the twisted rocks with glorious exuberance. At dusk, they reached a spot called the Overseer's Cottage and after they'd settled in, they met on the terrace where Kheto again commented on the commotion at the beacon.

"Through Michael's gestures, the followers of Mokolo have now felt the strength of Anor. The powers of the Stealthstars are invisible to most, but I witnessed them. As you could see, those possessed by evil entities can feel and fear them as well. Please be careful on the way back. When he recovers, that young man may not recall the events, but his girlfriend will tell him what happened and the message will reach the witch who will, in turn, report it to Thanatophor, thus exposing Michael."

"A young woman tried to take a photo of Michael with her cell phone when were leaving them," Lorelei recalled.

Kheto nodded. "If I am right; the witch will soon be after you. It's best that you're leaving the country tomorrow."

"I had no clue he would react so dramatically. I just extended my hand. It was quite extraordinary, to say the least. But where does all this leave us? What is Master Sanath's advice?"

"Master Sanath is inviting you through this encounter with me to join again in the great adventure and, at this moment, friends of yours are in Bangkok, fated to open the Casket of the Yellow Feather with him."

"True, Jonathan's wife is in Bangkok. How do you know that?" Mike and Lorelei were excited and curious about the events in Bangkok, but they were unable to obtain more details. "You seem to have penetrated many secrets. Will we know all the secrets of your Order one day?" Lorelei's curiosity was whetted again.

"Some secrets are meant to be revealed," the elder responded with a twinkle of good humor in his eye, "and others are meant to remain secret. I sense the children will soon know more than their elders.

Otherwise, we shall face our doom. *Homo sapiens* appeared on Earth about a hundred thousand years ago. The average duration of a species is ten million years. At the rate we're going, we will never last that long. We are already exhausting the resources of Mother Earth well before our time is up." Dusk seemed to accentuate the looming threat in the elder's words.

"But we believe the Goddess is here now," asserted Lorelei.

"She is here, yes, but where are we?" was the stern reply of the Xhosa with a vast gesture of his arm pointing to the sprawling city of Cape Town that now looked like a fiery dragon studded with multi-colored jewels in the engulfing night. It ensnared the mountain in its coils, beautiful, yet strangely oppressive.

I invited you to this piece of paradise, lofty and solitary, a flat table where the book recording our deeds will be opened, as will be the case for the human brain." He paused.

"Why do you mean?"

"The purpose of the legend is to reach the House of Ni, to open the brain to a reality greater than it now apprehends. The human brain is like this mountain—both are surrounded by the confusion and falsehood in the world. Like the lofty mountain peak peeking out over the clouds, modern man tries to keep his head above the surrounding fog, the consequences of his own misdeeds, strangled by the accumulated effect of his mistakes.

Everything is being activated now, and moving faster. The Yellow Feather is the channel of willpower on which the white man climbed, and all the other races followed. The situation is dangerous because the movement is linear. Without balancing the ascent through the properties of the Blue Feather, which are stronger in my race, the movement is recoiling; the whole system is on the verge of collapse. The great boat of modern civilization, with its marvelous technology is simply capsizing."

They climbed down the steps of the terrace and sat on a lovely patch of moss between spherical boulders, the lights of the city at their feet and the stars a canopy above their heads. The vastness of the scene filled Lorelei's heart. "This world is so beautiful: it is just a matter to fit in again, to complement this beauty, to feel it once more." Michael looked at her with complicity and tenderness in his eyes; he loved the way his fiancée could connect with her own inner depth.

Michael and Lorelei shared the sandwiches and drinks they had brought with them in their backpack with Kheto, and when the time came to part, they felt sad and dejected. They hadn't seen Sanath for some time and the reassuring presence and gravity of Kheto had provided them with the same sense of guidance and protection that they so appreciated in the presence of the wizard.

Lorelei shrugged. "Our vacation is over, and we will leave the country tomorrow. Is there anything else we need to know? Leave us your phone number please."

Kheto responded calmly but his tone was sad as he had taken a liking to them and would miss them too. "I have no phone, no address and I leave no traces."

"Uncle Kheto, when shall we see you again?"

He replied with a smile, "Only the stars know. But if you want to visit my home, come to Namibia, to the Ameib Guest House in the

Erongo Mountains. When you reach Elephant's Head Rock, my people will find you. This is where I have my refuge, a place of safety and well suited for rest."

"Elephant Rock again? As in Delphi?"

"Yes, just as in Delphi. There are a number of such places emitting a hidden power that only the Stealthstars and the children of the Goddess can feel."

Kheto sighed and concluded, "Our ancestors said that a day would come when a rainbow appears in the sky and the great Goddess will appear in its midst. We keep faith. If man is to experience the Golden Age, he must do it by entering a unified field of consciousness. I will not give up the fight until Mokolo is defeated."

He moved his hand over and around them, drawing the shape of a rainbow while saying cheerfully, "Ten o'clock and all's well, sleep under my cloaking spell." Waving fondly to them one last time, the Xhosa elder disappeared into the shadows of the night. Only then did they notice the furtive silhouettes of some members of his tribe who'd followed him, shadowing him discretely to provide protection.

The two young people spent that night in the Overseers Cottage in deep sleep in which Michael found himself in a vivid dream.

He had entered an ochre colored, circular room. He saw, lined up against the walls of the rotunda, the likeness of the ten high thrones of stone on which the Daskalian Masters, the teachers of the human race, had once sat. The reddish hues of the walls glowed softly, indicating a place of magic. This was the way the underground dwellings of the Avathas received their light in the ancient days of Dagad Trikon.

Before the ten thrones, he could see a circle of seven smaller arm-chairs of pink stone, a child sitting on each. Before the children, on the floor, he marveled at an odd sight: white, wooden, toy horses like the horses that children ride on merry-go-rounds. He heard a voice speak "I am Dikayoson, the Herald of the Chamber of Maat. Behold the celebration of the Fifth House that brings the many into one."

He looked intently at the children and was struck by a similarity in their features. They had large eyes, magnetic, black and shiny, which graced their handsome faces with an extraordinary liveliness. He trained his gaze on the child who was closest to him. He had a regular and sweet face yet, there was something terrible about his expression too. He turned towards Michael and said,

"I am Udurlan, Herald of Anor. My son Aliskhan was slaughtered before the Cave of Wonders when the hordes of the Evil One invaded

Dagad Trikon. But Aliskhan has already been sent, and I shall be back soon."

Michael was shocked and captivated, staring at this child who revealed himself as his father for he knew that he had previously been Aliskhan. He listened intently to the messenger of his own clan, the proud House of Anor.

"The purpose of my House is steadfast, and it is to connect the many tribes together. In this age of demons, the crooks, the sycophants and courtesans who joined them defeated us. The fifth of the Dark Riders gallops for them. Until this day the devils have maintained their challenge to Anor through treachery and divisiveness. But Anor shall prevail."

An aching pain in Michael's throat almost suffocated him, but it gradually dissipated.

When Michael and Lorelei awoke the next morning, Table Mountain was bathed in a fresh mist. They decided to go down through the footpaths to avoid the cable car station, and they followed the trail through forested ravines flanking the city's southern suburbs. Again, Lorelei believed she caught a glimpse of a ghost frog at the beginning of the trek, but could not be sure.

Back at their hotel, Michael found that his flight had been cleared and, after settling their bill, they took a taxi to the airport. He had a long chat with his brother Jonathan in Washington, who told him that new developments had taken place. Jonathan was planning to go to a NATO meeting in Brussels, but first they would meet in London.

CHAPTER NINE

NOT MUCH TIME LEFT

Brussels - where Jonathan O'Lochan and his friend Bernard review why mankind does not have much time left, while in Bangkok the search for the remaining Avasthic caskets is about to begin after the meeting with the wizard Sanath.

Millennia after fighting with the Avastha rescue army against the demons who invaded Dagad Trikon, Olophon of Elnur, reborn in these times as Jonathan O'Lochan, landed at Brussels Airport after 6 p.m. Shortly thereafter he checked into the unremarkable Hotel Bedford, rue du Midi, in the center of Brussels. The heaviness of the weather and strong winds announced an approaching storm. He dined with Bernard, a Belgian diplomat, and former colleague and friend, at the Place Chatelaine, a square that had maintained the distinctive charm of old Brussels. The trendy place was full of young people and noise. No one paid attention to them except for a sleepy Ethiopian waitress.

They dined on beef carpaccio and fettuccine al'tartufo and Jonathan noted, not for the first time, how Italian food always tastes better in Italy than anywhere else. Bernard, an ambassador for his country, was now posted in the ministry, so it was impossible for them not to survey the state of world affairs with broad strokes. Bernard commented that the Belgian capital is a living illustration of European contradictions, the capital of a disunited kingdom while, at the same time, hosting institutions of the European Union. The tissue of the city had been punctured by offensive monuments of concrete and steel that sheltered the sprawling Kafkaesque structure of the European Commission where bureaucrats spun endless reams of regulations in their attempts to make uniform the once rich diversity of life on the European continent. The industrious Eurocrats were disturbed to have lost the confidence of the European people who, throughout history, had strived for and thrived on diversity. But these Eurocrats were isolated in their golden cage, too well paid and insulated from reality to escape.

Jonathan vented his frustration, "The Israeli soldier who reads his tiny bible on top of his tank near the Litani River and the Hezbollah fighter who rains down his Katiouchas on Israeli civilians, after bowing to Mecca, are worshiping the same god and killing civilians in the name of that god. Hezbollah is happy to transform the civil population into martyrs around their launching pads while the IDF is bombing women and children in self-defense. I had to deal with this when I was posted in Cairo, and I cannot bear this idiocy anymore. Extremists help each other's logic; they work to build up self-hypnosis. The madcaps are winning while the sensible men and women are squeezed in the middle and lose ground. In the meantime, and elsewhere, our soldiers are discovering what it means to move in full battle gear at 115°F in Shiite insurgent suburbs. Poor kids. I fear the specter of Vietnam, a meaningless war: apocalypse then, apocalypse now."

Bernard turned the conversations to global threats, "Speaking of which, did you see the latest report of the International Panel on Climate Change? Higher sea levels are threatening two billion people because four out of ten people in Asia live within sixty kilometers of a coast. How do you cope with that?

"I know. This is part of my presentation tomorrow. What exactly are the latest projections of NATO on the relationship between global temperatures and sea level?"

"Projections are notoriously tricky to get right; but a team of geochemists is looking for clues to the future. Before the most recent ice age, the earth went through a warm period that lasted ten to fifteen thousand years, a little warmer than today but not as warm as the temperatures that climate scientists expect with greenhouse gas emissions. Research strongly suggests that sea level then rose seven to ten meters higher than today. We just don't know how the ice sheets in Greenland and Antarctica will behave in the next three hundred years, when and if they'll melt and how fast that will happen."

"Five million people will be on the move very soon but the authorities will only take notice when the migrants show up at their door. And then what will they do? Send in the army? If the scientists' studies are right, it is hopeless." Bernard answered.

"I would find comfort in the fact that this is not exact science, and I agree that forecasting ice sheet decay is difficult, but we are sending heat trapping carbon dioxide into the atmosphere far faster than anything the planet has seen for over fifty million years. What can we expect? Climate diplomacy has failed; we have already lost our chance for complete prevention. We have burned our bridges. Our politicians have let us down. The road ahead takes our coastal cities to Atlantis. You know what happened in the USA after the storms Katrina and Sandy. At least tell them the true state of affairs."

"I will show the multiple feedback loops with the breakdown of social security, the return of poverty and the resulting risk of violent conflicts."

"Ecology, economy, politics, society, everything shakes. The Middle East is toxic. We are moving into a perfect storm. The Templars, Marx and the Third Reich all believed in the final struggle. This may very well be the last one depending on how much will be left afterwards."

In warm rain, they took a brisk walk around the square and back to Jonathan's hotel where Bernard dropped him off. It had no air conditioning and Jonathan, who decided to keep the window open because of the heat, soon came to regret it as raucous partygoers from a nearby club filled the street with drunken songs for what seemed like most of the night. The next morning, yawning profusely, he boarded the bus provided by the organizers of the classified NATO Science Security Forum. Delegates presented their ID at the entry gate of NATO's aging H.Q., passed though metal detectors and gathered at the Luns Press Theater. It was unusual to host such a meeting on a weekend.

A professor from the center for Ecological Noosphere Studies in Armenia began by recalling what Jonathan already knew: that two-thirds of the services provided by nature to humankind were in steep decline worldwide. The benefits reaped from our engineering of the planet had been achieved by running down natural capital assets. Unfortunately however, the living machinery of the Earth has a tendency to move from gradual to catastrophic change with little warning.

The UNESCO Director for Natural Sciences concurred. Geo–political realignments were going to have to be significant to cope with the addition of one billion people due to demographic expansion, mostly in lower income countries vulnerable to climate change. Starting in the next decade, water stress and yields decrease at lower latitudes would affect billions of people depending of the severity of the temperature increase.

Meanwhile, the rapid impoverishment of northwestern countries is crippling the efficacy of any coordinated international response. The effects of hurricanes on New York and the Tri-State area cost billions, money that no one has, given indebtedness and the already overstretched public spending budgets.

All this sounded depressingly familiar. A little bored, Jonathan checked the quality of the simultaneous interpretation, in this case in French and Russian. Next, a retired Brigadier General from the US Army Command and General Staff College introduced a model for a defense analysis perspective on emerging security threats, noting that not much had been done over the last decades. On a twenty-year timeframe, the future trends of asymmetric warfare included greater outreach of transnational organized-crime groups involved in drugs, weapons and human trafficking. He pointed to the intensification of cyber war. The breakdown of law and order in failed states would increasingly be linked with terrorism and, possibly, the spread of weapons of mass destruction. The resurgence of maritime piracy would endanger our international shipping routes. Military technology would lead to wider deployment of electromagnetic and blast effect weapons. The increased engagement of unmanned capabilities to influence military operations points the way to robotic warfare.

When it was his turn to speak,. Jonathan delivered his presentation, backed by an array of statistics and maps. Access to essential resources such as food and water can no longer be ensured; the risks of hunger, riots and conflicts will increase. In the drylands, entire cities may soon face the need to evacuate. Large southern European cities will be affected by food shortages. The massive deployment of solar captors and wind energy on the Atlantic coast of Morocco can provide supply for energy starved Europe but providing them required an immediate and costly investment as part of a comprehensive strategy to create local jobs and reduce forced migrations.

In the discussion that followed the presentation, Jonathan responded to several questions. Finally a young woman from the Marine Research Station in Aquaba, Jordan, asked him, "Dr. O'Lochan, I am not sure I got you right but if your statistics are correct, it is too late to change course. We are heading for a multiple scenario catastrophe aren't we? What should we be doing?"

Jonathan paused, allowed the silence to permeate the room. Instead of giving the usual stock answer: an incantation to technological progress and international cooperation, he said, "We must accept the obvious.

Climate change is not the problem; it is man who must change. I am an optimist, and I believe it can be done. I even believe that, for many ordinary people, change is on its way though they don't know it yet. But," he added somberly, "the biggest problem is that our élites are hiding a simple fact: we are working under a tight deadline."

That was it. Jonathan did not really know what else to say. He knew he sounded naïve. To the other participants, his response was unsatisfactory; his proposed solution was not rigorous enough for a scientific forum. Changing human behavior sounded like an even greater problem than climate change. But, how could a lecturer at NATO HQ tell his public about the Deep Way, a new way of living where man could enjoy more with less?

They would simply not be willing to hear it and he was not willing to face ridicule for nothing. On the other hand, by not letting them know how the Deep Way could transform individuals, he was failing his audience, just as politicians had failed us. He simply did not know how to convey the great news that the Deep Way was now open and available to everyone. Jonathan stepped down from the podium. Chasing away a vague feeling of guilt, he just wanted now to rejoin his companions, his fellow Stealthstars. But on the way to the airport with Bernard, he began carefully sharing elements of the Dagad Trikon discovery and was encouraged to find the Belgium diplomat quite receptive. After all, maybe there was a readiness out there to look into the promises of the Inner World.

Tracy was there to meet him at the airport in D.C. and while he was pleased to see her, Jonathan did not rejoice at returning to the East Coast. A suffocating heat wave was shattering all-time records for electricity use across a wide swath of the United States. The heatwave was the main topic of conversation during their drive home.

The heat wave prompted utilities and government officials to issue renewed emergency warnings for energy conservation. From Pennsylvania to Indiana, cattle and poultry were dying by the thousand. The heat index at Washington's Reagan International Airport indicated 115°F and 91% humidity. The stifling temperature in Washington, D.C. had been in the three-digit Fahrenheit range for weeks now and the population, surviving in large part on air conditioning, feared a disastrous breakdown of the electricity supply such as had already occurred in the borough of Queens in New York City. That power cut had cost twenty thousand lives - mostly elderly people who'd died of dehydration. Many people refused to report for work in Manhattan, unwilling to bear the suffocating temperatures in the subway stations, and there were regular reports of people who had braved the heat, fainting or breaking into tears out of sheer desperation.

"If you go out in the street; it is as if you're breathing molten lead," lamented Jonathan. "I wonder how Lakshmi and the baby are doing in Bangkok, I'm glad to hear it is much cooler there."

They sat in the living room of their little flat in Georgetown on a comfortable cream-colored sofa in front of the TV and channel-switched from the weather channel to breaking news, checking for updated information on the heat wave. The telephone rang. Tracy picked it up, laughed and exclaimed joyfully, "Bingo! You two are telepathic. Jonathan, you really don't deserve this," for it was indeed Lakshmi calling her husband from Bangkok. Jonathan switched on the speakerphone and Lakshmi told them the news about their daughter, a full account of the encounter with Sean and what was happening in Bangkok. The outpouring of news and the reappearance of Sanath suddenly cheered the Georgetowners. They were curious about the new friend, Sean, in Thailand, and the appearance of the South American Hllidarendi, Mariluh. They wanted to know everything in detail.

Soon after, Lakshman phoned Tracy on her cellphone. Her flushed cheeks and happy tone of voice showed clearly to whom she was talking. She went out on the balcony with a jug to water her beloved plants; brothers can be a nuisance when you want to chat undisturbed and you don't always want them to overhear your conversation. She came back from the terrace bubbling with excitement, "Hey guys; it sounds like our dear wizard is calling us again; he is reassembling the Yuva Platoon."

"Except we are not that young anymore," noted Jonathan.

Meanwhile in Bangkok, Sean took some time off work. He headed a well-drilled team, and they could operate without him for a couple of days. He looked absent-mindedly at his family, absorbed in the ethereal memories of his journey with the Glorfakir that had unexpectedly taken him so far back in time. He still could feel the emotions, recall the smells, and the dramatic force of the vision. The experience tugged at his heart-strings. But a few impressions were already escaping him, bundled in a haze within the ochre, high cliffs of the desert mountains. He'd mentioned that he would narrate his meeting with Sanath later as he was not ready to share it yet. Full of expectations, the cousins drove with him to the Oriental. Lakshman knew of the hotel whose fame dates back over a hundred and thirty years, when it first opened its doors as a mariner's lodge along the Chaopraya River.

In the lobby, they paused to admire a magnificent arrangement of orchids climbing up the center of a circular, lotus-bedecked fountain.

They found Mariluh in an elegant crimson, silk sarong, waiting for them at the entrance of the River Wing. As a wizard, she was able, at will, to slip in and out of appearances and identities, and her entire bearing looked completely different now. She guided them to the atrium known as the Author's Lounge in the older wing of the hotel. The whiteness of its high walls served as an elegant setting for afternoon tea and the lush greenery of bamboos and palm trees provided a comfortable freshness.

They recognized Sanath sitting on a large white leather, bamboo armchair. Lakshmi felt her heart leap with joy when she saw again the familiar face with the high cheekbones, the short, bushy, gray beard and the penetrating dark eyes. He stood up as they approached and Lakshmi discreetly noted the impeccable, cream, linen jacket, the delicate hues of a foulard, for the wizard had not lost any of his distinctive classiness, his sartorial elegance. They embraced their mentor effusively. Lakshman beamed with joy at meeting Sanath again whereas Sean greeted him in a more reserved, Eastern manner.

Sanath then took them to the Cio Italian restaurant on the marble terrace by the riverside, beside a luxuriant garden. The terrace was secluded from the hotel by compact vegetation and offered enjoyable privacy. The river was high and the fast-flowing, brown water was almost level with the terrace, giving the impression that they were floating on it. Colorful and noisy, long tail boats, small craft, rice barges and ferries with pagoda ceilings crisscrossed the river.

The cousins updated Sanath on the latest news and brought him the best wishes of the O'Lochans in D.C. Lakshmi smiled while narrating, "Aliskhan and Esitel are ending their vacation in Africa; we spoke for hours yesterday. They told me they also met a member of your Order there. With Chief Kheto for Africa and Mariluh for Latin America, things are really speeding up. We're hoping you'll tell us in what direction."

"Who? What did you say?" Sean, taken out of his daydreaming, reacted to the unknown names with unexpected vivacity.

In the comfortable familiarity of the encounter with the master, Lakshmi had absent-mindedly mentioned the Avasthic names of Michael and Lorelei and now felt embarrassed for Sean.

She registered an approving nod from Sanath and explained, "Oh sorry. Since the revelations made at the battle of Jetzenstein Castle, we often call each other by our Avasthic first names, as nicknames: my husband Jonathan is Olophon, his younger brother Michael is Aliskhan. My cousin Lakshman is Etakir. We sometimes call Lothar von Jetzlar, Hanomkar and his sister Lorelei, Michael's fiancée, Esitel.

They call me Erilie, she added almost shyly, the Sheravalian. It's just a play you know."

The moment Sanath was waiting for had arrived most naturally, and he intervened with a touch of gravity. "Chasean Aryaputra, you fit so naturally in the team. I see that you have absorbed the lore of the Great Mother. Since last night, it must be clear that the legend belongs to you too. I am not surprised by your skills, given who you were before. The team is complete at last." The group exchanged glances, struggling to make sense of these words.

"Then he would be, then he is…" said Lakshman, jumping to his feet, "Lidholon of Anor, from the Yuva Platoon!" he completed in amazement.

Lakshmi, with a flicker in her eyes added, "Yes. I knew; I knew there was something! It is normal that you react to the name of Aliskhan. You were the closest of friends, both squires of the same House, but you do not remember. You are not even aware that you moved with him in the Bardo, the twilight world, to bring us from Delphi to the underground fortress of Elnelok and the temple of Maat. She couldn't contain herself any longer, "I need to hug you! Michael and Lothar will go crazy when they hear this!"

"Yes. Sean was Lidholon of Anor, son of the Nizam Aslerach," Sanath said simply. An explosion of joy and laughter immediately interrupted him. "Lidholon, dearest among his brothers-in-arms made his landing in the human race, having chosen the country that worships the Buddha. This has much to do with the errand that brings us all here."

Sean endured vibrant moments of hugs, explanations and more questions. He was quite embarrassed but slowly warmed up to this moment of reckoning. It made sense of many of the weird dreams that had visited him since his childhood. Instinctively he felt the sense of belonging to this group, and that his own fate was catching up with him. He mentioned how the Glorfakir had taken his attention back to the vision of the last days of the Rock, he shared a flood of recollections and turned to Sanath, "I must say one of the overwhelming emotions I experienced in my journey to Dagad Trikon was my despair in learning that one of the great Avastha lords could betray us. I still do not understand how this was possible."

The wizard felt this question was important; he was determined to answer it and explain the mechanism of our failings, "It was quite simple. As you know, there is a saying that the greatest cunning of the devil is to make believe he does not exist and the greatest stupidity of man is to believe it. In pride, we lose the awareness of evil so that evil can, unnoticed, influence our desires, thoughts and actions. Then we may see the traces of evil in others but not within us. In this darkness, evil can breed and grow. The Avastha who fell from grace made this human mistake. The Governor thought that he could make a deal with Thanatophor. However, it was not so and we keep repeating the same mistakes. Thanatophor takes full advantage of our naivety. He is usually smarter than those who bargain with him, a point Goethe made in *Faust*. We lost too many deals, and now we do not have much time left. Fortunately, the power of the Great Mother returned in full force and you, the Stealthstars, are reassembling."

Sean happily turned to his companions, "I thank the Great Mother that we are back. The team has indeed been re-formed..."

"...as an ancient thread that was broken but has again been tied. There is still work to do," added Lakshmi with a broad grin. "Whenever the great wizard invites one to a meal, expect surprise guests. Last time in Jetzenstein the demons came for dinner. This time, mercifully, a missing Stealthstar of our own blood reappears as we join him for a delayed brunch."

"Time is what we don't have," responded Sanath, "and I am so glad we found Sean because the Avastha prophecy states that, in the last days before the great transformation, the scattered Stealthstars shall join again. I sense that the pace of our discoveries is now going to accelerate."

The conversation on the river terrace of the Oriental Hotel was bubbling; questions mingled with laughter flew in all directions. In this animated discussion, Sean wanted to draw attention away from himself and asked Mariluh, "Please could you be more specific about the flame of the Buddha as you called it the other day?" Sanath nodded his consent to Mariluh; the question was bringing him closer to his next purpose.

CHAPTER TEN

THE FLAME
OF THE BUDDHA

Where Mariluh explains why the reserve energy, beaming from the head of the Buddha, can be awakened in everyone, and how Sanath reports on his meeting with Confucius and Lao-tzu, and extends an invitation to a momentous encounter at the temple of the Emerald Buddha.

Mariluh had spent some time in Thailand; her investigation had been exhaustive. "Consider this, giant statues of Buddha with the flame jetting out from the top of his head are found all over the entire country. At their base is an engraving of a comma, the symbol of the three and a half coils of the sleeping energy, the sacred serpent.

In the temple school near Mukdahan, Buddha is sitting in the *dhammackra mudra*; that is, a special position to uphold the order of the universe. He is in front of an ornate Wheel of the Law that he sets in motion. The Khao Takiap image, in the southern beach resort of Hua Hin, is higher than a two-story building and faces the sea with both hands raised in the *abhaya mudra*, the gesture to allay fears and calm the Ocean of Illusion. Normally, this should have kept the fury of the sea at bay, but consequences of evil have recently stirred earthquakes and tsunamis, so the protection of this specific station is no longer effective. The gold Buddha of Tha Ton, perched on a hill close to the border with Myanmar in the north, is seated beneath the multi-headed naga, the sacred snake. The snake changes skin; an allegory of death and resurrection. The white Buddha near Phan is a recent construction, and yet it captures the right coefficient to express sovereign detachment in the Buddha's smile. These varying postures conform to conventions from the scriptures whose meaning has been lost. The living mechanism manifesting the Deep Way is unknown to most monks. I activated the energy field of the statues."

"Pardon?"

"I moved from one statue to another to awaken them, to clear the clouds of surrounding ignorance and the heat released by uninformed priests. I awakened in these effigies the subtle energies corresponding to their mudra, their ritual posture, so that people who pray to them with an innocent heart may be blessed. The small statue you bought is particularly powerful in storing the waves of energy."

"How come? These are man-made effigies only; you cannot trans-form them into Sao Iambus, the living stones!" exclaimed Lakshmi almost indignantly. She glanced quickly at the smiling Sanath for his approval.

"I agree but the magic that blows in the wind is rising," continued the priestess undisturbed. "I made a great discovery in Bangkok: I found out that the capacity of the statues has changed; they have begun to release the waves of energy in the temples around the hall where Sean's group practices meditation. This has never happened before."

"Extraordinary indeed," noted Sean, surprised to learn that their spiritual practices had an effect he did not begin to suspect. "I know this country has more to offer than luxury beach resorts to be visited by for-eigners, and, on occasion, tsunamis. However, this is news to me. I wish that more people could feel it."

Lakshman, bemused by the news and still somewhat skeptical, noted, "Materialism has chased away real spirituality. Are you saying that spiritu-ality can now penetrate matter? If so, something important is happening. Would you take it as a sign that the bridges between the Inner and the Outer Worlds are being rebuilt? And if, so that we, after all, will see the end of the split between matter and spirit, this long misery that we, the Avasthas, used to call the Foul Rift?"

Mariluh's eyes sparkled with life and energy, "The transformation has begun but I don't know for certain what the consequences will be. Much understanding of the Deep Way was buried in the myths of Asia. I am in contact with Buddhist monks who are sincere and eager to redis-cover the true teachings."

Sean asked, "Could you please describe how the flame of the Buddha is working in practice?"

Sanath answered, "The power of this flame opens the *vilamba*, the space of silence between two thoughts. This is the entry point into the space of meditation that is so hard to find because it is hidden in our head, wrapped within the Lily of Anorhad. How would you paint energy? How would you render it in a sculpture? On a Byzantine icon or Persian miniature, it is represented by an aura of fire or light. In the statues of this part of the world, it is sculpted as a flame jetting from the head of the Enlightened One."

"Nevertheless, these symbols aren't only found in Asia."

"Of course they're not," replied Lakshman to Sanath's explanation. "Consider the painting by El Greco in the Prado museum in Madrid. He painted the apostles at Pentecost with tongues of flame coming out of their heads. Look at Florentine symbolism: you'll see the flames above the heads of the angels painted by Fra Angelico."

"You're right," Lakshmi exclaimed slightly bemused, "how was it that we never made the link? Where else do they portray energy coming from the top of the head?"

Sanath laughed, more than willing to share his insights with his eager students, "Everywhere. If we start on this topic, we'll sit here for hours. Pallas Athena was born from the head of Jupiter. Why? Take the underwater archeological excavations near Alexandria. It took a fifty-ton crane to raise the pink, granite statue of Hapi Heracleion that was retrieved from the sea near the mouth of the Nile. He was an important god of the fourth century before our era. He was responsible for the annual flooding of the Nile and hence, the fertility of Egypt. He is described as carrying a crown made of three papyruses but, actually, the effigy represents the triple force of the feathers as the serpentine energy jets out."

As an archeologist, Lakshman delighted in the subject and had a special fondness for ancient Egypt. "I believe there are other Egyptian symbols for the energies of the Deep Way. For example: the serpent is an emblem of both Isis and Athena, the great goddesses of Mediterranean antiquity. Look at the Hemhem war crown of Harpokrates, son of Isis, the Horus of Edfu. The ram's horns express the needs for the two lateral energies to open wide the vertical passage to the apex of the brain. They are surmounted by three papyrus sheaves with solar discs, framed by two feathers and two erect Ureus snakes. The Hemhem crown carries a reference to the blue and yellow feathers but who can understand this today? Certainly not our most eminent French archeologists."

Mariluh added, "The reserve energy is usually represented by an undulating snake; in all these effigies, there are hints, left by ancient cultures and indigenous customs, clues for the mastery of the Inner World. Master Sanath asked me to help restore the core knowledge and spiritual value of this vast and diverse heritage. Keeping the codes of the human tribe was indeed the purpose of the great myths and of the religions that followed."

"It's a shame Tracy isn't with us to hear this," Lakshman said. "She is passionate about this research. This is what the Oikos project was meant to retrieve but ultimately failed to achieve."

"Precisely, and so did everybody else who tried," Lakshmi continued, "religious dignitaries mean well perhaps, but they can't access the inner codes. Not only have they lost the content of their heritage but worse, they don't even believe in it any longer. Who today has access to the Buddha's flame?"

Sean intervened, "The Great Mother explains that the flame exists within us, but lies dormant. It waits, for the moment of *sammadhi*, when the consciousness connects with it. By the time he received his enlightenment under the banyan tree, Siddharta Gautama was totally cleansed and completely pure inside. His energy rose up like a rope made of a thousand strands. Our experience of the Deep Way is of the same nature but not at the same level. Our energy rises at first, no more than a few strands. His flame was a burning fire, ours a flickering candle. The strength is less."

"Perhaps I sound ridiculous, but let me ask: does all this really tell us that ordinary humans can now access the state of the Buddha?" No matter how much Lakshmi wanted to hear 'yes', she couldn't quell the incredulous tone in her voice.

Sanath replied, with compassion and understanding. "Siddharta Gautama was a much higher being. The emerald color of his effigy in the main temple of Bangkok tells us that the Prince of Kapilavastu, worshipped in all Asia, was, in fact, the son of the Emerald King you saw in Vaikuntha. He incarnated on earth out of compassion, to show us the way, the middle path of the White Feather."

Sensing their puzzlement, Sanath continued, "Beings from above never force their way on us; it is up to us to pick up the clues. Some say God cannot have a son. How do they know? As Adivatar is almighty, he can do as he pleases. He also lived among us incognito, walked on the earth just like one of us. He can have sons and daughters if he wants to, no matter what bearded or bald theologians may say. Some priests would have us believe that he is far away, existing as a heavenly abstraction, an inaccessible entity and that only they are fortunate enough, only they are authorized to explain his obscure will to the common folk. But it is not so: he gave us the power to be his children, to open the Lily of Anorhad so that the flame could rise to its destination…if we so wish."

Since it was such a long time since any of them had seen Sanath, Lakshman asked, "And you have been sent to help us in deciphering them. May I ask please, where have you been in recent times?"

"I was summoned to China by the Assembly of Daskalians. They are, as you know, the supreme Masters of the Deep Way. I stayed in a city near the southern mountains, living in the cottage of an Italian architect who works in Shanghai and who is also a student of mine. He took me to a magical cave on a sacred hill, with a small replica of the Hall of the Daskalians that you visited in your past adventure; however, there were only two thrones. The hall was visited on that evening by the holographic appearances of the two Daskalians who had been sent to China: Lao-tzu and Confucius."

"Please tell us about it!" They remembered their visit to the Temple of Maat in the valley of Dagad Trikon and were astonished at the recurrence of an event they had considered unique.

"In a nutshell, this is what transpired: the dignitaries of the Dark Council of Thanatophor are not bothered by the defeat of the two demon kings at Jetzenstein because, in accordance with their plans, their seeds have now sprouted worldwide in the brains of human beings. They push for war in the Middle East; they take it for granted that the Western countries will fall into their hands. An onslaught has been launched in other parts of the world that has the potential to drive the trends of history. If they manage to get hold of the caskets releasing the energies of desire and action before we do, all is lost. The Daskalians want us to prevent the War of the Feathers. This is why they gave me indications about the locations of two of the lost caskets containing these Avasthic relics. Their destructive power is such that it could wipe out human civilization. In order to open the caskets and receive their content, I have recalled the Stealthstars. We need to work quickly."

"Now humans have grown up—but still, the story of how they deal with the perilous feathers is not yet clear to me because they are determined to continue their own dangerous experiments," said Lakshman.

"That's right. The Daskalians conversed on such topics as the Agnya chakra, the 'third eye'. We could follow their exchange because they wanted to pass on a message. Lao-tzu observed that imbalances created by the negative forces were already destabilizing the weather, provoking monstrous typhoons, floods in the south, fires and drought elsewhere. Sandstorms bring airborne particles from the Gobi desert up to the shores of Canada. Confucius hoped that human institutions could quickly reform under the pressure of the emergency and evolve in a cohesive body of dedicated, competent and wise administrators."

"So they were optimistic?" Lakshman asked, trying not to sound cynical.

"Lao-tzu, known as the author of the *Tao Te Ching*, was of the opinion that China could not resist the repeated visits of the Dark Rider of greed, which is now trampling its cities, taking a larger size on each occasion. He suggested that the Chinese people must return to their native, subtle ways to perceive the dynamics of contradictions and balance that effect their story. Confucius laughed and reminded Lao-tzu that China had been bruised by Mao Tse-tung's brand of Taoist dialectic teachings. Lao-tzu agreed and said that this is what happens when aspiring heroes lose contact with the Deep Way, which he called Tao. When the heroes leave the middle path, the blessings of the path leave the heroes."

"Why was the focus solely on China?"

"Remember, these two Daskalians fashioned the China of today, and the Dark Riders are now turning their attention to this large and ancient nation. They are only seven of them as you know, but working together, they remain the most effective fighting machine of the Evil One. The rapid acceleration of wealth and concentration of power in few hands create favorable conditions that are propitious for the Riders to enter the human mind, in China today as well as everywhere else."

"Did they see grounds for hope?"

"They seemed both concerned and confident at the same time: They say the power of transformation, the power of the flame of the Buddha is being rediscovered now that the Goddess is walking upon the Earth. This is why, by the way, I had asked Mariluh to come to this Buddhist country."

"So is it about Buddhism?" Lakshmi looked so surprised that Sanath couldn't help smiling indulgently.

"No more so than about any other religion. They also spoke of Yeshu, the Son of the divine breath and of the faith brought to Asia by the Apostle Thomas. Christianity was taught in the monastery of Da Quin as being the religion of light. They recalled its seven-storied pagoda where the Christian monk Alouben wrote in the year 635 A.D., under the Tang dynasty, about the northern wind of holy energy. There are many paths but one destination; many languages but one story."

"What else did you hear from the teachers?"

"They also spoke about Chinese food. They said it was not as varied but much better tasting in the age of Confucius. He observed that the art of cooking with love definitely brings peace through the stomach. It was all most interesting. But then they debated a matter that is not easy to convey. In fact, I have witnessed many wonders in my long life but what they said astounded me greatly. I do not know how to explain but after we pay a visit to the temple of the Emerald Buddha, I will try. Let us meet tomorrow morning," he said. "And please bring with you the statue that Mariluh sold you."

The evening ended, and the cousins hurried back to the flat where Ananya was waiting for her mummy. Sean, somewhat dizzy with the pace of revelations, was glad to go home. Nevertheless, he shared with his mother and sister everything he had learned, as they were also students of the Great Mother. Their spiritual inclination made them receptive; they trusted Sean's judgment and the good faith of their visitors.

The following morning Sanath and his party boarded a boat on the busy river to reach the famous royal compound and temple complex. Lakshmi carried the statue bought from Mariluh, wrapped in a silk cloth in her backpack. On their way, they admired the Temple of Dawn with its massive and ornate central Stupa.

Lakshman asked, "The sailors on this boat are wearing yellow T-shirts as do the staff of the supermarket and also so many people everywhere. Why?"

"The King is ill and every Monday, the people wear the colors of the yellow royal banner to express their dedication and best wishes for his good health," answered Sean. "He is the oldest serving head of state and a remarkable personality."

Sanath nodded, "This is truly the case. The love of an entire nation for its king is rarely seen these days, and it reminds me of things long past. The allegiance of the common folk to a righteous ruler has not been seen much since the era of Lord Rama, who ruled in India after the departure of the Avasthas. You see, Southeast Asia is *Ramayana* country." He added with reference to India's most ancient and popular, classical story. "The Kings of Thailand from the Chakri dynasty took the name of Rama, which is now found on so many streets. The King's colors refer to the Yellow Feather.

"The sun rises in the east and sets in the west; the location of the caskets reflects this. The feather carrying the glow of the sun was initially brought by a Lord Rider of Falkiliad to the island of Japan, the country of the rising sun. However, its effect there, vibrating in the soil for a long time, was too powerful. It was then entrusted to an order of Zen monks who brought the Casket of the Yellow Feather to Thailand. The worship of the White Monkey and of the Buddha developed here because of the direct link between them and this feather."

"I didn't realize there was such a linkage until I saw ballets here based on the theme of the exploits of Hanuman, our dear White Monkey, a key hero of the *Ramayana*."

"That's right, Lakshman. The *Ramayana* contained many secrets of use to the human race. It was a huge, epic tale meant to maintain the contact between the region of the world it covered and the tenets of the Deep Way."

"Does this mean Thai people do quite well?" Lakshmi wondered.

"Not really," replied Sean with a sigh. "They have the signs but the signal is too faint yet to pick up the path. Their minds want places to go. Lust and greed, the cavalry of Thanatophor, are mercilessly trampling many Asian families. You see; King Rama stood for the successful human model, being notably a loyal and loving husband. Too many Thai men adopt frivolous lifestyles. The more you grab the less you get. Womanizing destroys the confidence of their women and the happiness of families. If relationships cannot be fully enjoyed in trust, lost is the world of precious feelings and refined expressions is gone. In this age where darkness still rules, every nation goes against the code that was provided for its emancipation. Thailand is no exception."

Mariluh who had been sitting silently, her enigmatic face resembling an oriental mask, added, "Buddha here is more of a symbol than a reality. He was and manifests complete detachment; he taught freedom from hankerings and wants. Here, the newly rich run crazy after possessions. When the attention is on the latest gadget and the next courtesan, it is unlikely to settle on the keys to the Inner Gates. The flight forward in the Outer World throws them out of the inner reality, it diverts them, makes them players in the world of their own virtual game."

The lapping of the river, the squawking of birds, the display of vivid wing colors, the scent of the water—like so many tourists before them, they thoroughly enjoyed the welcoming ambiance, the cool freshness that the river offers to the over-heated metropolis. Young boys, having fun, jumped and splashed in the water.

The boat arrived at the Tha Tien Pier. Mariluh wanted them first to visit Wat Pho, the oldest temple in Bangkok featuring the largest reclining Buddha in the country. Seen by all and known by none, the flame of destiny was clearly jetting out from the top of the limbic area of the Buddha's head. Sanath and Mariluh showed their companions the many secret symbols engraved on the soles of the feet of the giant statue and concluded,

"Buddha is represented here in the state of *nidra* yoga; that is, he is said to meditate even while sleeping. This means that, during the sleeping state, we can recharge our spiritual batteries."

"Should I say, referring to Jung, 'through direct contact with the universal unconscious?' The ultimate wellness program," commented Lakshman with envy. "Ideal isn't it?"

"Yes, however, being completely effortless it is not easy," Sanath words carried a sober warning. "When the magi of the last age achieved it in the waking state, they became *nishkriya*: they did nothing, yet everything worked for them. Whatever happened to them was for the best."

Always curious, Lakshman noted that the location of the subtle centers of energy indicated on the sole of the Buddha's feet corresponded to the parts of his own feet where the relaxing massage given this morning by the girl in the supermarket had released physical well being. "Again," he muttered, as though to himself, "they know something without knowing about it."

They took a cab to the entrance of the Grand Palace, established in 1782 A.D., housing the royal residence and the Temple of the Emerald Buddha. Banners, flags, a procession of limousines and a large military presence heralded the festivities conducted in the palace for the Queen's birthday. Surrounded by four walls, the compound covered an area of over two hundred thousand square meters and encompassed many buildings that represented two hundred years of elegant architectural experimentation. The white sky of Bangkok had cleared and now a backdrop of light blue enshrined the splendor of the gold-covered Stupas, the glittering statues and the multi-tiered roofs of the pagodas and temples covered with tiles of exuberant colors. The impression created by the ensemble was both magnificent and cheerful.

The surrounding courtyard of the Wat Phra Kao, the temple of the Emerald Buddha, was enclosed in a rectangular gallery, which housed the epic tale of the *Ramayana* unfolded in a long fresco. "The story of the father around the house of his son, how befitting!" commended Sanath. They passed three groups of young monks in saffron robes. Lakshmi normally liked the traditions of this fascinating country, but she suddenly noticed a strange sensation of heaviness in the back of her head accompanied by a wave of heat, which seemed to be coming from the monks who were chanting repeatedly: *Buddham sharanam gachami, dhamam sharanam gachami, sangham sharanam gachami.*

She looked interrogatively at Sanath but the wizard, obviously undisturbed, only grumbled, "Monks, mullahs, muftis, priests—they all have the words but not the meaning, the concept but not the truth. Only the truth is helpful for survival, as Merlin used to say."

Sean nodded, "It is the same everywhere: I heard the Great Mother saying that teaching religion is against religion. You can only imbibe it on your own and…"

"By the way, here She is…"

Sanath interrupted Sean, pointing at a statue of Kuan Yin, the Chinese mother of mercy, with an opened lotus on her head. She was sitting before the temple, her back against a high pillar of stone bearing a lotus with many petals. "Here is the Mother, facing the house of the Son," he completed, gesturing towards the Emerald Temple.

"Yes! It is strange," Lakshman recalled, "She looks like the Goddess I saw in my vision in Amsterdam, on the dark-blue ocean, releasing a harmony and balance that was lingering on the waves. I was able to absorb the wellness pouring out of her through my body."

They walked briskly towards the temple entrance that was usually filled with a throng of waiting pilgrims. On this day, the surroundings were empty because the temple was closed for restoration. However, a guard at the entrance seemed to be waiting for Sanath and allowed him to come in with his companions. This wizard had many tricks; he had prepared this moment in advance.

Sitting in solitary grandeur on a high golden throne topping an elaborately chiseled altar, the Emerald Buddha was waiting for them. Following Sanath, they bowed then sat on the marble floor. Sean opened his hands towards the altar, and the cousins instinctively did the same.

Gradually, the sense of expectation eased and they relaxed. The wizard seemed to have withdrawn inside himself and had closed his eyes.

After some time, the wizard, guided by the instruction received from the Daskalians in China, arose and scrutinized the large pedestal in the middle of the temple. He activated a secret mechanism at the base of the statue of the cobra king flanking the throne, and a piece of wood slid laterally outwards. Sanath withdrew a small, richly ornate gold casket at the bottom of the altar. As he placed it in their midst, his hands trembled slightly.

"This casket is dangerous. Its content is lethally toxic to most people. The casket was originally under the custody of the Lord of Falkiliad. It is the one Hangker sought for thousands of years, the one the Sernatil tried to bind with his own spell. It can be opened only when a powerful enough counter power manifests on the Earth. This is now the case."

Lakshman felt reticent for he hadn't expected to pursue his discovery of the caskets in this manner. Events were moving way too fast. He felt they were too few in number to take on the qualities of the casket. Where were the others, Tracy and her brothers, Lothar and Lorelei von Jetzlar? When the Dagad Trikon fellowship was fully gathered, as at Jetzenstein Castle, he felt more confident and reassured.

"Please remember Lakshman; you are Etakir, who consigned and retrieved the Avasthic weapons. You can also retrieve this casket consigned to fate by the ancestors. Now I beg you, open this box. Press the spot at the center of the Star of David on the lid, and do it carefully."

Lakshman advanced and his unease dispelled. He knew that the wizard would not open the caskets himself but that his formidable magic was protecting him.

The casket was of pure gold. Its ornamentation was different from the Thai style of decoration of their surroundings. It reminded him more of the geometric signs and symbols of the two caskets he had already discovered: the Casket of the White Feather he had found in Iceland and the Casket of the Wheel retrieved from the Vatican's art collection. The center of the lid was adorned with the design of a star with six branches.

With slow and careful movements, he followed the instructions and opened the gold engraved lid of the gold rectangular box.

"What do you see?" asked Sanath.

With a sense of trepidation, Lakshman responded, "I see a yellow feather."

CHAPTER ELEVEN

THE WAKING OF THE CHAINED DEMON

Where the opening of the casket awakens the demon Hangker in hell, and how he contacts his agent in Bangkok to prevent the Stealthstars from being empowered by the magic of the Yellow Feather.

By opening the lid of the casket of the Yellow Feather, Lakshman triggered a reaction a few kilometers under the earth's crust where hell's vast, torrid prison network is heated by the nearby magma. It is a place of dread, veiled from sight by the sulfurous vapors that constantly float in a huge cavity. A sinister structure rises in its center, a massive iron fort built on a granite buff.

The right and left hands of Thanatophor, Hangker and Belzebseth, are each chained in two separate towers. The two demons had been thrown into hell after their fight with the archangels over the Rhine valley in Germany. In front of Jetzenstein Castle, high on a cliff, Gabriel had defeated Hangker while Michael had subdued Belzebseth. Hangker's prison is placed ominously on a rim above a boiling sulfur lake. In his cell, deep beneath the brown steel of donjon, Hangker, the sulking overlord of buried arsenals, awoke with a sudden jolt.

"Ha! What is this?" he asked, raising his right hand upwards. The chief lieutenant of Thanatophor arose abruptly from his couch. He sensed both a decisive opportunity and a fatal danger. His light-blue eyes darted towards the Earth's surface, searching for the source of the disturbance with his fearful, supraconscious sight, and he felt within his bones that his chance to escape from his prison had come at last.

Thanatophor's armies and minions were, of course, the secret rulers of the Dark Age, but what he and his demons wanted was open and unchallenged dominion over all humans. Who can fathom the amplitude of the power of the solar casket to which the Second House of the Avasthas had pledged allegiance? It spreads in all directions, including towards Hangker, a destination that was not anticipated.

Amplifying his powers of clear sight, the devil gradually saw, through a light mist, the colorful roofs of pagodas and temples. "I know this place," he thought. Straining his sight further, his gaze entered the temple of the Emerald Buddha and seized on a group of human silhouettes, the root of the commotion. This hazy vision caused him great excitement and some alarm.

The Demon King, who rules over the egos of men, could see, placed on the floor of the temple the one casket that was now his to win. Hangker embodied the will of Thanatophor to enslave the force of the Yellow Feather for this was the very same magic box that he had been looking for since he invaded the Rock fortress with the complicity of Serapis Sernatil, Governor of Shalamphur, many millennia ago.

He had managed to subdue the Governor by sending him the seventh and greatest of the Dark Riders, the Rider of Pride. The Sernatil, not realizing he had been thus foiled, had even introduced a small element of Hangker's substance into the casket before it had been sealed and sent away by the Nizam; and this therefore, was the one Avasthic artifact that Hangker was connected to. He knew that some of its secrets, consigned long ago to this magnificent Avasthic casket by his ally, were pushing human consciousness towards the trap prepared through their ego. This could still work to his advantage. He was right but not certain.

The moment of the opening of the casket could easily ruin the plans for his deliverance…or hasten the moment of his triumph. For such was the ambivalent power contained in that magic box. Opening it could either release heaven or hell. He knew that.

Hangker was never far from the treasure he coveted but the casket had constantly eluded him. Through the ages, the Order of the Hllidarendi had foiled his attempts to gain the casket, always keeping it in hiding. But his ancient enemy, the Sand Keeper of Dagad Trikon, was at this moment sitting on the floor surrounded by Avasthas warriors facing the open chest. This was the moment for him to strike.

After the epic battle at Jetzenstein Castle in which Hangker was thrown into the nether worlds, the fearsome guardians of hell, the servants of the god of death, were keeping Hangker secluded in the complete isolation of its prison. But they could not penetrate the scheme through which the demon king had foreseen the potential for his eventual escape. As with all great plans, it was quite simple.

He was the inspiration of those who constantly say "I, me, mine." Most of mankind was already in his clutches. Long before his defeat over the Rhine at the hands of the Archangel Gabriel, Hangker had spread the microscopic seeds of his own essence and through the errands of the Dark Riders he had injected the will to dominate into the egos of people. These seeds of aggressiveness germinated and multiplied and were waiting until a critical mass would be reached. Indeed, he had already succeeded in reaching substantial numbers of the human race.

The demon had taken full advantage of the fact that unpredictability is a necessary part of the unfolding of the Grand Scheme. Mankind's freedom, kept intact through the twists and turns along of the way, had given him opportunities he eagerly seized. Human beings, while advancing on their evolutionary pilgrimage, had made choices and thus mistakes. Mistakes have consequences; they are not without effect. This is the Law of Maat that the lieutenant of Thanatophor wanted to turn to his own advantage. Having largely penetrated the ego of man, Hangker's influence had pushed humans into making such blunders that calamities were bound to follow. He wished to achieve what the gods on Mount Kailash would have wished to avoid: the degradation and consequent destruction of the human race.

In this age of iron, whether or not the devils would stay in hell any longer depended not on the angels or the gods but on human beings. Humans were either the jailors or the liberators of evil, and this is why Hangker was so hopeful. The opening of the magic casket was the tipping point. The strength of his essence had now reached the given threshold of influence over human consciousness, when the devil was about to be sucked back to the surface of the globe, leaving but the emptied envelope of a mere ghost still floating in hell's chains.

He had dearly aspired to return to the Earth's surface and to feed again on the dominion he exerted on men through those who want to dominate others.

The demon had been patiently waiting for this hour. He knew it was approaching, and the certainty of his potential coming triumph had kept alive his steel will that was hidden from his captors by his usual somber mood. Soon he would bring more disasters, pestilence, broken societies and wars to this arrogant race that considered itself the owner of the planet.

Hangker's powers of sight allowed him to see beyond the clouds of sulfur and the Earth's crust, to the scene within the emerald temple. He saw two warriors Etakir and Lidholon, looking somewhat puny in human form, bending over the casket. He also saw the Lady Erilie, Captain of the Sheravalian Guard of the Lady of the Rock, who, before his assault on the Avasthic fortress, had escaped on a winged horse with the Casket of the White Feather. The Avasthas now looked simply human, quite diminished indeed, and he felt nothing but contempt for them. He then saw something else, something much worse from his perspective: sitting motionless behind Etakir, the leader of the Yuva Platoon, he saw a gracious silhouette that was not human: the shape of a small white monkey emitting light.

The sight of the Lord Hanuman, the one who, in his angelic form, had thrown him into hell, caused him deep anguish and wrath. The huge gate of the grim tower shivered under the waves of hate that rolled from Hangker's roaring. Together with the power of the Yellow Feather, he could have reduced the willpower of these few Stealthstars, even in the presence of the wizard. However, the watching presence of Hanuman was quite another matter. A prisoner of hell he still was, not equipped to face such a formidable foe and, although he was close to succeed, much now was outside his clutches. What could he do?

He telepathically alerted the abbot necromancer in the temple complex who had been of great help to Belzebseth and himself since the birth of the Dark Age.

It is not rare that crooks and villains find it expedient to appear as saintly and the Abbot Tuchpamonporn was no exception. He had reached the higher echelons of the Buddhist hierarchy at a young age, being famous for extra sensory powers not mastered by other religious dignitaries. He had since developed a group of worldwide followers, well beyond the confines of his own monastic order, able in these times to make full use of the possibilities of web-based networking. Invoking well-sounding causes, he was a successful fundraiser and his influence was felt an the upper levels of human social institutions and hierarchies. Who could recognize in this sleek operator one of the highest mages, president of the Dark Council, mentor of the witches, a man clothed in a sheath of sorcery, one who could instill fear at will?

Tuchpamonporn eagerly received Hangker's message and concentrated to decipher it with more clarity. Reception was blurred given location and distance; he heard whispers in his ears, the name of the Sand Keeper. The abbot reacted to this angrily. Indeed, he too was hell-bent on again finding a trace of Sanath for there was a personal war between them that had stretched over many centuries, and nothing mattered more to him than the destruction of the Sand Keeper.

They had fought many inconclusive battles and the inability of Sanath to defeat him said a lot about the might of Tuchpamonporn. It had grown through many lives in which he had helped strengthen the grip of his two masters over the Dark Age. He still had the ambition to extract from Sanath the solution to riddles that his own sorcery skills could not provide. This important agent of the demon kings arose, sensing the call from hell, shaking with excitement, sniffing the smell of his prey with the help of extra sensory enchantments. Slowly, his body turned in the general direction of the nearby temples and with a guttural sound, he called his henchmen who were posted as sentinels in the courtyard of his lavish personal residence.

Not everything was lost for the two demon overlords. Their escape route from hell had taken much skill and planning. Their Riders were galloping throughout the globe, gaining strength every day. Anger, Greed, and Vanity responded to Hangker while Lust, Attachment and Jealousy worked for Belzebseth. However, they always joined their forces in a variety of combinations and permutations, preferring to attack together for optimal results. As Hangker had infiltrated the dominion of the Yellow Feather, Belzebseth had done so in the realm of the Blue.

Thanatophor's lieutenants had relied on their demented cavalry to haunt the minds of men. The Dark Riders had been elusive, no angels could stop them, let alone destroy them, and they had registered great success, six of them, the enemies of the soul, galloping with the seventh, the Rider of Pride, the enemy of the Self. He was the mightiest because he knew how to imprison human consciousness in the delusion of selfishness. All were doomed to fight goodness, all were eager to do so, riding to pluck the spoils of the onslaught. Hangker still had faith in this flying cavalry and those who obeyed them. The abbot, so convincingly camouflaged, was foremost among them.

Centuries of experiments had given the demon lord the proof that with the help of the Riders, men can easily be distracted, weakened and turned to his purposes. Avasthas who became humans should be no exception.

CHAPTER TWELVE

THE PITFALLS OF THE YELLOW FEATHER

Where the force that drives the rise and fall of empires is revealed within the cosmos and the human body too, where it stirs the might of the demon Hangker and how the power embodied in the little statue of the Buddha helps subdue its effects.

The Stealthstars heard Sanath's voice speaking softly, "This is the Yellow Feather. It contains the power that makes the Earth spin. Now please close your eyes so that you may enter the vision." The brightness did not subside. As they basked in the glow of the Yellow Feather lying in their midst, they found themselves in a golden radiance, not knowing whether they were sitting in the hall or in the casket.

How does one spend time outside of time? In Bangkok's sacred temple, Sanath and his companions were settled in a golden serenity that flowed from the casket. It seemed they'd spent some time in this quiet state before the feather revealed itself. The first recognition surged as waves, a power in motion, an immense energy.

They saw fields covered with yellow mustard flowers and felt the blossoming of spring in their limbs. They were connected with nature, a roaring force flowing, the entire creation vibrating with music of buoyant energy, an energy that was theirs too. This power was binding electrons and neutrons, the five elements within matter and creation at all levels. Nothing was static.

They felt pulsating dynamics within themselves, a cosmic will at work arranging both order and chaos. They sensed and were connected to the energy that was behind the creation of the universe, the movement of the stars, galaxies and even the tiniest atoms. It was ebullient and awesome, too vast to comprehend because everything that was created and activated had been set in motion with only a fraction of this force. Scientists, artists, scholars, and entrepreneurs, doers in diverse ways and forms were all using this force, although mostly unaware of it, and oblivious to the fact that the results of their work were under its power. The feather carried the conviction that every future can be conquered; every goal can be reached. It projected the magic of creation and generated aesthetics, knowledge and arts under all its forms. The sensation was exhilarating, the attraction to move along with it, commanding. It was the force to think, to act, to create and to achieve sustained by the melodious notes of a cithara, or so it seemed.

However, as Hangker's attention darted towards the temple, cracks appeared in the consistency of the vision. A tension field affected the golden splendor that sustained this well-being. The sumptuous tissue of elation began to palpitate and crumble. Another aspect of this reality appeared as this world was now seen from a very different angle, through the prism of greed taking diverse shapes and forms that illustrate objects of human desires: possessions, land, armies, cities, kingdoms, beautiful men and women. The impulse to grab, to possess and to control was surging. The mood became agitated and more chaotic. A centrifugal force sucked human volition and desires in many directions: lust, greed, and aggression. Then slowly, a compulsion emerged above all desires: to own the Yellow Feather and its inextinguishable power.

Was this at all possible?

Gradually, the trap laid in the Casket of the Yellow Feather by the Sernatil on behalf of Hangker revealed itself to the companions: dynamics turned into disorder, breeding competition, everyone twisted by envy, pursuing a compulsion to overcome, to command beyond any limit. Ambitious and egocentric people bent under its sway, incapable of mastering the course of their own motion while taking charge of society. People endowed with high education, wealth and the ability to dominate were the ones most attracted by its appeal. The Stealthstars tried to resist the formidable pull. Being in the temple of the Buddha, they instinctively prayed to him. The Enlightened One had taught desirelessness and detachment. Was this not the way that women and men could resist the temptations offered by the Yellow Feather?

Through all his many lives since he had been Etakir in the remote days of Dagad Trikon, Lakshman had battled with this power. His past achievements in the Deep Way were unmatched by the other Stealthstars and this was why he was the one to receive the full blast of the casket's revelations. The companions received the contents of this casket but with different shades of insights. However, the opening of this particular vessel of Avastha magic was especially significant for Lakshman. It dawned on him that the total wealth of this field was available, but on one condition: he could have the power provided he did not want it! This hidden stipulation inserted in the Casket by the Lady of the Rock itself granted access to the mastery of the Yellow Feather. What a paradox and what an ultimate locking system. Could he claim to have achieved this? In this uncompromising light, he could not hide himself, nor hide the bite of his own desires. He started feeling destabilized, tense and uneasy.

Although a part of Hangker's own substance had been consigned in the treasure chest, the content of the casket had been prepared under the supervision of the head of the House of Falkiliad together with an Aulya who could handle the *Bibliotheca Diabolica* and had penetrated the most secretive methods of the demons. It is easy to underestimate the trickiness of the devil; it is far easier to underestimate the efficiency of goodness. He felt a heavy pressure in the center of his forehead that distributed pain on the lower side of his brain, towards the left side of his skull. His eyes began aching.

These sensations emitted by the Avasthic security system were perceived in his own body, activating a protective reaction. He became conscious of an approaching danger. The warning revealed the rise of a malefic presence that was feeding on the turmoil of the will to power, a presence of dread he had faced in the hall of the knights in the castle of Count von Jetzlar.

A historic fresco was unfolding at a speed that was overwhelming. Lakshman's body was very hot: his shirt was wet with perspiration. He had realized that an avalanche of formidable forces was contained within the feather, a force that had swept through human history making, shaking and dissolving empires and nations.

An old English nursery rhyme resounded in his ears, "Humpty Dumpy sat on a wall, Humpty Dumpy had a great fall…" His vision carried him to Europe in the last years of the nineteenth century. Imperial Europe was at the peak of its power, having colonized the rest of the world and then launched itself into a formidable phase of industrial development. A continent under the sway of the fateful feather and propelled by its impetus, equipped with steel and fire, was now on the brink of entering a devastating war.

He saw Emperor Wilhelm II of Germany, pompous with his waxed moustache, dragging behind him the old Ludwig III, King of Bavaria. The many feathers crowning their absurdly theatrical helmets, in this vision, were all yellow. They were followed by a retinue of generals and princes in dazzling military uniforms, reviewing their troops, who were on their way to the front in World War I shouting "*nach Paris, nach Paris.*" The Emperor and the King were taking the salute. The flag-waving crowd exuded confidence, enthusiasm, excitement and dynamism.

But the vision moved on and delivered a harrowing truth. Lakshman witnessed the return of the defeated German soldiers a couple of years later, maimed, hurt and hungry; he felt the gloom and anger of broken lives and dreams, the turmoil of the communist uprising in Munich and the desperate King of Bavaria fleeing the revolution.

The King and his ailing Queen are alone in a coach, about to take refuge in an estate in Hungary. The color of the feathers on his helmet has faded and turned as grey as his beard. The rule of the royal House of Wittelsbach is over. A small group of plotters from the retinue of Hangker, wearing brown shirts with red swastika armbands in a beer shop in Munich prepares for what will become World War II.

Lakshman experienced torture as he felt the properties of the unfolding scenes in his bones.

The Blitzkrieg announces the curse of a new world war. The Prussian military class driving the Wehrmacht raises the banner of the Third Reich on the Acropolis of Athens. Mussolini, chin thrust forward, stands on the balcony above the Piazza di Venezia in Rome, clowning his way to Roman imperial grandeur. In Asia, the Japanese enter Nanking and Singapore.

Lakshman agonized at the Holocaust brought about by the Nazis' cold and demented rationalization, the harrowing scenes of the Soviet invasion of Prussia and of the fall of Berlin.

He saw that the intoxication of power is such that without an antidote, mankind never learns. Pushed into excess, the feather was increasingly under the control of Hangker. Swayed by the negative aspects of the Yellow Feather, the Europeans had destroyed many civilizations, and they were now destroying themselves.

The scenes of Lakshman's successive animated visions continued through the twentieth century. History repeats itself on a grand scale, like a dumb narrator who knows only one plot. The feather or, rather, its curse of domination escapes Western Europe and zigzags from one country to another, its tip writing the annals of mass slaughter. In the Soviet Union, Stalin fills the gulags, followed by the great yellow leap forwards of Chairman Mao. Placing his concepts above facts, he causes the death of some thirty million Chinese.

The forces unleashed by this feather cannot be tamed. Nostalgic for the bygone days of Islamic conquests, Arab fanatics try to reestablish the Caliphate of the faithful. Iranian mullahs want the nuclear bomb, Turkish reactionaries dream of Ottoman grandeur while ultra-Orthodox Jews refuse to give peace a chance. Attracting speculators to the stock markets, bringing gains and losses, its movements are causing the overstretching of American power and sowing the seeds of its abrupt decline. Deploying a kleptomaniacal financial system, the capitalist dragon devours its own tail as Marx had foreseen.

Lakshman, sitting in the temple of the Emerald Buddha, realized that the United Nations were in complete disarray. As was the case before WWI, rumors of conflicts and wars spread far and wide; and every potential belligerent is convinced that God and right must be on his side. Everything that could be done for love is converted into hatred.

The frieze vanished and Lakshman returned to the present, compelled to register the effect the power of the feather had on him—and it was extraordinarily powerful. A force coming from nowhere now inhabited Lakshman. He was the center of the galaxy, and everything was moving around him. He was pervaded by the sense that his will could bend and crush anything; he felt strength and light beaming from his body. The awareness of his super strength was a physical sensation. He was elated by the premonition that the world was his to seize and command. This preeminence was due to him, and he truly desired it.

Lakshman wanted the power to move and shake; he wanted that power. Who could stop him? Not this old wizard sitting behind him, too afraid to approach the casket. Sanath needed a rest; the time had come for him to step down, for Lakshman to replace him. New blood and new strength were now needed to lead the fight against evil. Yes, it was his destiny to achieve great things, his destiny to lead and the destiny of others to follow.

Such was the detonating alchemy contained in the solar casket that, while this drama was unfolding in Bangkok, the grip of hell's chains on Hangker loosened. He started to float in his cell, levitating at first just a few centimeters above the ground. As the awaited pull lifted him slowly upwards; a cold jubilation surged in the demon king. His plan was functioning. In a few moments, he would be free.

But something happened back in the temple, something that could possibly close his channel of access to human minds. And a voice whispered in Lakshman's right ear, "The frontier is within you."

Being a Stealthstar, the built-in reaction of Lakshman's organism absorbed the warning of the White Monkey. The Yellow Feather could nurture Botticelli, Handel and Einstein, art, beauty and science. It could also produce Attila the Hun, Pol Pot and all dictators, leading to oppression and cruelty. It had caused the building and burning of cities, the rise and fall of civilizations. Such a vast potential, such open-ended possibilities and within it, just a tiny, narrow thread to keep to the right path.

It was highly unsettling for Lakshman to realize that the main battlefield was within.

It seemed that Hangker was approaching within the tumult of this uncontrolled might and Lakshman understood why hell could never quite contain the demon. Hangker would be called to ride the movements of the feather as soon as the human attention crossed a certain limit. Panic seized and convulsed Lakshman. Pain scorched his liver.

He regretted that he had opened the casket and released its devastating magic. Hands sweating, feeling pressure in his head and nausea in his stomach, he was relieved to hear the loud voice of Sanath, "Etakir, close the lid of the box, close it at once!" Etakir obeyed immediately and the pull emanating from the casket subsided. Sweating profusely, Lakshman opened his eyes, turned towards Sanath, happy to acknowledge how much he still needed his protection.

All attendants to the opening of the Casket of the Yellow Feather had broadly similar experiences, in that they first enjoyed its glorious splendor, and then discovered the other side of its deadly pull. Simultaneously, they breathed heavily and paused, experiencing the aftermath of the casket as a commotion in the brain. The wizard was looking at Lakshman with concern, "In this particular emergency, you have registered a signal from the Lord Hanuman as an intuition. He was sitting silently to your right. I saw him. He is now busy on another front, trying to blur the messages that Hangker is sending to his servant in the monastery of the temple complex to delay his intervention."

Lakshman feeling dizzy closed his eyes again. His companions were slowly recovering from their trip to the frontiers of the province of the psyche that feed the ballooning of the human ego. His mind was still racing with a mad momentum, separated from his will. It was speeding randomly, propelled by the surplus of energy, processing at full speed a caravan of images and thoughts, 'The Thais assume the flame of the Buddha is just decoration…it's a pity Jonathan is not here with Lakshmi…I need to pick up my laundry…the price of gold is high…we shall reconsider the launching of the next jewel collection at the Basel Fair taking into account Chopard's latest design…I liked this necklace of black diamonds and pink heart-shaped sapphires that was launched at the flagship shop at 709 Madison Avenue…the other one that featured twenty emeralds the size of almonds was just too flashy…the lady at the pier was selling emaciated chickens…I wonder how Sean experienced the casket, Oh what a headache!'

Turning into an overheated engine that dries out all moisture, his brain went into overload and there was a pressure on the right side of his head, which tore into his left eye. Again, he felt nauseous, as if seasick. He heard his own voice reverberating in his head, "I see my world, and the white man's world, dried out by its allegiance to the Yellow Feather. Modern men and women look alike, cold and mechanical; they work in their buildings of steel and glass, bound to the terminals of their machines. They do not even know what they have lost. They heat up eventually through surges of lust; it is all heat, no warmth. Subtle and beautiful emotions of love are missing. Nevertheless, they still think somehow that theirs is the best model." Opening his eyes helped to chase away the voice.

Lakshmi distracted her cousin from his dizziness by asking the wizard without her usual courtesy, "Please tell us, what is going on with this Yellow Feather?" She too had experienced a very bumpy ride.

Sanath arose to stretch his legs and responded while pacing back and forth, "We experienced the untamed solar power of action."

"Did it belong to the Avasthas? Did they know how to control it?"

"To an extent, yes, they did. There is a mechanism for this. The Avasthic and human inner structures are the same. In both species, the inside has been conceived like a building with a number of stories and main channels to irrigate it. Each of these levels can bring to man a piece of satisfaction; each one has in store for man a specific kind of gratification, or we may say, it emits a certain flavor of joy."

Sean asked, "The same story as in the Avasthic library?"

"That's right," responded Sanath who knew the others could not quite understand this question. "The story connected to the Yellow Feather corresponds to the Second House."

"Did the human seers know about this?"

"The Emerald King visited our planet in the form of the sower; he was called Krishna and spoke about this raw energy and the mechanism to control it; you can read about it in the holy book of his teachings, the

Bhagavad Gita. The yellow force you felt was called *rajo guna* in the ancient scriptures of India. This is what you experienced when we opened this casket.

"I felt complete dynamism," said Lakshmi, "an intense happiness. It was strange, powerful. But then the field of its vibrant harmony splintered like broken glass."

"I loved it; I was swept off my feet; it was like riding a wild sea wave," added Sean, who had a better trip than Lakshman.

Sanath nodded, "You were more firmly stabilized thanks to the use of the Sadhan shield, because the Great Mother has taught you how to remain within the shield of your meditation." He developed the analogy. "Wide variations occur in the manner in which men seek satisfaction on each floor of their inner structure. The second floor is under the watch of the House of Falkiliad, custodian of this casket of the star with six branches. The corresponding subtle center within contains and distillates the essence of the joy of action or the thrill of creativity in the brain. It fuels the sport of doing, projects inspiration for music and poetry, animates thinking and activates the potency of will and discipline. In the modern world, many people experience this intoxication at a much lower level, becoming workaholics, bosses and business tycoons."

"Sounds okay to me, but why my headache?" Lakshman asked restlessly.

"We can only absorb this force at homeopathic doses whereas what we received just now was the force at full blast. Left to itself, the power can be hijacked by Hangker; normal people who taste it always want more," the wizard explained, noting the companions' reaction of incredulity at the strength of the energy they had sensed coursing in their veins. "The center of the six-branched star can be inebriating: it also releases into the yellow channel the opium of the doers; that is, the yearning for control and domination. This is what overcame the best of the governor of Shambalpur. This is a story that constantly repeats itself."

"Like what?"

"World history, what else? Various nations in history have progressed under the auspices of the Yellow Feather each one in a specific way. For instance, the Jews took the star of Falkiliad as their national symbol and borrowed many talents from this feather; the French drew from the star their fondness for analytical rationality, the Spanish their lofty pride, the Germans their cult of efficiency, the Japanese their need for social structure and the Russians their vitality. In the United States, it represents the invention of a country. But in any case, at some point, if you cross a line, it exaggerates."

"If it is an Avasthic casket, there is goodness in it. We just need to learn how to maneuver it, but how can we get it right?"

"Very difficult. The stoical philosophers of Rome like Seneca and the Emperor Marcus Aurelius advised us to achieve complete detachment and self-control but who can achieve this today? The Buddha gave us the best clues: we must balance the properties of this feather with those of the other two. If this feather spins into a one-dimensional loop, it is finally cut from the subtler source of energy and inspiration. We end up stressed and sick; eventually, we die of a heart attack or liver cancer. Unfortunately, we lost the true Buddhist toolkit."

At this point, the invisible White Monkey who was listening to the explanations of the good wizard shook his head and whispered in the wizard's ear, "Once a teacher, always a teacher; but you don't have much time left. Dear friend, don't forget how corrosive the content of this casket is. Humans cannot handle the force of the Yellow Feather. Please move on."

Indeed, inspired by the opening of the casket, Hangker half emerged from hell and beamed his message more forcefully. His correspondent, the chief abbot of the nearby temple was online. Time was running short. Hanuman moved Sean's backpack just slightly. The wizard stared at it.

"Speaking of which, the moment has come to test this celebrated statue." He turned to Sean, "Kindly place the casket before the altar and you will see a rectangular slit on its lid; slide the base of this special statue you received from my Kogi sister into the slit. Please recite aloud the prayers that the Lady of the Rock has taught you in order to call for the help of the Buddha. I believe we have not yet exhausted the potential of this casket."

The small statue fitted neatly into the gold engraving and covered the six branched-star. Sean recited aloud three times: 'I take refuge in the enlightened consciousness; I take refuge in the law of right conduct; I take refuge in the community of the twice-born.' He then recited a prayer unknown to the Stealthstars, as a prayer linking the name of the Goddess to the name of the Buddha.

The turmoil subsided; the tempest they had felt in their limbs was over. They felt a faint breeze coming from the altar and to Lakshmi, it was singing a soft tune. The pressure in their eyes and foreheads was receding.

The silence grew deeper. Each enjoyed a feeling of relaxation. The temperature of their bodies cooled down. They closed their eyes again and bathed in the returned presence of a golden auspiciousness surrounding them. At the center of the vision, the flames on the top of the small statue and of the Emerald Buddha were flickering softly with a multicolored radiance.

At first, the images of the White Monkey in the frieze of the *Ramayana* from the neighboring gallery danced before their eyes, as if the character had become alive. "Accept to lose and you may win. Strive to win and you may lose. The Buddha is now helping you to rise higher, just watch," they heard Hanuman whisper. Then the walls of the temple disappeared, and they felt an incomparable mood of golden elation.

There was a pervading feeling of gentleness; the light of the sun brought clarity to all things. From within this light, a formidable presence was uniting strength and clarity through meekness. They heard Sanath say, "I don't understand. I...I am returning to the place I love. This is way beyond what we ought to experience. This is not in the Casket of the Yellow Feather."

CHAPTER THIRTEEN

THE LIGHT OF THE LAMB

Where Lakshman and his companions are taken beyond the realm of the Yellow Feather and are given passage through the narrow gate of the Lily of Anorhad beyond which truth is no longer a pursuit but a reality in which the Lamb of God is revealed.

The Temple of the Emerald Buddha was no longer to be seen. The revelation of this light projected a new landscape within his head, and Lakshman found himself floating on a lake whose surface was agitated and troubled. He wondered where he was and looked up at the sky. Through swirling clouds, he could see two gigantic feathers, one blue, one yellow, fanning the strong breeze that blew on the waves. His swimming was tentative; at first he worried about drowning but then, from nowhere, a sentence came into his head, a memory of the years he'd spent in college, translating ancient Greek: *"Truth is at the bottom of the well."* The intuition was clear: truth was at the bottom of the lake.

His preoccupation with himself was keeping him on the surface, floating like a cork on the waves. When he relaxed and abandoned himself to the water, he began to sink. But instead of drowning, he found himself at another plane of the liquid, as if on a different level, a more placid lake, a second lake that was being revealed under the previous one. The breeze was gentler. Swimming vigorously now, he distinguished a shape emerging through the swell. He progressed towards a small island that had appeared as a possible refuge, relieved to find it surrounded by still water;

he noticed that his mind too, was calmer. He passed between two swans and after walking a short way on firm ground, he contemplated a circular structure at the center of the island.

He entered a ten-meter high dome crowned by a top of crystal with walls made of mother of pearl. Three entrances carved in the rotundity of its inner shapes offered him three distinct choices. The central passage facing him was much smaller and narrower than the two flanking ones. A child was standing before its door; his face emitted a purity that evoked the portraits of angels by the artist William Blake. There was a calm strength about him as he addressed the visitor, "When you reach the gate of paradise they will not ask you how much you have done but how much you have loved. My name is Isaprem of Anorhad. The one who asks for the truth should also want to know. Love is the truth and to pass this gate you must love the truth. Man wants to know only what suits him, as do the dwellers of the great cities, gyrating in their own thoughts. These thoughts are the fuel of the fire that shall eat their cities because they do not really want to know the truth. This is why their world will pass into smoke and shadows." He leaned towards a white, wooden, toy horse by his side and asked, "How shall they withstand the light?"

The child stamped on the ground with his right foot and beams of light and hot vapours fused from the nostrils of the small horse. Lakshman became frightened and walked towards the entrance to the left of the child. He approached the door to find it consisted of a central pole with long lateral filaments undulating gently. This gate looked like a vertical, bluish-colored feather, and not exactly welcoming; but a vague sense of unease could not stop Lakshman's curiosity.

As he ventured through the curtain, he felt as though the feathered door had cast a nasty spell. A strange sensation enveloped him as if he had been punished for trespassing. Deep gurgles and rumbling noises alarmed Lakshman. The place was not unlike an autumn valley under fog, where the mist dims the light and blurs the shapes. The atmosphere was eerie. Had he crossed a forbidden passageway to another space?

He registered the sensation of being swallowed by the atmosphere of the wet grotto; small ghostly shapes were flying around him. On both sides, he could now see barriers, looking like rows of large, sharp, clasped teeth. Had he entered a living organism? He sensed with increasing fright; this cavernous tunnel was nothing less than the mouth of a dragon. Straining with all his might, Lakshman hurried out to find himself in the central hall, but then, he could not stop his movement and this time, he crossed a yellow, feathered gate on the right of the child.

He noted immediately he had again entered the mouth of a dragon, but a different one. The atmosphere was tense, electric; the light was very sharp. He could smell the stench, sense the heat, becoming gradually aware of the threat of the fire contained in the belly of the beast that could burn him at any moment. The belly, he realized, contained the shapes of various likely futures.

He glimpsed a large digestive machine, pulsating with the breath of the dragon, into which humans were plugged like little robots. This was not where he wanted to slide. In order to interrupt the movement pushing him forward, he had to make an enormous effort to reverse his course and progress back towards the exit of the dragon's mouth. It was more difficult to cross the entrance curtain in reverse but binding all his energy; he managed to do so and found himself in the hospitable dome. He breathed with relief, freed from the smell of rotten eggs.

Grateful for the newfound freshness, he faced the smaller entrance to the central corridor. He stared at it. Now the entrance looked more inviting than the larger gates defended by the feather curtains. Ysaprem of Anorhad moved to the side, inviting him to enter. Squeezing himself with much difficulty through the narrow gate, he slowly climbed the first steps of a staircase.

All the while, outside of the Temple of the Emerald Buddha, danger approached. Walking though the courtyards, Tuchpamonporn took time to find out their exact location. The Ghost Riders who guided him had secretly reached the entrance of the mother-of-pearl-covered dome. In front of the gate, they stopped. They could not pass through, for only those who were authorized could cross the narrow gate of the sixth House of Anorhad. Its hermetic locking code blocked the will to power left in the casket by Hangker and the Sernatil. The gate was also denying access to Belzebseth's black magic.

Lakshman was now in a space that looked like the hall of a temple. The combined effect of the casket and the effigy of the Buddha had propelled the scope of the vision to another plane, to one beyond the realm of the feathers. The casket and the statue had now disappeared in the brightness that filled the entire hall. Above all, there was a presence that remained, stunning, invisible, yet pervasive, like a crystal container reveals itself when all the colors it reflects are withdrawn. That which is essential but never truly perceived was now surrounding them. "Who is this, who dwells in this light?" Lakshman could hear the question in his head, could feel a pressure in his forehead dissolving slowly and he was liberated by a sense of lightness in his entire body. Liberation was the pervading feeling and, in the light of this moment, his vision revealed the secret of the three feathers.

Undulating lines of varying hues shifted and changed until three graceful shapes appeared. He saw the three feathers elegantly twirling around, playfully dancing with each other as if the contents of different caskets were flowing into each other, fusing into a new dimension of integration. They were much larger than the one in the casket. Gradually, they joined, the yellow on the right, the white in the center and the blue on the left. The slight bending of the yellow feather suggested its gentle taming by the Buddha. His small statue had asserted a spell that subdued the power contained in the casket. This control over the yellow feather permitted a new choreography.

In a movement of grace, the two colored feathers stretched slightly sideways as if to leave open the path for the white feather to rise up, forming the tricolor Lily of Anorhad, emblem of the Sixth House. Desire and feelings combining in harmony with thought and action formed that point of equilibrium through which consciousness can break through to the other side. This psychic alchemy was opening to man the passage to the Higher World. The feathers had revealed their innermost meaning and delivered their secret.

The vision fascinated Lakshman and his companions who had each gone through a similar experience. They would have been weary had they not experienced a sweet reassurance dawning within them, the feeling they were accepted, away from any harm. They felt like children. Yes, that was it, they were just as children. Thus, the majestic light absorbed them. With the blessings of Hanuman and the Buddha, the companions had escaped the trap of the Yellow Feather, and thus they had been allowed by the guardian of the narrow gate to crack open its cipher. Lakshman, incredulous, registered the tune of a famous English hymn, quite out of place in Bangkok, or so it seemed at first. It was playing softly in his head as if to help him come down to a more familiar plane.

'And did those feet, in ancient times, walk upon England's mountains green. And was the holy Lamb of God, on England's pleasant pastures seen.'

England? Was this the destination? The Lamb? Was He the Master of Anorhad?

Recognition flashed into Lakshman's mind: why was it that the meek had the power to bind all the strengths together? During the entire Dagad Trikon saga, never did he approach that riddle. "Agnus dei qui tollit peccata mundi, dona nobis pacem: Lamb of god who carries the sins of the world, give us peace..." The children of the West used to repeat this prayer in their churches but who could feel that wonderful relaxation within their limbs? The Lamb was the solution! It was this apparent weakness of egoless modesty that maintained balance in the harmony of the cosmic order, and kept the tremendous powers of the Yellow Feather under control. Dwelling in the Sixth House brought sensations of freedom and relief; there was no need any longer to win, to prove anything or to perform.

The antidote to Hangker's poison flowing into the human psyche, the answer to the riddle of the Yellow Feather was…humility. Humility was the crown of true kings; it graced the true masters of the Yellow Feather with rare nobility.

The Stealthstars dwelled in a physical perception of vacuity, felt the lightness in their body, as if their load had been taken away.

The vision they shared acquired a new magnificence. The presence within the sun manifested in the shape of a man of dazzling splendor.

In the unfolding of the Avasthic vision, the lily formed by the feathers was now serving as a delicate pedestal for the One who resides in the sun. He is standing, a rider waiting for his horse. No cross to carry this time. He is the King who destroys the impediments and foes of the ascent. He is blameless and controls the door to the heavens of the higher consciousness, the House of Ni. It is His prerogative to grant passage to the highest house, the Seventh, from where Buddha sent his beacon to announce the coming of the new world. The meaning of this beacon was now being revealed.

They heard the voice of Sanath, "We produce our thoughts when we travel in the fog, but we receive our intuitions when we soar in the sunlight. See through the eyes of the elders of Anorhad; the Casket of the Cross has been opened." Spiritual strength was spreading outside. Shadows and creeping servants of Thanatophor and creatures of darkness dissolved in its brilliance. Sanath continued, "When the children reach beyond the powers of the three feathers, then the flame coming from the top of their heads will ignite a force that was never known before on this Earth."

And the fire, high in the sky, the complete energy of the sun could now be received, enlightening all earthly things. The enlightenment beamed knowledge inside and a refined culture outside, opening the advent of a radiant civilization that would more than match the past glory of the Avasthas. Crossing the Lily of Anorhad allowed humans to absorb and administer the solar power wisely and this capacity was lending its glow to the age to come: a Golden Age.

Each of the companions present around the casket received the Anorhadan prophecy in a slightly different manner, corresponding to their specific level of intuition. When the solar radiance faded in Lakshmi's vision, the scene turned to the shadows of an approaching night. The setting sun diminished in size and ended up as a red dot at dusk. Suddenly, Lakshmi was back in the sari shop in New Delhi and she was staring at the vermilion dot on the forehead of the Lady. She returned for a while into the stream of feelings she had experienced on that occasion.

Sean received the prophecy in a state of deep silence. His body felt extremely light as if he was floating towards the top of his head. Everything stood revealed in clarity, the truth at last, inside and outside, goodness and evil. It was plain that man had to fight evil and to promote good, as was the case when Rama ruled in Ayodhya. There was no ambiguity or relativity left, no hanky-panky, or rationalization possible, no fears, no doubts, no hypocrisy, no small compromises, no thoughts.

Sean's attention encompassed the students of the Great Mother, his friends around the world. He saw dark shapes hovering above them around the gate of Anorhad, fiendish wraiths, galloping ghosts, one of them a powerful greenish witch. Many obstacles and risks were left on the way but honesty, the light within, would guide them in good time. They heard a soft voice coming from very far away.

"*Stella matutina, laudamus te.* Star of the Morning, we praise Thee. Can you see the star of the morning? It announces the new day." The light of the sun had receded so they could indeed see the faint light of dawn and admire the shine of a bright star. These words concluded the prophetic vision, marked the end of their meditation. They opened their eyes, back again in Bangkok, and looked at Sanath interrogatively. Who had spoken?

"Praise to the White Monkey whose presence again protects us. The time when we can claim victory is not yet here. Keep the memory of this astounding moment in your hearts while we revere the Anorhadan brilliance that does not scorch but enlightens and..." Sanath stopped brusquely, turned his head towards the entrance door where one of his men was frantically signaling. Without appearing alarmed, he motioned everyone to arise. In one swift gesture, he replaced the small statue in the backpack, opened the casket, and took the Yellow Feather, which vanished into his pocket. With an agility no one would have suspected in a man of his age, he rapidly embedded the casket back into its former place.

There was no time for explanations. "Quick, they are coming. Let's get out of here at once!"

CHAPTER FOURTEEN

SETTLING THE SCORE

Where knowledge that is not sought for the sake of truth has turned a scholar into a traitor, and how the wizard decides to take care of it for the last time.

The wizard and his companions rushed out of the temple and exited its surrounding square. Looking over his shoulder, Sean saw a group of fierce-looking, shaven-headed priests wielding long sticks running towards the entrance they had just left. A group of Russian tourists were in their way, delaying their course. What captured Sean's attention was the leader of the monks: he was the young monk from the market, now wearing the saffron robes of a high abbot.

Sanath led them at a fast pace out of the compound. As they stopped, by the side of the road, his expression was stern.

"Who are these guys who're searching for us?" asked Sean.

Sanath said, "I'll tell you later, let us leave this topic for the time being. The important thing is this: until today, I always understood that the caskets had to be opened to release their own specific powers but, in opening this one, we were propelled beyond its content. There seems to be a gathering force that operates on its own. I will have to reflect on this, but I think now I shall rest. I propose that we take separate routes and meet this evening at the Oriental. There we'll revisit what we have just witnessed."

He nodded in the direction of a dark blue, chauffeur-driven limousine that was parked in the shade of a nearby tree. The driver and the man sitting next to him looked Caucasian. The limousine pulled over, the

121

wizard got in and waved them goodbye with a flickering smile and the car drove off. Lakshmi, Lakshman and Sean took a local taxi. Looking through the rear window of the cab, Sean had the distinct impression that a Range Rover containing two monks was following them. With the promise of a generous tip, their driver jumped a red light with perfect timing, sped up the access lane to the overpass, took the next exit and stopped abruptly at the entrance to a crowded vegetable market from where they watched the Range Rover speeding along the overpass oblivious of their maneuver. They left the cab and hurried through the busy market. Sean took them to the taxi stand under a range of trees in a back alley where they boarded another cab. If more than one team had been shadowing them, their followers could not have kept up with these maneuvers.

Back on the veranda of the Aryaputra home, still immersed in the magic journey at the Temple of the Emerald Buddha, the three friends discussed the events of the day. That evening, they joined the wizard at the riverside terrace of the Oriental Hotel. Various types of marine craft were cruising on the Chaoprayha as passengers took their leisure at dusk under the spectacular display of a dark orange sky.

Sanath and Mariluh had also reviewed the events of the day and they seemed particularly serene. Sanath reprised what they'd seen and experienced. "We have seen the tricolor Lily, received the Anorhadan prophecy and felt the glory of He who controls it. I was yearning for this vision, but I did not expect to receive it here, for it belongs to the content of another chest, the Casket of the Cross, buried under the sacred oak tree in the forests of Byelorussia. That the casket here is releasing the content of the Byelorussian casket too means that the magic oak has finally died. This is the sign of the end, the end of this age."

"Is this now happening to all the remaining caskets?"

"I cannot see that part. You see, Lakshman; it may be that the caskets are releasing their magic without Avasthic intervention as originally planned; something or someone has stepped up the game in the revelation of the legend. It means the forces are combining, the substances they contain are mixing, flowing into each other; the connections are being established. This is ahead of the content that had been poured into the caskets, beyond the power of the Avasthas. It is really beyond me."

"Is our mission over? Is it now futile to look for the remaining caskets?" Lakshman was shocked and counted off those still missing: the casket of the four-branched star of the House of Kalabham, the casket of the six-branched star of the House of Falkiliad, the casket of the twelve-branch star of the House of Eleksim, the Casket of the Discus of the

House of Anor and, of course, the Casket of the Cross and the one of the Blue Feather.

"Frankly," responded Sanath pensively, "I think we shall soon know."

"Why did you say you are getting a rest?" asked Lakshmi.

"I have lived for over one thousand years, most of them quite busy ones. Don't you think I deserve a break? Besides, when the king returns and visits the land by himself, what is the need for a messenger?" The wizard was now in an excellent mood, as someone who has just received great news or better, a fine insight.

Before they could further revisit the content of their visionary experience, Sean, with a worried frown on his usually smooth forehead, wanted to clarify something that was bothering him greatly. He returned to the cause of their swift escape, "Do you know those we saw running towards the temple?" he asked, "and what is the reason you rushed us out?"

"You saw the driver and the bodyguard in my car? When I left China for Thailand I asked my old friend Ivan Sadaka to give me the protection of his Russian security team. Since the explosion of my house in Holland, I am at war with an invisible foe. I was on my guard, as I knew that tackling this casket was dangerous. It could jolt up Hangker, free him from wherever he is, because of a treachery that tampered with it in ways we could not fully understand. His followers were alerted to our presence, and somehow the devil warned them. I guess his telecommunication system isn't as effective as it might be because they came too late to catch us; besides, we were again under the special protection of Lord Hanuman. We escaped just in time. Those priests are under the command of Hangker. They master sorcery and cursing spells but with the feather in our possession I guess that this devil, for the time being, is still stuck in hell."

"I asked because something reminds me of my travel through time with the Glorfakir, and more precisely what happened in the den of the Sand Keeper at the time of the fall of the Avasthas," continued Sean, "I remember clearly this part of the dream I had in your hotel room. If I may, I would like to ask you if you remember that as the Sand Keeper you had told me that no one had permission to get close to the *Bibliotheca Diabolica*. I remember Lidholon, and I was surprised when your attendant showing us the library mentioned the colors of the books it contained. Should he know such details? As I became suspicious, I stayed awake during the night and saw a shadow accessing the library but could not catch up with it. And today, I had a quick look at the group rushing towards the Emerald Temple as we were leaving."

The cousins could not make out what Sean was talking about, but he did not pay any attention to them. Looking feverishly for his cell phone, he continued, "The leading monk today was the one who was shadowing us in the Chatuchak market and since my vision in the room of this hotel, I have a nagging suspicion I now want to clarify once and for all. Here it is," he added, finding the picture he had taken of the monk at the Chatuchak market on his cell phone. "The picture is pretty clear. It reminds me of my visit to your highland retreat in Dagad Trikon. Can you see this mean-looking fellow?"

Sanath studied the photo for some time and closed his eyes. He looked absent and they didn't dare disturb him. After some time, he released a long sigh and said, "Thanks Sean, you have been immensely helpful. Do you know this man? Have you ever seen him before?"

"Yes, he reminds me of the librarian to whom you entrusted the custody of the Avasthic library."

After another thoughtful pause, Sanath volunteered a full explanation. "So it is; we finally meet again. I will have to take care of him this time. It is, literally, a long story. I have spent more energy than I would have wished over the ages dueling with a few characters, and this one is indeed known to me. A long time ago, in the days of the Rock, he was my closest assistant, and single-mindedly devoted to the pursuit of knowledge. I trusted him completely. His name, you may remember Sean, was Agnorth and he was a nobleman of Falkiliad. You saw the last days of the Avastha fortress and I think I should now tell the whole story to your friends.

"When we escaped to the Himalayas after the fall of Dagad Trikon, all of us stayed in an ashram in the upper catchment area of the Ganga River. I noted that Agnorth's behavior became increasingly bizarre. One misty morning, I decided to spy on him as he left early, ostensibly for an errand to the nearby village. But instead, he followed a mountain trail leading to the grotto of a feared tantrika, a practitioner of the dark arts. I managed to make myself very small, almost invisible, and followed him. There, to my horror, I found that Agnorth was the teacher; and the black magician the apprentice. Agnorth was in possession of manuals of the *Bibliotheca Diabolica* he had stolen before the burning of the Avasthic library. It was one of the worst moments of my many lives. After Serapis, now Agnorth—this new betrayal was like a second death for me. I was devastated. When he returned I confronted him, he who had been my favorite disciple, but I was so distraught that I could not use my full powers on him. The affection I once had for him weakened me greatly. He cast terrifying curses, which put me in great difficulty.

"Both of you, Lakshman-Etakir and Sean-Lidholon, returned from a hunt just in time to save me. Of course, you've forgotten this, but I am an Aulya among Avasthas and keep the memories of my previous births. I keep the burden of such treacheries. Agnorth was neutralized, but his fame grew among the shamans of the mountain valleys. Still today a shadow of his sorcery is practiced in remote monasteries by some Tibetan lamas."

Sean asked, "What happened to us; I mean when we caught Agnorth? What happened after this?"

"Ekatir, Lidholon and Esitel did not wish to live any longer after the fall of their world; they resolved to plead with the gods and to leave on foot towards Mount Kailash in the Himalayas. Evenyl had been wounded during the battle with Agnorth; she could not recover because of her previous ordeal and was too weak for the journey to Kailash. So, with a heavy heart, she let her friends depart and was desolate thereafter as no traces of them were ever found. I had left her in the custody of my only remaining Pushpak chariot and being still unwell; she returned with my other attendants to the remnants of the Rock, to offer the use of this flying machine to the Nizam of Elnelok, the underground citadel of the Elnorians. I presume that she spent the rest of her life with the last Avasthas."

"This is a sad tale, Master. What became of you?"

"I would not go to Mount Kailash without being summoned, a point the younger Avasthas in their desperation would not observe. The Sand Keeper moved to Tibet, lived as a hermit and was venerated as a great healer by the population of nearby villages. He passed away not long after the departure of Evenyl, whom he had come to love as his own daughter."

"What happened to the evil books that had been stolen from the library?"

"I never found them again. I very much feared that Agnorth had returned them to the demon kings because we see traces of the application of these dark treatises in the modern age. I found out later that Agnorth also enjoyed a rare respect from the Council of Necromancians as he served both Hangker and Belzebseth. This story is one of my most abject failures. Thereafter, we battled through several lives. I feel responsible for my disciple's failing because without me he could not have achieved his dangerous command over magic. I finally understood what went wrong."

"And what was that?" Where could one feel safe if even the favorite assistant of the wizard could be turned around? It was plain that a world they had deemed pure had been soiled.

"In the days of Dagad Trikon, the six enemies of the soul did not inhabit the ghostly horses and their Riders. Lizards carried them."

"Why six? I thought there are seven Riders."

"I shall explain another time. But to return to the subject at hand, I once saw Agnorth playing with lizards outside my den, one green and one yellow, I remember. I scolded him and told him never to do so. I thought he did not know of the dangers of this, but he disobeyed me. The Avasthas seers know because they love, and they want to know more in order to expand this love. I did not know that Agnorth was dedicated to knowledge for the sake of fierce self-promotion, as represented by the yellow lizard, not for the sake of love. In that context, jealousy in the green reptile turned him against his teacher who knew more than him. But he concealed his game so well that I never suspected him. He, like Governor Serapis Sernatil, betrayed his race for the intoxication of the Yellow Feather. However, I see from this picture that he has lost some of his strength in this life."

"What should we do?"

"Nothing, nothing at all. Thank God Sean helped me to identify him," replied Sanath. "The time has come for me to put matters right. I think it must have been Agnorth who pierced my disguise as Baldur van Jetzlar in Vassenar and I might credit him with blowing up my house in Holland. You know that I have amassed a solid wealth and can take care of my security. Ivan Sadaka and his party of Russian bodyguards have gone underground, but they still assist me with superb efficiency. I will ask Ivan to take care of this fellow. After all, an ex-cardinal would know how to deal with a high abbot! These people understand each other. Excuse me a second, please."

Sanath's memory could process information across long periods. He recognized that he could not afford to let Agnorth escape yet again. The occasion had presented itself to him, as a collateral blessing of this latest episode. Indeed, he now seemed pleased to have picked up the trail of the renegade disciple again, because if Agnorth had been looking for Sanath, the reverse was also true.

This game of hide and seek had lasted so long because both foes could resort to exceptional camouflage skills. He foraged in his pocket, dialed a number on his cell phone and conversed with the recipient. After a time he rejoined his companions at the dining table.

"Warm greetings from Ivan in St. Petersburg. The end of this game must come. The abbot will reap due reward for his treachery. But let's forget about it for the time being and have dinner together." Sanath's mood had changed. He was now relaxed and behaving more as an exquisite host than a high wizard; such was his fondness for his guests. He was delighted to entertain them.

"What shall we drink?" he asked gently. "I can recommend the 'yoga blend' fruit cocktail with guava juice, fresh mango, strawberry and banana. They mix it in such a way that it tastes both sweet and sour, indicating perhaps that yoga is found between two flavors. And now, let us talk about serious things." The wizard ordered the drinks and the rest of the meal.

The lights of the fifty-story high Peninsula building across the river sparkled in the water. The small pagoda-shaped ferries busily crisscrossing the river shone with garlands of lights.

Sean narrated all he could remember of his time travel back to Dagad Trikon carried by the Glorfakir sword. He conveyed the mood in the den of the Sand Keeper, revealed the treachery of the Governor and described the Avasthic library. It was a sad tale for the cousins, but greatly appreciated as it provided an explanation for the episode with the monks and the missing pieces of the Dagad Trikon puzzle. Later in the night the wizard took his leave saying, "You will please excuse me as I have some business to attend to, but we shall meet again tomorrow evening, same time, same place."

CHAPTER FIFTEEN

THE SECRET OF THE PORTALS

Where the connection between hell, earth, and the heavens are the subject of enquiry, and how a dream reveals the role that women play in the network of cosmic portals.

The O'Lochan family, in Washington, D.C. discussed what Michael had told them about his experiences in South Africa. "Mike said that Kheto had quoted Jean-Paul Sartre saying, *'L'enfer c'est les autres.'* – 'Hell is other people'. But he said that a clever guy like Sartre ought to have said, *'L'enfer c'est nous; c'est pas les autres.'* – 'Hell is us, not other people.' Blaming others does not help because we can only change ourselves."

"Heavens and hell seem to mix, how do we move from one to the other? How can one find the exit from hell? Or open heaven's door? I bet many would want to know. Some of us spend moments in hell or paradise, but we are not always conscious that we visit these places, even though we do."

"One thing is sure," said Joseph in response to his sister, "the wizard believes that hell and its people exist and he seems to spend much time fighting it. You mentioned he always creates a new disguise so as to better conduct his investigations and pass unnoticed behind enemy lines. We never quite grasp what he is up to, but whatever it is, he definitely has enemies who are trying to get rid of him. He talked about the six Dark Riders, who could penetrate human brains and defile the characters of people, about demons active in leading the legions of the living dead to possess the human psyche."

Tracy added, "He also told us we are heading, with open eyes, into a climatic meltdown of our own making."

"He said everything was connected, remember? He's right; it's not just about the climate. The climate is, in a way, the result of other things that have been going wrong for too long."

"I know Jonathan, but people don't want to see the subtle connections which brought us to where we are," said Tracy in tired annoyance. "We tried hard with the Oikos project but when it started to challenge the way we produce food or run our transport systems, we were taken down by special-interest groups and funding was withdrawn. No one was interested any longer. I'm frustrated, but if the world has to burn, well, I guess hell is winning."

"When the quest for the caskets was initiated and Lakshman went to Reykjavik he had no clue what he was getting into. For us, unveiling the legend of the Avasthas became a matter of urgency. In the session of the Council of the Order of the Hllidarendis in Jetzenstein Castle, Sanath told us there is little time left. What did he mean? I believe it is also about identifying the portals between the three worlds: earth, heaven and hell. Two years passed by, and I see no progress. What did we get?"

"We achieved a lot," replied Tracy, "in retrieving the Avasthic caskets, we discovered 'the Gift', the key element of the Avasthic prophecy, the highest prize of the game of evolution: the heavens are within ourselves, we are the legend. We uncovered the mechanism for self-empowerment hidden within us. Really, that's a lot. The medieval minstrels declaiming the tale of the Holy Grail in the *Roman de la Rose*, would have been amazed to know what we now know about the subject."

Joseph said, "I guess junkies, too, would love to know that the Holy Grail is the unlocking of the juice of bliss in the limbic area of their brains! Who would remember that gods and demons have fought perennial battles to get this ambrosia? I know some of us went to the heavens for a while, we got it for free, but we lost it again. I mean the state, the feeling of bliss. It's gone isn't it?"

"We don't command it Jonathan, it comes and goes, like the White Monkey. Sanath told us we have yet to learn how to stabilize our attention's access to the Inner World. But Lakshmi can't forget the taste of the nectar of blessedness. Shortly before we married in New Delhi, she met this...this," he searched for the right words, "this Great Lady in the likeness of the High Lady of Dagad Trikon in a sari shop."

Tracy replied, "Remember what she said she'd felt: a complete immersion in pure love. How wonderful is that?"

"How could I not remember," responded Jonathan. "It was so strong; she could hardly bear it. and she was in tears. The Lady in the sari shop carries the Gift, walking incognito on this earth. But can She bestow the Gift to Her human children if they are not ready to accept it? And how shall we find back our way to this place of bliss? I know it is there but is it within our reach?"

"The Gift is something we receive, not something we achieve," said Tracy, who added, "Mike and his fiancé had this wonderful encounter with an African member of Sanath's order, that's exciting. And the news from Countess Laira that the oak tree in Byelorussia is dead is perhaps more worrying than exciting—if I remember Sanath correctly; but any news of the legend is good news to me. And Mike had this wonderful dream."

"Oh yes, what was it?" asked Jonathan "I wanted to listen but was interrupted by a phone call."

"Mike saw you in Avasthic armor, wearing a helmet adorned with the wings of a sea bird, defending a portal to a canyon behind which women, carrying a large amphora, took refuge. Your green shield was decorated with the ten golden-wheel-naves of Elnur. Warriors around you carrying long spears were lined up in the canyon, facing the evil host. I heard the voice of the commander next to you, and I somehow knew it was the Sea Lord, Philtalas, telling you, 'Raise the Aim, Rim and Klim war banners.' Three flags, red, white and dark blue, were raised high in the wind above the spears."

"Sounds spectacular," said Jonathan, quite pleased but almost envious. 'Aim, Rim Klim'? It sounds like Sanskrit. I will ask Lakshmi what it means. I wouldn't mind having a dream like this again. Michael always connects fast to the Legend."

As they went to bed, the temperature had mercifully gone down. Everything was quiet in the Georgetown flat. In Tracy's bedroom, a book on Southern Algeria lay open on the night table. Before going to sleep, she had picked it up for no other reason than to recall a journey she had made when she was twenty-one. Tassili, in the Touareg language, meant the table-land of the waters and the name was resounding; the Tassili of Assekrem. Lying in bed, she remembered she had traveled by jeep from Tanmarasset up to the Hoggar with three other students, the driver and the guide from the army who also served as a bodyguard. They had progressed slowly on the bumpy trail crossing sandy flatlands where occasional shrubs punctuated the desolate landscape and herds of goats kept close to the wadis that captured the scarce moisture. After a few hours, the trail climbed gently and then became a steep, curved mountain road. Here, there was no vegetation, the earth was ochre and the mountainsides that had withstood erosion were dark brown, as were the huge boulders that had fallen off the cliffs, resting on layers of crushed black and purple stones.

The temperature had slowly dropped; the air became crisper and the colored peaks and rocky needles at their feet were ablaze from the light of the setting sun. Above two thousand five hundred meters, the jeep had climbed the Assekrem and reached the simple hermitage of Father Charles de Foucauld at the top of the pass, an Alsatian playboy aristocrat who'd become a reclusive saint, who was assassinated in 1916. His hermitage now served as a shelter for travelers.

Tracy admired the breathtaking view on the dome of Tahat and the Ilamane peak, the grand organs of their basalt columns rising towards the sky. In the mineral solitude of this cataclysmic landscape, there was no sound, no sound at all. Heaven and earth fused at dusk in a silent immensity. It became intensely cold, and they were glad to enter the refuge. The innkeeper was cooking on an open fire. Tracy exchanged impressions with an Italian traveler who was happy to hear her speaking in his own language.

Before retiring for the night she went out to see the sky. It was freezing cold and the sky was clear as crystal, there wasn't a grain of dust in the air and millions of stars were shining brightly in the black sky. People sometimes say that the sky is the limit, but here the sky was limitless. *Allahu Akbar!* She was puzzled by the sheer grandeur and she felt she understood Islam, understood why people of the desert had such awe before the greatness of God. She returned to her small room and slipped into her sleeping bag, her eyes filled with traces of the starry night, and she was able to melt into this grand beauty, and to touch eternity.

Tracy, now asleep in D.C. with a smile on her lips, was bathed in these beautiful memories. She dreamed she heard a door creaking and sensed a faint light on her eyelids. She awoke to find an old woman in a Touareg robe sitting in the doorway of her room staring at her kindly. An oil lamp was beside her on the doorstep, and the flickering flame revealed her great age. She had seen this woman in the small kitchen and had assumed she was the innkeeper's mother. "Why are you sitting on my doorstep?"

"This is a portal, and you are a portal too."

"Are you a portal too?

"Yes I am, and this is why I have come to you. Long ago, my ancestors came from a magic place to the nearby oasis fed by the Atakor summits, which surround this place. There was more water in those days. They were brave and gentle people. They came from underground hiding places and worshiped the stars, expecting their people to return and take them back to

THE BREAKING OF THE SEVENTH SEAL

the stars, but it never happened of course. They left paintings and engravings in grottos and caves, and their legends died with them but a message was passed on by word of mouth, and now I must pass it on to you."

"What is the message?"

"We are women!"

"Yes, I know."

"We are women, and we are the secret. If we do not find our secret, the world shall perish, as the world is perishing now."

"Is it only up to us? Don't men have something to do also?"

"Men? We give them birth. We give without asking. We feed and we carry them. But we do not know how to sustain them anymore. Women are the carriers of love. Men can love too, but it is impossible for them if we can't. Women can. We can love even when they can't. This is the difference and in this difference we can make love sprout, even more when the ground is not so fertile. The secret of how to till the land of love is lost when today women can't love as they once used to."

"What is the secret?"

"Unconditional love. We can transform the world through our hearts if we can rekindle the sheen of the spirit in those we love. When we can emit the power of selfless love, the best among men can too. They grow. They express unselfish love pouring out of their simple but good hearts, and we are fulfilled as well. Women start feeling how much beauty there still is, even in those who are covered by the shadows of the Evil One. Then we shine on men, and they shine on the world."

"Well, it's not happening is it? I mean, not in the real world."

"This real world isn't real at all; it is just a gigantic illusion people have blown up like a balloon around themselves. This bubble shall pop. Lots of us live in a hidden hell of unhappy bonds, unfulfilled hopes. We live next to each other instead of together, many women thinking it's better to suffer silently, but they are not ready to remove the core of their suffering.

Devils know that in order to destroy our men, they need to destroy us first, or at least, they need to weaken or minimize the love power in the world—in women. The Evil One does not want men to be uplifted or transformed, does not want their egos to melt into that love. The dark force operating against the universal power of true women attacks us because it attacks our capacity to channel the divine power into this world. Love is this power."

Tracy was fully awake now—in her dream—feeling a tickling sensation in the center of her chest. The power of love? Yes, but how? She answered the old woman, "The love you talk about is not on their radar;

132

they love to take, not to give; many women are uncaring, demanding, thinking they are as smart as hell."

"This is only because they don't know hell, not yet."

"Perhaps we sell ourselves short and cheap; perhaps we try to capture the love of men, yet we lose them because we lost the way to ourselves, not knowing what is our own strength."

"And not understanding how destruction works: from the loss of our own self-respect to the breakup of family life," added the woman. Her responses indicated she understood perfectly well what was going on. Tracy was surprised that the grandmother did not speak as a member of a Touareg tribe would, but seemed quite modern and well-informed.

"We lose, my young lady, because we try to win this enormous, universal battle through our egos, not through our hearts; unable to forgive our men, unable to give them so much real love that there will remain no space for negative entities to stay in the presence of our strong love. The Evil One has constantly attacked us by various means because he is very much afraid of the power of a woman who has managed to preserve it."

"But how can we love men who behave like brutes, like idiots or nomadic copulating bulls?"

"That's the trick of the devil isn't it? He fashions them so that we can't love them any longer. Everything is so confused in these huge bubbles of illusion that people nowadays call their lives! Tell them it's not their fault; it's not anybody's fault. We, the women, we have to forgive in order to break this vicious circle, but with our hearts, not our brains."

"That's it? Do you really think this can work?"

"It can't work for all women because there is now a parting of the ways. Two races are being formed, and two tracks are being traced. This bifurcation is the judgement. There are those who shall evolve further with the power of love. If our men come around because they can still feel real love pouring from us, and many do, we have won and love has won with us. And there are those who shall regress without love's redemption to lower forms of awareness. If men's hearts are dead and cannot be revived, if they insist on insulting us, we shall leave them to their own devices. The devil has won with them, but they shall not rejoice for long. They won't be able to enjoy outside of the bubbles of illusion."

"At times it seems that men and women either walk away from one another or they exist in a state of war.

"They walk away because they are at war and they fight because they have parted in their feelings. Even lust has become a sort of war. Frankly, women can win this war of the sexes but in this victory, they will lose what made their lives worthwhile."

Despite this alarming theme, Tracy felt wonderful in the clarity of the old woman. The presence of the legend was so tangible. Weren't these teachings those of the Lady of the Rock? Wasn't her ancestry a group of Avasthas who would have finally left the hidden fortress of Elnelok?

Thinking about the transforming power of love, putting it into words immediately takes half the magic away but Tracy wasn't thinking; she was simply dreaming. In the lucidity of the dream, everything looked so clear, so obvious and plain, so easy to perform in everyday life...she absorbed it all: the message of the ancients of Assekrem who probably came from Dagad Trikon, the benevolence of the grandmother, tender and wise, the benevolence and trust of her own emotions. She asked, "What sort of portal am I?" But the voice that answered this time was not the voice of the elderly Touareg lady. It was a voice from far away, "You are a portal between the legend and this world." Tracy sat up bolt upright. Her intuition had served her well; this woman was indeed a descendent of the Avasthas of Elnelok. And this voice, this voice...

"Assume your powers as a woman. Be bold, have complete confidence in yourself that you are a portal of love from the stars. Love is from the heavens. It is there, just find it. Find this energy within you, enjoy it. Tell all women, they really are the portals of the greatest power. They just have to believe in themselves and they will transform this world."

Tracy felt a surge of power through her entire body; was it not the voice of the Lady of the Rock speaking of the Deep Way? But at this very moment, the old woman who was sitting on her doorstep turned her head as if something was happening behind her. She stood up quickly and disappeared.

The floor creaked slightly. A shape emerged from the shadow of the small corridor and, suddenly, someone else was sitting on the doorstep. The light of the oil lamp became much brighter and revealed a new, uninvited guest. He was a boy of about seventeen years old, with curly black hair framing a handsome face. His voice had the pleasant softness of velvet, "So, she told you the big secret, did she?"

They stared at each other. Tracy found that the boy was very cute; perhaps one of the goat herders from the Assekrem, but there was something about his eyes she didn't trust. She did not know how to reply.

"You heard the so-called 'secret' but it isn't true, you know; men cannot be won by love. You will just be used and abused as usual."

Tracy had a flash of intuition: use and abuse? This was the clue in the boy's eyes. She stiffened and said, "You have entered my bedroom without being invited. I don't even know your name. At least you could introduce yourself." The light of the oil lamp brightened.

"Lesser mortals call me the Evil One. Those better informed call me Thanatophor."

There was a long silence. Behind the amiable shape of the young boy lurked something else, something formidable that, at times, his charming eyes could not conceal. However, Tracy, at this moment, felt completely filled by the words of the Lady of the Rock. These words had affected her in their meaning, clarity and reality. She answered simply, "You can't touch me!"

The handsome shepherd looked at her pensively. He answered, "I know, I was just checking." He stood up and disappeared from the doorstep.

Tracy arose and closed the door.

Awake in her bed in Georgetown, although still under the mood of the powerful dream, Tracy felt strong and energized at having faced the greatest of all devils without the slightest fear. But she soon found herself crying, not only for herself, who did not know how to approach the man she loved, but for all those who thought they had found him, and allowed themselves to accept a life which is a half hell, willing to bear the unbearable: the slow and cold end of love. How could the women of today refresh love? How could they speak to those who allow their love to be diffused, exchanged for money, or for so-called material comforts?

The wizard had already exposed the pincers of this general attack: role models and trends destroy the innocence in young girls; the media lure the female ego in silly suffragette or masculine postures through entertainment, fashion and other means; emancipation from common sense reinvents freedom; money and the seductions of this superficial world capture the once-innocent and quickly spread from the West to other countries. All are losing their precious traditions and heritage.

She was exhausted, but soon her tears were of relief because she was reminded that the power of love, hidden as it may be, is still there. "I can't wait to tell this dream to Lakshmi and Lorelei; this is the legend visiting me."

She felt such certainty: it's never too late to forgive, to stop being blind...to keep the heart open without fear that it will be hurt again. There was just one leitmotiv; "We have to be aware of it, aware of what is happening here, why and who is behind it and for what purpose. Once we are aware, the negativities don't baffle us easily. We don't blame anyone, we can have a desire pure enough to solve the mess with men and it will happen! Everything is possible now. We are portals of the energy of love that operates in the heavens and in all of us. So let's grow, let's forgive."

CHAPTER SIXTEEN

THE WISDOM OF ASIA

Where the Stealthstars agree that we know less than we assume, and that our ancestors knew more than we suspect. How the wizard explains that Asia had received wonderful teachings concerning the Dance of the Feathers.

They had gathered again at their usual meeting place by the riverside, and this time they noticed Ivan's security team discreetly monitoring the area of the hotel lobby. They felt tired but stimulated by the lore that had engulfed them since they had absorbed the Anorhadan prophecy at the Temple of the Emerald Buddha.

"I am overwhelmed by the meaning that was revealed at the end of the vision, when we went beyond the Feather. What a state, what splendor; did it not bringing us hope, a promise that our race will succeed?"

"Perhaps, Lakshmi, but in that case do we need to go on chasing after these caskets?" wondered her cousin.

Sanath seemed to agree, "Something is affecting our mission and the way the legend was meant to be revealed. The energy within this small statue, the movement that carried us beyond the Feather, everything indicates that the Great Mother has intervened; She is activating spiritual energy within matter." Sanath responded. "Yet, if She allows some of us to search a bit longer, possibly with the help of the Yellow Feather, we may elucidate a few riddles still hidden in the legend. In this way, could we recapture some of the science that was lost so long ago in the burning of the Avasthic library?"

Lakshman commented, "Perhaps we should let this magic rest. Sean, you absorbed the casket best, but you told me it was because the Great Mother taught you how to use the Sadhan, the shield of meditation. I was overpowered, snowed under. I experienced such strength in the feather that I felt its might was indomitable. Left to myself I could not have handled it."

He was puzzled by the contrast between the Lamb and the formidable sense of might and light, the modesty and the power. "The area of the Yellow Feather is intoxicating for most of us. I have been burnt by the revelation of this casket and feel vulnerable. I see a fatal paradox, a power that cannot be resisted and a quality that cannot be achieved. Action is a linear force; it takes over. Let's get real. Everybody wants to be a winner yet how many of us want to be humble? Buddha was a prince who did not mind begging for his food, but don't you think most people would rather be princes than beggars? I wish I could be humble but, honestly, that's not how I would describe myself."

The wizard smiled indulgently, "Perhaps, but knowing our weakness is the way to erase them. You see that you still need to improve. This places you in a category where you would wish to be: together with all those who are willing and capable of learning."

"The 'younger brothers' are slow learners," observed Mariluh. "Under the compulsion of this feather they want to take action, to create and to succeed. Soon they cannot stop thinking and worrying, instead of learning how to navigate through life like the Kogis elders who move like a feather: easy, light and free."

"Kriyafel Kurion, the Head of Falkiliad was a model in this respect," added Sanath with a touch of nostalgia. "He was elegant and light like a feather, yet full of creative energy, immensely capable and foremost among the learned ones, yet childlike and playful. The Circle of the Aulyas would call him for advice but he always remained humble."

"Competence with modesty? What a rare blend! Do you think the Great Mother might instill this level of excellence in the human race? However, I seem to remember…didn't you allude to this in your last Council in Jetzenstein Castle?" asked Lakshmi, her eyes now sparkling in the light of sudden recognition.

"I did. Look around and see how the horses from hell capture the Yellow Force and ride with it. CEOs and politicians bask in the feeling that winning is all there is to it. Bankers will grab money until none will be left around. Men spent stormy millennia fighting and killing to enjoy these specific sensations. Moderation and modesty are not popular; Lakshman is right, of course. This Feather was the bane of Napoleon and of conquerors before and after him. But the linearity of its force is broken by the spell of Anorhad. The Mongols, Tatars, Swedish, French and German invaders were each, in turn, humbled in Russia because this is where the Casket of the Cross was buried."

"Can I please return to the extraordinary role the statue played in the events of this afternoon? What sort of power had it released to subdue the randomness of the Yellow Feather?"

"My sister Mariluh will take this question from Lakshmi," Sanath said as he gazed up at the sky. Something had happened on this day in the temple that had brought him a new level of detachment. It was mostly expressed in that he was obviously enjoying himself more than previously. Gone were the tensions or even the frights endured in past episodes.

"You see the Buddha you bought is no ordinary piece. It was found in an antique shop of the left bank in Paris by an Iranian follower who offered it to the Great Mother at the Delphi festival. She accepted it, took it in Her hands and willed that some of Her powers should pass into the statue. Since then its magnetic current has been switched on, and here it recharged the effigies of the Buddha so that pilgrims to his temple would be sweetly blessed in the future. I was its respectful custodian for a while and made good use of it. A clairvoyant monk discovered it and reported to the young abbot. I guess he recognized the properties of the statue and was planning to steal it. I hid in the market. I felt the danger and this is why, under instructions from Master Sanath, I was so keen to pass it on to you. The specially charged statue, containing the vibrations of the feminine power, could also subdue the dark side of the Yellow Feather."

"What exactly did you do?"

"The devotees coming to holy places unknowingly seek a charge of spiritual energy that brings them elation. This is the reason, for instance, for the popularity of the Kaaba in Mecca. The stone is sacred because it does contain power."

"Like a Sao Iambu?"

"Precisely and this is exactly how this little statue is working. You see, Lakshman, it's like getting online. When people come to pray in temples or churches, usually they are not connected. It all depends on their sensitivity and on the efficiency of the Deep Way's communication equipment available in those places. As a rule of thumb, it helps if these instruments are vibrating. Our Buddha statue recharged the figure of the Emerald Buddha, and thus it will emit for a while. I trust the simple pilgrims will be better able to trigger a response through this effigy." She paused and added, "It can be a rather frustrating affair: the connection in temples, pagodas or churches does not work effectively because the heat of the priests who are in charge usually spoils the delicate vibratory energy."

"Genuine old priests like me are not supposed to meddle in their affairs," sighed the wizard with an ironic smile. "In the Buddhist countries as anywhere else, religious charges, rituals and practices are often a source of wealth or political influence for the keepers of the temples."

Sean added, "It is down to business, and they are serious about it. I know good monks who complain about the state of religion and society, but they do not know how to bring about change. The entire continent of Asia is torn between the vanishing traces of its wisdom and the fierceness of modernity.

"Is there anything during this holographic audience near Shanghai that you might share?" he asked the wizard.

Sanath reclined comfortably in his armchair and willingly returned to the lessons learned during his trip to China. "The Daskalian knew that the Lily of Anorhad is formed by the Three Feathers. Isn't it plain to us that the references to the yellow and blue areas of the Avasthic legend correspond to Lao-tzu's teachings on the yin and yang? The yin being the feminine and lunar power and the yang, the male and solar power. If we use them separately, they are pulled apart, in different directions making it easier for the Dark Riders to storm into the gap."

Sanath reiterated that the Deep Way has to be felt, experienced and imbibed and went on to explain that the course of destiny was not pre-ordained. We move in a space of uncertainties, and we are free to live our lives ignoring the fact that more powerful forces than ourselves exist though we cannot see them. Or we can chose to explore the landscape of the Deep Way to discover and master the use of these forces. There is a subtle abstract of the cosmos existing within us in complete purity, a sort of hidden map of the underlying reality existing in the form of vibrations. The Three Feathers are embedded in the human body as a network of energy channels. The wizard concluded that the proper working of the Three Feathers establishes a subtle balance between the three organs.

"Three organs?" This explanation was getting more specific; more concrete and this was what Lakshman was looking for.

"Exactly. I thought you knew this?" replied the wizard reading an expression of curiosity on their faces. "The heart, the liver, and the brain to be more precise. The heart projects the sentiment, which has the capacity to touch reality from inside.

The liver projects the attention, which has the capacity to grasp reality from outside.

The brain projects the intuition that integrates all this into our consciousness. It sounds simple enough, but integration is difficult to achieve. Students are often too agitated; their attention needs staying power to achieve the necessary fine-tuning." Inner silence is the space where higher knowledge is accessible."

"I must say, I was overwhelmed by the force of this Feather. If the blue one is as difficult to tame, I wonder how we can get it right?"

The wizard answered, "To get it right Lakshman, we need to use the positive powers of both the feathers. For instance, using this power of dynamism, Hanuman, the messenger of the Emerald King, helped in your quest."

"Perhaps, but we can't always count on the magic of the White Monkey, as was the case in Philip's castle when he emerged from the tapestry to save us. I would still like to understand more clearly what you mean by the power of the Yellow Feather. What does it look like?"

"Didn't you feel it? An enormous but temperate strength controlled by innocence and mildness. Hanuman's help brings endless dynamism, a deeper intelligence, the intuitive capacity to focus on the essential, to understand what to seek and what to avoid. A man who has mastered this feather is a man of character and determination, a man of steel. 'Steel does not move on its own,' the Lady of the Rock' used to say, but under the impulse of a magnet." Sanath paused for a while as if to give more weight to the next thought. "The custodians of the magnetic force which control the Dance of the Feathers are the scions of the House of Kalabham. If we can unearth their casket and access the lost lore of Kalabham, it would give us the key to the entire unlocking system of the seven seals. I had been doing research in this direction with the help of members of my Order and sent one of them to Uluru, Ayers Rock in Australia, but now I cannot say because I am no longer sure we are fated to unearth the caskets of all the great Houses. However we must definitely unravel the mystery of the Three Feathers."

"So Lao-tzu wanted to teach the Chinese about the magic Feathers? Maybe the most knowledgeable Chinese scholars understood the magic, they got it and this is why they are respected in the whole world for their wisdom."

"Yes Lakshmi, such was the purpose of Lao-tzu. Tao contains the dance; and the Dance of the Feather opens the Tao of Anorhad: the higher harmony of the brain. Men must use the feminine within them; care about others, use their capacity to nurture, look after the community, sustain and protect those who need support. This was the higher calling of those proficient in warfare and martial arts: commanders who cared about the welfare of their soldiers are followed; they call on the power of the yang to exert their yin in an optimal way. On the other hand, women must use the masculine within them, the yin assertion to project their qualities, and fully manifest their capacities to transform and inspire."

Sean added, "This was also what the Great Mother told us: breaking the code of the gate of passage is not just about shifting back to the other pole but the blending of the feathers, awakening the feminine within the male and vice versa."

"Yin and yang, male and female intertwined. Yes, there were references to this in the *Apocrypha Gospel of Thomas*."

Lakshmi made a mental note: she wanted to spend more time with Sean to find out about the teachings he had imbibed. "And I suppose this has nothing to do with physical inclinations nor does it mean we must undertake transsexual surgery in a specialized clinic."

Lakshman remembered disputing the insistence of a gay friend at being the next frontier of human evolution.

"Right," agreed Sean, "it's nothing to do with sexual preferences; it is much more essential; it has to do with optimally using the two hemispheres of the brain represented in the symbol of Taoism. The next synthesis is not of the flesh but of the spirit."

Sanath agreed, "Confucius was the synthesis maker, the grand architect of harmony. This is where Lao-tzu joins Confucius to build the solid foundation of Chinese philosophy. Tao reveals how the feathers work out; the triple rhythm, mingling emotions and reason, feelings and thoughts, desire and action to reach harmony and joy. The three feathers were described as the three gunas in the *Bhagavad Gita*, thousands of years back: *tamo guna, rajo guna, and sattwa guna.* It's a simple trick: if you can use them together, you achieve self-control. *Tamo guna:* use only this channel and be under the influence of the blue feather; that is, you are under the control of someone or something else. *Rajo guna:* use only the yellow one and you want to control others. *Satwa guna:* access this channel and all three work in harmony. Really, people were more sophisticated in those days. Materialism breeds such ignorance, such arrogance."

"Thank you for this, Master, it makes it clearer for me. I recall the Great Mother explaining, as Lao-tzu did, that no feather can function properly without the other. Activating one or the other unilaterally spins further one-sidedness and confrontation. When we move far away from the central channel, we cross the invisible limit between normalcy and excess. We do not even notice it. A good example of this in China was the unlikely student of Lao-tzu, Chairman Mao, who sent millions to their deaths, people who did not fit into his own dialectic schemes."

'How lucky he is to have imbibed all this directly from Her,' thought Lakshmi looking at Sean, feeling again, to her discrete shame, a tiny bite of jealousy. After all, Erilie of Eleksim had been a maiden of the Lady of the Rock and now Lidholon knew more than she did. She felt vaguely left behind and looked around for diversion from these unpleasant thoughts. But Lakshman had no such feelings. He listened to Sean, feeling congenial, comforted in this argument by the first-hand knowledge he had acquired while opening the Casket of the White feather in Iceland and Amsterdam. All pieces of the cosmic puzzle were falling perfectly into place.

The night was full of scents and rumors; the glittering cruising vessel, the Royal Chaopraya Princess, was passing by loaded with tourists, blaring out Western pop music. Coming from the opposite direction another cruiser resounded with loud Indian bhangra music. For an allegoric instant, the sounds mixed on the water in an exotic cacophony, expressing the merriment of their fun-seeking cargoes. Lakshmi pulled herself together, smiled, and remembered again how blessed she was.

Lakshman shared his quiet jubilation, "The distance in the Grand Scheme, as the Avasthas called evolution, is thus created by the space between the feathers. When they were too far apart, the Great Schism occurred. In learning to play the Game we learn the movement of synchronicity between them. Consequently man and woman achieve essential equality; society develops solidarity instead of competition. We do not destroy ecosystems; we feed them. We move away from class conflicts towards integration, from separation to synthesis. Is this not the way to understand Rousseau and real democracy? The way we can move into the Golden Age?" Lakshman was bringing the Tao of the Feathers to the field of politics. They agreed this could open a practical perspective for society.

"Mysteries were revealed in the Temple of the Buddha for a good reason. It was the *Vairocana* aspect of the Buddha that was the power to awaken the universal harmony of the cosmos. I suppose you understand that the aspects of the Buddha represent the various states of mind we can achieve through the Deep Way." The wizard smiled to tease them gently and continued, "For instance, as the *Bodhisattva Ratnasambhava*, the Buddha maintains balance in all things. When we activate his power within our brain, we come close to the White Feather. At one time, the Asians knew so much about it, but they've lost it all now, it seems. Finally, as the Buddha prophesized, it belongs to the enigma of *Maitreya* to make it tangible, universal, and accessible for all of us. The Buddha figured it out: he was the overlord of the Yellow Feather because he had mastered the properties of the Blue one. Such was the wisdom of Asia."

Noting that his interlocutors did not fully understand him, Sanath moved to his conclusion, explaining, "Siddharta conquered the Yellow Feather in his form as the *Boddhisattwa Avalokiteshwara,* where he displayed his thousands arms of compassion. This aspect manifests the power of heavenly yin, femininity at its best. It is within us all and is carried by the Blue Feather. One controls the other and vice versa. This is Tao."

"What happens now to the Yellow Feather?" asked Laksman. "Do you still have it?"

"Oh! I almost forgot," responded the wizard. "I was waiting to complete this little ceremony." His right hand foraged in the deep pocket of his white, linen jacket and extracted a silk handkerchief. He placed it on the table and opened it carefully. They all looked at the small feather. Sanath took it in the palms of his hands and softly blew it in the direction of the river. The feather twirled around in the breeze.

"Look! Look!" shouted Lakshman, jumping from his seat.

"What, what is it?" asked Sean. For the feather had disappeared into the night and he'd seen nothing.

"I ... didn't you see? I glimpsed the white shape of Hanuman! He jumped, swiftly opened his mouth and swallowed the feather but now... now, I'm not sure." Lakshman peered into the night in vain. He sat down, looking like a dejected child, embarrassed for having said something that adults cannot grasp.

"Oh I am sure you are right," said Sanath coming to his rescue with a broad grin. "This Feather belongs to no one, at least to none of us, to no human. But to him, that's another matter. The Feather will just follow its course as it always did, under the watch of the Archangel. It's that simple."

The wizard of Dagad Trikon was watching them intentsely. The Stealthstars were advancing. Perhaps the Great Mother uses them as rangers, he thought, to probe the frontiers, to crack the codes, to unveil concealed pearls of knowledge. He concluded, "When the feathers dance together, when you let the powers flow without interference, whatever is best will happen to you. Through humility, you achieve *Ta Yeou*, the possession of greatness as indicated in section fourteen of the *I Ching*, the esoteric Chinese book."

At that moment, the full moon emerged from behind the clouds, bathing them in milky light, pouring a diffuse sense of comfort upon them. Sanath said softly, "The lights of the city chase away the light of the moon, but which one is mightier? The legend is like the moonlight, for the stuff of the legend shall never die."

As if to make the point, the hanging silver laces of the black clouds moved around the moon in reverent procession, offering a dramatic backdrop above the Normandie restaurant on the top floor of the east wing of the Oriental. The night was mild, moist and enveloping, the scene beautiful. The companions felt mightily happy: on top of the world, and confident that their quest would be blessed. They could take on the world; they could do it. Sean felt that all his life experiences were converging. Lakshman was happy to have faced the pitfalls of the Yellow Feather; he now felt stronger. Lakshmi was in an uplifted mood. She had touched the magic joy again, she had felt the delight of the proximity of the White Monkey that shadowed them in the temple; but also, beyond the pangs of separation, how much she wanted, just as iron dust is attracted by the magnet, to be close once again to the Great Mother. Yet the Lady in the sari shop had told her she needed to investigate some more. "Well," she thought; "I am making progress."

"How magnificent the power of the Blue Feather must be; I wonder how it feels," she said dreamingly, looking fondly at the full moon whose invitation she had unconsciously imbibed and welcomed.

"We need to travel to England to discover that," was the quizzical response of the elder of the Hllidarendis.

CHAPTER SEVENTEEN

ACROSS THE VALLEY
OF SHADOWS

Where the companions discover the casket of the Blue Feather in dreadful circumstances and how the magic it contains takes them to an extraordinary destination.

A beam of early morning sunshine illuminated his glass of orange juice as Jonathan O'Lochan breakfasted, and with a sense of anticipation, greeted the new day. He had slept well on the flight from Washington, D.C. to Heathrow Airport, London traveling in business class with what was left of his free air miles.

The plane circled above Reading, waiting for permission to land because of the usual air traffic congestion around Heathrow. He looked down at the landscape where patches of light illuminated the ground through a fragmented bluish fog. The panorama absorbed his attention.

The scenery emitted an enchantment he could sense high up in the sky. England looked like an awakening sleeping beauty. He enjoyed the promise contained in this moment for soon he would meet Sanath and he relished the prospect of being with Lakshmi and their daughter Ananya again. Through long conversations on the Internet, he was fully informed of the events in Bangkok.

He readjusted Tracy's blanket. She was still asleep beside him in the adjacent seat and a curtain of auburn hair hid her face. Jonathan envied how easily she could sleep on a flight. He leaned against the window and enjoyed how the sun caused patches of bright color and shade to paint a fairytale countryside below him. He could see the River Thames, a castle here and there, the brown rooftops of scattered cottages, and the colored dots of early morning cars, moving like small toys along the roads. A white rectangle that seemed to be a large tent was set ablaze by the light of dawn not far from the river. The green hills rolled leisurely, caressed by the freshness of early light, and carried on their waves darker areas of copses and thickets where night still lingered. England's beauty revived memories of childhood, when he visited his maternal grandparents in the countryside. Fondly, he remembered how proud he was to ride on the stone lions that flanked the staircase descending from the terrace to the French designed garden in front of his grandfather's stately home. Back then he was the lion king, a feeling that did not last too long for life is about reality checks and packs of hyenas. But, he concluded with a flicker of a smile, life is still good.

He was completely alert and recalled the exchange he'd had the day before with his best friend Lakshman, who had shared the wonders of the Casket of the Yellow Feather. By virtue of the closeness of their bond, elements of Lakshman's experience had entered him through some sort of conscious empathy. With the emergence of the latest casket he felt again this old surge, this caffeinated resolve that his life would not be for nothing; he knew and liked the feeling. It was a will to take on life, a refusal to accept compromises and mediocrity, and the knowledge that somewhere, deep inside, a force was sustaining him to make the world a better place. After all, was he not a Stealthstar, a returned Avastha who had come back to snatch away from the clutches of rascals, all the goodness that still palpitated on this wonderful planet?

He closed his eyes and felt Lakshmi's love gently tickling him; he felt her sensing the approach of his plane. It was so good to love and to be loved by the same person. The flower in your own garden emits the most enchanting fragrance. This was going to be a good day. He stretched. Jonathan was eager to get to know Sean who had arrived the day before from Bangkok and was staying at the Marriott near Heathrow with the rest of the wizard's party. Tracy had taken a call from Lorelei just before boarding at Reagan International airport: Michael had also booked a room in the Marriott on his way back from Cape Town and Lorelei, flying in from Frankfurt, would be arriving soon after them. The good wizard would not gather this special group together without some specific purpose.

After landing and a speedy customs and immigration clearance, Jonathan and his sister hugged Michael waiting for them in the arrivals hall and they took a cab for the short drive to the Marriott. Lakshmi was standing in the lobby with Ananya when her husband arrived. He kissed the baby profusely, his wife more discreetly and in the light of Lakshmi's eyes he read more tales than poets could write. "Absence makes the heart grow fonder," they taunted each other. They were slightly disappointed to realize that Sanath was still resting in his room and that they would have to wait till the evening to see him.

They went to their rooms and later met in the restaurant. There was much to exchange and ponder. Sean was introduced to the rest of the group, Jonathan and Tracy, Michael and Lorelei, Lakshman and Lakshmi. The complicity between them bubbled up in conversation and laughter.

Sanath, carrying a copy of the *International Herald Tribune*, joined them for dinner and showed Sean a headline that shocked him. A Bangkok power broker connected to the ruling party had been found drowned in a city klong and the police suspected foul play. It was the body of the high abbot Tuchpamonporn that'd been found in the canal.

They sat around the table and celebrated the ancestral connection among them that Sanath could so clearly feel in the energy circulating in the room.

Lakshmi asked the wizard, "When Lidholon was revealed in Bangkok, you said the team was complete but one of my sisters was missing. We were three sisters of Eleksim who joined the Sheravalian Guard, three to fight the devils: Erilie and Esitel have been found. Evenyl was with Lidholon in the last days of the fortress but we lost her; perhaps she did not incarnate again?"

"Perhaps she did and perhaps is now listening carefully."

"Oh my goodness, yes, it's Tracy, isn't it?" Lakshman shouted joyously, turning to his friend's sister as Sanath nodded. These O'Lochan Stealthstars, luckier than others, had managed a group landing so that they could comfort each other through the proximity of family bonds. When this happy commotion was over for the benefit of those who'd missed it, they asked Sean to again describe his time travel back to the burning of the rock citadel. Sean, in the re-telling, was now able to see a faint resemblance between the traits of Evenyl in his dream and the features of Tracy. While sharing his recollections, he was moved by strong emotions in seeing how deeply Tracy was affected by the account. When Sean narrated the episode of the reading of the *Kavach*, Sanath explained that the protection of the *Kavach* was the reason Evenyl had never been found by the demons. Sean again saw her delight when Etakir reappeared and joined their small group in the den of the Sand

Keeper after the battle. Tracy, listening intensely, felt goose bumps over her entire body.

They stayed at the hotel overnight and despite the jetlag no one went to bed early; there was too much to catch up on. The next morning, the English member of Sanath's Order was waiting for them. They immediately sensed his quiet dignity. He was thin, had slightly curly white hair, and his aquiline profile underlined a noble face softened by a mildness in the eyes that reminded Lorelei of Kheto the African. He introduced himself as Ian Ildemar and a member of Sanath's Order. Lorelei acknowledged the natural elegance that seemed to belong to all members of the Order. She asked politely, "Are you the English Hllidarendi?"

He responded with a twinkle of humor, "British if you please because, I have the good fortune of being Scottish. I am thrilled to meet you all." Turning to Sanath, he said, "Please, Master, follow me. Everything has been arranged as per your suggestions. Our search was long and sometimes painful but it finally bore fruit; three days ago we retrieved what we believe to be an Avasthic casket, possibly the one that had reached the shores of the Western islands, the one that was in the custody of Merlin. However when we approach it our limbs become heavy like lead and we almost froze."

"Releasing the Yellow Feather creates an imbalance in the cosmos that must be corrected by unearthing the one that complements it, the Casket of the Blue Feather. The planning of these two events has to be precise."

The wizard turned to his companions, "We have no time to lose, the moment is dictated by the opening of the Casket of the Cross and though none of us was involved in it, its content is now filling the ether. We saw it in the temple. I guess you can easily understand; it takes all three to manifest the Lily of Anorhad. The sixth seal has been broken and the narrow gate is open. Let us clarify what it is that we really found. Our Stealthstars may now risk opening it. But I must warn you. This feather carries its own dangers, different but no less terrible than those you approached when you discovered the yellow one. This zone is the one that opens on the collective subconscious that is directly connected to hell."

"Speaking of which Master, please talk to us again about the Riders. The more we know them; the better we face them."

"You are right Lakshman. As we have advanced deep into the Dark Age, the Riders are no longer a mystery. People even make movies, thinking them to be creatures of fantasy, but they do not know their nature nor realize their effect.

"Listen please and listen well.

"Lust is the first, creeping and tenacious; it takes away freedom, auspiciousness, and the freshness of attention.

"Anger rides second, fierce and impetuous; it destroys peace within and without.

"Greed charges with great speed, pushes one to grab, to own and possess but denies true satisfaction and fulfillment.

"Attachment ensnares as a creeper around a tree and takes away the space in which love can live.

"Jealousy, the perfidious green witch, moves in a sneaky way, it prevents enjoying the merits of others and achieving unity.

"Vanity in its gallop takes you into a labyrinth of mirrors and creates artificiality, a delusion that hides true identity.

"Six enemies of the soul, riding together if they can to bring human consciousness to the demons.

"But Pride, the seventh, dearest to Thanatophor, is the mightiest of all and the bane of the mighty; it is the enemy of the Self because it imprisons one in selfishness. Together, all seven multiply and generate their likeness in the minds they can penetrate."

"Indeed Master, there is no mystery here. Formerly, these Riders had Sanskrit and Latin names; it seems that they have been around as long as our race existed. And yet we do not seem to make them out, or to recognize them. That is the mystery and the reason they multiplied. But still, I do not quite understand why you make a difference between the six enemies of the soul and the seventh, the enemy of the Self?

"The six enemies of the soul prevent us from realizing our full potential, which is to reach our destination: the heaven within us. But the seventh, pride, replaces this destination by another one. The Self, the heavens within, is our true destination. But, pride replaces the Self by the ego. With pride, the creature takes itself for its own end. Thus, further evolution is not possible."

"Yet, as you said, they tend to ride together don't they? How do we fight them?"

"They are called the Dark Riders because they roam in the valley of shadows, they cannot gallop in the light. The two Avasthic weapons have been revealed, and they are now within the grasp of everyone and can equip the minds of those who seek their protection. The Sadhan shields the attention within the safe space of meditative contemplation. The route of the Riders is blocked. They cannot pass. The use of the Glorfakir sword can be turned within, and this practice is called introspection. When the focus of the inner glance is powerful enough and focuses on a Rider that has already entered within us, it reveals the Rider in its cloak of deceit. The foe loses strength and finally dissolves because it cannot stand the light of knowledge. When, however, the Glorfakir is turned outside, it allows us to see, without reacting, the aggression of the Dark Riders that are projected from the minds of others, and when we do not react to it, their effect cannot enter us. It is through our reactivity only that we give to outside aggression the right to affect us."

"How true," said Sean. "I remember one day, I was in struggling with my troubles, and the Great Mother simply guided me with these words, 'Don't react, just see!'"

Ian nodded in sympathy at Sean's comment. "With these warnings there is nothing more to say. Master Sanath wants us to move on; and this is why he gathered us here. Let's do it. I am sorry you have no more time to rest, but I shall now take you to our destination. For some reason, the casket must be opened at the location where it was found. The day will be very full because we may indeed have another important errand later in the evening. A stretch limousine is waiting for us."

Clearly the pace of the quest was accelerating. Finding the Casket of the White Feather under the Icelandic glacier had been such a difficult and spectacular venture. And now, to their surprise, the casket of the mysterious Blue Feather was simply waiting for them.

Squeezing in, they boarded the limousine. The mood was light and full of expectations. On the road to London, Sanath leaned back and, looking at the sky, enjoyed a state of quiet jubilation. He turned to Ian, the Hllidarendi of the Western Islands, "Have you unveiled, dear Ian, the subtle qualities of these islands?"

"What do you mean?"

"I have traveled far and wide and everywhere the state of meditation is of the same nature, but in certain places I discover delicate nuances, shades and differences."

"It would seem that there is only one state of consciousness in the Deep Way…"

"… but it has different coefficients. Let me give some examples. For instance, when I land in India I am greeted by the smell of its earth and a deep silence, despite many sounds and noises; I feel lighter already at the airport and, when I reach Haridwar, bathing in the River Ganga is like entering a flow of blessedness. When I meditated in the basement of the Basilica of the Nativity in Bethlehem, there was an adorable presence, a feeling of sacredness; I was touched by so soft a grace, the sense of a delightful and blessed innocence.

And then again, when I visited the Topkapi museum in Istanbul, I went to the chamber where they keep the objects that had belonged to the messenger of Allah. There were many objects, but none affected me. But, when I stopped before the glass case where the sword of the Prophet was kept, it was a different matter. I sensed the vastness of a rumbling sea within; I was completely filled by the rise of majestic power, a sensation that is the hallmark of the Daskalian Masters.

You should come one day to the ridges of the Himalayas. When I was meditating in front of Mount Sagarmata, a long time back, a lofty feeling of vacuity could shelter the joy that pervaded me. I was like a pearl, and the nature around was my oyster. If I meditate here in England, once I dissolve the lingering confusion, the state is of delightful coziness, comforting, almost like an enveloping holiness. And so it goes on my dear. The ocean is one but it contains much variety. Can you feel it?"

"Yes Master, at times I am blown into the heavens and at times I struggle. It is not easy working in London but may we all one day visit the world and drink at the everlasting beauty of its secret sources."

The driver had played the *Vespro della beata Vergine* by Claudio Monteverdi. Sanath looked now very far away and the passengers respected the silence of this lonely, grand old man.

They crossed the Thames and traveled south. As they were nearing Clapham, the limousine dropped them in front of an old house in Chelsham Road. It was a dilapidated, three-storied house of a dirty-grey-brownish color, dating back from the time of the Industrial Revolution. A moribund tree in the small front garden testified to poor shape of the property. They pushed open the creaking gate and Ian opened the door. Through a narrow hallway, they entered a large room at the back of the house. The house had been uninhabited for years, and the earthen floor was littered with piles of dirt, shovels, and wooden planks, and to the right side, a large rectangular hole in the ground.

"This is where we unearthed the casket," indicated Ian. "This room has a particular feeling to it, as if it had been occupied upon a time by tenants who knew the Deep Way."

On a solitary table, they saw an object that immediately filled them with awe: it was an Avasthic casket in a shiny dark blue alloy. It was of a circular shape with a delicate silver trident engraved on the center of the lid.

"Congratulations Ian. After centuries of careful research, we managed to locate this object. Lord Ichwaril of Eleksim on a winged horse first brought it to these western islands. The seven fairies that guard the seven sources of the River Thames, up country, near Cheltenham, were keeping watch over it. On their advice, Merlin buried the casket downstream, not far from the river. He did so on the day after the fateful battle between King Arthur and the felon Mordred. The son of the king was under the influence of the witch Mokolo who had taken the form of Morgan. She stirred up his jealousy and hatred for his father.

Let us sit on these blankets and settle down. I shall request Lakshmi to open the chest."

Laksmhi's heart missed a beat at the wizard's invitation, and she glanced furtively at her husband for they understood each other well and shared the same malaise. The reference to Arthur was painful to both of them. The story of Lancelot of the Lake and Guinevere was a lingering wound in their common past. To carry in your bones, the legacies of a doomed love that brought down the fellowship of the Knights of the Round Table was not a pleasant memory. Seeing how scared Lakshmi was, Lakshman wanted to encourage her. Trying to hide her embarrassment, she responded,

"Master, I am surprised; isn't Lakshman the one appointed to open the caskets?"

"Pain cannot heal when left hidden. Sometimes to conquer the past we need to open the lid that covers it," responded the wizard. "Besides, this is the casket of the Blue Feather. It must be opened by a woman; the feather for the blue zone should reveal the feminine side of the force."

There was no hiding from the wizard. Lakshmi looked at Tracy and Lorelei as if to draw strength from her Avastha sisters and waited for a moment. She studied the casket for some time and opened it hesitantly. Following a ritual by now familiar to them they closed their eyes and held their breath.

Tracy felt the pangs of Lakshmi without knowing the cause. Her attention moved to the back of her head which now felt like a subterranean domain. Many corridors and cavities linked her brain to obscure and cloudy realms. She traveled in the network of nerves but was soon carried to an unknown place, a newfound inhospitable realms where she sensed she was not alone. She felt a cape of lead falling on her, felt increasingly paralyzed and, in the moment, her attention sensed the approach of danger. With all her strength, she recalled her dream in Georgetown and the sensation of anguish was immediately interrupted. The words of the Goddess in her dream brought her back to herself and to the room in which she was now sitting.

Lakshman had a similar experience. His attention was located in the entrance hall of the crystal dome of Anorhad, but it very soon moved to a place whose symmetry with his previous vision could not be missed: the rows of teeth, the same organic matter…he was again in the mouth of the first dragon he had briefly visited, a great, dark blue beast containing the past. This time he could not exit but was sucked into the dragon's arteries, filled with colliding images of people of a past age. He followed a tunnel draped with spiders' webs that announced an ominous presence. As he fell into a hole he saw a bat hanging over him, slowly opening its wings. He experienced fear and, at the end of the tunnel, someone was feeding on that fear. His only escape was to open his eyes, and he did so. He found himself back with his companions who had still their eyes closed. Only a brief moment had elapsed since Lakshmi had opened the casket.

She turned to Sanath and said, "It is practically empty, Master, there is only a small scroll." Sanath instructed her to read it aloud and she complied. The brief text surprisingly written in old English characters read, "*Walk across the street and enter the cottage on the opposite side.*"

Without a word, they followed Sanath, who'd headed for the narrow entrance hall.

Sean exclaimed: "We are trapped; we cannot exit."

They hastily retreated for a dense spider's web now sealed the entire entrance of the house with the except for a small free space just above the floor. An enormous spider was crouched in the upper right corner, its body a sinister black and violet, its legs a dirty color somewhere between yellow and orange. All of a sudden the house seemed even more derelict, darker, more inhospitable, and now freezing cold.

Lakshman shrugged, but he preferred fighting the spider here rather than in his brain.

"What is this?" asked Lorelei with shocked revulsion.

"We have landed in a nightmare," stuttered Lakshmi.

Sanath observed, "This doesn't start too well. Something did happen as we opened the casket; is this old Merlin's mischief? We have definitely been thrown deep into the blue zone. We are trapped by an offspring of Arakna, the witch of paralysis."

"What shall we do?" asked Michael. "Should we try to sneak through the opening at the bottom?"

"I wouldn't try," answered Sanath cautiously. "Look at the web carefully. It carries glue that is very sticky, but it has other interesting properties too. I don't smoke, but I always carry matches." While they hurried to prepare torches from wooden sticks, cloth, and paper that were lying around, the wizard commented, while keeping the spider under close watch,

"This happens when we are caught in the tunnels of the past. Arakna casts a fearful spell on those who are imprisoned there by the effect of their own mistakes or by bonds of old emotions and attachments. She is one of the main operators of Thanatophor in the blue territories; but the Glorfakir sword can defeat the spider."

Sean stared at three dark shapes hanging in the northern corner. "These are no spiders," he thought, and looking intently he realized they were bats. Restlessness and anxiety surged through him. A combination of guilt, depression, and despair recalled the nausea of feelings left by the harrowing experiences of the worst moments he went through in the last days of the Avastha desert fortress.

"There is another one!" Lorelei pointed at a spider on the floor before the exit door. Simultaneously Lakshmi exclaimed with alarm, "Sorcery! Look at the ceiling, it has become darker!"

The dusty beige ceiling of the living room was turning dark-grey and seemed to palpitate. It had all the appearance of another web in the making, inhabited by a yet invisible but clearly hostile presence. Michael and Sean lighted their torches. Lorelei shouted, "Sanath, behind you!"

In the days of the Rock, the Aulyas had recognized that Elkaim Ekamonon, the Sand Keeper, was the one among the paladins of the Goddess who knew hell best. He had mastered most of the cardinal works of the Avasthic library and, as one of the warring Aulyas, he had also a good grasp of the *Bibliotheca Diabolica*; something even Agnorth did not know.

The wizard turned quickly as a third giant spider, emerged out of nowhere, a few inches away from his legs. Pointing at the beast with his right index finger, Sanath, the Sand Keeper shouted in a terrible voice, "By the fire of Bhairawa, freeze!" The torches lighted suddenly with a bright yellow fire. The spider instantly stopped, shriveled, and desiccated from the inside.

In a low voice Sanath commented, "I know they'll start multiplying, they always do. We need the fire, so I tuned into the Archangel Michael. I'll explain later. We are ready it seems; quick, quick, let's get going."

Now was not the time for discussion. Michael and Sean put the flames of their makeshift torches under the web, which quickly caught fire. Sean, shaking his torch, caught the spider before the entrance door as it moved laterally and with a lightening speed pierced the wriggling beast with the tip of a burning stick. With a swift blow Michael caught the other spider as it tried to flee up the wall. They rushed past the mess, without daring to look at the wriggling remnants of the frightening insects.

They pushed open the door and, with immense relief, found themselves in the street. It was a pleasant and sunny day. But a further surprise awaited them.

A carriage drawn by four horses was standing before the tree, the foliage of which was now magnificent and the rows of houses on Chelsham Road had disappeared. They could not understand how they now found themselves in a leafy garden suburb. And how was it that the street was now cobbled?

Looking to the north they saw ancient timber yards alongside the Thames, and to the south, rows of poplar trees. In the immediate vicinity of the house, there were only a few buildings surrounded by open fields, market gardens, and marshes, and, opposite the road, was a row of solid red brick houses. The domicile with the number thirteen on the opposite side of the street was a Georgian residence on three floors plus a basement.

Baffled by the changed scenery, they ventured to cross the street, as enjoined by the Avasthic scroll, when a party of four people exited and walked to an awaiting carriage.

They wore cloaks, knee breeches and wigs, dressed as gentlemen from the turn of the nineteenth century. Curiously, they appeared not to see Sanath's party. Although the Stealthstars were at a distance, they could hear their conversation. They were obviously talking about the occupants of the house they had just left,

"He is gratified to have moved here and seems to greatly enjoy his garden. He already planted a fig tree and a grape arbor. This area of Surrey, south of Westminster Bridge is now being developed. The Archbishop of Canterbury owns most of it and resides sometimes down the lane at Lambeth Palace; His Grace intends to make the most of his estates."

"Maybe, my dear," responded the second Londoner walking with a silver topped walking stick, "but I would be surprised that this rural Lambeth Vale will bring our friend to his senses. I find him amiable, but even the initiated ones can scarcely understand his poems, and I dare not describe his drawings. There are elements of genius, I confess, but he is evidently insane, suffering from the vapors of self-delusion…"

" …But he is so gentlemanly and full of genuine dignity though without a penny. You must admit he is a gifted artist, a triumphant engraver although he goes sometimes further than good taste suggests he should," intervened the third member of the party. "I find him to have a most singular mind, with a remarkable combination of mystical ravings and great mental powers…"

"He is a decided lunatic and an inspired poet but he does not seem to know how to sell his art," concluded the fourth one. "Yet, Wordsworth was surprised when a well respected gentleman spoke highly of him, at a dinner given by Lady Caroline Lamb last Saturday. He told Sir Joshua Reynolds that his engravings are of the highest merit, extravagant, and sublime, and that…"

The conversation became inaudible as they boarded the carriage. Jonathan said, "This landscape, the costumes, this conversation: we're in a different time!"

Sanath commented pensively, "I think this is very promising."

CHAPTER EIGHTEEN

RETURN TO LAMBETH VALE

Where, in another century, Sanath and his companions meet with an Archangel who came down from the heavens to be like one of us, and how they discover that he is one of the game changers of history.

rossing the street and a couple of centuries, the companions followed Sanath into the Georgian house, surprised to find themselves on such a strange itinerary, in such a strange environment. It was not unlike traveling through time that had brought some of them from Delphi in Greece to the Temple of Maat and the basin of Vaikuntha, following the opening of the Casket of the Wheel.

On the ground floor, they found two square rooms of generous proportions with many roomy cupboards and walls, elegantly wood-paneled to a meter height. A marble mantelpiece adorned a spacious fireplace. A stairwell led down to a back door, which opened on to a long garden.

They entered a paneled studio, encumbered by a range of artist's and craftsman's tools. There were oilstones, pots of wax, candles and a magnifying glass, racks of gravers, burnishers, etching needles and hammers, tools of the engraver's trade. Strong smells of soaps and turpentine to clean the ink and *aqua fortis* to etch the copper mixed in the air. The bulkiest object was a heavy wooden rolling-press with its great arms for pulling the plate beneath, a shelf beneath holding pots of ink. Cupboards overflowed with thin sheets of copper and expensive handmade paper. Dirty rags for wiping off excess ink were scattered on the floor. Everything seemed to have its purpose in this admirable chaos. The temperature of the room was rather cool, and they felt it as a pleasant freshness within themselves.

There was a consistency in the effect of opening the caskets, the fluidity of time and space. The legend was taking the Stealthstars into a continuum that unfolded into another dimension, where every episode had its own appointed role.

They crossed the studio and reached a small living room. The personage who was clearly the master of the house was wearing a worn out high collar coat with odd lapels and a white shirt. His graying hair receded from a peak on his domed forehead. Under the arched eyebrows, the piercing eyes were striking, gently inquisitive. A wide mouth and round chin expressed a mix of kindness and resolve. He was sipping a cup of tea and conversing with a woman and a male friend who had stayed behind.

None of them noticed the group of Stealthstars, who stood in a corner of the room, who it turn did not register how odd it was that they took up so little space and received so little attention. Sanath seemed transfixed by the appearance of the lord of the house and whispered to his companions, "The blessings of the Avasthas forefathers are with you! This is what I guessed. You are very lucky indeed. Behold the prince of the Blue Feather. Oh, am I glad to meet him again?"

The gentleman who had thus enthused the wizard vehemently addressed his visitor, "My dear captain it is about God, God's glory, my friend: what else is there to do? Do you understand?

Does the rain have a father? Who fathers the drops of dew?
From whose womb comes the ice? Who gives birth to the frost from the heavens
When the waters become hard as stone, when the surface of the deep is frozen?
Can you bind the beautiful Pleiades? Can you loosen the cords of Orion?
Can you bring forth the morning stars in their seasons or lead out the bear with its cubs?"

"He is quoting from the *Bible*, the *Book of Job*," said Sanath. The visitor responding to the name of Captain John Gabriel Stedman now addressed the lady, the wife of the tenant. She was wearing a tired old dress, reclining affectionately on the high back of her husband's chair. In her youth, she had been a lovely brunette but the toils of life and poverty were starting to show on her traits.

"How fortunate you are, Mrs. Blake, to find yourself in the company of this great man."

"I have very little of Mr. Blake's company; he is always in paradise."

"No Kate, it is paradise which is always with me," responded William Blake with a grin. The companions of Sanath realized that they were looking at the poet, artist and engraver whose visionary work gained fame long after his death.

"I am chagrined to hear that my *Marriage of Heaven and Hell* is misunderstood by those who say I treat good and evil indifferently. There are errors and mistakes that beget evil but judging and condemning beget more of it. The marriage takes place because the heavens are coming down to help us out of this hell. I said that God becomes as we are that we may be as He is. The marriage in this case, my dear Stedman, is of divine mercy and forgiveness, and it dissolves the fruits of evil."

"Forgiveness for the Lily of Anorhad, the gate to paradise," Jonathan whispered to his wife. Blake's words comforted them. Guinevere and Lancelot, somewhere in their subconscious, still needed to reach beyond a mix of unease and guilt to be washed pure again by sweet mercy. The invisible group of seven intensely followed the exchanges in the engraver's parlor as he continued with a fiery outburst, "The clerk, the lawmaker and the priest, the state, the tribunal and the religions, all plot together to impose on us their reasonable unity. Thinking is not the solution. True oneness cannot be achieved by the mind. Reason did not comprehend Jesus and cannot comprehend unity. The mind separates and shall shrink in its own iron chains.

With firing limbs and flaming hair, the spiraling column of delightful energy will rise in splendor, like a blazing furnace, and make all things new so that unity may be restored. Its vivid brilliancy alone, my dear Stedman, can generate what Swedenborg described as the Great Man, the advent of our own divine humanity, the one God in all, and all conscious in the cosmic One."

His attention captured by Blake, Lakshman whispered, "The delightful energy? Does he also belong to the Lady of the Rock?" But Captain Stedman obviously didn't have such insights and asked, "This rising energy you describe, Mr. Blake, is it the French Revolution? Some said in the house of Mr. Thomas Butt that you sympathize with it. You should be careful in expressing such views for here in England these beliefs are held to be seditious, against God, King, and country."

"The French? Diderot, Voltaire, d'Alembert are trying perhaps, but I don't think they shall succeed. They trust their brains too much; I hesitate to trust the French."

Blake seemed oblivious to the fact that Stedman was not quite following him. He continued in a visionary mood, "I cherish the fair luminous mists from where emerge my dreams and parables. My visions and my imagination are reality, not these wretched states and shadows that fill their world of toiling. He brought his joy to us, and therefore, I repeat, God becomes as we are that we may be as He is. We are coexistent within God, members of the divine body; we are all partakers of the divine nature. But this is discovered through the immortal heart, not the fragmented brain. It is wrong to try explaining this to the rational faculty. Socrates and Dante knew this well."

"And so did Eve in Eden," Tracy noted, totally fascinated. "Experience, feelings, this is the invitation of the Goddess, to dare taste the fruit of the tree of knowledge." But no one paid attention to Tracy, as they single-mindedly concentrated on Blake's words, who continued, "The heavens are here, I told them in poems but no one can hear or see," and he began to sing loudly, his eyes brightening, with a strange but beautiful melody:

"My eyes more and more
Like a sea without Shore
Continue expanding,
The heavens commanding,
Till the Jewels of Light,
Heavenly men beaming Bright,
Appeared as One Man
Who complacent began
My limbs to unfold
In his beams of bright gold;
Like dross purged away.
All my mire and my clay.
Then those in Great Eternity met in the Council of God,
As one man, for contracting their Exalted senses
They behold multitude, or Expanding they behold as one,
As One Man all the universal family.

"Mister Blake, this is a mighty song."

Catherine looked at her husband with an innocent, adoring glance that erased the tiredness and strain from her face. Sanath muttered to himself, "This song...he is spelling out for us the riddle of Anor."

After a pause, Blake concluded, "You see, my good Captain, it is through the spirit that we can access the great mystery that is now in the making. The next millennium is not far away and when it shall come, what was sealed shall be opened, what was hidden shall be revealed."

Stedman nodded though visibly clueless and Blake continued, "This is the secret of my art. I have no earthly fame, and many call me a madman. Those with eyes that could see my spiritual glory have not come yet. But I am quite contented. I rejoice in the exceeding joy that is always poured out on my spirit. By the performance of spiritual acts I keep the mirth of the spirit dancing. The expansion of our spirit will manifest, in a hymn of roaring joy, the birth of the Great Man."

"What does he mean?" whispered Jonathan to his wife; what does he mean by spirit?"

"Truth, Consciousness, Bliss! Connecting with it at last, drinking the feel of it! Blake invokes the Holy Grail within our head, the Gift; all that was revealed to us in unfolding the legend of Dagad Trikon. Look at the two objects on this circular table, a small blue feather in a velvet box and this antique cup. I guess this is Sangreal, the cup of the myth. It is with him." Lakshmi continued with a pressing tone, "Can't you see it? He is fully connected with the heavens; this is why he seems a stranger in this lower world. Look at the aura around his body; he is emitting a fairy light."

Yes, the light was indeed defining the dimension of this room. The light of several candleholders mingled in the light emitted by Blake. And in this light, they saw the darkness, including, most unexpectedly, the darkness within them. This wasn't pleasant but clarity was useful.

"Much of our burden is stored within, it's better we start noticing it," whispered the wizard.

The light from the heavens is too strong for mortals, and they can feel rejected when they are not prepared. Lakshman touched his loneliness, reaching the buried wound of being an orphan, born but not loved, afraid of losing the connection with the Lady of the Rock. Lakshmi had loved to doom and death and remained frightened of her capacity for passion. Would love burn like a fire that should have cooked the food but instead had engulfed the house?

Sean and Michael observed how their bravery was a sheath of willpower cast above the secret anguish of failing their destiny, a wound the two esquires had carried since the fall of the Rock.

Jonathan similarly spotted a floating tedium for existence, struggling with a sense of his own meaninglessness. At this moment, he even remembered his fondness for Nietzsche and Jean-Paul Sartre.

A restless Tracy remembered the ease with which Thanatophor had approached her in her dream. Lorelei went back millennia to live again the dread she had experienced as Esitel, when she felt raped by the malicious eye of the demon in the opthalir, the seeing jewel that belonged to the witchcraft toolbox of Belzebseth.

Above all the Stealthstars were carrying the fear to live for nothing. They deciphered together their collective psychological portrait. It is not fun when the past seems to have been much greater than the present, no fun to have been the first born when you aren't the first any more and don't quite know what it means to be the last. Because they were made of the stuff that forged brave men and women, the Stealthstars had high expectations of themselves, often squeezed between heroism in the making and nothingness in waiting. All these emotions, hidden in the blue zone were suddenly overwhelming because revealing the baggage of the fallen Avasthas.

But this is where the shadows were misleading them because in the smoky corridors of the past, emotions get corroded, twisted or distorted, hiding the graceful nature and comforting benevolence of the Blue Feather.

What the present and the coming moments were going to offer would outshine the sorrows and uplift them way beyond their conditionings. The aura in the room was liberating, bringing lightness and mirth. Distinguishing these moods with the beam of their attention, the Stealthstars spotted sentiments in their hideout, setting their inner eye on the psychic states that were stored in the hidden corners of their emotionality. This was therapeutic. The heaviness lurking around the Blue Feather being slowly exposed began to dissolve in them, burnt in that light which converged from the artist and the small feather. Weight, darkness and sorrow dissipated like shadows above a dancing fire. Being thus liberated, they experienced something like elation, the fury of joy.

"Behold the Master of light and fire," whispered Sanath to his party, "he is truly foremost amongst the great angels, the killer of devils, dragons and of Arakna. His sword is of the fire in which the Glorfakir was forged."

Yet there was such meekness and bonhomie in Blake that they could not discern in him the hint of a formidable angelic warrior! They watched the scene in sheer fascination. The animated conversation between Blake and the captain continued for a while. They discussed the engraving plates that Blake would prepare for Stedman's book. As the conversation ended, the visitor effusively thanked Blake for sharing his visions and insights and took his leave. Catherine Blake, likewise, left the studio for the kitchen.

Alone, Blake gazed at an abstract, unfocussed horizon then turned slowly and trained his large and brilliant black eyes on the corner of the room where Sanath and the Stealthstars were huddled together. The Stealthstars had been accustomed to see without being seen and it came as a shock when, suddenly, they realized they were seen. They felt naked.

Blake had turned his attention on them and was watching them attentively. His appearance was now exuding a profound dignity, and the group was even more intimidated when Blake addressed them.

"You are coming from the future aren't you? I do converse with spirits from the past, with Celtic druids, with William Wallace of Scotland

and his enemy Edward I, and with the Earl of Warwick, tutor of Edward IV. I have had much intercourse recently with interesting characters, but I do not peer into the future, which is the province I leave to Gabriel.

A light of contentment dawned and danced in his wide eyes and he continued excitedly,

"I am highly delighted to recognize a mentor of our race; if I am not mistaken this is the noble Aulya Elkaim Ekamonon, the wizard coming from the vanished Avastha kingdom blessed is its memory. Am I right to understand that he is bringing with him scions of the primordial race? Would those lovely beings that graced the earth before the fall of the ancient world now come to visit me from the future? How very odd," he said.

With profound reverence, Sanath, with joined hands, bowed towards William Blake and his companions promptly followed. It wasn't often, they thought, that the great wizard would bow to anyone. Sanath's voice was charged with emotion, "In those days I called you my friend but I did not really know you. Please forgive me." His greeting became unexpectedly solemn:

"Obeisance to the saint patron of the Western Islands,
Obeisance to the carrier of Uragni, the mystical fire
Obeisance to the wielder of the Flaming Sword,
Obeisance to the Dragon Killer,
Obeisance to the prince of the Blue Feather,
Obeisance…"

William Blake, his mouth open, looked baffled at this ceremonial address but he now interrupted Sanath vigorously. "No, no, stop this! Not here, not now."

Sanath interrupted his litany at once, and Blake continued, "These are things behind the veil, things that should not been uttered when I am still in the faint shadow of my natural life, in this prison of matter. I have not yet returned to my kingdom nor have I retrieved my weapons of burning gold. What is your errand in my humble house, Master of the Hllidarendis?"

"O magnificent one, the opening of the Avasthic Casket of the Blue Feather revealed you to us, so that we may understand the fate of the prophecy left behind by the gentle folk of the Avasthas."

Blake laughed. "O, yes, I remember now: Merlin must have played a trick. He emptied the casket of its content and left this note, so you would come to me." He laughed again.

At this, even Sanath looked shocked. He grumbled, "So this is then what old Merlin was up to," and turning to Blake asked, "My Lord why did he do such a thing?"

"The elders of the first race who sent this casket, stored in it the art of loving and being loved because love is what moves this world, the essence of our deepest emotions. To know whether it would be safe to release its content to the humans, Merlin secretly prepared a few drops of an elixir, derived from the formula contained in the casket and served it to the Queen. You know the rest of the story," he said, looking with fondness at Jonathan and Lakshmi. "The genie jumped out of the bottle and the love between Lancelot of the Lake and Guinevere sealed the fate of Camelot. The quest of the knights for the Holy Grail was foiled."

Jonathan and Lakshmi felt like shrinking in misery. Would this past life of doomed love always haunt them? He sensed their dejection and gazed at them with great sweetness:

"The raw power of this Blue Feather is desire. In these days of fallen angels, no human, except Galahad, had the purity to handle the content of this casket, and this is why the search failed. The time was not ripe yet. Arthur's companions failed and so did those who came after them. Merlin was mischievous, of course, but you two are not guilty."

It was up to Blake to reveal the enigma of Eleksim; looking straight at Lakshmi, he added, "It was your House, Eleksim, who was keeping the protocol of love and this is why you had to face the love that hurts and suffer the hurdles of love through the great corrosion of this Iron Age. My dear fallen angels, all of you have one thing to do today and this is to get up, arise!"

Gesturing at the circular table that had caught Lakshmi's eye Blake informed them, "Joseph of Arimathea brought to the shores of Albion the goblet that contained the holy blood of Christ. Since the Middle Ages, some called the Grail 'Sangreal,' meaning 'royal blood'. These islanders are the custodians, but they do not know. The purity that is still in them, even though hidden and covered, remains alive but buried in their hearts. Tell them to awaken, tell them that Albion is the heart, the immortal heart that can receive the nectar of the Grail."

The damsels of Eleksim were extremely moved. Lakshmi finally realized that mistakes are not fatal. She felt forgiven, resurrected by the words of the prophet who had the power to send her back to the intensity of feelings she had experienced in Vaikuntha and the Delhi sari shop. The mercy flowing from Blake was telling her that she and Jonathan had passed the trial of Eleksim, how to love in full innocence and security. Sensing the release of tension in her, Jonathan relaxed immediately too.

Tracy recalled her vision in a glorious flash, "Yes, women can bring men to the Grail when they accept the glory of their womanhood, assuming

themselves as those portals of love that bring purity to the hearts of men."
Lorelei felt light, floating in a golden dust, bathed in a mellow love.

The genial artist paused and suddenly looked frail and tired, a trace of helplessness in his voice, "But when my dreams are over, this world is still with me, and I must bear it. Satan is every day increasing the distance between man and the love of his Creator. Farewell now, friends of this long journey, you must leave me. As I see you, I start receiving glimpses of the age you come from, and I fear the great labors of Urizen have molded your world. I do not seek to venture there."

He looked with a tender admiration at the Stealthstars. "Gabriel had told me in this very parlor that the children of light of the ancient race would return because of a higher calling and lo, I see you have come. I daresay, such a thing never happened before. Farewell, my shooting stars. There is great joy among the angels that you became again dwellers upon earth. And remember, children, the love you come from: live your light in merriment and fun."

Leaving Blake was heart-wrenching. He was so noble, the Stealthstars wanted to reach out to the chained spiritual giant, to console him somehow, but they were released by his last words. The vision blurred, and they took their leave in the bluish mist of a few tears. As they came out of the red-brick house, they found themselves in front of the house on Chelsham Road, back in the twenty-first century, with Ian and the limousine waiting for them.

They turned and saw that Blake's house did not really exist; they had, in fact, come out of what used to be the dilapidated house behind the moribund tree. But that house in Chelsham Road had now been restored, infused with a new life and youth, its facade refreshed.

They halted, silent and profoundly moved, still deeply under the spell of Blake. They were shaken to part from someone they had met for a brief moment yet someone they felt they had loved for so long. The experience of his presence had been so uplifting that, now back within their physical bodies, they felt incredibly light, as if their feet were not touching the ground.

Sanath observed in a low voice, "Have you noticed how our weight seems reduced? In his challenge of matter, the angelic Blake overcomes the law of gravity and we partake of him for a brief moment."

Ian too could sense the lingering majesty of the moment. Without saying a word he invited them with a gesture to board the limousine.

They drove north. Lakshman looked at his watch. Hardly a few minutes had elapsed since they had entered the derelict house at Chelsham

Road, and this could mean only one thing: time had stopped as soon as they had opened the Casket of the Blue Feather. The wizard observed, matter-of-factly, "You can travel through time only where you step out of it."

"What a giant! There was an air of inspiration about him; he did look like his portrait by Thomas Phillips," observed Jonathan. Still profoundly moved but slightly incredulous, he asked Sanath, "Excuse me please, but there was something about the way you addressed him? Why 'dragon slayer' and 'patron of England?'"

"Saint Michael, Bhairava or Saint George, yes, the man you saw was the passing expression in the human race of that heavenly warrior who, through millennia, has fought Thanatophor, the one that Blake calls Satan. In entering the process of human existence, he accepted the loss of his own angelic splendor. This is, I submit, a poignant tribute to the compassion the denizens of heavens have for this greatly confused race. The fact that the leader of the angelic hosts came into our race as a penniless but genial artist to help us expresses his incredible generosity and mercy."

"So," said Lakshman, "with a touch of incredulity, "you are saying that Blake was not a human being?

"He was, and in so doing he took upon himself some of the weaknesses of a human being. At the same time, he was much more than that. And aren't we all in the end, if the end can be achieved?" Sanath responded in his typical elliptic way. "Blake's poetic and artistic world shows a fiery splendor. Likewise, the Archangel Michael who patrols the blue zone is represented on Brazilian paintings or Russian icons bearing a sword of fire. It all fits nicely. I cannot really start to explain the world of the Avatars."

"Avatar? So he was an incarnation of the higher world, isn't he? What exactly did Blake do for us?"

"He transformed history with a poet's rhymes and a painter's brush. You see, the advent of the Prince of the Blue Feather at the juncture of the eighteenth and nineteenth centuries triggered at the subtler level the rise of a higher desire. From Blake's lifetime to the modern age, this human puzzle of existing, two souls in one breast as Goethe lamented, has been intensively explored by the human mind. His vibrant enthusiasm for our own infinity sprinkled the yearning for infinity in the unconscious of the modern race. He almost cured the French of the sickness of being reasonable. The search for infinity stirred their doomed poets, the spleen of Charles Baudelaire, the rage of Arthur Rimbaud, the melancholy of Paul Verlaine or the longing of Stéphane Mallarmé. But it was Germany that picked up on his prophetic visions almost immediately."

Lakshmi seized on the point, "You must be speaking of the German philosophy of history in the nineteenth century: Herder, Feuerbach, Hegel. Are you saying, Master, that Blake inspired their theory of spiritual evolution?" Well-read and insightful as usual, Lakshmi could not resist digging into these references. "Hegel was born not long after Blake and clearly formulated this hypothesis in his *Phenomenology of Spirit*. Then we have Bergson and his *élan vital*. Do you see a link, Master, all the inspiration flowing from Mr. Blake, although it was too subtle for anyone to notice?"

"You are right. In an age of superficiality and trivia, true game changers aren't noticed, and his century passed by without anyone knowing him. The singular spiritual energy of Blake influenced contemporary thinkers because he could permeate the unconscious. His seminal intuitions flew into us. Blake is the hidden code breaker for our age, yet few could break his own code. Not many understood his warnings."

"Warnings?"

"Blake lived at the dawn of the Industrial Revolution. By being born in our race, he discovered our problems. He prophetically warned mankind about the emerging dangers, the satanic mills of modernity. Single-minded and devoted, Blake merged the genius of creativity and the impetus of emotion. In his inspiration, he vainly endeavored to free us from conditionings and mental concepts that keep blocking our spiritual energy from ascending through the Lily of Anorhad. If the gate is shut, the Lily is a dead end, seen from his evolutionary point of view."

"Was it because he sensed modernity was going to be the product of mental concepts, a sort of huge virtual world?" asked Jonathan.

"Quite so. Blake saw the primacy of reason emerging in his own time; with the Encyclopedists and the French Revolution. At first, he thought it was a good thing to take the mind beyond the superstition of the church, but then he sensed the threat from the other side."

"What side?"

"The old church was in the blue zone, a thing of the past. In his frightening visions, Blake saw the monstrous might of Urizen of the Yellow Feather coming, a new church of mental constructs, heartless and efficient, logical and cold, dried up and spiritually dead. Urizen is the modern Titanosaur, a potent energy that began rising at the time of Blake: the pretense of man to rule the world only with reason."

Lakshmi waited impatiently for the end of the explanation because another question was already whirling in her mind, "Didn't we have a glimpse of Urizen in Bangkok?" she asked earnestly, "because somehow, the casket had been tampered with by the Governor of Shambalpur?"

"Indeed. Urizen is the state of mind of the ruling class and the ruling trend in the state of mind. It shapes modernity to the bitter end as the masters of economics and finance drive rich countries to their ruin. Behind it, we find the work of the demon Hangker.

"Are you saying Urizen created modernity as we know it?"

"Yes, with many achievements certainly, but also the alienation of thoughts from feelings, man from woman, paralyzing conflicts between ecology and economy, nature and society. Blake saw it coming. Knowing how to combine the dance of the two feathers, he fought Urizen. He wanted to free us from past beliefs. At the same time, he understood rationalism would lead the modern world, then in the making, into yet another illusion. Urizen created a world that would belong to the rationalists, the accountants, and they shall ruin it. Global wealth, created under the blinding sun of the Yellow Feather, is siphoned away from people and exploitation breeds exclusion and violence."

"What could Blake really do about it?" asked Lakshmi, intrigued by Sanath's explanations.

"That is a brainteaser, isn't it? How to undo Urizen?" Sanath paused to ask his own question. "Remember the lid of the circular casket? What was engraved on it?"

"A trident, I think."

"That is the answer. Blake summoned a counter force. He called for the great power flowing from the Master of the Trident who resides on Mount Kailash: the power of pure desire. He invited the entire human race to dream bigger dreams and rise with higher desires. That was, my friends, the point of this casket."

CHAPTER NINETEEN

UNCOVERING SUSAMSKARA

While not everyone knows how to make the best of it, we all have a past and how Susamskara helps in making the past work for the present.

S
anath knew he had one weakness left. As a teacher he was too attached...to teaching. He loved his pupils like his own children and there was simply so much that he knew and wanted to pass on for the benefit of future generations. He remained absorbed in his own reflections and could hide his perplexity. Were the days of his mentoring now numbered? If so, so much would be lost. The Stealthstars had yet much to absorb, but Sanath could not know precisely how deeply or how much they could take in.

The caskets contained the deposit of the accumulated knowledge of the Deep Way under the protection of magic spells. The Stealthstars had to retrieve the codes to claim their inheritance. Each casket was supposed to release its content in a gradual revelation but something had tampered with this mechanism. The Avasthic prophecy was no longer unraveling as the Avasthas had planned.

And the Order of the Hllidarendis had now apparently nothing to do with it. He admitted it is hard to know which way magic will flow, but the process was escaping him. Other forces were at work, greater than those consigned by the gentle race of Dagad Trikon. It was highly unexpected, for instance, that the Stealthstars would move up to the entry of the Lily of Anorhad and beyond. Sanath was puzzled that, while dealing with the Yellow Feather, they had been sucked back to the axis of the central channel, the White Feather.

There was something glowing with power and fateful about this day placed under the sign of their meeting with Blake, the archangel who had come to face the foibles of our modern era.

Sanath sensed that the quest was reaching its destination, and he would use the time left to say more about the forgotten arsenal of the Avasthas. Again, he was attentive to the conversation around him.

Lakshman recalled his own activity as an archeologist. "I turned over many stones and opened a few graves. Some places were laded with bizarre energy fields. Ritual for the mummies, cults of ancestors, conversing with the dead, paleonto-climatology, psychoanalysis, or analyzing skulls...some of man's avenues to his past are truly bizarre."

"Are you saying it could be dangerous to get into the past?" asked Tracy. Sanath interjected, "What can be truly dangerous is when the past gets into us."

Lakshman wondered, "This is the other side, isn't it? "The casket unearthed in London is dangerous, like the one we found in Bangkok, but in a different way; the spiders, the tunnels..."

"You are right; the tunnels are the real problem." Sanath shrugged, as if to shake off fragments of unwanted memories from his mind.

"If the corridors of the blue zone are swarming with spiders, I'd rather keep out. What are these tunnels?" asked Tracy.

"Neural pathways within our brains, also paths that are taken by our minds. We each have our private map. Much of our life, we dig in and out of our own tunnels without understanding the lurking dangers. The tunnels are carved within our nerve synapses, the neuron-transmitters. We go on building a sort of psychic network, spreading through our neural pathways in many directions, reaching way beyond the frontiers of the conscious mind."

"Where do they lead?"

"Well, this is a delicate question for sure. But are we ready for this?"

"Were we ever ready for any of this?"

"All right, as a matter of fact, part of the network can connect us to hell."

"To hell?"

"Not everything from the past is pretty. The tunnels of the blue zone connect the right hemisphere of our brain all the way to the content of the entire subconscious, including the parallel worlds where unpleasing beings are lurking. It is the job of Belzebseth, his minions and the ghostly cavalry to make sure that the tunnels lead there."

"I guess you are saying the tunnels can be traveled from both sides," observed Jonathan, who noted that the wizard was bringing the debate to the territory of psychic warfare.

"This is the real danger," the wizard acquiesced, "we go places and once we have visited somewhere it creates a trace, a facility to follow the same route. Inadvertently, we may follow these roads again. But, the true peril is this: once a tunnel is dug, others can burrow in it from the other end and gain access to our innermost mind."

"What do you mean by 'others'?"

"The Hllidarendi Kheto, whom Michael and his fiancée met in Africa, is our specialist in fighting this black art. I wish you would spend time with him one day. We are talking here about entities that are not in flesh but exist in the strata of the past, which, so to say, float around the subconscious mind. When we put ourselves in a vulnerable spot, they try to penetrate us with their own awareness. They are unsatisfied souls that want to enjoy emotions or sensations through our own nervous system, in our physical body. They have none of their own; they are parasites."

Lakshman observed, "I remember the guy from the FBI in the dacha near Moscow at the meeting of the Oikos project. He spoke of the 'psychic compulsion viruses' in serial killers, pedophiles, and the like."

"These are extreme cases of PCVs," noted Sanath. "The sly, depraved, or aggressive ones are not the kind of tenants a landlord is looking for. Other PCVs are more common. A power-hungry fellow will lurk around ambitious bureaucrats. Alcoholic ghosts can hang on at the door of the pub waiting for the next binge. Slaughtered soldiers don't go away. There are all sorts of permutations and combinations. The ghost of a woman can enter the body of a man or vice versa. Then, gender confusion follows."

"We went through this already, but we heard more about the disease than about the cure," remarked Lakshman.

"Not all attempts to gain from the past must be faulted. Luckily, our inner architecture can be secured with a bit of engineering work," replied Sanath to reassure them. "In these corridors and vaults, we can mine deposits of precious stones, we uncover arsenals of methods to defeat evil. The hints left by the great ones are scattered along the road traveled by the existential rangers. You can discover the clue to the mastery of the future within the past of the human race. The Blue Feather can transfer that knowledge that enriches the DNA of a race. The Aulyas called this pool of experience *Susamskara*."

"What exactly is *Susamskara*?"

"Positive conditionings. *Susamskara* is the inbuilt benefit of acquired knowledge. Consider it precious because it gradually deposits in the consciousness the long-term survival skills of a species: it leads the adaptive process of evolutionary learning. *Susamskara* helps us to play in the Grand Scheme."

"I am afraid we are not given the choice to play or not to play; the real choice is to win or to lose."

"That is the question Jonathan. When we learn the rules of right action—Avasthas called them *maryadas*—from good parents, teachers, or elders, we benefit from past lessons learned over centuries. Then, we see the merits of imbibing virtues that strengthen the tribe such as honesty, generosity, the capacity to respect, reliability, loyalty, solidarity, and forgiveness. These are social qualities that are linked to love at a subtle level, and they restore in us the properties of the six great Avasthic Houses."

"Love is the centripetal force isn't it, that which keeps things together?"

"Well-spoken Tracy. By nurturing the ways of love, *Susamskara* brings us closer to the central channel of the White Feather."

"What we used to call morality?"

"Morality? You will frighten modernists with this unpopular word," responded Sanath with a broad smile. "Yes, there is a link; true morality, not the one that hypocrites talk of, protects an ideal coefficient of security of love in the density of relationships. Confidence and feelings nourish each other; *Susamskara* is the sum of everything positive that happened to us, so, it includes also the benefit of the practice of morality. By discarding it our ego turns the odds of the play against us."

Lakshman observed, as he computed a range of anthropological references, "I believe this knowledge is still prized today in the less modern societies. Maybe this is why you asked the priestess Mariluh to reawaken the statues of the Buddha in Thailand, to bring back what was holy from the past."

"We are not too successful," observed Tracy. "As you know, the Oikos project was an enlightened attempt by governments to reconnect to the best in the traditions and history of our species; but it failed for lack of funding."

"My Order, like Dikayoson in the earlier age, was meant to keep *Susamskara* alive," Sanath revealed, "but we failed because the tide of modernity overcame our influence. Thanatophor seduced man and defeated him. Blake saw it coming. Today harmful conditioning is powerfully mainstreamed into the accepted lifestyle. Unsuspecting consumers start adopting what is trendy but where do these trends lead? Many tunnels are narrow, and that is where the offspring of Arakna are waiting to capture us."

"Oh right, I forgot! What is the story with this spider?"

"Arakna spins the bad conditioning. She doesn't kill, but imprisons until the victim is emptied of all self-substance. She freezes the power of man to choose, to change, binding him in the web of conformism, pettiness, and routine. She ties the silk chains of habits, which bind perceptions. Man is petrified in matter; he cannot manifest the living Self. It all ends in decay and death. This is finally what the word 'Thanatophor' means: he is the one who carries death."

"How does Arakna affect humans? Can you give an example, Master?"

"Through the taste buds, for instance."

"I beg your pardon?"

Sanath, a mischievous twinkle in his eyes, laughed at the puzzled looks of his companions. "Look at eating habits: they are so normal and powerful that men don't notice them. However, if Arakna achieves the slavery of the taste buds, eating becomes a compulsory habit; it spreads and becomes an urge of the entire body. And what is the result? Pandemic obesity is part of it.

"It's just an example. The main job of Arakna is to weave dependencies in human behaviors that prevent mankind from evolving and learning. We are stultified by conditionings of one sort or another. This may seem innocuous; the web is still invisible but if Arakna is so dangerous, it is because she uses poison. Indeed, once victims are immobilized, Arakna injects venom, which is the chemistry of dependency. Therapists know that the dominion of Arakna grew formidably over these last decades with the spreading of all kinds of addictions, toxic mania and substance abuse."

"There is a way out, isn't there? You used the fire of Bhairava to stunt the spiders."

"That's right. His sword of molten gold is a terrific weapon. The heavenly goldsmiths collected some of its sparks and used them to manufacture the Glorfakir. Spiders loath Uragni, the mystical fire in the sword of Bhairava. Today, Arakna wanted to prevent us from meeting her archenemy."

"Can we do the same; I mean, neutralize the spiders?"

"With the Glorfakir, yes. Its blade is forged in the concentration of the conscious mind; it strikes with the sharp edge of attention coated with willpower. There is always hope if we chose to use the Glorfakir. Men and women are learning to use it in various rehabilitation and recovery programs. It is the sword of sharp attention that cuts through the thickest webs of intoxication. In the Avasthic military college of Shambalpur the cadets who wanted to join the Yuva Platoons were duty bound to pass exams in fencing classes."

Lakshman appreciated it when the wizard recalled such little episodes from the esoteric Avasthic heritage, and asked for more details.

The teacher had to be a respected swordsman who had achieved a state of initiation known as the *Chittanirodh Podium*. It imparted the fine art of controlling one's attention, solidly established in inner silence, keeping the projection of thoughts under complete command. Only a weapon under complete control can be put to full use.

"Angels are helping us all the time, aren't they?" asked Lakshmi, her heart still drenched in the sweet comfort she had received from the audience with Blake, the human form of the Archangel Michael.

"They are," responded the wizard, "if we allow them to. Our guardian angels take us forward, out of the silk prison of Arakna, where we become prisoners of bad or painful memories; we lose self-esteem, chained by our own deeds. And if we are worthy, they lead us in a treasure hunting tour to uncover the footprints of divinity within nature, science, and history. When we discover this wonderful legacy, we realize the blessings of the Blue Feather."

Lakshman said, "For most of us, we are born; we die, and that's it. But in the meantime we try to squeeze plenty in between. This should not all be lost. It would be a relief that much of what we did, of what happened in the past can work for redemption; I mean, how do we build *Susamskara?*"

"Pay attention, chose what you want to become, form good habits, watch your own behavior and in so doing, the right hand will help the left. Although influences, conditionings, and wrong behaviors created the tunnels, there is a way that helps us to erect the *Susamskara* protective walls of positive conditionings. We put our house together stone by stone, step by step. Even if our inner barriers have been pierced, we can repair them and restore our integrity."

Sean added, "When the Deep Way flows into our neural pathways, the Great Mother says that it switches on the inner instrument, our attention is no longer confined to our brain. We can pay attention through all the centers of our body. It is a new step in cognitive evolution."

"Does it work for those who are burdened by the weight of their mistakes?" Sanath answered Jonathan.

"Even if unwanted visitors have entered our networks, we can throw them out. And even if we have been thrown off our mind's horse by wrongful attention, we can climb back into the saddle. Never give up. We were born to make mistakes, but we live to correct them."

"May I please ask why you never spoke about this before?"

Sanath replied, "The notion of *Susamskara* is not new. Remember Dikayoson, the herald of the Chamber of Maat who watches the proper functioning of the Wheel of the Law, the boundaries of ethical behavior. *Susamskara* redesigns and realigns the networks through which we experience our emotional body in conformity with the script of the Law of Maat. We are then fully guided because our behavior resonates naturally with nature, with the Grand Scheme, with the whole."

"A crash course in inner repair work is required in the modern world; I am glad you confirm it. The Great Mother says the same. No matter how badly we have been attacked or how many times we have fallen we can always get back on our feet." Sean informed them.

"How? Tell us more, please, tell us all about it." Lakshmi put her hand on Sean's arm, shaking it slightly, as if the sister was pleading for knowing all that a brother knew. Sensing the longing tone in the young woman's voice, Sean had to offer a disclaimer, "We learn to meditate but we don't know what happens when we meditate. We use the Deep Way without knowing much about it. The wizard sees things that we don't."

Sean turned to Sanath, "I hear you saying that the Glorfakir can burn the carriers of fears, creeping things, creatures in the shadow. Are you also saying that even addictions, the combined effect of the spiders and the Dark Riders, can be defeated? It is easy enough to land in hell but difficult to exit."

"Difficult but possible my dear friend. As *Susamskara* restores the integrity of our inner architecture, we reach the upper floors: we gain confidence in ourselves. Confidence in turn brings a versatile weapon that belongs to the House of Anor. Those who master it can break the Fifth Seal, the one that releases the expansion of consciousness."

"I'd really like to know the teachings of the Great Mother on the process of Self-healing. I understand that much won't be conveyed by words, but still I hope Sean will have time to tell us more."

Sanath threw a reassuring glance at Lakshmi, and the light in his grey eyes gleamed with mercy. He knew it wasn't easy for Erilie, the first of Sheravalians, once so close to the Lady of the Rock, not to be among her disciples in this lifetime. She depended on her own inner quest to keep up with subtleties of the Deep Way, and Sean seemed more familiar with it now. Sanath knew that, no matter how much she respected the Hllidarendi and his wisdom, it was the feminine power of the Goddess that Lakshmi felt increasingly attracted to. And he knew this was right for that was the true source of his own power.

Sean smiled by way of agreement to Lakshmi but returned to the words of the wizard, "The weapon of Anor?"

"Ideally I would have waited to touch upon this subject until we approached the Casket of the Discus but I fear there is not enough time left for this. The weapon I refer to is precisely...the discus, which is the Sudarshan discus, the power of auspicious vision. When it is thrown, it cuts through evil and the goodness we project returns to us like a benefic boomerang. The Sudarshan places us definitely beyond the reach of Thanatophor and of the swarms of ghosts. Then we master a lofty quality that bridges the narrow passage to the House of Ni.

"What quality is that please, Master Sanath?"

"Faith. Faith, however profane this word has been rendered by the churches of recent centuries; it is a quality in the custody of the Sixth House, a quality that explains the strength of the Anorhadan seers. They called it *shraddha*, and I shall explain more about it later. Faith in what came before us because it also contains meaning and greatness. Faith in what is yet to come because whatever happens has its purpose.

But, faith also means faith in ourselves, dear Sean, and for the one who saw the fall of his clan and the end of that fair age."

Sanath had witnessed the agony of Lidholon after the death of his friends. Like all those who had seen countless struggles, and many defeats, Sean knew man couldn't prepare for success alone. Suddenly, the wizard added in German, as if uttering a warning brought forward by peeping into the battle of the immediate future:

"*der Untergang des Abendlandes!* The decline of the West is ineluctable, but it may lead to a greater future. Faith must, likewise, grant resilience to the men and women of the West in the moment of reckoning. With faith, they shall overcome."

"Master, you are talking about us, about them, about the fate of individuals and common history, moving from the particular to the general, from one levels to another. Sometimes it is really difficult to follow."

"I know Michael. The legend is like a Russian doll, a meaning within a meaning. I try to explain it well for you, I daresay, but what you encounter isn't difficulty but density, the sense—either confusing or exciting—of packed and layered meanings. In bringing to you *Susumskara*, I want to make it easier for you to realize how the past is within the present and how it can help us. Often, the state of the past is the cause and our action is the effect. Knowing the cause we better control the effect. The past is a formidable storehouse with diverse contents that affects the state of society. Some of it is very helpful. Those who ignore from where they come may not know where to go."

"Where do we come from?" Lakshman had been rejuvenated by this exposure to the concept of *Susamskara*. A weight had been lifted from him because he now realized that not all the past is a burden, on the contrary. The goodness that it contains can also sustain us. "Let me tell you where I feel we come from. Sometimes in winter I go to Geneva on business and whenever I can, I rent a car and drive to the mountains, to spend a few days in the snow. The last time I did this I stood outside my hotel at four o'clock in the morning, well protected against the cold, and just looked at the sky. It was a moonless night, extremely clear, so dark, so splendid, sparkling with stars, twinkling stars, shooting stars. Gradually, I lost myself in the vastness of this grandiose dome, and it seemed that my gaze could go further and further, seizing the constellations and the Milky Way and then, I saw it all as a single palpitating membrane, the protection of a womb around me. A thick mantle of snow cushioned the earth, and the sense of safety I enjoyed was just wonderful. I shall not forget the gentleness of this Christmas night. And now comes the best part: when I returned in my hotel room, I closed my eyes, and I saw them all, all the stars, sparkling within my closed eyes. And this vastness within us: I feel: this is where we come from."

CHAPTER TWENTY

MORE THAN REASONABLE

Where we can and must do more with our awareness than just being reasonable—to reach our destination and to bring fulfillment to our destiny.

T he Friday traffic in London was slow. Their limousine had crossed the Thames, and as they passed Westminster Cathedral, they paused to buy some fast food. Michael said, "Goodness, the power is very strong here. It's strange, I feel it all over my body and yet we are in the midst of a city." Ian smiled, "Yes but it is not the church. Sean could tell you that someone very great had lived in this vicinity."

The vibrations in Michael's body increased as if strengthened by this remark. The space within the car seemed filled with a strange white mist in which Sean's black hair suddenly looked much lighter, as if floating on the top of his head like fair filaments. In a split second, he found himself sitting next to Lidholon in front of the Cave of Wonders listening to the parting words of the High Lady, "...after many years endured through the passing of shadows, you shall carry the return of the light and in those future days, the great Avatar shall awaken my secret power in the children gathered on a green island, in the heart of this planet, where some of you shall meet Me again..."

"Where are you, honey?" Michael smiled at Lorelei to signal everything was fine. He was back in the limousine and enjoying the present moment, the traffic in the street, the passing clouds in the light blue London sky. Did the High Lady mean England? Could this country famous for people with their stiff upper lips really be the heart of the subtle energetic structure of the world? Slightly puzzled he looked again at Lidholon-Sean as if to see whether he too had caught this glimpse of the distant past.

Sean was intrigued that someone who knew the Great Mother was also a member of the Order in England, a keeper of the legend. He had never met Ian Ildemar before and wondered how much he knew. He asked, "How does the Order of the Hllidarendi function?"

"The Order has waged a long, losing battle against Thanatophor. It keeps but a shadow of its former strength. Membership is now much reduced and aged, as the qualifications for membership can no longer be met. The last initiation took place in a little red church in Finland forty years ago. Members are required to be able to stay on the *Chittanirodh Podium*, the crystalline space of vacuity and freedom from thoughts and emotions. However, the Order still works as a collective force. Its members are loners but telepathically integrated."

"Telepathically?" In a flashback, Sean remembered his dream about the soccer stadium, when everyone present was integrated by the power of the moment. Was this the same thing? The answer suggested the contrary.

"We don't meet by focusing on the same object but by joining in the same vacuity. The shield of the Sadhan is activated through the Deep Way. No outside interference can penetrate this silence. When in meditation, we use the second Avasthic weapon, the Glorfakir. Without thinking, we move our attention to a specific problem. We seize it through the inner sight. This sends a message to the telecommunication department that regulates the Game. When we reach the right threshold of focus, it is wonderfully efficient. Invisible beings and energies respond. I believe it works for the Stealthstars and the students of the Great Mother too, as a function of their rate of absorption of the Deep Way. We are spontaneously synchronized when there are no interferences. Good things happen; things work out. Human beings normally do not have access to this reflex action system yet, but they would get there if they only imbibed the Deep Way."

"Incredible! So you don't even need to meet?"

"We meet physically now and then, sometimes for work, mostly for the pleasure of friendship and the Grand Master pays me a visit from time to time."

Michael and Lorelei had described their incredible encounter with the great genius most critics of his time had considered a gifted but eccentric artist. Lorelei asked Ian, "The extraordinary thing to me is that you do not seem at all surprised now that we are telling you about our experience of meeting Blake. How come? After all, a ticket to a bygone century can't be bought at the nearest subway station."

Ian responded with a broad smile. "I am a member of Sanath's Order, but I have also become a discrete follower of the Great Mother whose feet are now walking the hills and dales of England. She told us that Blake had been an angelic envoy and revealed much about him. He had such faith in the soil of England that he wanted to build the New Jerusalem here, a community of enlightened and free visionaries."

"Why didn't you go with us to open the Casket of the Blue Feather or to meet William Blake?"

"I was not meant to; I am the Hllidarendi from the Western Islands, and I have been around for some time, although not as long as Master Sanath. I met Master Blake when he was alive as one of his fervent young admirers in the Shoreham group that gathered around him towards the end of his life. I am not meant to meet him again before I leave this body."

"So you once knew him well?"

"I don't remember very clearly, it's been some time ago," he added with a wistful look, "but, yes, I can enter his thoughts, which is hermetic for most, and I get his message. Blake was not only ahead of his time he was on time."

For a moment, Ian stared into nothingness, lost in his own recollections. And then, he opened his bag, "Oh I forgot, I bought a present for you. He took out a book of the *Illustrations of the Book of Job* with a commentary by Dr. Udo Szekulics. Lorelei admired the engravings. "Marvel at the innocence of the faces; they look so luminous, so pure. Let me show you these two plates, number thirteen and seventeen; what do you see?"

"How beautiful. God is laying his hands on the top of the heads of Job and his wife."

"Correct, Lorelei. What do you read on the top of the plate?"

"She read, "*We know that when He shall appear we shall be like Him for we shall see him as He is.*"

"It's clear, isn't it? He points to the destination. You can see the Archangel left his clues: the hands of God, above the limbic area of the brain indicate the location of the house of Ni where we shall know Him and know that we really are in His likeness. Blake was both a heart and an eye-opener, he wanted us to feel and to see."

"I can see this but he lived just like one of us, not at all like an angel, didn't he?" Lorelei breathed a sigh of amazement at what such a life must have been. "Did anyone ever notice?"

"Not in his lifetime. Imagination was contestation; he fought to integrate the global divine world in the limited space created for us by modernity. He pushed hybrid forms of knowledge to access the Deep Way, pulling the innovative levels of art to bypass the gatekeepers of state and religion. They mocked him in his time but today the students of the Great Mother venerate and bow to him."

Lorelei turned to Mike. "He is connected to the Goddess; just as he was on the Retable of the Dove, don't you agree? Grandpa used to say that it is not by chance that Michael, like Gabriel, is portrayed as an attendant of Mother Mary; he said archangels constantly interact with the Eternal Feminine."

"I suppose they do, replied Michael, and your grandfather had gathered in his castle all these beautiful and symbolic objects with the help of the wizard to leave a physical trace of the legend, in statues, paintings, and manuscripts." He recalled his experience in Blake's house, "I am glad to bear his angelic name. Please, Master Ian, tell us more about him."

"On the bidding of the Great Mother, Blake came to unchain our race, to free us from the wrappings in the blue zone: he came to challenge all conditionings: political, aesthetic, and above all, religious. Fossilized beliefs and religions have distorted the messages of the divine beings that these religions pretend to worship. They have covered us with restrictions and superstitions. Religions forged the worst bonds of conditionings. It is not surprising Blake was not well received. He wasn't appreciated, he was more mocked than praised, and he struggled against poverty his entire life. At times, he even felt despair."

Despite the elated feelings they had experienced, Michael surprisingly, now felt dejected. "Is religion breeding the biggest spiders? What shall we do? William Blake was of a much higher level than us and just consider the reality of his life! Blake was buried in a pauper's grave, as was Mozart; and van Gogh went crazy. There is no money left for the genuine creators but plagiarists, harlots, crooks, rotten politicians, and exploiters bathe in wealth. Gandhi, Lincoln, Martin Luther King, Sadat and Rabin were assassinated, but Khomeini the fanatic, has a golden mausoleum. This is a wretched world. What can we do, Master Ian, what can we do? Are we to suffer as these great ones did before when they attempted to bring peace, knowledge, pure music, or even pure art?"

Ian's reply was supportive but firm, "Yes, Michael, it's tough. Men walk in darkness and don't recognize it because they are now under the spell of Thanatophor. He leads a great army of entities and found a way to enter their brains. The holy war, the jihad is now in the mind and they don't know it. Human beings have difficulty in grasping what the devil is up to: the six dark horses that could penetrate brains and defile the characters of people, the seventh that invites them to challenge their creator, not to mention the many demons still active in leading the legions of the living dead to possess the human psyche.

You are better equipped than others because of your Avastic background, but you don't have the power to turn this tide. Today, something is happening, something that never happened before. The Great Mother has come in a human form. Seekers are the salt of the earth. She is giving the Gift to all those who seek and come to her, irrespective of where they come from, no matter how high or low they may be."

"If so, the job of the Stealthstars is over?"

"No, but you will merge with them because by now you are too few to succeed, too diminished to turn the tide from hell. You shall be safe in their midst."

"Are you telling us that, in cracking the riddles of Dagad Trikon, we understand that our mission is to discover that we cannot complete it?" There was a trace of bitterness in Michael's voice.

"Blake shows us not to give up. He opens up the way of courage. He fought with his enemies and their conditionings his entire life: on the left, the priests, on the right, the rationalists. Things have not changed much. They fight the Great Mother today as they fought Blake in his day. I must say, I understand the rationalists," Sanath added with a chuckle.

"I don't," replied Lorelei incredulously. "Why did you say the rationalists are attacking the Great Mother?"

"Over millennia Thanatophor destroyed most of the Avastha legacy, so religion became at best, a solace for the stupid, and at worst, a control mechanism for the devil. Now, She reverses the trend. Straightforwardly, She brings the keys to the Inner World to the common man and woman, not just to the élite. The ordinary people take to it more easily than the upper echelons of society. This is such a bold move that the devil is caught off guard. In uncovering the Deep Way, the Great Mother reveals spirituality through states and sensations felt on an individual's central nervous system; this is a new science, objective and transferable to all. Moreover, She makes it fun and joyful. Rationalists don't like it because She demolishes their principal claim: that spirituality is subjective and irrelevant to the intelligent mind. Their creed was the pedestal for the monument of Urizen."

"Is conditioning the same as Urizen?"

"No, conditionings are spun in the web of Arakna," replied Ian. "Urizen was a new energy that rose at the time of Blake, man's pretense to rule the world with reason. Blake saw that it would become the religion of modernity, casting the previous ones aside, with freemasons as the new class of dogmatists, the apostles of rationality. Rationalists despised the old priests whom they considered to be guardians of dead beliefs for sweet idiots. Indeed, Christianity faded away during the modern age."

"But these priests of reason are now forced back to the drawing board simply because She destroys the possibility for reason to deny the spirit."

"Yes. She wipes out the cardinal article of the rationalist faith. Is it any wonder they fear Her? Just think about it: a woman from a faraway land brings verification to the hypothesis that Blake was offering: that divinity within man can be tangibly experienced! And She transforms people. This is revolution and it's quite normal that many in the ruling class oppose it," added Ian. "This is about God, you know, unknowingly echoing the words of Blake they had overheard in Lambeth. We need to be more than reasonable to get there."

"That conclusion," said Michael, "would greatly please Chief Kheto. He said on Table Mountain that you wanted to prevent the war of the feathers. Beyond materialism, we fast forward to the core of the Dagad Trikon prophecy, correct?"

"Preventing the war of the feathers means we can access the path of the White Feather that leads to the narrow gate of Anorhad. We must pass through it or perish. The Lady of the Rock had hidden Herself in the triangular sacrum bone, within each one of us, the reserve energy for this verification. Then, invited by the hand of God, as Blake showed us, the energy rises until it reaches the House of Ni." Sanath paused to give time for his words to sink in, for them to comprehend what he was saying. "When we develop the feminine within us: we find our depth; with the masculine, we find vastness. When depth and vastness combine, we enter Tao. Thus, we dance with the feathers. Our destiny is fulfilled."

They were now driving through Chelsea, but they did not pay much attention to the lovely surroundings. While they were absorbing the implications of this exchange in an appreciative silence, their car halted, their way blocked by a police officer. A motorcade of dark limousines approached at high speed and, in the third car, a black Rolls Royce that bore the royal crest of the Windsors, they caught a glimpse of the Prince of Wales and his first son, William, Duke of Cambridge, the future king of England.

Ian sighed. "What a coincidence! So near and yet so far. I know the Prince of Wales; he has an enquiring mind, a seeker in his own way, but I could never really talk to him about this transformation my Order would like to facilitate. Charles' son, William, is a good man. If only he might know how much work is accomplished by the divine powers in our islands, he would have faith in Albion despite the surrounding corrosion and decay. There is a prophecy that King Arthur will return to rule England."

As they passed Heathrow Airport heading in the direction of Reading, Lakshman asked, "Where are we going exactly?"

"We are heading for Henley-on-Thames where I have the sense that the highlight of the day is yet to come," answered the wizard.

Lakshmi was puzzled. "How can you say such a thing? How can we surpass traveling to the eighteenth century and meeting an archangel?"

"We shall see, we shall be seen," answered Sanath, waving away Lakshmi's queries with a gesture of his hand. "Ian is waiting for a call, but first we'll stop over for a short rest and to get a bite to eat. I didn't have breakfast this morning and didn't eat the fast food. Ian tells me there is a fine inn down the road."

They had now left the M4 and the passengers were distracted by the scenery as sunshine, showers and brisk breezes alternated in a display of typically English weather. On leaving Windsor, they reached the end of the A404 and turned into a narrow country lane where they were hemmed in by tall hedgerows.

They passed through lovely villages, ancient country houses half-hidden behind beech woods, then turned into a lane and stopped in front of a solitary, gracious building. They had reached the old coaching inn of the White Horse conveniently situated three hundred meters from the road, a restful retreat from the rush of modern life in beautifully land-scaped grounds. Rooms had been reserved for Mr. Baldur van Jetzlar's party. As usual, Sanath's planning was perfect to the last detail.

The well-proportioned inn displayed the exuberance of protective porches, conic turrets and escalating rooftops so typical of Victorian architecture. It was a meticulously maintained hostelry that offered a haven to relax; for the enjoyment of fresh country air, and not too far away from London. The travelers were happy to check into their rooms and then strolled around the landscaped garden.

CHAPTER TWENTY-ONE

THE MAGNETIC
DEFENSE SYSTEM

Where we hear about the youthful adventures of the wizard, and of the magnetic defense shield whose effectiveness will make the difference between the evolution and regression of the human species.

The wizard's party gathered around a heavy rectangular table at the far end of the dining room. Sanath ordered a delicious snack; home-baked delicacies, muffins with marmalade and cookies, newly laid eggs with bacon, tea, and freshly brewed coffee. The cozy room, empty of other diners, had white wooden paneling decorated with nineteenth century engravings that depicted scenes of the rural gentry by the River Thames.

Sean cleared his throat, as if to apologize for opening a topic unsuitable for the amiable milieu of the inn. His question arrested the leisurely conversation at the table and everyone's eyes turned to him, "Master, we saw some bats in the house in Chelsham Road after we'd opened the casket and were trying to leave. I sensed a diffuse but very real threat. What did their presence mean?"

"The house where we found the casket is on the magic map, a place where the legend is being processed and has revealed the circuitry of the blue zone. You know; we are more vulnerable in the tunnels because of the traps."

"What sort of traps?"

"Tripping traps. You see, when we make a big mistake, when we stumble and fall, when we experience defeat or failure; our subconscious becomes loaded with a painful memory. This memory creates a trap into which we can trip when we next try to ascend. Each one of us have some of these holes; the holes of the ratavolars."

"Pardon?"

"Ratavolars are entities, bat–like creatures that wait for your attention to cross their path. When it does, they strike and their bite releases the lineaments of guilt, diffidence, or loss of self-esteem. They whisper in your inner ear: 'remember how low you fell? You are a failure, bound to fail; you can't make it.' They suck the blood of your spiritual strength, which is the basis of self-confidence."

"I know what you mean," said Sean as he dimly recalled the sensations of his trip through time and the acute dejection of the young Avastha lord who could not prevent the fall of his clan.

Jonathan added, "And all the while the Dark Riders don't just vanish. They are still around too."

"That's because they can inflate or reduce their size. They can become microscopic and travel the tunnels unnoticed, trying to push our attention into the spider webs or the ratavolar's holes."

"We were surprised to discover that most of the powers of the Dark Council can still be operational against the students of the Great Mother," commented Sean.

"However as they learn to build *Susamskara*, the students gradually close the tunnels and plug the holes. Evil does not go away because we pretend it does not exist." Sanath wanted to build on Ian's comment and continued in a tone that betrayed an unexpected shyness, "For the first time you will hear a confession from me."

"That sounds good," thought Michael, who had been attentively registering the teachings of the day. "If a high wizard has things to confess; lesser mortals can be forgiven for erring."

"When I was a young wizard; I was rather good at it and, frankly, more than pleased with my skills. Success smiled at me and so did most princes and wizards of these long bygone days. I was gifted with healing, enchantments, and equipped with magical weaponry. I had killed the assistant of Belzebseth with a spell of my invention and frozen his giant purple lizard. I loved it. In disguise, I entered the capital city of the demons, on a spying mission on behalf of the Nizam of Dagad Trikon. I had to learn more about their practices in the realms of the blue zone. In those ancient days, I didn't know the panoply of the devil's charming deceptions. I thought nothing could affect me; I was so sure of my strength, of my innocence. I did not know about the tunnels, and quite unexpectedly,

I became ensnared by the charms of a most seductive girl. I was taken by surprise, and fell in love. I fell rather vertically."

This startling twist of the story commanded an even keener interest of the audience.

"Her name was Chupaquarni." The very way he pronounced the name, with almost unconscious regret that had survived centuries, impressed Lorelei and Lakshmi. They exchanged appreciative looks, curious as to this new, unknown side of their dear wizard. "She was older than me but an enticing creature, and later on I concluded that the greatest experts in casting spells for capturing the attention are of the feminine gender." Sanath smiled as he could see the puzzled look of the listeners. They obviously had assumed that the high wizard was above this sort of thing.

"But she wasn't an ordinary witch, I must say, not at all," he added quickly as if to reassure not only his audience but also himself. "I learned too late that she was from a high demonic lineage. If I had known of her ancestors, I would have been more guarded. She was the daughter of the sister of Ravana, King of Lanka, the woman who had vainly tried to seduce the Lord Rama of Ayodhya and his younger brother Lakshman.

Chupaquarni was slim at the waist and generously endowed elsewhere. She fitted the ancient canons of feminine beauty, and her feet hardly touched the ground when she walked. Her figure was not unlike those of the celestial dancers depicted in the frescoes of the caves of Ajanta in Maharashtra, and when she was singing she could catch your soul. Before she'd become a tool of Belzebesth, she had been his victim. She captured my heart by offering me her vulnerability. I did not realize that her other side had learned to play with it. I became ensnared because of my desire to help her."

The companions were deeply affected by this all-too-human account of a not-so-human wizard. They became very still, listened motionlessly as if afraid their movements might disturb the flow of Sanath's memory. Even the approaching waitress who'd come to pick up the dishes, sensed the change in the room, and quietly tiptoed back to the kitchen.

"I was rather bold and had no clue that she was a connoisseur of men; she could detect their strengths, tease their virility, sense their weaknesses. I intrigued her. Being innocent does not mean being naïve, but I was betrayed by my own presumptuousness. I was learned but certainly not an expert on women. She was sensitive and perceived another force in me, something she did not get from the other men she knew. She decided to own it, to absorb it for herself. I became her music teacher, and the agents of Belzebseth who were patrolling the streets of the city watching her pavilion became familiar with my daily visits. The spell of attraction she cast on me was effective because she could display innocence enrobed in sensuousness, fragility dressed in the ploy of enchantment. Worse, she knew it.

"I don't want to defend her," Sanath stressed with a sigh, "but if evil was simply boring, it would not have won this age. It knows well how to mix with other features, beauties, or enchantments, by which it becomes desirable and spicy. Evil cannot seduce without draping itself in the appeal of goodness. I just want to say," as if to excuse himself in a touching manner, "that things are sometimes not as black and white as they may look at first sight. We often become so entangled into such dilemmas that we lose our path."

"You," said Sanath, unexpectedly turning to Jonathan, who was enthralled at what he was hearing, completely absorbed by the tale, "must have pity on this plight because you also discovered eons ago that love is fickle if not handled carefully. Whether one loves the Queen belonging to another, as you did, or the temptress bent on robbing one's very substance, as I did, there is such a thing as loving in vain. But, love is only wasted at one's own peril.

"Chupaquarni was herself put to a severe test. In the process of seducing me, she herself was seduced too. I think that in a way, she really liked me. But, her innermost nature was to conquer and not to give. She also was bent on delivering the proof of her loyalty to her sorcerer lord. It was quite a dilemma for her but a worse one for me. Indeed, her flame had burned many times before, whereas mine was fierce because it was new and unspoiled. I was overwhelmed by such intense feelings.

"What a fool I was, forgetting that evil camouflages under the allure of delight as bait to capture us. I justified my attraction to her by my strong desire to protect and rescue her from the tentacles of the Dark Ones, certain of my own magical powers and skills.

"In short, I was lost. Drenched in emotions, bound by all my senses, I wasn't even aware of the dark side of the blue zone; my energy dropped to that of normal human beings and my cloak of stealth dissipated: some of Belzebseth's spies began to suspect me, were close to piercing my disguise, and they reported our romance to their master. He rejoiced greatly. The minister of darkness did not know for certain who I was, he thought that I was a mage from Dagad Trikon, perhaps even an ancient Aulya. Belzebseth was clever enough to wait to see whether I would reveal more of my hidden world through the artful seduction of Chupaquarni before resorting to his torture machines.

"Determined to use her beauty to entrap me, he instructed his courtesan, and infused her with the ghosts of many female seducers to increase the potency of her enticement. She was already gorgeous, as I already mentioned, but after she became possessed by spirits, her stunning beauty was enhanced to a new level. Now, it bent attention and will: it captured; it captivated; it became utterly irresistible. I was an élite wizard capsizing like a small boat in a violent tempest, slowly drowning in attachment and obsession, in a vain attempt to save her by my magic, or just by my love.

"It looks easy for a person on a spiritually higher level to be able to lift another person higher. I tried to create so much light around my beloved that all her shadows would vanish. On such occasions, when her ghosts left her alone, Chupaquarni seemed to have forgotten about her subjection to Belzebseth. With an angelic smile on her apparently innocent face, she attentively listened to the words of my teaching, showing a keen interest in spiritual progress and in everything I was so eagerly trying to transmit to her. Perhaps she meant it, perhaps she allowed herself to love me, and thus it was even harder to escape her formidable arsenal of temptations. Hard though it is for me to fathom now, I even wanted to initiate her into the Deep Way, which would have revealed to Belzebseth the innermost secret of our race. Fortunately for me, the necromancer made a mistake.

"At the point when she would bind me forever, the specters Belzebseth commanded reported something that alarmed him—it was the capacity I displayed in reviving her innocence. He feared this, and tried to possess her even more. Fortunately, he did not realize how weakened I had become, my magnetic field deactivated by the penetration of misguided desires. He made a stupid mistake in the subtle mixing of good and evil that is the supreme art of a great sorcerer; and the overdose of evil revealed his plot. I had to witness helplessly how the black side of Chupaquarni prevailed and overpowered her, making her more lustful and demanding, turning her into a completely different person to the one I thought I knew. Torn between attachment and despair, my energy dropped to still lower levels and so, my defense mechanisms in the blue zone were dismantled.

"She surrendered to her parasitic ghosts. They were now so present that I could see them despite my weakened condition. And, when I saw a party of trolls posted to watch the gate of the city I knew my time was up. My mistress planned an ambush, and her house was surrounded by the guards of Belzebseth, waiting for the order for the assault. I was about to be delivered to the Dark Council.

"Having realized this, as I lay for one last time in silk and satin comfort, I tenderly promised that I would reveal to her the next evening the secret of the nectar that can emulate bliss higher than that of physical passion. This was the Holy Grail, the real prize that the demons were after: how to trigger the flood of the bliss carrying juice flowing from the brain. Chupaquarni, mystified, asked her master to spare me just a little longer so she could uncover this secret and he agreed to postpone his plan. That night I went to the stable where I kept my stallion, one of the earlier lineages of horses belonging to the Avasthic lords, one that gallops with the speed of the wind. All the gates were closely guarded but he jumped the walls and swiftly carried me away, in a moonless night, that protected my last-minute escape."

The confession was now complete but not it's teaching. The women, fearing they may miss the lesson the Master wished to impart, implored in one voice, "What happened to you and Chupaquarni, Master, do please continue."

"How dry this world would be without women," Sanath smiled, "and how less complicated." And he continued in an easy tone, "Hiding in a remote mountain cave to heal my wounds, I discovered that my seducer had dug deep tunnels and opened inroads into my very soul. In these tunnels, the chemistry of the spiders was beginning to poison me. I was being invaded. All my spells were ineffective. I was yearning for her, I could not sleep, I could not eat, and I was obsessed, having lost my freedom. Even worse, other creatures of enticement could now visit my mind from the very tunnel I had opened through my foolishness."

The sense of astonishment was now palpable. Sanath, a man of such gravity and wisdom, seemed so much above the fray that somehow, no one would have imagined that he could have ever been caught in this kind of net. Now, after his open, sincere confession, everyone felt great sympathy for the honesty of the grand old man who didn't hesitate to share the memory of the passion of his youth, however embarrassing and painful it must have been. Lakshman quickly came to his rescue.

"The feminine charms, when fully deployed, are rather hard to resist. Listen to this story in the legends of India. Demons and gods were lined up, facing each other. The demons were going to win the competition with the gods to obtain the ultimate prize of the universe, the gift of the elixir of blessedness that was called soma, which, by the way, is precisely what you had promised your enticer. The demons were strong and clever, but the Emerald King did not want them to get the prize. He descended to the place of the contest, transformed into a gorgeous female shape whose eye-catching appearance completely captured the devils. Mohini was the name of this enchantress. As the gods shyly looked at the ground to protect the innocence of their attention, the jubilant demons lost control over theirs and, while they were distracted, she snatched the prize away from them and distributed the soma to the gods."

"The winners were those with the better mastery over their attention," agreed Sanath. "This points to the importance of the *Chittanirodh Podium* to win the last struggle, the one that must be fought inside."

"Look at Samson and Delilah! The Jewish chronicles tell a similar story: the fiercest, strongest man being defeated by the cutest girl." Lakshmi said. "The annals are full of such stories but then, Master, what happened to you, how did you break away from the tunnels and traps? And what about Chupaquarni?"

She suppressed the vibrancy of her sympathy. She herself had once dealt with the fire of passion and found it beyond her control. Perhaps she would learn something from the wizard's story.

"As for Chupaquarni, I never dared to explore what had happened to her in those days. But because our old loves may not leave us completely, no matter how happy or unhappy they were, I can again sense her presence in this life. She visits me in dreams at times, in a wedding ceremony that can never be. The worlds of shadows and of light can play with each other, but they cannot fuse. I am not the one to save her, although she may be saved if enough goodness returns in this world. I had to forget my romance with evil to become serious about my love for God. Fusion with love itself is what one should want, not just fusion with someone and definitely not through the dance of seduction." Sanath became silent and no one dared to say anything, but he composed himself enough to be able to return to the first part of Lakshmi's question.

"There is a reason I recalled for you the memories of my youth, and we are coming to it now. I was about to be banned from the Avasthic fraternity of junior wizards, but the Kiledar saved me."

"The Kiledar?"

"Yes, this too is a memory." Sanath paused. "A good memory that brings us back to *Susamskara*: the Kiledar is the 'Master of the Fortress.' It is one of the titles of Chanta, the Warden of the First House, Kalabham, and worshiper of the Elephant God. The elder of the tribe of Kalabham occupies the high office of the Kiledar, to keep the fortress safe; that is, the fortress of our own being. Keeping invaders out of our brains is part of the Avasthic craft."

"How did Lord Chanta help you?"

He took pity on me and initiated me in the teachings of the Elephant God, the one who is still worshipped in India today as the Son of the Goddess under the name of Ganesha. He revitalized innocence in me and helped to keep my fortress safe. Cementing the orifices in the tunnels was part of it. The keeper of the fort controls a spot at the back of our heads, which regulates the optical chiasmas and can expel intruders who enter through the eyes. The Kiledar knew how to deploy a subtler magnetism to coat the walls of *Susamskara*. Only years later, when he was fully satisfied with my progress, did the Kiledar propose me to the Circle of the Aulyas for the Office of the Sand Keeper, the custodian of the magic of the Triangle Rock."

"Did the Kiledar have a location on this planet, where we could find him or his power?"

"The casket of the four-branched star is a casket we have not recovered yet. We sent search parties towards Uluru, the holy rock in Australia where we suspect it may be buried, but there is also a similarly special mountain in the Swiss Alps. When you see its location from space, or look on a map at the mountainous formation surrounding it, this Matterhorn is placed at the center of a swastika of rocks, surrounded by snow and glaciers. The giant effigy of the elephant is turned to the north, is curved trunk quite explicit, and it looks at the mountain called the Jungfrau, the virgin. Surprisingly, a chain of mountains, oriented towards the sacred peak, projects the profile of the bull Nandi; he is one of those who carry the lords of this universe. You see this figure clearly from the road leading to Zermatt. The power is strong in the area of the Matterhorn. There are many other holy places around the planet to sustain and beam this energy field, not to mention the Sao Iambu stones."

"Are you saying that the First House is the one that controls the secret of the planet's defense system?"

"Correct, Lakshman. The blessings of the Elephant God protect *Susamskara* with the force of pure innocence and project a magnetic screen that seals the entrance of the underground channels. It shields the conscious mind from the invasion of the living dead, the ghosts, the witches, and the demons. The First House tunes into the field of divine magnetism that maintains the cohesion of the universe. If we cannot reinforce or re-establish the field, there is no reason for Mother Nature not to press the reset button. It can erase our civilization and destroy our race, and it's getting very close."

"Innocence is a word that no one understands today, and I fear there is no time left for us to realize its meaning. How can we revive its effect?" asked Lakshmi.

"Innocence never dies, don't worry, it is eternal, and a powerful source of life's vitality; it can be restored at the core of our inner being.

When established as spiritual magnetism, it beams rays of inexhaustible force. It flows as a brook in springtime with the foam of spontaneity and pure fun, so much so that it makes people less dependent upon pleasure."

"Is pleasure a bad thing?"

"No, but you get more pleasure by going beyond pleasure. Pleasure is the fickle master for quick gratification. With innocence, enjoyment becomes a natural disposition, not just depending on external stimuli."

"Oh I see, this is why it was said we cannot enter the kingdom of God if we are not like children; now you are telling us the same thing."

"Absolutely. The entire legend is contained in the smile of a child. This legend is for the lost children, the children of God. As men become children, they can master the challenges that would bring them to their doom; it is the children who are fated to begin the new age. Then the goodness of this world will throw the devil back into in the furnaces of the nether realms."

"They will try to fake this too, and self-certify themselves as children of God and twice-born because they hear an evangelist's ramblings on radio or television."

Lakshman and his companions were still struggling with the distance between the words of the wizard and the reality of the world around them. The wizard paid attention to the interruption and continued, "To be a child of God for them is but a metaphor. For the one who has experienced the Inner World it is a reality. The world that people believe to be real is an illusion and the world they deem an illusion is real. The Houses of Kalabham and Anorhad are allied and defend the field, the Gate of the Elephant, and the rite of its passage. The Deep Way is the one to remind us of our supernatural origin; when accepted within the magnetic field of the Elephant God, we become the children of his Father."

"Isn't the art of the Kiledar lost today? It is not easy to be spontaneous; our minds are overcomplicated, too structured to move with the flow. This ascent is not a one-shot affair. I am not sure: Are we going up or down?" asked Jonathan. "We still mess up, trapped with loss of self-esteem and guilt in one of these hidden ratavolar holes. The constricted passage of the Anorhadans, behind the forehead, can easily be blocked again! The narrow gate, Christ warned us about."

"Why should it be such a surprise, my dear Jonathan? Climbing is always a delicate affair and past mistakes only make the ascent slippier. You may recall that some in the past had reached high levels and still came crashing down. Ego can catch up with you on the higher levels, as with rulers of men, the twice-born saints, or even angels. This is why the Avasthas were always using the Glorfakir for introspection."

But Jonathan was not convinced. "Do you really think this is going to work? Most people I know, in the so-called real world, have lost their sense of innocence without even knowing it. If they have kept some sense of it, for them it is mostly about missing the innocence they have lost. Where is the Kiledar today? I tell you, we need help."

CHAPTER TWENTY-TWO

THE POWER
OF THE AVAHAN

Where to manifest the Deep Way requires the art of calling for help from the invisible energies of life and love that surround us, and how Lorelei experiments with this power within herself.

At Sanath's invitation, they relaxed in armchairs, and had tea on the porch. The mist had evaporated; the clouds moved aside, the scene cheered by the late-afternoon sun. They admired the private grounds, designed in cottage garden style, a quintessential example of civilized country living. A profusion of trees, shrubs, lilacs, flowers, and climbers displayed a multiplicity of colors, sometimes subtle, languid, often striking and vivacious.

Michael and Sean had escaped the group for a while, explored the garden and their respective life stories. The human brain cannot comprehend how friendship can endure for millennia; but it was here now, from somewhere deep within them. They had a lot of catching-up to do, the Avasthic reminiscences of Aliskhan and Lidholon, memories deeply buried in their unconscious: re-awakened by their ethereal travels and caressed by a flux of emotions.

As they strolled along, a casual observer might have noticed the movement of their heads appearing at the top of the hedgerows in rhythm to their conversation. Curved, and angled lines provided nooks and crannies in which to hide, and from the porch, the rumor of animated chatting and laughter could be heard, which scared birds to flight from their nests. Trees, in clusters between a round pond and a pergola, oscillated softly in the breeze.

The group convened under the pergola whose distance from the inn afforded privacy and seclusion. The wizard was relaxed, in the manner of someone getting close to the end of an assignment, anticipating a transfer of duty and an ensuing break.

It had become an established practice during these encounters to squeeze as much information from the wizard as possible, and this time he responded as never before. He proved to be more talkative than he had been in Jetzenstein Castle, and Lakshmi, for one, could sense a change in his relationship with them and was worried about it, without knowing why. As he became more intimate, she sensed that they were about to lose him. Wizards only exist with distance, secluded and separate from common mortals.

Sanath could sense a certain frustration in Jonathan and Lakshman, but he could not give them the answer: he could only help them find it for themselves. For this, he needed to provide more clues. First, he asked Ian to describe his experiences with the students of the Great Mother. Although Ian was astounded at the powers the practitioners of the Deep Way had acquired, his unprejudiced assessment had identified some drawbacks.

"The Great Mother has perfected them as instruments, no doubt, but I observe that they often do not know how apply what She taught them because they have not adjusted their external behavior to their new inner mechanism. At times, it is as if they aren't using their knowledge. Their bearing power is limited. They still react to their surroundings, so they can be tricked into leaving or losing access to the central channel of the White Feather."

"'Bearing power?' please explain?"

"It is the force of sustenance within love. Think about a good mother, her strength and her care. Her bearing power is nurturing. It's the capacity to look after everyone. A good student will revere the teacher who, with all his heart's desire to raise his pupil up, imparts precious knowledge. Great leaders are willingly followed, and soldiers are prepared to lay down their lives for their commanders when they feel they carry that power. That feminine quality of motherhood makes men who imbibe it truly exceptional. With the strength of our heart, we take our stand under the umbrella of the White Feather, and the capacity to bear enables us not to react to outside pressures or burdens, to withstand the lateral tractions of the Blue and Yellow Feathers."

"That is true," added Sean, "we forget that the choreography of the Blue and Yellow Feathers cannot succeed without the play of the third feather. For instance, there are still those who are trying to use their inner powers for their own gain in the Outer World. In such cases, the force is diverted by the play of the Yellow Feather."

"Sean, do you think the seekers, can make it? I mean, can they emerge from the tunnels, repel the sneaky ways of the demons and change this world because otherwise, the Stealthstars shall surely fail."

"I don't know for sure, Mike. We seem to conclude that we know nothing; we recognize that we cannot possibly fathom the inscrutable ways in which the Great Scheme unfolds. I must admit the majority of the pilgrims who reach Her door benefit tremendously. Those who come with an open mind are healed, counseled, comforted, and spiritually grow. Many progress, enjoying themselves, purposeful and steady, yet affectionate and fun loving. I'd put it this way, the most learned among us become increasingly humble because the vastness of the spiritual power we're uncovering is breathtaking. Frankly, what is strange and encouraging is that we often make mistakes and take wrong turns but somehow, it all works out. When we are honest, things end up all right through the working of an invisible hand, and the results are always positive. It's quite amazing!"

"So the 'Invisible Hand' is not only for Adam Smith's market place?" Mike retorted, half jokingly.

"I've seen it also works for the spiritual pilgrim. This hand from above can multitask and work fast, and thank God for it because the perils hovering over us are not waiting around."

"How can we explain that the Riders of Thanatophor can pursue us even though we have crossed the Lily of Anorhad?" asked a perplexed Michael.

"Because we go in and out of the Inner World. Practitioners are too often careless. They are meant to focus attention and consolidate the new stage of consciousness," responded Sean. "Students are slow to climb on this *Chittanirodh Podium* and so, it's no wonder that some followers of the Great Mother can lose the passage to the Inner World and thus, the benefits of the initiation."

"However, when the Lady quits the Triangle Rock to lead the way, the gap between the Outer and the Inner Worlds is bridged. This, I thought, was the content of the Avastha prophecy. Surely, this is a sign that we are reaching the end of our quest?" asked Michael.

"Yes, but it is not a guarantee," commented Sean, "learning about the mechanism of the great inner transformation does not yet mean that we can trigger it at will."

For beginners   How to grow.

This was the moment that Sanath chose to share the subtler content of his insights, and he focused his powers of concentration on what he wanted to pass on.

"If the force for their transformation is weak and returns to the triangular bone, they need to heal, to practice meditation, and to grow inside. As Jonathan said, they still need help, help from above. And they need to learn how to call for that help."

Sanath now wanted to take them to the next level. However, at this moment the innkeeper appeared. "Two visitors have arrived. I believe they are from your party."

"Please ask them to join us; I'd almost forgotten," said Sanath with a bright smile of contentment."

The silhouettes of two people appeared. Chief Kheto greeted them with a warm grin and Mariluh's sparkling eyes expressed how pleased she was to join them.

"I did not tell you they were coming. I wanted to leave a little surprise for you. The Daskalians in China instructed me to call this meeting. Our Order is at a crossroad in its lengthy history. We shall hold the Council of the Hllidarendis tomorrow." After further exchanges of affection, Kheto and Mariluh retired to their rooms to rest after the flights from Cape Town and Bangkok, respectively.

Lakshman said, "Your reference to the Daskalians reminded me of something I meant to ask you. At the Oriental Hotel in Bangkok, you mentioned a particular insight of the Daskalian teachers without telling us what it was. I must say you teased my curiosity. Can you convey now what was discussed by Confucius and Lao-tzu in China? I am much intrigued."

"I was coming to it," answered the wizard looking pleased at the delicate tuning of their mutual attention. "It is both a fine and an immense subject whose significance could easily escape human understanding. The moment is ripe to explain how human magic can rouse the heavenly forces. You have already seen it at work. I have to tell you about it otherwise you may never grasp this finest aspect of the Deep Way. I will speak of one of the properties latent in the Casket of the Blue Feather."

"I remember the trident engraved on the lid of this casket. In the legend, the Master of the Trident is the one who blesses the power of pure desire. But please Master, is it something to do with what you witnessed in China?" asked Lakshman.

"To begin with, do you recall how the Archangels, before fighting the demons in Jetzenstein Castle, first appeared?"

"Of course, we remember that splendor! Gabriel and Michael were in attendance of the Virgin Mary on the Retable of the Dove. They materialized, created a gale with their giant wings that pushed the demons out of the windows of the knight's hall. The demons perished in a mid-air battle above the Rhine valley. The moon was full, and the battle happened against a balletic backdrop of black clouds; how could we forget it? It was magnificent," responded Lakshmi.

"Poetic and correct, but not precise enough. How exactly do you think the Archangels materialized?"

"They were awakened by the touch of the White Monkey who descended from the tapestry above the entrance door," replied Lakshmi.

The wizard was using the Vani power, the creative, magic power of speech, but he could not always know how this force affects others. Its spell now worked in an unexpected way. Lorelei had been exposed to the demons in her past, and this recollection had unexpectedly opened one of these infamous tunnels in her.

She was following the exchange but now recalled her confrontation with the demon lords. Brutal sensations surged through her, the same sensations that she'd experienced in a past life, revulsion and terror, both demons within her. She closed her eyes, and faced the horror. They appeared so fast, for an instant she feared for her sanity. Her heart pounded, her face was covered with perspiration, and her breathing was labored and heavy. A sickening mist of depression, anxiety and, finally, a panic attack enveloped her. Were the demons entering her just as easily as they had entered the great hall of Jetzenstein? Dark clouds fogged her mind and she heard voices saying, "You are doomed, you cannot escape us."

Dizziness overwhelmed her. She opened her eyes to break free. She gasped for air. She was Esitel, trapped in Belzebesth's opthalir. However, she remembered the reassurances given by the archangel, in the form of William Blake. She would not yield; she would not fear, and now the voice of her dear love reached her, "Are you sure you are well?" Michael sitting beside her anxiously scrutinized her startled gaze.

"I am fine, just fine." Michael's concern had called her back to the present. She patted his hand in appreciation; pleased to be back in this friendly environment, content to have him by her side—in this lifetime. Sanath, on the other side of the oval table, paused as he scrutinized her, aware of the young woman's distress, but she smiled to reassure him that she could face the challenge.

To bring them to the desired point of enlightenment he continued as though nothing had happened, "This is accurate but not sufficient. How was it that Lord Hanuman jumped down from the tapestry?"

The cousins looked at each other and appeared perplexed. This was magic but how do you explain magic to a wizard? After some time, Lakshman answered. "I am not sure Master, I remember that you bowed."

"That's it. Precisely," exclaimed the wizard with a spark of contentment in his eyes, "and this time we come closer to the point. I bowed, and the power of this bow summoned the Archangel because it contained the authority of the Avahan."

"What's Avahan?"

"The Avahan is a special calling that projects the strength of our heart through devotion and surrender and this call, coming from the desire of the heart, triggers the response of the heavenly forces. The Archangel reacted to it because love, trust and faith were packed into this wizard's bow. That the White Monkey is a connoisseur in this matter is at the core of the Hindu, Thai and Indonesian legends, which tell of his dedication to the God King Rama. He could not resist the Avahan appeal because he felt the intensity that it projected. Do you understand the force of this bow that challenges the divine powers to respond? Have you figured out the core of the Avahan, the subtler power that can access the realm of the gods, beyond the reach of the rational mind of Urizen or the smartness of the Demon Kings?"

Lakshman hesitated, "I am not sure that I do, or frankly, I am positive that I don't. I believe this is powerful conjuring indeed: beyond our grasp. You are a wizard; we are now mere humans aren't we? How can we trigger a reflex action from the higher worlds? In the knight's hall in the castle, it all happened within a second. The connection was instantaneous. It is a complete mystery, and may I say please, you have not yet explained what this has to do with the discussions of the Daskalian Masters."

Sanath could not miss the trace of impatience in Lakshman, but he knew it was more an expression of helplessness than impertinence.

"It has to do with the way one bows! Thus spoke the Daskalians."

At this moment, Lorelei squeezed Michael's hand hard and closed her eyes. Within her, the whispers of the ratavolars in the area of the Blue Feather soiled by the intrusion, stirred with compelling emotions, but she now called the attention of her conscious mind, wielding the Glorfakir and with the edge of concentrated attention, transformed Sanath's advice into her psychic reality, recalling the power of the Triangle Rock, "Mother, I am a Sheravalian, your daughter bows to you, again and again. Your daughter is inviting you," she repeated three times.

Perhaps it was the glance of William Blake upon her, or the determination of her heart; perhaps it was the company of Stealthstars, or the Avahan that worked out. She sensed a response from her own force, something rising from her sacrum bone and she now searched the tunnels in her sinews to confront and chase away the unwanted visitors, "Get out! How dare you! Go back to hell!"

Calm returned, her heartbeat normal, only a bead of perspiration remained as a trace of this intense, brief battle. She smiled feebly at Michael, who was looking at her with loving concern. He knew what dread she had experienced at Jetzenstein Castle under the clutch of Belzebseth. She smiled and whispered, "I am fine, my love; just practicing."

Lakshman continued, "I missed this. Do you mean the Daskalians were speaking about the power of Avahan?"

"They were. For it was devotion that was released in the calling of Avahan that I used in Jetzenstein but what I heard from them was beyond my own imagination."

"How come? For you, venerable wizard to learn something new, it must be something exceptional."

"The Daskalians, Lao-tzu and Confucius, were talking about the Goddess Kuan Yin, the Chinese mother of mercy; they expressed their astonishment at Her taking a mere human form. They then discussed Her work and teachings on the Earth. For the first time, I heard about magic higher than anything I'd ever conceived possible. I heard them saying that, essentially, the Goddess bows before human beings."

"What do you mean? She bows to 'us'?"

"I listened carefully because this, in its simplicity, is the subtle trigger. When the Great Mother meets seekers, She begins by doing *namaste*, and saying I bow to all the seekers of truth. And She bows. People think it is some sort of Indian courtesy. They're wrong. They simply don't understand."

"Understand what? Please Master, could you be more specific?"

"The Daskalians say that when She bows to us, She peeps into the glory of our future, to the moment when we become the beauty that we really are, and thus, She fast-forwards the process. What She acknowledges and sees will come to pass because She surrenders to our capacity to rise. Beings from the higher worlds trust mankind. She who is omnipotent bows to us humans with complete love, trust and faith. She calls us. The Daskalians simply revealed to me the magic of a mother's love. Her surrender compels the divinity in man to rise in the same manner that the surrender in man compels the divinity in the heavens to respond. It is our divinity which stirs when She bows to us; our secret energy rises; the flame of the Buddha in us is awakened and, in some cases, glows at the top of our heads."

The group registered how the energy around the pergola was gently rising, in a slow movement, as if a higher presence was joining them; and surely enough, all present experienced a profound silence.

Lakshman felt it, and in this moment, his questioning was gone. The questions previously in his mind were now directly answered by his state of being. He noted that the wizard identified now with human beings, something he didn't recall him doing before. He added after a serene moment of contemplation, "It is amazing that the Kundalini can be awakened just like that! It was hidden in man, sleeping within the sacrum bone, out of reach. It does not rise easily. It wasn't easy even for high ascetics to access it."

"I know, Lakshman. This is something unheard of, even on top of Mount Kailash where the all-knowing gods congregate. In Jetzenstein, I bowed to the gods and my Avahan brought the Archangels into action. Can we imagine the supreme force packed in the Avahan calling of the Great Mother? Listen to this: as She bows to mankind and its freedom, She does what the Lady of the Rock had promised to do before disappearing in the waning days before the fall of Dagad Trikon."

"What did she promise?"

"To touch our hearts. The calling is from heart to heart."

Tracy recalled her dream and closed her eyes. The vision was now complete and she wanted to share it. "When She touches our hearts, all the heaviness carried by the Blue Feather dissipates and we are freed. Transformation is linked to the deeper feminine within all of us, the serpentine power, which responds. The warmth of the heart can awaken the spiritual reality of the feminine in everyone. A new world will come into existence when we reconnect with the Eternal Feminine."

After a pause, Ian said, "This strange modern civilization basks in the projections of mental concepts, the cold sun of Urizen. It is fitting Master that you reveal this to us on this, the day you met Master Blake in England given that he came on Earth to defeat this mechanical world."

Sanath nodded and continued. "She is the One who sends help to us. Everything depends on Her. This was expressed through the Retable of the Dove in the knight's hall of the castle; on this medieval triptych, Michael and Gabriel are the attendants on both sides of Mother Mary. This has a symbolic meaning. She is the pure feminine power to which the Archangels are fully devoted."

"So everything converges?" wondered Lakshmi. "The Lady of the Rock who was hidden in each of us now emerges from the sacrum bone? Master, why don't you write about everything you know?"

"What would I write?" answered Sanath sadly. "I would be laughed at. Moreover, when we write, we arrest what is dynamic; we freeze what is ever moving, in constant flux. No, writing is betrayal. Exposing the treasure of the heart is the secret of the House of Eleksim; only the rays of recognition moving through the moisture of love can reveal the rainbow. The Great Mother is now revealing the core of the Dagad Trikon magic: the beauty of the encounter with one's Self in the innermost chamber of the Inner World, the House of Ni. This is where we become Swatantra Avasthas, in command of ourselves."

"So the prophecy of the Avasthas has eventually come true? "Lorelei loved the reference to Eleksim and she intuitively felt its sheath of affectionate protection. After all, it was her House.

"It has, my child. This energy rises as you could see in the Temple of the Emerald Buddha. Ordinary people become vessels in which they contain the Buddha's living flame. The legend has become reality. It rises in the presence of the Lady of the Rock, the Great Mother, as children do in a good and proper school when a teacher enters the room."

"It is true that the Great Mother usually addresses a gathering with the greeting, *I bow to all the seekers of truth*, but I never understood it literally, I just didn't realize it has such a profound meaning," Ian said with some puzzlement.

Sean asked, "I thought it was just Her grand courtesy. I did not consider it as deep as you say it is. If She is surrendering to human beings and their willingness to ascend, then the question for us must be: how shall we respond?"

"Surely Her surrender must be met by ours, but here, don't you think Sean has a point?" enquired Jonathan almost impatiently. "Somehow I sense the beauty in what you say Master, but I wonder how this Avahan magic can be passed on to normal human beings. Surrender seems the key word here but, in military language, surrender means capitulation and defeat. No one wants to surrender! A city, which surrenders, loses the protection of its ramparts; it can be ransacked and burned, turned into a desolate abode for ghosts and roving dogs. Sorry for being my usual doubting Thomas self, we've already had this discussion, but I am not sure that surrender sounds that attractive to common folk."

"This is understandable because they dwell in the City of Man," the wizard said patiently. "I would not surrender in that city either. Surrender makes good sense only in the City of God. Once you pass through the inner gates, you enter that city and benefit from its security system. You are fully protected. Then, there is a way to let go, to surrender, which gives you ownership of the world."

"Master, this Avahan may work for you, but it is beyond what people know, it will not work for us. I agree with Jonathan." Lakshman had again forgotten that the Deep Way does not operate in the realm of thinking.

"It is very simple: you must have seen how a mother responds to the cry of her infant child?" interrupted Lorelei.

"Yes, but...?"

"Learn the calling," said Lorelei, forgetting that Lakshman, as an orphan, had never experienced this protection. She had gone to the inner place where things really happen, quietly admiring the craft of the wizard: she had noticed that his words had unlocked these movements on the battlefield of her Inner World. She was smiling, without paying much attention to the questions the men had been asking. She was following this exchange at a different level, taking it in spontaneously. Is it so that men tend to turn outside and women inside? However, Michael returned her smile and she felt he knew what she was feeling.

She had seen the tunnels from the subconscious where strong emotions condensed. In a brief moment, memories of dread had invited the presence of the evil she'd feared from ancient times. She had felt in the depth of her being, the emergence of the approaching devils, and spiders progressing behind them, and she'd fallen into the ratavolar's trap. However, she had brandished the fiery steel of the Glorfakir to fight the intruders and resorting to the Avahan, calling with the full intensity of her innocence and sincerity, she had stopped evil in its tracks. She was amazed at the swiftness of the effect. Now, in tune with Sanath's discourse, the soothing power of the Blue Feather unfolded within her heart. It was the capacity to receive the response of love from above. A sweeping feeling of self-confidence, security and faith had immediately cleared the intruders from the tunnels. Her subconscious mind was filled with the pleasant comfort of the protection of love. Looking down, she was amused to see a couple of spiders disappearing through cracks in the pavement.

The analytical mind is not as fast as the receptivity of inner intuition. Lorelei was yet to hear what she had already learned. Sanath's teachings were unfolding. And he sensed that, despite the twists and turns of his agile mind, Lakshman was progressing.

"Do not think that surrender leaves you defenseless, on the contrary. The White Horse," and here he interrupted himself with a smile, "you will have noted the name of our inn? The White Horse protects he who loves the truth. I told you about the White Horse at my Council at Jetzenstein, didn't I?"

"Yes and you seemed much worried then," recalled Jonathan, "because somehow you linked it to the death of the sacred oak. It was something I never quite understood."

Sanath said, "I didn't fully explain it at that time. The death of the oak is a symbol for the death of Christ. Think about it. After His death comes the resurrection. Today, over two thousand years later, can we see the sequence? The Father was worshiped, and then the Son came to pave the way and to open the gate. Now the Great Mother surrenders to human beings and freely grants redemption.

"Some try to play smart for their own purposes. Children always try to take advantage of the mother. However, in this case, misbehaving is most unwise. At the time of Her apparent helplessness, She is served by the fiercest power. The power of the White Rider encircles Her movement of redemption. He protects but He also punishes."

The companions, captivated by the wizard's depth, learned how the revelation of the tabernacle of Ni was under a mysterious and terrible protection that safeguarded the path, testing the sincerity of both those seeking to enter and those who had already entered. It was an immense force of destruction cloaked in the power of illusion, an unfathomable force floating in and about the House of Ni.

"Master you go too far and too fast for me," said Lakshman. "How do I move from understanding as an idea, to it being a powerful force working within me? I understand the concept of accessing the higher powers and securing their protection, but there's a difference between appreciating a concept and manifesting it in reality. I still do not understand how you managed to call the archangels in Jetzenstein? It is wizardry to me. I am still clueless how to establish the higher connection through the Avahan."

Lakshman felt dejected. The art of the Deep Way seemed so elusive, and now he felt desperate, almost rebellious. He had enough. This was just too hard. An old tune played in his head, "How does it feel, how does it feel, to be on your own..." He thought, "Aren't we all rolling stones under the hoofs of the Dark Riders?"

CHAPTER TWENTY-THREE

THE SECRET OF THE ANORHADANS

Where the unlocking mechanism of the Lily of Anorhad responds to a combination of living faith and surrender, and how it relates to the experience of connecting with the higher powers.

Jonathan continued, sharing his friend's mood, unknowingly bringing this discussion to its appointed end. "I feel stuck, as if the walls of life are closing in on me, removing my options. When I was small, I wanted to do something big with my life. Whether it was childish or child-like, I don't know; but that determination kept me going as I went through more difficult times. I always felt that I didn't want to let that little boy down, but it just gets harder and harder. I'd better leave that dream behind because I just end up frustrated. In any case, like every other Tom, Dick or Harry, other things keep me busy, like the price at the gas pump and the rising costs of health insurance. Life beats us with reality checks, and many are trapped with dull jobs or joblessness, which is not remotely exciting. So much for wanting a grand destiny, I feel more like a dog left outside in the rain."

"Maybe, but there is always an umbrella moving above you!" Jonathan looked perplexed at this unexpected remark from Tracy, who was smiling at him.

"They are finally getting closer," thought the wizard who was following the discussion between Lakshman and his best friend, trying to hide a smile. "Thank God for the women. They pick up on intuitions faster than men."

"You or I may imbibe the legend; however, I doubt if we can pass it on to others. We have discussed this many times: the world is like a play of shadow puppets. The Inner World is the reality behind the screen and whatever is projected as shadows on the screen of the material world becomes the Outer World, the only one we can see."

Sanath felt it was time to intervene, "You are missing an important point and without getting it, there is no way to understand the practicalities of how to transform within. Can't you see what it is? What did you learn from me?

Lakshman had been keeping notes throughout the day. He had just completed his observations on the astonishing encounter with William Blake and wanted to sum up the fruits of his recent discoveries. He read aloud, "Dear Master, thanks to your help, we have now uncovered three caskets for the three feathers. We understand better how the three energies function within us: they design our psychosomatic landscape and govern a wide variety of feedback and interactions at different scales of thoughts and emotions. I think we can describe them as complex adaptive systems, which are dynamic, self-organizing with emerging properties corresponding to the principles of the Avasthic houses."

He looked up from his notes to see whether people were following him, and continued. "It seems to me that they are constantly intertwined, co-evolving in the face of both exogenous and endogenous forces. They relate to the Outer and Inner Worlds. However, if these drivers put too much lateral pressure and rupture the inner balance, their action becomes linear, and this opens tunnels in our synapses, hence the danger zone patrolled by the Dark Riders. We then face disturbances, crises or sicknesses. Alternatively, if the force of the White Feather in the middle path of the spine prevails and reverberates on the others, our energies become highly integrated, and happiness occurs.

"The only trouble is that in the world in which we live, our attention is constantly drawn away from the central channel. It is impossible to stay on that axis, and we are easy prey for the devil."

Sanath replied with a touch of amusement, "The jargon is good, but forget it! The one simple thing I wish you to understand is this: we cannot defeat Thanatophor, but we can take refuge in the house of the One who can. Is this clear? There, we find the two weapons with which to defend ourselves. The ability to deal with the three channels does not depend on these concepts but on the ability to use the Glorfakir—the sword of attention—and the Sadhan, the shield of contemplation."

"Of course, Master. I just wanted to summarize." Lakshman smiled at Tracy. He suddenly understood the reference to the umbrella: refuge, protection, the Stealthstars were not alone. He felt a change of heart and replied, "You and I miss it because it is obvious Jonathan. Someone or something invisible is looking after us, someone we must meet, someone we must now see. Perhaps we failed because we wanted to fight alone, to win alone, but this was just a dream. We dream in the darkness of the night, but we must wake up in the light of the morning. I tell you, we will all have to wake up. No one will sleep or dream through the dawn of Anorhad. I remember the brilliance of my vision in the Temple of the Emerald Buddha? There is no escape, no place to hide. Time is not static. This is certain: and thank God for it. We are moving towards the breakthrough."

Sean was always articulate, and spoke as if trying to explain things to himself. "The Great Mother could see Thanatophor in hot pursuit of us. She gave us the key of Her house in the limbic area of our brains, not because we deserved it, but because we needed shelter: we were in danger. She decided to save Her children no matter what. Even though we were not sufficiently prepared, She initiated the process, and now leaves it to us in our freedom to complete it. It is a testing that the Great Mother had foreseen. There is a lot left for us to do, not to do, or even to undo."

The good wizard looked at his pupils. His purpose was challenging: to plant the seeds of the subtle principles contained in the treatise of Anorhad, which had vanished from the Avasthic library in the last days of Dagad Trikon. The men were somewhat slower than the women, but he had finally brought them to where he wanted, so that they too might solve the riddle of Dagad Trikon, a riddle that the devil had made hard to solve. Some tenets of the lore would remain hidden, but now was a good time to reveal more.

"I see what you mean," Jonathan said, "well, I suppose I do, but, frankly, it is not real: to see is not to become. Your vision belongs in another world and an invisible glass barrier separates us. The question is, how can we activate the Avahan power on this side of it?"

With a solemnity that infused his speech when he deemed it necessary, the wizard offered just one word. "Trust."

"Trust? That's all? You, you mean like on the old one-dollar bill where it was written, 'In God we trust,' between the pyramid and the eagle?" Jonathan said with a mix of insight and incredulity.

"That's right my friend," Sanath acquiesced with a broad smile, "the solution to one of the baffling twists of the Deep Way is written on that one-dollar bill, no matter how much it has lost of its past value. Some of the founding fathers of the U.S.A. met in good time with a certain Hllidarendi," he added with cool satisfaction. "I enjoyed long discussions with Jefferson in his home in Monticello. I always had a fondness for the Blue Ridges of Virginia. My dear Lakshman, it is trust that is the key to solve the puzzle of existence. Trust is the big mystery. It was smart of us to put trust on that old one-dollar bill, but ultimately it was withdrawn from circulation."

"If it were that simple, we would have solved this mystery a long time ago," interjected Lakshman.

"I grant you this point," conceded Sanath with a disarming grin, "the gods wouldn't make it too easy, would they? We aren't talking here about trust as understood by the average person. The trust that we are speaking of carries more meaning than the name found on the one-dollar bill. The trust that calls the protection of the heavens is faith, and not the blind faith invoked by the priesthood. I speak of *shraddha* that I told you about; real faith, of the kind that is not based on mere belief."

Lakshman asked, "Could we say that it's knowledge based on experience; this is your point, isn't it?"

"Undoubtedly. This is the only basis for real trust. Experience nourishes faith, and faith opens the possibility for vaster experiences. Thanatophor and his delusions can only ride the rumors of our minds; within the silence, they cannot find us. When we experience the consciousness that is beyond thought, we become connected with reality; we are wired into these wonderful energies that shape our worlds. Things start working for us. We become confident and strong: a virtuous circle is put in motion as we reap the rewards of *shraddha*. No wonders the devil relies heavily on our doubts and fears to prevent us reaching the stage of experimentation."

Lakshmi observed, "I find it ironic that the devil of the modern world, who manipulates so much of technology and science, rejects the scientific approach, don't you agree?"

Jonathan replied to his wife's question, "This is because he plays with the science of matter, but he cannot control the science of the Deep Way."

Lakshman insisted, "This doesn't sound like a big secret to me. Faith is the mainstream topic of a great number of books that were printed in the earlier centuries and see where faith landed us."

"I concede this point too. At last we touch on the tale of faith and the devil, the most artful deception of Thanatophor. Under the notion of religious faith, the devil managed to pack into the blue zone of conditionings so much ritualism, narrow mindedness, fanaticism, intolerance or violence that, naturally, man finally became allergic to the very notion of faith. As we said earlier, in the eighteenth century, after years of religious wars and abuses by the churches, modern man began crossing to the territory of Urizen. He was pushed, from the left to the right, into the clutches of Hangker. All the while devotees kill and torture while shouting '*God is great*'. Using religion to block the path to a spiritual union was a stroke of evil genius and it worked brilliantly. Today's atheists are among the victims."

"Are you saying that when the blue zone is corroded, it automatically throws you at the mercy of the corrosion of the yellow?"

"Yes, and vice versa too. We needed to open this last casket to expose the demon's tricks. Thanatophor is logical," continued the wizard, "if man walks through the gate of Anorhad, evil has lost. He tries to prevent this by stretching the forces of the two feathers. Let me recap. When we were in Bangkok, we saw the effect of Hangker on the Yellow Feather. Modern man in his own world drives at full speed, an amnesic who has forgotten the last accident. He has lost his memory. Without memories, we cannot learn. Without learning we miss the potential of our future. He who does not know his beginning cannot choose his end. With the Yellow Feather, we look only outside. We want to master others, not ourselves. We see the failings of others but not our own. We blame the societies of others; we don't improve our own. It is truly useless. Read the newspapers, this is the stuff of world news: money—*das Kapital*—becomes the capital punishment of capitalist countries, yet they refuse to face up to the reality and still wait for the next terrorist to come along. It sounds like a joke but not for the many families thrown into poverty."

"But we can correct this with the power of the Blue Feather?"

"Indeed, with *Susamskara* there is a treasure of experience that can take us forward if only we can retrieve it. But, in London, we faced another plot affecting the blue zone. Belzebseth uses the mass of inertia to stop the advance of mankind from matter to spirit. Tunnels under his influence bring us to behaviors that divert, pervert and degrade us. And then rumors and shapes of thoughts from the tunnels play tricks on us: they carry inferiority complexes, diffidence and guilt, clouds of confusion."

Sanath paused to add weight to his conclusion, "The devil wanted to snatch away the Gift from the gods, and failed. He is not enjoying the thought that the heavenly beings now want to share it with the mortals— in his scheme; he is battling us with more success as both feathers combine to bind us in clouds of delusion. What is worthy today is invisible; what is useless steals the show. The inner mechanism of psychic energies is either blocked, or it malfunctions. We don't see that when we hurt others, we hurt ourselves. We need to master the art of the calling for the help of the energies of life and love."

"Please explain again why 'trust' is your magic word?"

"Remember the one-dollar bill? *Shraddha* is trust in God, and this is the antidote for a simple reason: it is linked with the truth, to the clarity of the White Feather. The world in delusion can be seductive for a while, but it inexorably leads to ugliness while reality opens the gate of beauty, and this is not delusion. Trust in our destiny means simply that we confidently look for the truth."

"Our great thinkers say there is no absolute truth, but I guess this is exactly what Thanatophor wanted them to think isn't it?"

"And for good reason, Jonathan. What is liberation? It's the truth for those who follow it. What is destruction? It's the truth for those who don't. The Outer World is an animated entertainment, a pantomime of illusions that humans believe to be real because it is their personal creation. They believe in this artificiality but the worst liars are those who believe their own lies and who dress themselves up in the appearance of sincerity."

"Yes Master, I understand. It seems that our ego lost the perspective: we love our own creations and forget to love ourselves, perhaps because we are the creation of someone else?"

"It is by looking inside that we can find who has created us. The inside of the watch reveals the watchmaker. Anorhadans know that in the Sixth House, we must have the courage to look for the hidden truth of the Inner World, and *shraddha* is the aptitude that carries us there. It helps deploy the Tricolor Lily; it expresses trust in the goodness of life, in the beauty of this universe, no matter how much ugliness Thanatophor pours into it. Finally, *shraddha* expresses the experience that we are children of God. Sheltered under such a bounteous genealogical tree, we can no longer be affected by delusions. When *shraddha* is established the foundations of the fortress are unshakable; we have done the job; our blue zone is shielded."

Tracy turned to the wizard and said, "So this is the formula for the Avahan call to reach the heavens: surrender and *shraddha*! This is how you invited the White Monkey isn't it?"

"Yes, and with this understanding, you have entered the protected territory of the Anorhadans. *Shraddha* opens the left petal of the Lily. Surrender opens the right petal. These are the qualities that made the Anorhadans so rare, even among the Avasthas. This is why they are positioned on the last portal, the closest to the supreme destination, the House of Ni."

"There weren't any books on the Seventh House in the Avasthic library of the Sand Keeper. Why was that?" Sean asked.

"Because you need the power of the Lady of the Rock to break the Seventh Seal, and this was the secret. The seers were not permitted to talk about it, lest the devil try to spoil this too by using his tantrika practices to disable the inner instrument."

"This was then, what about now?" asked Michael.

"Sean can tell you. To settle in the House of Ni, the Goddess is reintroducing, through the gift of experience, such a thing as real faith to our miscreant world. As the Buddha Maitreya, the Mother of the triple feathers, She is permitting the rise of energy that calms our thought processes and activates the pure insights that propel the Great Scheme. *Shraddha* brings us to our true identity, which releases a tremendous joy because we become so much more than what we expected."

The meaning behind the wizard's words was slowing sinking in.

Lakshman nodded in assent. "I sense the truth in what you say. We have been knocking on heaven's door but the handle to open it was on the other side. Someone must open that door for us, and that's why we need the calling of the Avahan. It makes sense. However, I must confess, going back to the miracle at Jetzenstein Castle, I would not have been able to invite the White Monkey to surge from the tapestry and to materialize into our world, standing there with these two terrifying demons breathing down my neck."

"I know," said the wizard softly, "but this is why you are not the Master. Day by day, step by step, enjoy your life and rejoice in your faith: faith in yourself, in life, in the love that you can feel. If we don't dare to become what we, in truth, really are, we won't know the glory that awaits us. Trust that you can go within, trust in your truth, trust that you will find: reality is good, is beautiful, is true. The middle path will open much faster. It will widen before your steps when you progress with the sincerity of your desire and the depth of your experience."

Sanath hesitated but continued on his course, "Reality will open to you, and one day you may see the White Monkey smiling at you outside the legend. Or perhaps, as the returned Avasthas meet up again, they may feel the presence of another of the great ones who visit us from the heavens. If they do so outside the legend, know that the age of delusion is over and the Golden Age has arrived."

"Are you saying that all the heavenly beings will help us again, as they did in the days of the Avasthas, when they attended the great festivals of Shambalpur?"

"They do already. Their actions are all around us, attentive, subtle, delicate, and they respect our freedom; this is why people do not perceive them yet. The heavenly beings will help if we cross over into their territory. Their realm is beyond thoughts."

"You mean to say that they have a place?"

"Yes, their place, their home is the House of Ni."

Simultaneously, they realized that the wizard had used higher magic, or maybe it was the magic of his subject because, when he pronounced the word "Ni" a soothing wellness entered into them and rose to the area at the top of their heads, a fountain of coolness, freshness and benevolence.

The day had been intense and ended in a splendid display of mellowing light. They returned to the inn and disbanded. Sanath, Ian, Kheto and Mariluh, sat in the ochre lounge and prepared the agenda for the next meeting of the Council of the Order of Hllidarendis.

As dinner was about to be served, Ian took a call. He listened attentively and said simply, "Very well, we shall do so." His expression instantly changed: it became more interrogative, a shade luminous. He whispered to Sanath who looked visibly moved and responded with a sigh, "So it is confirmed: we come to it at last."

Ian nodded towards Mariluh and Kheto, and in a most unusual gesture of affection towards the high wizard, he gently pressed the shoulder of the elder in a gesture of support and encouragement. He called for the limousine and gathered the group together.

They were intrigued by what the wizard had to say. "I told you that more was to come. Ian informs me that the Great Mother is aware of our presence here and that She greets you all. She invites us, Stealthstars and Hllidarendis, to join the followers who will gather around Her tonight in Henley-on-Thames. This summons is of great importance for the fate of my Order and for my own fate. When legend and reality converge, legend dissipates like smoke in a breeze. Come, let's get moving."

CHAPTER TWENTY-FOUR

THE SHAWL OF ELEKSIM

Where the few Stealthstars, following the traces of the legend, find that they are not alone, and how Lakshmi rediscovers and enjoys the magic protection of a mother's love, wrapped in the shawl of Eleksim.

Ian was smiling. This was the news he had hoped for and expected as he had been seeking a clearance for the companions to attend the gathering in Henley. The impatience of the Stealthstars mounted and in the excitement, the tiredness of a long day disappeared completely.

They boarded the limousine in silence, and in contemplative anticipation, swept through a scenic landscape with the atmosphere of the grand finale of an orchestral work, majestic and definitive.

The summer sunset seemed to keep the dusk at bay, as though waiting for them to reach their destination, and painted what seemed to be the backdrop of a mythical tale in drapes of splendor. The dark clouds around the sun emitted nuggets of gold, and parting rays beamed through disparate black and orange shapes. They softly caressed the folds of the surrounding hills and bathed the countryside in a haze of powdery majesty.

They followed the A4130 road to Henley-on-Thames immersed in a velvety light; amazed at the luminous tenderness that magically echoed the state they savored within. At the end of what had been an extraordinary day, nature was offering yet another happening, beyond any expectation.

Henley is a charming, riverside market town in yellowish grey stone, whose prosperity dates back to the twelfth century. As they crossed the

Thames via the historic, five-arched bridge, Sanath commented, "Like the Ganges, the Rhine and other special rivers, the Thames belongs to the geography of the Deep Way and carries with it a mystical property. I shall bring you to its source if we have time."

They turned right into Bell Street and were greeted at the entrance of Marlow Street by a sign which read, 'Welcome to the Swiss Farm International Camp.'

They arrived in a parking lot that was almost full, and followed, on foot, a throng of people streaming in the direction of the festival. They passed along a beautiful stretch of river where hedgerows and trees flanked the access path. Here and there, in sylvan spots, families enjoyed evening picnics. They skirted a fishing lake where ducks swam placidly among the reeds, and suddenly they saw their destination, a gently wooded park. Sited in rolling countryside at the foot of the Chiltern Hills, it descended from a border of thick forest down towards the Thames. Campers strolled amid multicolored tents and some queued at a field kitchen while others sat on blankets eating their evening meal.

Young mothers rallied children in the direction of a large white tent that had been erected at the bottom of the slope next to the river. The top of its multi-coned roof, surrounded by advancing shade, was still ablaze in the magnificence of the last rays of the sun. When he saw it, Jonathan stopped and looked perplexed. Lakshmi asked, "What is it, darling?"

He shook his head. "The white rectangle, next to the river, the hills around...No, there is no mistake, this is the place I noticed this morning as my plane circled overhead while waiting for permission to land. I had a strange sensation that England was calling me, as in the enchanted realm of a fairy tale. It was quite wonderful, the brilliance of the morning sunshine, and now in the last fires of dusk. Lakshmi, I tell you, this place has a light that beams for us."

Lakshmi gently pressed his hand. She was alert, empty of thoughts, entering the regal space of the present moment. "This feeling, this bubbling inside me, isn't this the signal that the celestial beings are not far away?" She raised her head towards the first night stars. Moved instinctively by her ancient Avasthic background, she was feeling the presence of the higher worlds. This night would prove to be a milestone in her life.

The air had turned fresh and crisp, and they felt a quiet happiness coursing through them. Sean enquired at the information booth in the middle of the field where a diligent organizer told him the Great Mother had left London and was on Her way by car and would arrive in less than an hour.

Sanath wisely decided that it would be difficult to remain together in this large congregation and suggested they moved as they please and to meet again at the end of the function, most probably after midnight.

At the mention of the arrival of the Great Mother, Lakshmi's mind went blank. This was all going rather fast for her. Together with Jonathan and Tracy she joined the growing throng of people of all ages and nationalities that was slowly approaching the entrance of the large tent.

The tent was almost full when Jonathan and Lakshmi entered, with women sitting on the right side on a carpeted floor and men on the left. Feeling a little intimidated and wanting to stay close to each other, they found a free space in the middle, not far from the front. Jonathan wanted to prepare himself, so he closed his eyes and almost immediately went into the inner space, that people around called meditation.

This was to be the night where the power of Eleksim, the Fourth House, would reveal itself to Lakshmi, and she subconsciously anticipated that something would happen. She felt increasing trepidation. "The goddess told us to come; however, there is no one to receive us. There is such a crowd before the stage. How will she find us?" She checked her hair nervously; her heart beat faster. This moment meant so much to her, how would she handle it? She should not miss a single detail.

The podium spanned the full breadth of the tent and was elaborately decorated with chandeliers, floral arrangements, and a large painted backdrop behind a throne.

A silver tray contained a copious display of fruit of many kinds. Attendants, young men dressed in white linen, and women dressed in rich silks, brought the last touches to the decoration of the podium in anticipation of the arrival of the Great Mother. The lights in the tent were as soft as candlelight and granted a sense of familial intimacy to the large gathering. Lakshmi did not know if she really belonged here. Her notion of intimacy did not fit with sitting in the midst of a thousand strangers.

Onstage, a tall, blond, young woman began playing a piano, and was soon joined by a singer who looked like her twin sister. They were accomplished performers who sang soulfully with a unique purity. Their command of their powerful and silky voices was wonderful, and in the vibrancy of their singing, they carried the emotions of the multitude that had congregated here to meet someone very much loved by all. A group, who sang rhythmical, Indian village folk songs, followed them and created waves of merry hand clapping. Excitement rose among the audience, but Lakshmi felt somewhat estranged: she could not quite join in the mood.

It was now the turn of an Irish singer with violin accompaniment. A young Englishman followed on harmonium and invited the audience to sing notes whose pitch would affect the frequency of the spiritual energy centers within the body. Lakshmi thought the claim extravagant, but she had to admit the relaxing sensations and vibrations along her spine. By contrast, the rendition of a Bach Oratorio left her with a sense of lightness in her head. She was surprised. Why was it that music had such diverse sensorial effects on this astonishing congregation? But yes, she remembered: the Avasthas worshipped music and this must have been the reason.

Clearly, art was a major medium of expression and energy for this assembly, and Lakshmi fleetingly remembered that Rasa music was at the core of the culture of the Avasthas. At least, this was a common point between the faraway past and the present, and she was about to enjoy one more proof of it.

The jovial master of ceremonies, who spoke in dulcet Caribbean tones, next introduced a group of two men on harmonium and guitar, and two singers who came from towns in the Czech Republic. Their voices were beautiful and melodious but what carried the assembly was the quality of the heart that poured through them. By the time they'd finished, the conversational buzz in the tent had completely stopped and the end of the performance was received in a deep, vast silence that finally broke into mounting applause. The musicians bowed, smiled timidly, and left the stage. After this highlight, a variety of songs, pantomimes and dances from all over the world kept melody and energy flowing.

Meanwhile, the other Stealthstars were still outside the tent. Sean, Saint Michael and Lorelei sat on the grass together. Sean had recognized many faces as soon as he'd arrived in the camp. Being a student of the Great Mother for a few years, he had made lots of friends. Some greeted him fondly. "Hi Sean, you're here, all the way from Thailand?" At that moment, a small group walked by, chatting merrily. "What boon would you ask from Her?" A man answered his friend; "I'd ask Her in my heart that I should learn how to type." The Stealthstars looked at each other and burst out laughing.

Sean said, "We don't know what everyone asks, receives or understands, but we have all received considerable powers, and it shows in the positive way that we can effect each other. I want to show you." He asked one of the young men to join them, inspired by a sudden idea. "Hi John, could you join us for a minute and help me. This friend of mine is 'new' and perhaps could you work on him for a little while?"

"Sure, with pleasure." John came closer and knelt behind Michael, who was sitting cross-legged on the grass. He addressed him with simple instructions, "Please, close your eyes, open your hands, palms upwards, and with my hands, I'll raise your subtle energy up your spine."

Three times, with his attention on Michael, without touching him, he slowly raised his hands from the base of Mike's spine to the top of his head, while quietly saying a prayer. He said, "You don't need to do anything; I feel a cool breeze coming from your spine. Wow! It's very strong." He paused for a while and added, "The Great Mother tells us that all of us have this energy. She is your spiritual Mother you know, the one who gives you the second birth. If I put my attention on you, I can feel a wonderful peace."

John was just enjoying this feeling and added, "I feel a fan of cool air flowing from the top of your head!" A smile appeared on Michael's lips. His eyes remained closed. After some time, he said, "I felt it, a movement from within my spine and my mind is silent."

"Everyone can get it now," exclaimed John happily, "but this is an truly blessed night." Michael shook his head and said, "I feel quite wonderful, quite amazing really. By the way, may I enquire, what do you do for a living," he asked John, "besides being an accomplished wizard?"

"By training, I am a plumber, but now I am a builder, a Golden Builder. This is the name of the company I work with. I do everything from the floor to the roof. I also do the pipes."

"If you work on them as well as you did on my inner channels, you certainly do a great job!" They laughed, and John joyfully waved them goodbye and disappeared into the dusk.

Sean had decided to join a band of young men at the entrance to the camp, to greet and escort the incoming motorcade with a procession of burning torches. Michael and Lorelei mingled with the people around them, walked up to the kitchen and ate a tasty snack, sitting on the ground in the company of others who were facing the river and taking pleasure in the mellow ambiance of the summer dusk. They engaged in conversation with a middle-aged teacher and psychotherapist from Elkstone near Cheltenham, and a pretty, young Chinese investment lawyer from Shanghai.

The Chinese woman told Lorelei and Michael that she had not met the Great Mother one on one, she'd just seen Her a couple of times within a large group. She'd been in similar festivals where thousands of followers would simply meditate in Her presence. However, the effect on her well-being was great, and this compelled her to come back whenever possible. She said it felt like waking up inside, opening up, everything becoming more real, more enjoyable, as if normal life, the life that is normal for most people, was a kind of sleep. It was both getting high while going deep within at the same time, just on meditation.

The teacher shared her good fortune: she had met the Great Mother twenty years previously at a time when She hardly had any followers in the West. She'd kept a diary to record her experiences and narrated how, just a few days ago, she'd offered flowers to the Great Mother at Heathrow Airport, who'd turned towards Her, looked into her eyes, smiled, and said, "May God bless you." But, the teacher recalled that she felt caressed inside by a deep kind-heartedness, as if indeed, these words were not merely polite greetings. She'd felt coolness on the top of her head and came away with a sense of really being blessed.

During the quest for the Dagad Trikon legend, Lorelei and Michael also had powerful experiences and known intense feelings. They would have loved to share their own history with these two endearing people. After all, they thought, the followers of the Great Mother had crossed the portals to the Inner World; they must know something about the Grand Scheme. But how could they tell about angels and demons, the Great Houses and the Three Feathers? Could anyone believe the Avasthic saga? They remembered their promise to the wizard. They would not tell.

The mood was relaxed; the wind carried merry laughter and fragments of conversations in different languages. The notes from a guitar mingled with singing floated down from a group sitting in a circle next to the forest. A young woman approached them, waved in the direction of a nearby rectangular tent and asked engagingly: "Have you already seen our exhibition on William Blake?" Michael stared, incredulous at the apparent coincidence, while Lorelei struggled, "Thank you very much, but we were there a little while ago."

"You saw the exhibition already? How did you like it?"

"Well, no—I mean yes! We liked it very much. Blake is such..." Lorelei swallowed, looking at Michael for the words, "such an extraordinary artist."

The young woman smiled graciously, happy for their appreciation of the exhibition that she, and her friends had prepared. "It was put together by Luis from Portugal, have you met him? He has been researching Blake for years and recently discovered the precise site of Blake's grave." She happily nodded goodbye, and walked away.

"Blake is a genius, you know," said the teacher in a serious tone. "The Great Mother says he came to England for a special purpose, linked to the Archangel Michael. Quite astonishing really."

Lorelei and Michael smiled politely and looked at each other with an expression of mutual helplessness. Wouldn't it be odd to share that they'd met William Blake in his home in Lambeth that very morning? The fiancés parted from their new acquaintances with some friendly words, and headed toward the tent where reproductions of Blake's engravings and etchings were hanging on exhibition panels.

"My goodness!" Lorelei exclaimed. "It's the story of Job again. Here are the same series of plates where God put his hands on the top of Job's head."

"Touching, isn't it, that he chose this story; he liked it so much. I guess Blake was telling us we were going to be tested but that everything would turn out right in the end. Look at the last plate, they sing and hold musical instruments in their hands: it is a happy ending."

Meanwhile Lakshman had brought Tracy to the tent entrance. On this evening their sense of mutual affection was softly converging and seemed blessed by the emerging night stars. He told her that he would like to remain alone for a little while before entering the tent as he wanted to prepare for the occasion, because he sensed that this evening could be an important turning point of his life. He had not approached the Goddess when they had reached the basin of Vaikuntha, and he wanted to make the most out of this exceptional occasion; he wanted to be rested and ready.

The best thing to do, he thought, was to take a short nap before the big moment. He walked along the large meadow near the border of the forest and lay on his back in the soft grass. He felt sleepy as the energy of the place pervaded him with a cozy torpor. He moved imperceptibly from sleep to dream and found himself gazing at the stars above his head. One star was clearly moving, and at first he thought it was a satellite but suddenly, two other stars were set in motion too. Gradually, a large number of stars began to perform a stellar ballet in the sky. Bewildered, he watched them regroup to form a shape: the shape of a horse, a horse in the sky. It is the sign!

The constellation of the horse appeared with chilling clarity, much sharper than the other constellations around it, which had slowly faded out of sight. However, there was something else, something buzzing around like a dark fly and coming closer and closer. "Oh no!" thought Lakshman, "it is one of those, one of the Riders, they have found us."

In this blessed place, he had forgotten about Thanatophor's existence; and he was both surprised and alarmed. He felt a paralysis overwhelm him and the flying shape was now near, hovering above the camp. It was hard to distinguish in the night, but he could now see the Rider, dressed in greenish attire. It had a woman's face, dark with yellow slanted eyes.

"The witch, this is Mokolo, the foe of the Fifth House." Lakshman was dumbfounded. Now, it seemed to him that the stars were falling on the earth; he was tossing his head from side to side, and these were not stars, but large icicles, and no, he was not in England but in Peru where snow and ice were raining down on the frightened population of the Inca fortress of Machu Pichu. He could not understand where he was, what was happening and then he heard the voice of Mariluh, "No, no it cannot be..." He awoke to the sound of a conch being blown, still shaking his head from side to side as he emerged from the lingering images of this powerful dream. Twilight had advanced, and the camp was embraced by long shadows.

A series of conches were being blown at the entrance to the park, announcing the arrival of the guest of honor in a motorcade. The last pilgrims, and a group of torchbearers surrounded three cars which had stopped before the entrance to the tent. Echoes of drums and singing came from inside. Lakshman arose and hurried down the slope.

The last pilgrims were pouring in and Lakshmi was happy to see Lakshman entering the tent because soon there would not be any place left to sit. Car headlights shone through the entranceway and torches of the escort party flashed against the tent walls. A curtain was drawn to hide the podium as the arriving party with the guest of honor entered from one side. The assembled crowd arose in one movement and stood before the golden curtain in silence.

Lakshmi had not yet dealt with the tunnels in her brain as Lorelei had done at the Inn, and a surreptitious fear was surging. How come that she, the maiden of Eleksim, could not open her heart?

Jonathan closed his eyes, and focused inwards, his body oscillating slightly, backwards, forwards, as if he was on a boat; he thought he heard the tide from the sea. Then he realized that the feeling came from a gentle pulsation within his spine. Lakshmi was staring at the curtain, her hands sweating. She almost feared this moment she'd prepared for and sensed that it would dispossess her of the legend in which she had taken refuge during these last years. She was afraid her neighbors could hear her heart-beat. Every emotion within was magnified. Images flashed through her mind at a fast pace: her daughter Ananya, how she wished she could be here; was this the end of the quest? At least, Jonathan seemed all right; why couldn't her mind stay at peace? She recalled nestling in the pink sari of the Goddess of Vaikuntha; the intimacy of the encounter in the sari shop in New Delhi; what was going to happen now? For no apparent reason, tears started rolling down her cheeks.

The assembly sang a song unknown to her, something reverential and welcoming. The curtain opened. Everyone bowed. A couple of tall women stood directly in front of her, and in any case Lakshmi did not dare to look. She sat down when the audience did and kept her eyes riveted on the ground. Finally, and very slowly, she raised her head. The palms of her hands were open towards the podium and she felt a cool breeze flowing in, and she stared intensely. The Great Mother was sitting upon a throne dressed in a creamy-white, silk sari with a red border and wearing a dark-red woolen shawl. She was gazing on the crowd and seemed both very near and very far.

The Lady looked very much like the person she had met at the sari shop in Delhi, and yet, at the same time, She seemed somehow different. Here She sat with a royal ease, Her head reclining back. Her gaze peered far above the heads of the congregation as if examining a gathering of invisible hosts suspended in mid-air at the back of the tent. Her silent presence filled the hall. She was aged, or rather, ageless, looking ancient and more remote than the affable, vibrant and welcoming Lady, who had presented her with a wedding sari.

Small children hurried to the podium in a sweet disorder that attendants attempted to control. The ceremony began with songs and offerings of such items as sugar, water, honey and milk.

Lakshmi's expectations had been so high and now, suddenly she felt anxious. An insidious apprehension crept in like a mist sweeping over her; had the ratavolars been fully cleared? In this moment, she realized with a fright that her luck might let her down. Feeling increasingly uncomfortable, she remembered that she was usually uneasy in the midst of large crowds. She found she could not even move her legs.

She experienced heat and unease in several parts of her body. She no longer felt the vibrations on her hands, nor was she anywhere near the state of bliss she had enjoyed in past times and at the beginning of the ceremony. The cozy comfort of the silk couch she had enjoyed in the basin of Vaikuntha, the velvet hospitality of the Goddess that had made her feel so perfectly at home was now a distant and painful memory in contrast to her present condition.

Lakshmi did not want to be drowned in the tide, a blurred shape in the faint light that bathed this multitude. Her entire body was straining as if to reach the podium to scream, "Let me out or let me in, please I am here, meet me."

The Great Mother did not listen. She was beyond reach. Tears came to Lakshmi's eyes, hot tears rolling down her face, messing her make-up and burning her cheeks. She bent her head further to hide her shame. "I am supposed to have been one of the elect, Erilie of Eleksim, Captain of the Sheravalian Guard, and banner carrier of the Lady of Dagad Trikon; I should be there on the podium with Her, holding that banner. Look at me...it is pathetic, what a mess!"

This should have been a catharsis, a festival of joy. Alas, she recognized the feeling that had slowly penetrated her. She recognized the bite of the ratavolar. It was this old foe, a foe she had known as a little girl. She was the one to seek fusion through love, and it was this fear again: the fear to be left out, excluded, to be left alone. She remembered the way she'd slipped out of the Vaikuntha water world as a guest in the wrong place who'd somehow outstayed her welcome. Her departure from Vaikuntha was understandable enough as one is not supposed to dwell too long in a place where one landed without a physical body. Nevertheless, this was different; she was sitting upon the ground of planet Earth, in her own world of blood and flesh. Was she also out of place here? Was she being discarded?

Fear is the specter that haunts the blue zone of emotions when the light of Saint Michael, the flame of *shraddha* is nowhere to be seen. As if matters could be worse, she began to relive the plight of Guinevere and Lancelot again, the love that hurts, the passion that destroys. Would hell grip her once more through the tunnels of her fears? Could the demons ride through them and seize her here, extending their iron grasp and snatch her?

She turned to Jonathan to plead for help. But her husband's eyes were closed. He had left her behind, passed the inner gates and was traveling inwards. His discrete smile suggested he was dwelling in that place she could not reach. It did not comfort her in the least; on the contrary, she felt lonelier. The pilgrims crowded around her were sitting tightly; she felt trapped. She felt a stranger now. The veil of that single fear was clouding everything: separating her from what she sought. Hurting badly, she then noticed that she was feeling cold. She was so cold that her entire body started shivering. In despair she raised her head again to look at the podium. What followed is a sequence she would never forget.

Without paying attention to the children who were pouring water on Her feet, She who sat on the throne leaned forward and said something to a woman by Her side. This did not interrupt the ceremony but the woman spoken to by the Great Mother looked into the crowd as if looking for someone. She took the burgundy shawl from the shoulders of the Lady and came down from the stage, walking hesitatingly past the first rows of the audience. She turned to the Great Mother as if to seek directions. The Great Mother gestured with Her hand for her to advance further. It was clear that She couldn't see Lakshmi sitting behind the two tall women, but when the attendant reached Lakshmi's row, the Goddess pointed to her. The lady-in-waiting leaned towards a stunned Lakshmi and whispered in slightly accented English, "Hi, I am Mihaela. Mother told me you were feeling cold." Without waiting for a response, she put the shawl of the Goddess on Lakshmi's shoulders in an ample and protective gesture. And without uttering another word, as if this was the most natural thing in the world to have done, she smiled warmly and walked back to the podium.

The Great Mother was now looking straight at Lakshmi with a playful smile. It expressed total understanding. Lakshmi felt the full blast of love within her heart; it melted the ice of her fears. Complete shyness overcame her; she bowed her head again, stunned by the speed of the relief. The tears flowing now were of blessedness, too intense to remain inside. When she raised her head again, the Great Mother was looking at the children on the podium. Lakshmi O'Lochan was in awe. Her inner eye had a glimpse at the serene face of William Blake. Blake—Michael, Mihaela, and the shawl...everything seemed connected.

The sense of exquisite comfort under the shawl was wonderful. She realized that her body temperature had changed. The shawl provided soft and pleasant warmth. She was now detached from hankerings, the fear of being left behind. The specter of separation, the grimacing ghosts had vanished; the tunnels were empty, the holes plugged. The ratavolar had gone. Fearlessness, bravery and courage returned with confidence in herself, the trust that love, what she most wanted, could not be lost because the reality of love was stronger than the delusion of doubting it. With *shraddha* firmly rooted in her heart, she could sense the depth of her own powers. She could see everything distinctly. The passing clouds do not abolish the vastness of the sky. The firmament remains in its own eternity; no matter how fierce the storms and tempests. Likewise, the love from above does not subside because we ignore it.

The audience sang a song, '*She does it all*,' and it echoed through her head like multicolor crystals releasing a flow of tumultuous joy. The happening was so direct and unexpected that she almost felt disbelieving, but she could not deny what had happened, because the burgundy shawl was on her shoulders, the legend was true. She had to control a surge of laughter. Just a shawl and such a shield, what a trick! And such a simple and motherly way to restore a world of protection and comfort. She caressed the soft pashmina texture. "It is red too, the color of the Fourth House."

She heard a voice behind her whispering, "This is the Shawl of Eleksim. This mantle of love poured the dust of stars that made our race and draped the great kings of yore in robes of grace. It is the Mother's commitment, the comfort of caring affection, the promise that we shall be safe, protected and under the bandhan of the heavenly powers. The shawl protects the human tribe, the togetherness of couples and families. Experience is the only way a human being can understand, and we are humans now: the time has come for them to discover and to trust this protection."

She turned. It was Sanath, right behind Jonathan. How so? He, who was the only one in the world left of his kind, the Aulya Elkaim Ekamonon, ancient Lord Wizard and Sand Keeper of Dagad Trikon and now the Hllidarendi Grand Master, was seated humbly on the floor with the rest of the people. Lakshmi felt he ought to have been recognized. But then she understood.

The message tenderly brought to her by the shawl signifies that love reaches you wherever you are. Being on the podium has no meaning for a worshiper; the place you occupy, the role you play has no importance. There is no particular spot to sit in the kingdom of the House of Ni. After all, it is hosted in the brain, a kingdom whose center is the heart and its limits nowhere.

Sanath's face beamed with such radiant energy that it seemed almost fluid. He looked so young or rather, luminously outside of time. Lakshmi felt reverence: she had the impression that she saw in him both death and resurrection. The magic was leaving him, but his true Self had now emerged in its own splendor.

Jonathan looked at his wife with fond affection. He had opened his eyes, distracted when Mihaela had brought the shawl of Eleksim, and from the depth of his meditation, the episode seemed to him almost natural. The Lady of the Rock, in Her present form, was simply greeting the returned Captain of her Sheravalian Guard. In doing so She was reminding the former leader of the young women holy warriors that she belonged to the House of Eleksim, to those blessed with the aptitude to activate and respond to the power of the heart. On the podium, two Indian women began singing a tune of love addressed to the ancient deities. The vibrancy contained in this song was indeed a splendid illustration of the Avahan faculty to call the world of the heavens.

Lakshmi registered that the simple music from disciples playing before the Great Mother was capable of such pulling power. Avasthas used music as a carrier of subtler realities and forces, to charm or to kill. The artists present had certainly learned this from the Lady of the Rock who was now resurrecting the lost lore. It was all here; she saw in a flashback the grandeur of the festival hall of Shambalpur.

The devotion in this music was a power that resided in her too. The singers were expressing her feelings; she was with them, and she could not stop flashes of intuitions happening collectively, like in the football stadium of Sean's dream but much higher, much more subtle. It includes them, me, it's all of us together; it's us, it is about us. The heart is the opener of the brain: I feel it. Eleksim, it's the secret of my House, the heart rising to the House of Ni within the head." The music weaved the palpitating fabric of collective consciousness.

The continuous, powerful and joyous serenity was in itself so remarkable. The former Avasthas scattered throughout the tent had entered a state of inner tranquility, feeling transformed, completely purified.

The end of the pujan festival came. Everything was done and accomplished; the last notes of the final song died. The Great Mother sat silently on Her throne looking at the assembly which was looking back at Her. Nobody moved: nothing was happening to the external eye in the Outer World. But the Stealthstars registered tsunamis of energies in the Inner World. In one movement that ended on the palm of Her raised right hand, the Great Mother was lifting up a flow of common pain and burden, dissolving hurdles, sucking in doubts and fears, sorrows and diseases from those who beheld Her. At the same time, in a movement originating from Her left hand stretched out towards the assembly, She was releasing the content of the cup, the elixir of joy, not in its ecstatic liquid form but in an ethereal gaseous consistency, bubbling in the open heads like a champagne of light and lightness. She was irrigating the united field of these hearts with the grand joy of the Holy Grail flowing from the House of Ni. She had hardly spoken a word during the entire ceremony.

Lakshmi felt a foamy well-being spreading from her chest, rising slowly into her head, carried by the sense of complete belonging she had felt in her vision of the Vaikuntha world when she had visited the abode of the Emerald King. The sensation carried *bhakti*, the word of her childhood that expressed devotion to God. It was sacred yet familiar, enjoying fusion with the whole; it was both physical and spiritual. Lakshmi turned to look around: a velvety smoothness had descended on the unity of the listeners engrossed in the devotional songs. "So this is where we finally find the lost Stealthstars," thought Lakshmi with pride. Her tears this time were tears of blessedness.

`Eventually, the curtain came down. They stood with the rest of the assembly, and the final hymn filled the tent, its parting words carrying the testament of the Archangel Michael.

Bring me my sword, O clouds unfold. Bring me my chariots of fire.
I shall not cease from mental fight, Nor shall my sword sleep in my hand,
Till we have built Jerusalem, In England's green and pleasant land.

The Great Mother left the tent, shortly after the completion of the ceremony. Lakshman being one of the last to have entered the tent was sitting next to the exit. The crowd formed an alley between the entrance and a white Mercedes. Pushed along by the movement of the throng, Lakshman found himself in the first rank. People of all ages, all races lined up next to him with flowers to offer and seeing he that had none, his neighbor gave him a white rose to offer. The Great Mother, progressing slowly, accepted each flower in turn, and passed them to an attendant walking behind Her. When She arrived before him, the Stealthstar offered his rose without a word and much of him went into this gesture. The Great Mother had been receiving the flowers with much grace, mostly silently, sometimes saying, "May God bless you." But when She reached him, She looked into his eyes and asked with a radiant smile, "How are you, Lakshman? It is so nice to meet you again after such a long time." He opened his mouth, but no sound came out. She was already accepting the flower of the next person in the line.

Lakshman enjoyed a sense of blissful vacuity and basking in this wondrous condition, he could sense someone's fixed stare. His eyes met Tracy's who stood several rows away, but the smile on her shining face spoke volumes. She was looking tenderly at him as if to say, "Didn't I tell you, the Queen never stopped loving you?" He returned her smile, bubbling with an overflowing joy that Tracy shared in this brief and unique happening.

There was great jubilation in the air and a joyous, relaxed ambiance filled the tent. Young women distributed fruit, cakes and candies. People began chatting and the scene was soon buzzing like a bee's nest.

Sanath and the members of his Order were the first to leave the tent after the departure of the Mercedes. Followed by Ian, Kheto and Mariluh, he went to a more secluded spot, and they sat under a birch grove next to the river.

CHAPTER TWENTY-FIVE

THE GAME IS A SPIRAL

Where the true nature of those who came to the Great Mother is revealed to themselves, and why the good wizard dissolves the magic Order of the Hllidarendis as a circle is completed and a new spiral rises.

A celebration of firecrackers ended the festival. Over a thousand people disbanded after the completion of the ceremony and close to midnight the camp was still animated.

Sanath's party did not join them for this had been a very long day. They gathered in front of the tent and walked towards the river looking for Sanath, each one eager to share their impressions of the evening.

"Have we moved in another plane?" asked Tracy? "It feels so wonderful, not quite of this world."

"Definitely," responded Lakshman. "She has taken us through the secret nerve that passes the constricted Gate of Anorhad. How can I say it?" He struggled for the right words, "The future is now: She brought an entire group of people on the central channel of the White Feather and into in the chamber of the House of Ni, a place that none explored before according to what the wizard said. A new story is being written."

"You can say a new history."

"And what about the shawl?" Lakshman asked his cousin merrily. "You are so lucky really; how did you manage to catch Her attention?"

"Touch it. Feel how soft it is. It kept me so warm. I didn't do anything, I can't believe it." Lakshmi halted; tightly wrapped in the Great

Mother's shawl she was in an expansive mood: happy to have a chance to recount the episode. "You know, I felt desperate. The shawl of Eleksim was Her response. I feel whole now: I feel complete. Everything is webbed together. It is amazing. She just knew," and she added with a grin, "Eleksim is the best!"

"When you reach the Inner World, a miracle is a natural thing, this is what the Avasthas used to say."

They stretched out their palms and felt the cool breeze flowing from the shawl. No one moved, not even an eyelid. They felt light and joyful. They continued towards the park's exit, and found the wizard sitting with the three members of his Order. The mood of the Hllidarendis was grave in contrast to their own lightness.

Sanath gestured for them to sit and invited them to share their experiences of the evening. Lakshmi, stars still sparkling in her eyes, related the miracle of the shawl, so grand in its simplicity. Kheto and Mariluh looked at her with affection and pride, as elders would at a favorite student on graduation day.

Then, Lakshmi added pensively, "There may be another angle to the Grand Scheme, and all the troubles of this world, the anguish, the pain we go through, the mistakes we make in coping with it." An intuition was dawning and she was about to follow its thread.

"What might it be?" asked Lakshman. He was used to his cousin, her incisive intuitions and her knack of speaking in riddles. "Yes," he said, "there are marvels to be revealed on this evening when the daughters of Eleksim connect to the magic of their House, the Fifth, that leads to the core of all things."

He looked instinctively at Tracy, as if his words held a message for her. She responded with a glance that carried her typical blend of insight and softness that he'd learned to cherish. Having been an orphan, Lakshman had a hidden fear of being lost for love. However, this was an evening for the sweetest that love can be, a time for love to express itself. Trusting in the protection, he felt that on this night he could let go and let his feelings flow.

Tracy saw the sheen in his eyes and returned his expression of tenderness. Unaware of the flight of Cupid towards her Sheravalian sister.

Lakshmi wanted to share the depth of her experience and began good-humoredly, "We know the Avasthas perceived the evolution of the cosmos as 'the Game,' a play that unfolds according to the hidden pattern of what they called the 'Grand Scheme.'

"The White Feather is the path that leads to the abode of the Emerald King and is under his control. In Amsterdam I had a vision that it's the path we must follow if we have to succeed under the Scheme, but I would love to hear your insight," responded Lakshman.

"I want to convey something that I now understand about that Scheme. However, first tell me what is the most constant ingredient of all great love stories, the most wonderful as well as the most tragic?"

"I don't know, passion maybe?"

Lakshmi shook her head at Lorelei's response and rejected the other suggestions of the group. "All right, I'll tell you: it is separation."

"Separation? What do you mean?" Jonathan asked with a mystified look at his wife.

"Come on, my dear, do you ever go to the movies? Shakespeare didn't change the plot, and it didn't change since Shakespeare. There is no great love story without separation. Separation hurts, but I think I just found out its meaning. Separation and encounter, being parted and reconnecting, finding each other again, or not: this makes the difference between the wonderful and the dramatic. In separation," she added with a smile, "there is misunderstanding, uncertainty, tension, sufferings, and searching, adventures leading to the maturing of desires. Finally, we hope for a happy ending like in the movies; I always like it when lovers find each other at the end of a story."

"This is a line drawn from the story of Erilie the Sheravalian," Lakshman observed light-heartedly, referring to his cousin's past Avasthic life, "and Olophon, the last admiral of the great Thalassean Fleet, first Nizam of Elnelok, the underground kingdom of the lost race, wrote of it ten thousand years before Shakespeare. It is a tale that was written for the rest of us too," he added, his eyes still cast on Tracy, who was hearing the last words of Lakshmi reverberating in her head, "when lovers find each other at the end of the story."

"But, can you spell out for us the link with the Grand Scheme?" she asked.

"Listen, the Game is built on this pattern, or rather, love stories are built on the pattern of the Game. In the Game, a distance must be created for the play to exist; the Master explained it in Jetzenstein Castle. If there is no distance, how can we travel? If we are not separate, how can we come together? There has to be an empty space between our goal and us, between our fulfillment and us. The Buddhists call this the Void or the Ocean of Illusion where travel is perilous. Separation creates the interval for the journey to exist. We had to be separated from the Inner World to discover it again, thus we could make it truly ours."

"But how does separation occur in the first place?" The Hlidarendis were following this exchange with sympathy, and Kheto asked the question, much in the Socratic manner, to elicit the knowledge from the awakening in the student. Lakshmi responded without hesitation, "You cannot play cards if the cards of all the players are known to everyone. Something has been left in random mode in the Grand Scheme and that something is us. No game exists when everything is preordained. A game needs randomness. Freedom creates the randomness. Combined with ignorance, freedom creates the space of separation. Without freedom, there is no distance, no story. Man is separated from his meaning so that he may find it and claim it as his own. He is separated in the same way that a lover is separated from a beloved one and man is severed from divinity. The Game of the Grand Scheme is seek and find; nevertheless, at its genesis, it is a game of divinity looking within our awareness for the return path to itself; Voila!" She concluded with a disarming grin as she faced the three men dearest to her and who had enriched her personality and her life. Seeing before her: Sanath, the mentor; Jonathan, the husband; and Lakshman; the cousin who was as a brother to her, Lakshmi felt gratitude for the many ways in which she could love. This gratitude was gladly returned for she always stimulated them with penetrating intuitions.

"So is it all about a ballet, a dance of freedom with love? The conundrum of our destiny is solved when we move from the freedom of seeking towards the necessity of uniting? We must fuse, mustn't we?"

Tracy felt a shiver in her entire body. On the one hand, she knew that Lakshman and Lakshmi were talking about the play of destiny, the wheel which moved the Grand Scheme, but, on the other, she wondered if Lakshman was explaining himself to her too, as a man would return to a woman that he had loved and left a long time ago. And as if to prove how right she was to trust her heart, Lakshman looked again at her, this time without shyness. Tracy could not sustain his glance and looked to the ground.

"That's right Laksh," continued Lakshmi, "the mystery of divine love is what mystic poets and Sufis wanted to bring to us. Most people see this play only in human love stories, when the lovers run toward each other through forests, hills and dales, adventures and perils, getting closer. Nevertheless, beyond our little love stories, there is a cosmic love story that powers the entire creation. I believe some guys could be a bit slower at grasping the Game because men do not understand women and the way they love. We do not love just for the murmurs of our senses. We love to find ourselves.

"Now think about it, or rather, feel it. In meeting the Self, we meet divinity within us. This is the happy ending for the longest of all love stories." The shawl that had enveloped Lakshmi had brought forward this recognition: finding oneself is most pleasant because it means finding love.

"As God is also a woman, She created for this same reason. She finds joy whenever one of us finds the Self. She finds joy when we can enjoy divine love, recognizing its intensity in the Gift."

"That's why you called your daughter Ananya?" whispered Lakshman with quiet admiration for his intuitive cousin. "You explained once that it means love without separation, doesn't it?"

Jonathan felt now that his wife had become suddenly shy for she had revealed a lot about herself. So, to take the attention away from her, he asked Lorelei, the other damsel of Eleksim who had not spoken, "What did you feel, what did you ask?"

"I was beyond asking anything; I felt that the trees, the animals, the hills can understand and feel this energy. Only the humans were not integrated but now they connect too." As it was nighttime no one could see that Lorelei blushed slightly, "I felt that love between man and woman is good, strong and powerful, it's a part of the whole."

"I was a bit disturbed in the beginning," began Michael, adding teasingly, "not as much as Lakshmi though because unlike her, I did not need to ask for a shawl. Gradually, the thoughts settled, and I became silent. At the end I felt, and still feel, amazingly good inside, in a quiet sort of way. It was a slow and gradual process and I cannot pinpoint if and when something particular happened. Well, thanks for that," he said softly to Lorelei in reference to her last comment.

She burst out laughing, "Oh well, we help each other practice."

"I should also mention," added Michael, "that I'd like to uncover the power of our own House, Anor, and find the Casket of the Discus. I have a gut feeling that there is more in Lakshmi's story than we can tell so far. If love can fuse two people, it can also fuse larger groups. There is much to discover. Tonight, under the gaze of the Great Mother, I felt powerfully my allegiance to the Emerald King who leads the Game with a sense that he wishes us to ascend higher, to achieve much more. Wouldn't we gain by finishing this task, by completing the circle?"

Sanath looked at Kheto, inviting him to answer.

"That's right Michael, you feel the call of Anor. My service to the Order," said the African Hllidarendi, "was to counter the attempts of evil to sow divisiveness in the hearts of men, and as I explained to you, in Africa, working for unity fulfills the purpose you are destined to serve. I do share your wish Michael, and if the story is coming full circle, it does not mean it is finished because the Game is not a circle, it is a spiral."

Michael replied, "When Sean sat next to me, I dived deeper into myself and into the silence. It is almost as if we had become one and the same being."

"It felt as if the top of my head had been removed," said Sean softly. "I did not know where I started and where I finished, I did not know where my being was beginning or ending. It is almost as if I was filling the entire tent. Who was this I? In Bangkok I told Lakshmi about a dream I had. It felt exactly like this."

They smiled; their grins would just not leave their faces. They were trying to put words on an experience that was one and the same, yet perceived by each of them differently. The wizard intervened, "You experienced the blessings of the Goddess according to the *tattwas* of the houses to which you once belonged. Eleksim is for the heart. Lorelei, Lakshmi and Tracy, the sisters of the Fourth House of Eleksim, feel the blessedness of love. Michael and Sean are scions of Anor. They entered into the mystery of the Fifth House that is yet to be revealed, the great oneness. Different aspects, different flavors but one energy."

"Sorry, Master, but you do not always speak in ways I understand," said Michael, finding in the ease of the night, a familiarity that he would otherwise not have dared, "what is a *tattwa*?"

Sanath did not mind. It's not a word known in English. "I forgot to explain it. A *tattwa* is a principle, that is, the ruling standard. How can I explain? Our world is a filigree of the higher one. The *tattwas* are the lines of the invisible world we can faintly perceive in ours. The main *tattwas* were hosted in the Avasthic Houses of course."

Sean asked the wizard, "Please speak about the *tattwa* of Anor."

"Anor is not about finding the deeper 'I' but the deeper 'us.' In the last centuries, only a few great human beings could get the Gift. They were mostly hidden from society, crossing into the Inner World after long years of practice and preparation. However, this was way too slow to have any effect on the world at large. We have to spot the beginning of the circle to understand where it will be completed. There was a meeting of the gods on Mount Kailash and the Daskalian Assembly, the meeting of the Primordial Masters was equally summoned. They all implored the Lady of the Rock to awaken Her power in those who would be willing to receive it. Only She could achieve this feat, dare such a transformation. And only then will the human race be free from the duality of the left and right feathers. In the emergency of this time, She must have decided to oblige.

Today something is happening, something that never happened before. The Great Mother has come in human form. Seekers are the salt of the earth. She is giving the Gift to all those who seek and come to Her, no matter where they come from, no matter how high or low in society they may be."

"If so, is the job of the Stealthstars over?" asked Michael.

"No, but you will merge with the seekers because by now you are too few to succeed. You shall be safe in their midst. Kheto please could you share your insights on Anor?"

"Remember, I learnt French," Kheto smiled, "and I read French books too. There was a mystical theologian called Theilard de Chardin, who had a mighty vision of the return of Christ whom he called 'the *Parousia*'. He envisioned the advent of a formidable collective force which shapes into a cosmic being, the omega, and the end of this cycle of history. Conditions for this to happen are now in place in various ways."

"That's right," said Sanath. "A spiral is made of an ascending circle but, from alpha to omega, let us see where the present circle takes us. With instant communication, continuous world news and the encounters in cyber space, human consciousness converges towards a kind of synchronicity. Information technology is supporting the junction of billions of consciousness streams. Increasingly, the people of the planet are thinking the same things at the same time. It is like flexing the muscles of what might happen if there would be a moment of perfect convergence.

"A convergence of our attention, everyone at the same time?" Lakshmi remembered Sean's dream of the football stadium.

"You can get a taste of it when there are events that capture the minds of the masses with great vigor, such as the mourning of the death of the Princess of Wales, or for example, at the time of the Olympic games. Consider the convergence of all those who partake in this fusion of minds, focused on the same point. It is more than just a mental process. The sense of communion is charged with emotions, an immense empathy. It involves everyone with a vitality that no one presently knows how to tap into, to use or apply.

"Compare it to millions of thin threads of light joining to form a luminous beam. It's immense consciousness energy, released, enjoyed, and soon lost. The meeting of minds is bound to a specific event in time and space that serves as a focus for it to emerge and unfold. It is there, with gusto, and then it fades within a few hours, and naturally it then disappears.

"Now just imagine what could be this phenomenon of global empathy if it could depend upon a state of mind rather than being an event-bound happening, if it could be reached by a quiet flux of fusion of enlightened consciousness. What could be achieved if the release of this considerable energy of consciousness could be applied as a laser beam for instance, to address the issues and challenges that mankind is presently facing."

"This would be beyond thoughts," Lakshmi commented "Wow! Just a state of complete oneness; what a wonder! Could we experience this elation flowing into action?"

"I think so," Sanath continued, "the formation of the collective mind is the new threshold in the pilgrimage of man towards its accomplishment, tuning into a cosmic awareness, stepping consciously into the game of Adivatar, experiencing a gratification that cannot be imagined. There is an episode in the Game that is about to open, one this world has never seen before. The Anor *tattwa* brings the next step in the Grand Scheme, the next frontier for the human race."

"Don't you think the people we mingled with tonight have started to move towards this frontier?" asked Jonathan, absorbed in a reflective mood. "Some of the followers of the Goddess are Stealthstars, some aren't, aren't they? What would you say Sean?"

"Yes, day by day, we are on the move but not quite out of the Ocean of Illusion, not entirely safe yet. Some swim, some sink, some will quit, and more will come. Some will grow, some won't. Many wish to ascend and some will betray the possibility of what they could become. It doesn't matter for there is a great force in motion. It cannot be stopped anymore."

"I believe every event, every movement finds its place in the Grand Scheme. The Emerald King is balancing energies, arranging this puzzle, developing options, and assembling a large reserve army of which we know nothing yet."

Jonathan's statement invited a comment from Sanath. "This foresight, bringing the feathers into balance, has much to do with the Third House, Olophon. You are from Elnur, a worshiper of the water world and a subject of the ruler of Vaikuntha who is the patron deity of the Third House. You grasp the fluidity of movements in the play of your King, the dance of time and seasons, and if you go further in this direction, you may see where it leads, you may see the future but I would not encourage you to do so."

Jonathan turned to ask his friend, "And you Lakshman, what did you feel? And, by the way, which Avastic House do you come from? I haven't a clue. We know only that in the last days of the Avasthas, Etakir was the leader of the Yuva Platoon." They turned to the archaeologist who had initiated the Dagad Trikon quest with great curiosity.

"I found my Mother. What else can I say?" he smiled and would not say more but they all knew he had said enough.

Again, it fell to the wizard to unfold the script. "Normally great archers were from Anor but in fact, Etakir is an Anorhadan. The children of the Sixth House do not own anything, not even a past. This is why he was the most accomplished Avasthic warrior, unleashing the full blast of the force that is contained in the present moment. This is why he appeared in this saga as an orphan. Those who cross the Lily of Anorhad carry no baggage. Lakshman came without any memories, and like other Stealthstars, he lost much of his strength in this wretched world. But now *Susamskara* shall restore him and with it comes all that is great and noble, all that he cherished."

"You mentioned that there are rulers or patrons of the Avasthic Houses?" Lakshman had not suspected what the wizard had just unveiled but did not particularly wish to be revealed or discussed, and he invited the wizard to pursue his explanation.

Sanath obliged. "I do not know if I mentioned this before? There is a specific guardian deity for each House. They are, so to speak, the owners. The Avasthic Houses control plexuses piled up around the axis of the spine, and they bring different expressions of higher worlds because they reflect the properties of the main operators of the cosmic machinery, the specific patron deities. They work in these plexuses but they congregate in the house of Ni. When we enjoy the properties of the Houses, it is as if we feel the reflection, the style or the specific coefficient or quality of the owner. Moreover, when we are clean, we can develop these coefficients within us: innocence or wisdom, spontaneity and creativity, serenity and harmony, confidence, generosity, compassion, forgiveness, there are so many qualities. The Avasthic houses are in the likeness of their owners. All this magic is now deposited in the subtle centers of the human body."

"As the ancient said, we are the microcosm that reflects the cosmos," observed Jonathan.

"It reflects the City of God! It encloses its citizens with the walls of heavenly magnetism. The water of life flows in multiple channels and irrigates the city with splendid energies. Pure knowledge paves a network of spacious pathways, the heavenly breeze blows though the portals of lofty houses and wish-fulfilling gems of delightful joy hang from the branches of its central tree. I bow to the great John of Patmos. He saw this in his vision of the Apocalypse and called it the New Jerusalem. The House of Ni on top of the brain is the temple of this city; those allowed into its core enter the chamber containing the Holy Grail. And these," the wizard shook his head with a last touch of incredulity, "these humans received Her clearance for this destination!"

"I am glad you reveal it so clearly because indeed, we felt this entire audience was equally blessed," observed Michael. He hesitated for a moment, tried a shy smile and summoned the courage to ask the wizard, "What did this magic night in England bring to you, what did you feel, Sand Keeper of Dagad Trikon? After all your own relationship with the Goddess is quite a riddle to us, isn't it?"

"Is it? Then we should perhaps leave it that way." Sanath paused but could not miss their disappointed look and so he finally told them what they feared to hear, "As we know, my dear friends of the Order of the Hllidarendi: we converged in England because I intended to call a meeting of our Order but this evening precipitated events, and to an extent, explained them."

It was now time for the wizard to offer his own account, "Sitting before Her tonight I understood why the Goddess, while directing me, keeps me at a distance. As I was running this mission, searching the world for the footprints of the legend, She kept me connected, albeit on a parallel track. In Her present form, Her magnetism is simply too powerful. If I would come any closer to Her than I was this evening, I might well dissolve. Yes, I would drop my earthly form, I would vanish, sucked through Her into the heavenly world."

"So it is true," commented Ian, "Merlin predicted that the Order would come to an end when the Lady of the Rock returned."

"This is correct. The time has come for me to dissolve our Order," confirmed Sanath. His bearing was grave but he showed no regrets. "This Avatar is absorbing all the magic of the world within Herself, like a cosmic receptacle, and She releases and distributes it in a new form to the human race! This churning is astounding. The seekers are the newborn of the Deep Way, still dazzled, equipped with a might they do not yet know how to project.

The heavenly forces operate the Grand Scheme through instant connection, sheer reflex action! Archangels, cherubim, seraphim, and guardian angels, all of them work in the split second of a moment, totally integrated among themselves. For instance, the Great Mother uses the *Avalokiteshwara* property of the Buddha, the wisdom of the all-reflecting mirror. She simply watches, as a witness, and Her seeing acts on the reflex. This reflex can also project a mood, a desire or a command: the angels instantly capture it, even before it is formulated."

"And so She does it all, as their song was saying," added Jonathan, "without so much as a thought. Wow!"

"This connection exists forever, and it is the foundation for all magic and miracles. Sometimes we perceive it as a legend; at other times we see its effect in the reality. We are here and there. In the City of God, I am a child, in yours, I am a wizard."

Lakshman had followed the entire exchange with a sense of gratitude to Sanath who had always been so helpful in deciphering meanings for them. He said with a quiet strength, "Of course, we need help and we'll get it too. Now only, I understand. The Avahan power does not work any longer like Master Sanath explained at the inn. It would have been too difficult for many of us. I saw tonight that the calling to the higher worlds is answered. The blessings descend on us simply because we meet; when we congregate, our energies mix. The Avahan works because we become one. This is when and how we complete this circle."

"See, I told you so," the wizard laughed, pleased with Lakshman's insight. He turned to three Hllidarendis and said, "when the Game moves into a new spiral, it is played with new rules."

CHAPTER TWENTY-SIX

THE BREAKING
OF THE SEVENTH SEAL

Where Sanath recalls in his farewell that the destination of the children of the Great Mother is the dawn of that beauty from where they all come.

"We need adjustment," the wizard explained, "when we move from one stage to another. Evolution is when we grow outside, but revolution is when we turn inwards. (R)evolution, the combination of the two, is when the movement inside triggers evolution outside. The letter 'R' becomes the symbol for 'Ra', the chief deity of Ancient Egypt, the new influx of energy. This is the only way to enter the Golden Age, because its foundations are a much deeper knowledge. I have served you in the age that has just finished. You do not need me in the age that is coming. Rejoice in its dawn."

This was a night for rejoicing but now the Stealthstars were alarmed. Sanath's might had meant so much for them, buttressing their sense of security. It was hard to admit that he would definitely withdraw. He, of course, could not miss this diffuse anxiety and invited the members of his Order to share their personal insights.

"We have all noted what has happened to us recently," said Mariluh. "It is a paradox: this evening the power was much higher, but all in all, I sense our magic abilities are waning. Don't you agree, Master Kheto?"

Kheto sighed but didn't say anything. He seemed deeply absorbed in his own thoughts, so Ian Ildemar broke the silence, and recalled with heartfelt emotion how the prophecies of Blake had announced the present moment.

They observed a grave silence that Kheto eventually broke. His tone was firm. "The demons are roaming in the woods near the camp. They now know where the Stealthstars are. They shall attack them, no doubt, and I feel in my heart that it's my fate to stand by the students of the Great Mother, with or without the Order. Can you also feel the Fifth Rider, the witch Mokolo, hovering above them with the specter of jealousy? I saw her tonight circling in the sky overhead." Kheto was alert to the movement of this enemy, fully aware that the warnings he had given to Michael and Lorelei on Table Mountain were not sufficient to counter its malefic influence.

"You did?" Lakshman stepped in. "I had a dream, and I saw her too; she looked dreadful. The students will have to learn how to deal with her deceptions, won't they?"

"Yes, they still have a few challenges to face by themselves. The witch is here; you are right; she preys on them, tries her tricks in different ways. This was to be expected: if she cannot break their unity, the force of the children of the Great Mother will become unstoppable."

Kheto had been sensitized by years of bitter warfare with the Dark Hordes, and his instinct was to keep on fighting. "When the ancestral foes, the wraiths of doom are still upon them, are we not to carry our mission a little bit further, shouldn't the Order continue to protect them?"

Sanath intervened. "No, it shouldn't. The Great Mother has gathered the children for the great banquet of this age, to stand before the eye of judgment. Don't worry. She is the One, as the Lady of the Rock, who sent me to protect mankind from Thanatophor. She will continue to protect them in awakening their personal wizard inside them. They are alone now, on their own," the wizard paused with a smile, "with the angels and the deities woven into their spines. However, you looked into your heart and I cannot overrule its guidance. You have my agreement, dear Kheto, to do as you please."

"May we drink love wherever it flows, in the sap of a branch of a tree, in its flowers or in its fruit?" Mariluh softly whispered, "Our Mother in the heavens is the source of the great stream. I feel every sentient being, the life forms, the joy in the bud and the fear in the rabbit, the totality of it. However I feel the pain too. Compassion is my deliverance. My Mother needs Her compassion to flow through one thousand brooks. We are these brooks, and we shall not let our Mother down."

"It us up to the humans now," added Sanath. "I must let go as the ancient race did when they gathered in the Givupatlast volcano of Dagad Trikon to leave the Earth for the stars. The Hllidarendis were meant to find the Stealthstars. Today I recognized many of them in the crowd, craftsmen of Falkiliad, sailors of Elnur, musicians of Eleksim or archers of Anor. They are transformed into themselves. The task is achieved."

"I am happy with this," nodded the priestess. "Ataui is the Aztec part of my name; it means 'Little Drop' and I always knew this drop was ultimately meant to dissolve into the ocean: I look forward to this merging, because like you, my beloved and venerable Grand Master, I read the signs in the stars of this wondrous night. What shall be your parting words?"

"You see; the fate of the wizard was linked to the magic oak." Now Sanath was speaking about himself in the third person, detached from his own subject. "The passing of the oak in Russia announced the end of his time. It died when the Casket of the Cross began to release its contents. He understood the time had come for him to bid farewell when he saw the manifestation of the Lily of Anorhad in Bangkok, respectively. What happened to him tonight is something he had anticipated, expected."

"You, our Grand Master of the Order, are the most ancient one, the Sand Keeper of Dagad Trikon, and the only Aulya still walking upon the Earth. You have been foremost among wizards, unmatched in your awareness of the enemy, fearsome, wise and crafty, defeating Thanatophor and his witchery." Kheto said in a sad but firm voice. "You lived for centuries and commanded great magical powers. Is this really the time for you to leave us? Must this blessed night be the moment of your farewell?"

His mournful note was well understood. Hllidarendis had been Sanath's life comrades, fighting together for the same cause. This had weaved a strong bond. Even though the members of the Order were great seers who could recognize the signs of destiny, their hearts were heavy at the prospect of parting. It was hard to believe that the Grand Master would just leave them, just walk away.

"It is to your advantage that I go away. It is better to have the Lady of the Rock in the reality than in the legend. As I said before, the legend unfolds at dawn or dusk, but it vanishes under the sunshine of high noon. True legends are like maps, holographic maps; they describe the way but they never are the destination. The time has come for the forces of goodness to manifest within us rather than being consigned to our mythologies." As he spoke, it seemed to the Stealthstars that, for a moment, the wizard was himself becoming transparent, like a holographic shape, not a human of flesh and bone but a being from higher planes that had been sent to guide and protect them through the hills and dales of this singular journey.

The stars sparkled so near, the hills and trees stood motionless, and everything was silent, yet alive. It was as if nature itself was at attention, listening to their discourse, as if it knew its fate depended upon the outcome of this night, when the legend faded away and the completed circle triggered the ascending spiral.

Sanath continued, "The world is no longer what it used to be. Something has changed. The animals can feel it but how far can the humans absorb the Deep Way? The teachers left their seats, and the children have taken their own. No more teaching, the time has come to transform. Witness the emergence of those who are masters of themselves, the Swatantra Avasthas. The earth dries up. The sea rises. The wind howls. Fire and frost bite. All this must pass, in a rite of purification, for the Golden Age to be reborn. It is going to be powerful...and for too many, it is going to be fatal. Wait until this is fully triggered! When the Tricolor Lily opens and the White Feather rises at its center, the seal of Anorhad will break."

"Then it is all about the Lily of Anorhad isn't it?" Lakshman wanted to be sure he got it right.

"Not at all. The gate is important but it is only a passage. We go through the gate to reach the destination. It is about the destination, not the gate. The alpha is the omega; our destination is the beginning. Lakshmi told us how this elliptical movement of return to the divine beginning is a play of love."

"Thus spoke the last of the Aulyas." Kheto said with reverence. "Master, I now understand that your task is indeed completed."

Bending slightly forward, Sanath with eyes full of love spoke his last words slowly, as if to check that they would absorb their meaning.

"The deities will beam and register their messages directly on the hands of the humans. A force is building up to a point where it will take a new shape. The moment the Emerald King in Vaikuntha wakes up is the tipping point of evolution, the ultimate game changer of history. Then the Seventh Seal will break in the heads of the appointed number within the multitude, and the properties of all the Houses will manifest.

When the children shall start dancing, with perfectly synchronized steps, the world, as you know it shall be destroyed, and the Game will bring forth the new one."

The Breaking of the Seventh Seal is the sequel to
The Legend of Dagad Trikon – to obtain a print copy, please go to:

www.dagadtrikon.com
www.daisyamerica.com
www.amazon.com

The Legend of Dagad Trikon is also available on Amazon in digital
eBook form. The link depends on which country you are in.

The author has a website at www.sakshi.org

Bearing Power – p.196
it's the capacity to look after everyone.

Catching p 194.
We go in and ot of the Inner World
Practitioners are often Careless
✓ To accend we have to be alert and
careful not to go in & out, but focus
attention + consolidate the new state
of consciousness. If not we can loose
the benefits of initiation.

243